Minutes

David Pyle

DAVID PYLE

FIRST EDITION

Library of Congress Cataloging-in-Publication Data has been applied for.

ISBN-10: 0615860516
ISBN-13: 978-0615860510

DAVID PYLE

To the Adventurous Soul..

DAVID PYLE

DAVID PYLE

Minutes

PROLOGUE

LOUNGING in his favorite paisley wingback chair, sipping on a cup of sorrows, Nathan Heart stared out over the neatly manicured front lawn.

Tock...

Tock...

Tock...

Mixed with the hours of oblique silence, that incessant sound of the antique clock was going to drive him right over the edge. If the immovable debacle wasn't a sentimental family heirloom, it would have been in the dumpster months ago. But the fact was, it happened to be a hard won prize between siblings after a lengthy cold war over his dead mother; Marion Heart's estate.

It stood like a vertical coffin, a constant reminder that time was slipping away, smoothly, silently, unnoticed.

Even though days ago he'd turned the age of thirty, Nathan had the morbid sensation of being dragged by a chain to the brink of the eternal. This loneliness had become an empty chasm with a razor's trim hidden by the darkness that had formed in his mind over the course of the last eleven months. It was the emptiness he couldn't seem to find release from.

With a deep breath, Nathan focused on what was in front of him for the umpteenth time. It was that ornate Heart Realty *For Sale* sign hammered into the ground on the distant front lawn that drew his annoyed attention. Standing just a little askew, there were several streaky deposits of white spew coloring the back surface, donations from recent clouds of blackbirds.

"Marion," he whispered under his breath, forcing himself to look away.

Such a free spirit. Nathan shook his head and chuckled to himself, then quickly repented.

It was Jonas Heart Jr., Nathan's elder brother, he truly missed after all was said and done. His relationship with his only brother was now non-existent.

As Executor of Marion Heart's estate, Nathan had been the one required, no..., sentenced, to act as negotiator, peacemaker, and referee to the five children of Marion Heart.

All the other children had *moved on* well before her passing..., yet here he sat, on the open veranda of the second story bedroom, looking out over the expanse in front of him.

Why hadn't he married early and started a family like all the others? Why didn't he move off to parts unknown, far from his childhood home?

Like a flood, all the memories of the last three years sprayed back into his thoughts, ever repeating in retching reiteration.

Their mother..., his mother, once vibrant, active in the community..., was finally at peace. First came the dementia, then memory loss, then the incessant chatter to her invisible friends.

He shifted uncomfortably in his seat as he took another sip.

Somehow, he had drawn the short straw by vote; probably an angry collusion between the others. He was the youngest, the one most *available* to be the caregiver. The estate had ample funds to pay for private care, but none of the other children were willing to watch their portion of the estate dwindle away to some local Rest Haven for an unknown length of years.

Yes, Nathan had been *available*. The most obvious choice. After Nathan's few failed relationships there was no marriage, no children, and no distant career in another state.

Available.

Now he was living in the old family estate in the middle of nowhere, house sitting, with his life on hold while there were no prospective buyers for miles. None of the locals would even consider purchasing the old home and property, because of the rumors..., and well to be honest..., the way Marion Heart died --

The way she died in the house.

CHAPTER ONE

ALONE in the dying rays of the evening sun, Nathan Heart sank further down into the wing back chair, pulling his wrap tighter.

It was one of the few remaining pieces of furniture from the estate. After the reading of the Will, the house had been all but swept clean of anything remotely valuable, leaving him to the empty footfalls of memories inside this long held family jewel.

♥

The evening air brought with it a chill of fall. September was officially here and along with it would come the religiously regular rainfall near the northwestern coastline of Oregon. For Nathan, it signaled another bleak winter season, alone in an unsold house and another season with his life put on hold.

Behind him, the telephone began to ring, along with every extension in every other empty room in the house. After the second ring, he casually looked over his shoulder, then back out at the last red cast of the sun on the horizon. The faintest of chatter began downstairs as the answering machine picked up the call, making its dutiful announcement for Heart Real Estate.

The family had reluctantly allowed him to setup his office here, temporarily offsetting his expenses. After all, he was maintaining an office and providing the service of selling the estate at the same time.

How thoughtful.

The blessing quickly became a trap and a curse of course.

Irregular visits and constant phone messages from his family, hinted that he wasn't trying to sell the house, or that it might be a good idea for him to buy the estate himself. Then he could divide the proceeds among the other four children and his portion could be the down payment.

Again, Nathan quipped angrily, "How thoughtful."

Oddly enough, his portion of the Heart Estate had never been spoken of after the furniture and valuables quickly vacated the premises. As a Realtor, he had seen this type of behavior time and time again. Blood was always thicker than water, but never thicker than greed among siblings.

Nathan stepped back pulling the chair inside, slowly closed the veranda doors, then intently listened to the downstairs recorder as his sister Josie's voice droned on. She finished leaving him a message, instructions actually, another inventive scheme to help him sell the house.

For two cents, he would gladly give up his portion and let one of the others, his faithful older brother or one of his three sisters, sell the house or get another realtor. At the very mention of this idea to his family, there was an immediate retraction of their comments and suggestions. There were extended realty fees and commissions to consider if another agency were to control the property. And of course, none of them could afford to drop their lifestyle to occupy or maintain the house or the extensive grounds themselves. There was also a small matter of pride for Nathan. The only other independent realtor in the town of Lumberton Oregon was his competitor....

How would that look? Allowing his only competition to sell a prime piece of property, a historical landmark, his family property, in his town? That would blacken his reputation and his pride.

But this house....

This house - two and a half stories, huge attic and basement, of creaky, noisy, elemental house. Nathan of course was accustomed to the usual creaks and moans. All old houses built during the early 1900's settle and shift, no matter how well they are built and maintained.

Heart Manor was no exception. Secretly, he had considered renovating it into a bed and breakfast, using the local rumors for advertisement. But then, what of the family name? Local whispers could easily become area wide conversation, even all along the west coast where all his family lived. The idea swept away quickly with the thought of more helpful phone calls.

Tomorrow was his routine trip into Lumberton. Groceries for one, he reminded himself. The usual delivery of firewood for the coming season was tomorrow, Monday morning. He forced himself out of his comforter, folding it neatly over the tall back of the chair, closed the veranda doors and began the walk downstairs.

He pushed the void away momentarily, but the flood of emptiness came rushing in again as his steps echoed down the staircase.

"Nathan...."

He paused midway of the stairs and listened.

He must have tuned out the ringing of the telephone and halted in the silence for next the ensuing message on the answering machine.

He turned and glanced to his left, down to his open office door, still listening. This was his favorite enclave; the only completely furnished room in the house besides his bedroom.

Nothing…, no sound…, not even a dying echo.

The house was silent except for the distant sound of the grandfather clock; its reminder of passing moments.

"Crazy old house," Nathan muttered.

Then he considered that the faux echo of his name could have been one of the many memories of Marion Heart calling out his name, calling for some tea, asking for one of her favorite books to hover over. She was such a creature of habit.

Then there were the other days where his mother would become a chatterbox, rattling on for hours on end about the past. Of all her favorite subjects, she always seemed to end up in some quiet reflections of Jonas Sr., the father Nathan never knew. Jonas Heart Sr. died when Nathan was barely two years old, in some field of battle; according to Marion during an act of heroism. She would point to the wall at the medals; the neatly folded American flag in the glass shadowbox on her bedroom wall. They were her most prized possessions.

Those days always ended the same as she finally drifted off to sleep while seated on her favorite loveseat, curled under a thick quilt.

His breath was short, his eyes unfocused, probably due to the hurried excursion down the stairs.

Nathan shook the cobwebs from his head and snatched his jacket from the coat tree in his office, striding for the front door.

The last two years came crushing down like a pressure cooker and it was the latches on the front door crackling that set him free.

He gasped in the chill air and bent over, hands on knees. If he didn't get out of here soon, he'd be the first to follow his mother to the grave. The youngest of the five. How ironic would that be? There had to be some way to be free of this duty.

As his breathing slowed and mind cleared, he ripped on his chocolate leather jacket and hurried down the front steps in the twilight. The fresh air always freed his mind of the past, that and the natural stone path that led around the perimeter of the estate. It was too late to walk the entire trek before darkness fell, but it was better than the darkness he'd just escaped.

Night came quickly, enhanced by the bosky tall spruce and thick noble pines around the periphery and along the back of the property. An evening wind was rising along the path, pinching at his cheeks, forcing him to return before his feet took him a few hundred yards.

A hopeful thought thumped him; tonight would be a good night for a drive along the coast and he rammed his hand into his jacket pocket.

"Blast," he hissed.

His car keys were on the desk inside his office. Despite his initial titer of hope, he'd have to go back inside to retrieve them.

As he rounded toward the front of the house, the outdoor lighting flicked on, illuminating the shrubs shrouding the spacious perimeter as well as the sweeping oval of the front porch. Two enormous shadowed lions cast in stone sat on either side of the two stanch pillars, mouths agape in a perpetual silent roar.

The telephone was ringing.

Nathan stopped at the bottom porch step and looked at his wristwatch with a sigh. It had to be Josie calling again. If he let the phone call go to the answering machine, there would be no end to the chides, no matter how valid his excuse.

The door clicked shut with a loud bump behind him as he hurried to his office.

"Heart Realty," he answered, snatching the phone from its cradle.

"You sound as if you were running. Did I catch you at a bad time?"

The sarcasm was unmistakable.

"Hello Josie. I was outside."

"In this bluster? I doubt that."

Nathan looked at the small ring of keys on the corner of his desk and snatched them into his hand. If only he'd had them pocketed in his jacket.

"The weather's bad there?"

"I didn't call to chat about the weather. I called to find out what you thought of my idea. Didn't you get my message?" she asked.

"I just walked in the house Josie."

Nathan heard the begrudged sigh of her voice. It was the first of September and evidently his eldest sister had just looked over her end of August tally. It was beyond him how she could have squandered her portion of inheritance so quickly. It was unlikely her husband Charles and two perfect children were the cause.

"I would ask you to listen to it and then call me back but that would be too presumptuous on my part. In any case, I spoke to one of Charles' associates and he assured me that mother's estate could have easily been sold by now if you had posted its availability in an MLS database. The listing is only around $8000, which is more than reasonable considering the estate is appraised at over five million. It serves as the total fee instead of the usual seven percent. He said he would be willing to walk you through the process if you don't know how."

Nathan gritted his teeth and held the phone away to suck in a breath before speaking. He was licensed in seven states, a professional, it wasn't his lack of experience or talent…, it was the house.

"We've been over this once or twice before Josie. If you want me to do the listing through someone else, then I'll call and get a quote. We can divide the cost between...."

"Divide the cost?" she spat.

Why, oh why didn't he let this call roll to the answering machine? His head began to throb along his temples.

"Josie, do you honestly expect me to assume all the expense, considering...."

"You've lived there in mother's old house for three years now, rent free I might add. How can you expect the rest of us to forfeit a single dime to assist in selling it?"

"Josie. Do I need to remind you that two of those three years were spent caring for Marion? For which I didn't receive a cent?"

He wanted to add that it was only Caroline, the youngest sibling that ever visited or offered herself during their mother's last days.

"Yes well, we all see how that turned out and you managed to have her alter her Will in those last few months, naming you as Executor to the estate."

Nathan felt the dizzy of his blood pressure rising.

"The estate was divided equally, just as mother intended."

Actually, it wasn't quite equal and everyone knew it. Josie Clarion hissed into the phone and uttered a mass of angry unintelligible gibberish to someone beside her.

"It seems you've drawn us off topic again Nathan. We were discussing the quickest way to dispense with that wretched property."

"If you think your husband's friend can sell the house any quicker, then I suggest you pay his fee and turn it over to him. I can move out within the week. As you well know, I only have a few items to pack and...."

"Nonsense! And leave the house empty and abandoned for derelicts or riffraff to destroy?" she grunted.

"Josie, what exactly do you expect from me?" sighed Nathan.

"I want that place sold. For the good of all concerned," she added.

"Believe me. So do I."

"Jonas and Rachael are with me on this."

But not Caroline, she wouldn't be party to this ongoing collusion. Nathan was ready to hang up and move out, possibly even abandon his only portion of inheritance in the old estate. But that would play right into his elder sisters' intentions.

"I have a dinner party arriving. I'll speak to you later this week. Maybe you'll reconsider my advice and have it sold by then."

♥

After Nathan hung up the phone, he slowly released an iron grip on the jagged tag of keys unconsciously cupped in his hand.

His palm stung from the death grip on their angry edges as they jangled noisily into a large ceramic cup on the edge of his desk.

When would this end?

He ran his long fingers through neatly trimmed hair, trying to see a means through the dark tunnel encasing him.

The old clock in the vestibule began to hammer out seven hard blows to announce the time. As the dying echo reverberated into to the empty cavern, his breath seemed to tighten in his chest and his head spun.

Nathan spilled the ceramic catchall across his desk and snatched his keys. Once again, he hurried for the front door, but not before kicking the leaden base of the old clock for good measure.

CHAPTER TWO

THE two eldest of the Heart clan had quickly claimed the twin gray Mercedes' parked in the garage the day after the reading of the Will. The two remaining vehicles were too…, *utilitarian* for their needs.

The truth was…, the bright red Cadillac XLR convertible and an older putrid green Buick Special were in need of repairs. Instead of auctioning them off for quick cash, Nathan was given the option to keep them. Which he did. The Cadillac was Marion's favorite. The compact little convertible was her poison of choice for Sunday drives along the Oregon coast. His black Yukon, geared for foul weather and unlovely terrain, sat quiet and rarely used in the nearest stall.

The convertible cranked without hesitation; he pushed the lever and made sure the tan cover was climbing into place. Then the heavy wooden garage door grunted smoothly into motion and Nathan ducked underneath it onto the paved drive.

He was met instantly with a stiff whip of wind and stepped out to have a look toward the lower elevations to the west. Far in the distant sky, there was a flicker of light that might have been the old lighthouse off Ramses Sound. The low rumble of thunder quickly dispelled that myth and he hurried back to the hungrily idling car.

He had to admit, he loved the thought of taking it out for a drive through the heavily forested roads, away from the memories and responsibilities.

Twelve twisted miles west of Lumberton, Highway 101 came into sight just as his windshield was pelted with cold splatters of rain. The car radio crackled and came on of its own accord at a nearby shard of lightning. That was nothing new; he let it play.

Another ten minutes and he was parked in front of the *Blind Pirate* watching couples make mad dashes through the encroaching rain toward the front awning. The old seafood tavern was the most popular along the pacific coast highway, with occasional live music and a relaxed atmosphere.

He folded up his collar and jogged inside just behind an elderly couple.

♥

"Nate! Heckuva night to see you out," barked the rotund bear of a man.

He stuck out his hand to swat Nathan's shoulder before hurrying back behind the long scarred bar.

"Hey Troy," mumbled Nathan as he sat near the end of the bustling room.

"The usual?"

Nathan nodded and Troy slid him a mug of cold draft.

Troy's speckled gray beard wiggled and he leaned close, "The sisters run you out of the house again?"

Nathan grinned over his first sip of beer, then nodded. Funny how some people were so gifted in reading others. It was probably because all the old bartender did during the day was entertain people's expressions.

"You gonna eat something or just lollygag here at the bar?"

"Just put me in the queue and I'll wait my turn," said Nathan.

Troy laughed and turned to wiggle a finger at one of his waitresses.

"Don't give me your city talk. With this landing pattern you'll be waitin' for a table all night."

A familiar young brunette worked her way through the milling crowd and leaned over the bar close enough to hear Troy blurt out his orders.

"Lisa, escort Mr. Heart here over to the corner table and don't take no guff off him either."

The quiet young girl smiled and took off at a quick pace through the crowd, Nathan hot on her heels.

As soon as he sat down, she plopped down a menu and grabbed Nathan's half-swilled mug and walked away. He caught himself staring at her long model's legs instead to hurrying to stop her. With the din of noise, it was probably useless to protest.

Soon a freshly filled mug was in front of him, he ordered, and the young lady quickly disappeared again.

The lights flickered and the walls rumbled a few times, then the world seemed to settle down to the steady volume of chatter as the storm front passed.

"Ya know, I could set you and little Lisa there up on a get together sometime if you're interested," barked Troy.

He sat down heavily in the groaning chair across from Nathan just as his food arrived. Lisa caught the last of the exchange and blushed while the platters of seafood clattered the table.

DAVID PYLE

"I think *Lisa* might have something to say about that," said Nathan, shoving a pinch of buttered lobster in his mouth.

Lisa walked away with an unmistakable smile on her face.

"She'd likely say yes," Troy laughed. "How're things with you this evening?"

"Better now," grunted Nathan. "The walls were closing in."

"Yep, 'magine so. I miss seeing your old mom in here with you. She sure loved the fried oysters."

Troy let his eyes follow Nathan's fork up and down a few times, "Ya know…, it ain't good for a young fella like yourself to be cooped up out at that old place…."

"Don't you have somebody else to give advise to tonight?" asked Nathan.

Troy grinned, "Yeah, but they most likely won't come back. You on the other hand; I can't seem to run you off."

"All I need is another critic," mumbled Nathan. "You know…, I turn three or four major properties every month, but I can't manage to give away the old Heart Manor."

Troy shrugged his wide shoulders, "Maybe it'll burn and you can collect insurance. Too many people around here know the history of that old house." He leaned over closer and whispered loudly, "You know…, about your mother."

Nathan tried not to choke on his bite while laughing.

"Don't mince words Troy. Why don't you just come right out and say what you mean?"

"I'm just sayin'." He grinned and raised his hand, waving Lisa back over and holding up Nathan's shallowly swishing beer mug when she passed by the table.

"Alzheimer's can be an ugly thing," mumbled Nathan, dotting his lips with a thick napkin.

"It weren't the Alzheimer's I was referrin' to and you know it," hissed Troy.

Nathan looked on angrily for just a moment, barely a moment, then let it drop. It wasn't worth an argument.

"I gotta get back to work. When you think yer done, come sit at the bar and jaw awhile."

Nathan nodded and threw a cash tip on the table.

The two men sat and talked over coffee between Troy's barking orders at staff members. They were an unlikely pair, but somehow Troy had formed a fatherly attachment toward Nathan over the last few years. He had especially liked the company of Nathan's mother, Marion. He called her a feisty old broad on several occasions, earning him sharp replies and a grin from the barely sixty-year-old woman. It was when she'd lost her favorite cameo pendant; that had been her last visit to the Blind Pirate and a defining milestone in her early decline.

Nathan looked at the time and stretched. No one from the family would be calling after ten p.m. unless it was an actual emergency. His cell phone was turned off, so there was little chance of them barging in on his evening.

"It's early yet," mumbled Troy. "Why don't you stay and chat with some of the hired help while I help everybody get ready to close up shop?"

Nathan knew exactly what he was referring to. Troy was always trying to play matchmaker between him and one of his *girls*.

"No thanks. I have a heavy schedule tomorrow," said Nathan.

The drive back didn't take nearly as long, even with rain darkened pavement and patchy fog hovering across the lower areas.

All the security lights were radiating the huge perimeter and the old garage door groaned open on its own while Nathan waited in the idling Cadillac. The air was still dripping mist in the aftermath of the early autumn storm when he sauntered across the crunchy green lawn.

A mist-infused gust of wind whipped him and he halted to wipe away the spray of water. Above him a light flickered and he glanced toward it just in time to see the lamp in his bedroom window fall dark.

Was someone in the house? He hadn't received a call from the alarm system. It was then he remembered his retired cell phone and turned it back on.

"*You have no new messages,*" chimed in his ear while he stood in the front yard; no text messages either. That meant the house was still intact; well at least the alarm hadn't gone off. What of the light?

He opened the front door and flicked on the glaring overhead lights in the living room. The massive chandelier instantly sparkled shards of rainbow over the empty expanse. The only sound was the steady tock, tock, tock, of the eight foot tall clock, idling away the time near his shoulder. He would have stopped the pendulum dead long ago if not for the advice of the clocksmith in Salem. According to him, a timepiece as aged as this one might stop working or keeping accurate time if it stood still for even a few weeks. The value would be far reduced on a non-working antique.

Nathan flicked off the heavy lighting and turned up the thermostat a notch to accommodate the seasonal change in weather. His footfalls echoed down the dark hallways as he walked into the kitchen to put on some water for tea. Above his clamor he heard, "Nathan…."

The echo of his name caused him to lower his head, waiting for the rest of the message on the answering machine. His eyes froze on the wall phone in the kitchen. It hadn't made a sound; none of the mass of phones rang.

Nathan turned off the heat to the whistling pot on the stove and hurried to his office. The bright red number 2 was flashing on his answering machine.

"Not tonight," he grinned.

Just to be on the safe side he walked through the rest of the empty downstairs…, four bedrooms with walk-in closets, a library, living room, formal dining room, den, four bathrooms, the breakfast nook in the kitchen as well as the walk-in pantry. The security system was working, so all the windows were intact, no sign of an intruder and no place for anyone to hide.

"You're losing it buddy," he grinned at himself.

Upstairs the story was the same. None of the cavernous seven empty bedrooms were bothered, still barren and echoing his heavy steps down the wide hallway. Then he came to the eighth, his bedroom door, and halted. It was ajar, just barely. Nathan bumped it with his palm and it clicked shut. All the doors were hung and weighted to close automatically.

He turned the knob and rushed inside, slapping at the light switch on the wall.

The air was fresh and chill. The window on the other side of the veranda door was up just over a half inch, letting in the brisk air. He was suddenly relieved the upstairs alarm wasn't armed.

Marion always asked for a window to be left cracked open even in the dead of winter. The thought made his head swim, even a little dizzy. The room looked untouched, immaculate.

His bed cover was still crisp, pillows perched where he'd left them. His clothes from the cleaners were still covered in clear plastic and hanging in the open closet. The veranda door was still closed. Heat began to gush in through the floor vent and he sighed a deep breath as he hurried to close the open window.

Just after it slammed shut, after he flipped the latches, just as he turned, the lamp beside the front window flickered on.

Nathan started, blinking at the soft glow of the lamp.

"What in blazes?"

He reached over and flipped the switch back off, then on again. It obeyed as he repeated the exercise several times. He shook the power cord and the light went off, then flickered back on of its own accord.

He unplugged it, quickly winding the cord around the base of the old ugly ceramic lamp, then sat it just outside in the hall. He didn't want Troy's prophecy to come true. All he needed was for a faulty lamp to start a fire and burn the whole place to the ground.

CHAPTER THREE

NATHAN...?

Nathan Heart stretched long underneath his covers, jostling himself awake.

"I'm coming...," he muttered.

It wasn't until his bare feet hit the cold wood floor that he awakened and understood he'd been dreaming. Dreaming of Marion calling for him in the middle of the night, just as she had those last few weeks. Those last few days when it became worse, when she was delusional, when she began to immerse herself in conversation with her unseen friends.

Nathan grunted and sat back down on the verge of his bed. It was almost four a.m. and he yawned painfully. After a quick trip to the bathroom, he slid back under the covers and drifted into a restless sleep.

The alarm went off at seven. A late start by his usual standards, but since the office was downstairs, he could afford to be a little lazy. He brushed away the cover and stretched, then shivered. He remembered distinctly turning up the temperature on the furnace to knock away the chill.

A billowing white curtain caught the corner of his vision; his only window across the room was raised barely a half inch. Didn't he close it, lock it?

He had other more important things to do today, least of all worry about whether or not he'd closed a window before going to bed.

A quick shower and shave ushered him on and soon he was seated behind his desk with a hot cup of coffee, looking over this week's list of heavy hitters. He had three potential sales and three pre-qualified prospective buyers, all in a two hundred mile radius. The commission for the one on the top of the list would net an even sixty-one thousand in commission.

With the housing market in a slump and the economy in the toilet, that was a Godsend.

The desk phone rang and he frowned, looking at the time. Not quite eight a.m.

"Heart Realty. Good morning. How can I help you?"

The phone line crackled then went silent, "Hello? Yes, my name is Renaldo Lucas. I'm calling all the private realtors in your state to offer nationwide visibility on any of your hard sell properties. We are *not* affiliated with the MLS. Plus we have a high success rate…."

Nathan yawned, sipped coffee, listened politely for a break in his sales dialogue to put him down easily. It was better than just dropping the receiver down and returning to his to-do list.

Finally, the man said something that piqued Nathan's interest.

"We offer a reasonable flat fee for each listing, no matter what the listing price or square footage and we only get paid if the listing sells. Does that sound like something you'd be interested in?"

"As a matter of fact it might. Can you send me some information?"

There was a smile in the voice on the line, "If you'll give me a fax number or an email address I'll have it to you within the hour."

He could use the Heart Manor as a test pilot. If the program worked as promised, he'd list a few other property dogs sitting on the back burner.

The day was looking up already.

After he finished his first cup of coffee, he gritted his teeth and punched play on the answering machine. The first message was his sister Josie to which he listened for a few seconds and tapped the delete button. The second message crackled loudly, then he heard a faint voice through a hiss of static. It sounded as if someone called his name, "Nathan…." Then the message ended.

"That was weird," he grunted, heading for a fresh cup of coffee.

He was reminded of last night's folly, hearing someone call his name. Maybe he really had heard someone call his name, maybe the phones didn't ring due to the storm and the answering machine picked up the call anyway. Stranger things had happened, especially in this old house.

While his thought was on phones, he set his empty cup by the coffee machine and snatched a fresh trash bag. This was long overdue, something that he promised himself several times. Room after room, he undocked every telephone and dropped each one into the billowing trash sack, both upstairs and down. Three live extensions were enough for any sane person with good legs.

True to his word, Mr. Lucas both faxed and emailed several pages of information along with a simple promissory contract protecting both parties. Their only inflexible requirement was that they would be the intermediary in any transaction, to make sure any property wasn't sold by circumventing their exclusive internet listing.

The forms were straightforward and he emailed several current photographs of the Estate and surrounding area.

That week went well. He sold two of the three properties on his list, with the third still a viable sale the following week. His sister Josie didn't call with her realty expertise.

All in all - a pretty good week.

Early Monday morning, while his coffee was still brewing, he received another call. After stumbling over his end of year filing boxes, he grasped his desk phone and announced himself. The other voice gave him the oddest sensation.

"Yes…, hello? My name is Madeline Stewart. Are you the man with the house for sale?"

Nathan almost laughed over the telephone at her smarmy southern dialect. He quickly cleared the morning gravel from his throat and took a breath.

"Yes, I'm Nathan Heart. How are you today Mrs. Stewart?"

"Why I'm just fine Mr. Heart and its Ms. Stewart. My husband passed on several years ago."

"How can I help you today, Ma'am?"

"Well, for starters, you can call me Madeline. I'm looking at pictures of this cottage of yours. It really is a charming little place."

Nathan cringed, "Little cottage? I'm so sorry Madeline. The photos you're looking at must be wrong."

"It is 18,700 square feet with twelve bedrooms is it not? Not including attic rooms and the root cellar?"

Nathan stalled again, "Well…, yes, but…"

"Oh my…. Please don't tell me you've sold it already."

Nathan shook his head at her southern drawl, amused at their miscommunication.

"No Ma'am, it's still on the market."

"Oh good," she gasped. "I was afraid there was some mistake. You see…, I'm looking to purchase a vacation home on the west coast and this one looks perfect. When can I view the property?"

This had to be a prank call. She didn't ask any of the usual questions.

"Why don't you tell me when it's convenient for you and I'll make arrangements to be here."

Nathan held his breath, waiting into the silence.

"Let me check my schedule. One moment Mr. Heart. Lindsey darling, bring me my little notebook. It's in my purse in…, oh…, it's right beside me. Thank you dear."

Nathan listened to a rusting of thick pages.

"Mr. Heart? How about tomorrow afternoon or midweek?"

Nathan nearly choked.

"That… would be perfectly fine. Where will you be coming from?"

"Here in Charlotte, of course. You know…, North Carolina? I was going to be in Sacramento on Wednesday anyway, but that can wait a day or two."

Nathan was about to commit the unpardonable sin of realty and ask this strange woman if she was sure she needed something this large for a vacation home.

"I'll be available either day Ms. Stewart. Just give me a call before you arrive and I can meet you somewhere to show you how to get to the Estate."

"Aren't you the nicest young man? That won't be necessary. Now…, you aren't going to up and sell it before I get to see it, are you? I'll be more than happy to wire you a deposit to hold it if I need to."

Nathan almost laughed into the phone. In nearly thirteen months, she was the first person to express more than a passing interest in the Heart Estate.

"You have my word as a gentleman. I'll hold the house until you have a look."

"Well alright then. I'll have my driver bring me to your doorstep first thing Wednesday morning…, say nine a.m.?"

"I'll see you Wednesday then."

Nathan nearly choked when the phone went silent.

Could the dirge be past? He wanted to run through the house celebrating victory, but reigned in his emotions, afraid he'd nix the whole matter.

"Two days?" he choked. He had barely two days to make sure the place was swept and immaculate. He hadn't explained his habitation of the property. There wasn't time to hire movers to get his things removed on such short notice. Hopefully this strange woman would overlook his occupancy in light of the circumstances. He snatched up the phone and called his regular cleaners to dust the house and wax the floors.

CHAPTER FOUR

NATHAN was awake and setting up breakfast by six a.m. Wednesday. Of all days, it was gloomy and overcast with heavy laden skies threatening rain.

Outside, the lawn and hedges were immaculately trimmed and the larger deciduous trees embracing the long drive were in high color, some already shedding their leaves. It was the most picturesque time of the year to show off the sheer beauty of the estate.

Inside, the hardwood floors were gleaming with freshly buffed wax, even the bannister and staircase was polished. His office was almost completely boxed and ready to move, but his bedroom was another matter. There was no way around it. If he moved everything and this client decided not to follow through with the purchase, or somehow couldn't afford it, he'd be stuck moving everything right back where it sat.

All the what-ifs plaguing his mind ended just before nine.

Ten minutes prior to the hour, a black limousine drove up near the house in the circle drive. Out stepped an austere looking lady in a floral knee length dress, her gray wool coat open and hanging just above her hem. She appeared maybe sixty, but not helpless looking by any means. Her slightly graying blond hair was arranged behind her head in a knot, making her appear all the more severe.

A young couple, probably mid twenties, exited the other side of the car, wide eyed and smiling at every nuance of their surroundings. That at least was a good sign. The young man was a little shorter than Nathan, about six feet tall, dark striking features with manicured chestnut brown hair. The young lady was blond, attractive, and delicate looking. Both seemed far more relaxed than their elder companion, wearing jeans and pullover sweaters. The young lady was tugging her red leather jacket closed and whispering a mile a minute at her partner.

Nathan peered through the curtains, watching Madeline Stewart pointing into the distance, a hard frown on her face. He was immediately glad he hadn't moved out completely. She seemed to be waiting on something or someone..., her arms pointing several directions as she talked.

Nathan hurried and opened the door, was about to speak.

"Well. I'm certainly glad you decided to greet us."

She might as well have slapped him, but he recovered as quickly as he could, hurrying down the front steps. Maybe this wasn't the prospective buyer he'd spoken to after all.

"I'm glad to finally meet you..., Ms. Stewart?"

"Did you forget my name already Mr. Heart?"

"Of course not...," he said, recovering quickly. "Would you like to come inside?"

"No, we'd like to have a look at the grounds first, if you don't mind. It looks like rain and if we wait until later..., well there may not be a later to look around, would there?"

Nathan shook his head in frustration, "I..., have an electric cart in the garage," he motioned. "If you'll follow me."

"That little cart of yours can't drive up here and pick us up?"

Nathan felt his mouth hang open, then nodded, "I'll just be a moment."

What in the living hell was going on? What happened to the nice cordial woman he'd spoken to over the phone?

The electric cart spun its wheels on the wet grass and he slammed on the brakes when he realized he'd forgotten to unplug it. The dongle of orange extension cord was trailing behind him like an obedient tail. Unplugged, he continued to the front of the house and everyone but the limo driver climbed aboard.

At least half the back perimeter of the estate was paved in a carefully manicured trail of native coastal rock, with the moisture in the air accenting each of their dark contrasting colors. Nathan did his best to be the dutiful tour guide to the home of his childhood, suddenly regretting the idea of selling it. After all this time, after all the harassment from his family, after everything, he finally had a chance to sell and move away. Yet, the lump in his stomach was growing with every item of interest he brought to focus.

"Now the property line actually ends at that rise of spruce and ash in the distance, but this is where the trail turns and heads back toward the house."

"I think its lovely Aunt Madey," said the young lady.

Madeline grunted and turned to Nathan, "You have grounds keepers?"

"Not on permanent retainer, but there are two reputable ones I use regularly."

"What about neighbors?"

"On all sides, but the nearest home is about two miles away," said Nathan.

"Good. Nothing worse than nosey neighbors," she scoffed.

"The estate is situated four miles outside of Lumberton proper and about fifteen minutes from Salem."

"What about you Henry? Do you like the place?"

His deep voice surprised Nathan, "Very much so. I believe it would make a nice addition."

Madeline Stewart nodded, "We'll take it then."

Nathan let the cart slow to a stop, "But you haven't even inspected the house yet."

"You live there, it must be habitable."

Once again, Nathan had to recover his dropped jaw. How did she know? What did it matter? She'd just agreed to purchase the entire estate.

Nathan slowly accelerated in silence.

"Don't be so surprised Mr. Heart. You were the one that told me you were occupying the place. When I asked to view the property, you said you'd be *here*, not meet us *there*."

Had he? Of course, it would be a natural slip of the tongue.

"At least wait until you see the inside of the house before you make your decision," said Nathan.

Even he heard the coldness in his voice. Did he *want* to spoil the sale? Two point two million dollars divided five ways was not something to scoff away over a personality conflict.

The cart crunched to a halt at the foot of the front porch steps and Nathan stepped off. Without any hint of politeness, he gestured the group inside and stood holding the front door open. All pretenses were removed from his face, he was not happy with this unfurling of emotions.

Ms. Stewart stepped inside, quickly followed by the young couple. Nathan closed the door and caught sight of the crinkled nose on his client's face.

"What is that godawful smell?" she asked.

Nathan sniffed, "I'm..., what is it you smell?"

"Is that the floor wax? It is. It's the floor wax. It reeks."

She fanned her hard featured hand before her face and began to walk through the rooms and hallways.

The young couple darted up the stairs like teenagers, clopping along at a brisk pace, talking in loud echoing bursts of excitement.

Maybe they would be the occupants and not this rabid woman.

"Mr. Heart, I see no reason to delay this any longer. Are you sure you want to sell this place?"

"Of course. Why would you ask?"

"I need to make sure there are no…, lingering attachments before we conclude our business."

There was a romp of footsteps descending the staircase, finally meeting with them in one of the front rooms.

"Someone is living here," said the young lady, trying to catch her breath. "There's a furnished bedroom upstairs."

Evidently, the young lady wasn't privy to the earlier conversation.

"How long have you lived here, Mr. Heart?" asked Madeline.

"I was raised here. I've spent the last… three years here," he answered.

"Alone?" she prodded.

It was bound to come out. If not by him, then one of the local gossips.

"Alone for the last twelve months or so," he continued. "I was my mother's caretaker for the previous two years. Before she died."

"Oh my. Bless your heart. No wonder you have such a strong attachment to this place. I ask you again. Are you sure you want to sell it?"

Nathan felt his head nod up and down, "My mother expressly stated in her Will that if all the children could not agree to share the home that it was to be sold and the proceeds divided equally."

"And just exactly how many children are we talking about?" she asked.

"Five."

Without hesitation, Madeline covered her mouth in shock.

"Good God. What was your mother thinking? It must have been a slaughter."

Nathan laughed before he could stop himself, his voice echoing through the house. Never had anyone caught him so off guard. He nodded, water suddenly dripping from his eyes.

"Were you the unfortunate Executor?" she asked.

Nathan could only nod at this point; pent up emotions uncoiled mercilessly in all directions. He felt utterly foolish with this sudden display.

"What a mess that must have been. I can envision a fleet of moving vans parked outside the very next day," she whispered.

Nathan laughed again, even harder, "Three of them. It was a circus."

Finally, after wiping away a flood of water, Nathan managed to compose himself. It actually felt good to be rid of the emotion.

"What exactly did you get out of the estate? That is if you don't mind my asking?" she said quietly.

Nathan pointed to the vestibule and covered his mouth for fear of starting another wave of insane behavior.

Madeline frowned, "The clock? You got a damn clock?"

Nathan could only nod and it was Madeline Stewart's turn to laugh herself to tears.

CHAPTER FIVE

THE young couple continued their extended tour throughout the house while Nathan and Madeline stood hovering over coffee and fresh sweet rolls by the kitchen counter.

"I was caregiver for my late husband," said Madeline. "It was a horrid experience. Oh that must sound so calloused, please forgive me. I did love my husband you understand. It was just so hard watching him die a little more day after day. I hope I'm lucky enough to fall down and break my neck. Get it all over with quickly."

Nathan felt his face fall ashen, with Madeline observing his every twitch. If his family and the house didn't end him, his memories would. He wasn't sure he'd ever get used to the frank candor of this strange woman and her southern euphemisms.

"I've never heard it put quite that way, but I think I agree with you," said Nathan.

He had listened to the many stories of hard fisherman and strangers at the Blind Pirate over the years, but this lady could hold her own with the best of them.

"Well, back to our business. I don't intend to haggle over the price. My lawyer did the research on the property values and this is house along with the two hundred and sixty two acres is priced well under market value."

Nathan nodded, "It is. If you're ready to put down some escrow money, I have one of the best lending agencies in the country on speed dial."

Madeline grinned and shook her head, "No thank you. I'll just cut you a check for the full amount. We can deal with the taxes as soon as the title clears. But I have one condition concerning the sale..., actually there are two. First, I need someone to stay here until all our furniture arrives. I collect rare antiques and I'd rather not leave the place unguarded while we're away. Did I mention that this was going to be a vacation home?"

"The house has a state of the art security system. I'm sure I can find someone...."

"No. I'd rather have someone stay here that knows the place and actually cares about it. Someone such as yourself."

Nathan's head was already shaking side to side in refusal.

"It's a deal breaker, Mr. Heart. Take it or leave it," she said with a shrug.

Nathan stared at the ceiling, tormented by the feeling of leaving his home, tormented by the feeling of being coerced to stay by yet another cunning manipulator. He was on the cusp; he had to finish this sale and be done with all his family rivalries at all costs.

"What about the attic or the cottages by the garage?" she asked. "Are they livable?"

"Of course."

"Let me give this some thought. You draw up the papers and let's plan on closing before the end of the month," she said, sticking out her hand.

"And the second?" asked Nathan.

"Oh yes.... There'll be no more floor wax with a fish oil base."

Nathan laughed and shook her small hand. It was warm and strong as most men's.

"I'll get the ball rolling today. If you need to start moving in before then, I can meet your movers anytime."

She turned her head in frustration, "That wasn't the deal. I'd rather you continue to stay here. In fact...."

Nathan saw her face turn into almost a trancelike stare as she mulled over something in her mind. After a few minutes, she smiled and began to nod to herself.

"I have the perfect solution," she said with a grin. "We're only going to be here four weeks out of the year. I want to contract with you to live here as caretaker, in the main house. When we visit, if you're uncomfortable with sharing, you could live in one of the cottages by the garage. The rest of the time, the house would be yours. You can keep your room upstairs just as it is."

Nathan grimaced, "I don't think it's a good idea. I've seen too many of these types of situations turn sour." Not to mention the fact that he wanted to get far, far away from here.

"So have I, where ugly people were involved. You're not an ugly person are you Mr. Heart?"

"I have two available properties in Salem. I could live in one of them and check on this place every week?" he offered.

She shook her head, "It's all or nothing. Besides, think about what your disgruntled siblings are going to say when you get your share of the proceeds and still get to live in your parent's home."

This woman was truly evil and he was beginning to like her. The begrudged relationship between his brother and sisters was the main reason he wanted to run screaming to some sort of freedom.

"Okay. You win," said Nathan. "On a trial basis."

"For one year?" she plead, almost whining.

Once again, the young blond lady appeared in the kitchen where they stood haggling out the odd terms of their deal.

"Is there someone named Nathan that lived here?" she asked.

"That would be me," he answered.

The young woman covered her mouth with her hand, "You're Nathan?"

A wispy blond curl of her hair fell down, dangling near the side of her face.

"What is it dear?" asked Madeline.

"I was in the east hallway upstairs, by…, the bedroom…, where…," she looked at Nathan, then continued. "When I passed the door, it clicked shut and I heard a woman's voice calling for someone named Nathan."

Madeline looked back at him with sudden interest, "Why Mr. Heart, you never told us the house was haunted."

He grinned, but only halfheartedly, "That's ridiculous."

"I *know* what I heard," said the young woman in soft defiance.

Her arms clutched tightly across her chest.

"Mind your manners, Lindsey. Mr. Heart may not be aware," said Madeline.

"This house is big and empty, sounds bounce around in it all the time," he said in defense, then he remembered waking in the night to the voice of his mother. Surely that was only a dream, brought on by two years of being nursemaid, after hearing her call him all hours of the day and night. Then there was the strange message on the answering machine.

"You don't sound too awful sure about what you're saying, Mr. Heart," drawled Madeline.

He shook his head, "I don't believe in such things. Surely you don't either."

Madeline's piercing hazel eyes stared at Nathan quickly turning to concern.

"Mr. Heart, not only do we travel extensively but we are from the Deep South, born and raised in superstitious surroundings. We've seen things that might curl the hairs on your toes. Especially if a little thing like a haunted house gives you pause. Personally, I think it gives the place character. It means people really lived here, not just existing from day to day."

"Just the same, I don't like the thought of it," gritted Nathan.

Ms. Stewart took another sip of her coffee and turned.

"I believe we have completed our negotiations, Mr. Heart. Now if you'll allow me to write you that check, we'll be on our way. I still have to pay a visit to Sacramento before we head home."

Nathan frowned, still not sure how he felt about the sudden abrupt end of the uncomfortable conversation.

"Would you tell Lester to come inside and get a bite sweetheart? I completely forgot about him due to all the excitement and you know how he loves his sweets."

Lindsey flashed her dark eyes somewhat angrily at Nathan for one more brief moment and hurried away quickly on her begrudged errand.

"Please don't mind my niece. She can be quite passionate over some things."

Nathan motioned Ms. Stewart toward what was left of his office, then led the rest of the way, "She reminds me of you. She could easily pass for your daughter."

It was Madeline Stewart's turn to belt out a surprised laugh.

"Now you're just trying to flatter me. I'd have expected that *before* our negotiations, not afterward Mr. Heart."

Madeline looked around at the stacks of boxes packed in haste.

"A little presumptuous of you don't you think?" she asked, with a little wave of the hand.

Nathan cleared a few boxes from a chair and offered it to her, "Excuse me?"

"It looks as if you were packing to leave even before our deal was struck, Mr. Heart."

"I..., Yes I was.... It was time for me to move on," he stammered, looking for a folder of documents on the old house.

"I've raised both the children as my own," she began, "Lindsey and Henry. Their parents met with an accident when they were only toddlers. I suppose if you're familiar with someone after too many years, you tend to absorb their mannerisms."

Nathan found the folder and handed it to Madeline, then cleared his chair and sat as well.

"The house is a registered historical landmark, which gives it a little more charm and future value. If you ever decide at some point to turn the house you should make an easy profit."

She pilfered through a few old graying photographs of the original homestead, a recent issue of *Homestead* Magazine, then flipped through the pages of the original title deed one at a time.

"After my brother and his wife were gone, the children were devastated. I was the only family willing to take them in at the time. It was the best decision I've made over the last half of my life. What are these?"

Marion tossed some photos on the desk.

"Oh, how strange. I don't know how those managed to get in there. Those are photos of my father, Jonas Heart, Sr."

Nathan stared at the three deck sized photos of the man in uniform for a few moments and dropped them aside. When he looked back up, Madeline instantly dropped the stare he'd felt burning into his mind.

"Mr. Heart," she began.

"Nathan, please," he corrected.

"Very well..., Nathan. Would you consider selling the old clock you have in the vestibule?"

Nathan had that same strange swimmy sensation that was becoming more and more prevalent.

"I'd be glad to make it a gift to you, along with the house, but..., it is the only thing I have left of my parent's estate. I guess I'd better hang on to it."

"I'd make it worth your while," she added.

Were her train of thoughts really so scattered, or was this some strange ploy? Then he remembered her pastime.

"I forgot that you collect antiques. Let me think about it a few days and I'll let you know."

"Lester, would you bring me my portfolio?" she barked, almost a yell into the echoing abyss of the living room.

Nathan saw the tall gaunt driver pass across the view of the office door, slowly headed outside.

"There's a little bible verse I like to live by that goes something like..., I'd rather you were hot or cold. If you're lukewarm, I'll spit you out. So you see, if we only live in the shadows, we're dead already. That's why I collect things which are *important*, not just *antiques*."

CHAPTER SIX

As the limousine drove away, Nathan held up the check for a quick inspection, to make sure he wasn't daydreaming. It was written out to Heart Realty in the amount of two point two million dollars.

After Lester retrieved Madeline's portfolio, Nathan watched her almost poetic scrolling penmanship fill in the information. Then she had Lester call for her nephew Henry. The account called for two signatures for anything over one million dollars, of which Henry and Lindsey were both signatories.

Such a strange family.

He walked straight out to the large black frame near the rural highway and plucked up the For Sale sign, carefully avoiding the whitewashing on the back surface.

Nathan hurried inside and placed the check and preliminary forms in an envelope then readied himself to drive to the county seat to register the transaction. He supposed that he should call his elder siblings to give them the news they'd been waiting over a year to hear.

Somehow, rubbing the finality of the whole matter in Josie's face didn't seem as pleasurable as he'd imagined. It wasn't until he was on the interstate headed north until he opened his cell phone and dialed.

"Caroline?"

"Nathan? How are you? Did Josie call you?"

"Yes..., fine, and she did. Have you joined her glee club?"

"You know better than that Nathan. Sorry I mentioned it. Hey, we'd love to see you. When are you going to visit us?"

"Nice diversion, Sis. Soon..., I promise. How's my favorite niece?"

"Allie started first grade without a hitch. She claims she's bored already."

"You should have her evaluated. She might be right."

The phone went silent for a few seconds.

"What's up Nathan? Josie getting under you skin again?"

"No…, yes of course she is. Doesn't she always?"

"I'll be glad when it's over and she can blame all her troubles on somebody else. You'd think the world revolved around selling mom and dad's Estate."

"I did it Caroline."

Nathan could hear her breathing for several seconds.

"You did what Nathan?"

"I'm on the way to the bank and the title company with the check. I sold the Estate. It's done."

"I…, don't know what to say," she whispered. "I'm happy and I'm sad all at the same time."

"Me too," said Nathan.

"Does Josie or Jonas or Rachael know? Have you called either of them?"

"Only you. They don't deserve to know just yet. Do they? Am I being as ass, Caroline?"

Nathan heard her giggle, just like she did when they were little. When the others bullied them incessantly and he and Caroline won some small victory.

"Anyway, it's done. I'm on my way to make it permanent. Why don't I feel the relief?"

"You will. When it hits you. When you put your share of the sale in your account and take a long, well deserved vacation."

Nathan felt his face smile unexpectedly.

"Yeah. I suppose you're right."

"Hey Nathan, I hate to do this, but I need to go. Don't beat yourself up. It's all for the best."

"Thanks Caroline…, love you."

"Love you too. Come see us."

Nathan dropped his phone in the seat beside him.

"A vacation?" he muttered.

♥

The business transactions went without a hitch.

Monday week, the check cleared and the process began its final methodical procedure.

Tuesday early, a medium sized moving van arrived and beeped its horn outside before a gruff looking individual stepped out of the driver seat.

Nathan stepped out onto the front porch, holding his steaming cup of coffee and wiping his bleary eyes.

"Mr. Heart?" the man asked, fidgeting with a folding metal pad.

"I'm Nathan Heart."

The man nodded and seemed to relax, "Got a delivery. Is this a good time?"

Another sedan stopped in the drive and two beefy men crawled out, tossing their jackets inside the car.

The driver of the van, turned, "They're the muscle. I'm supposed to have you sign this when we're done. Here's the Bill of Lading, the inventory list and a sketch of where it all goes."

He handed Nathan a stack of paper, the inventory list of items was two pages long, with their individual insured values.

Nathan wiped the crust from his eyes and frowned as he read the list; then the total value of the freight.

"You don't have to help, but I'd appreciate it if you make sure we put it all where it's supposed to go. I'm...," he thumbed over his shoulder. "We're..., a little nervous about getting this off our hands."

Nathan agreed readily, "I don't blame you."

He propped the door open and the men began trip after careful trip from the van into the house. There were delicate oil paintings still in crates that were disassembled on the porch before entering the house. There were specific instructions against scuffing the immaculate hardwood floors with the heavier pieces of furniture.

Nathan watched as a intricately hand carved armoire of original French descent, floated its way into one of the downstairs bedrooms. Two crates of rare books were carefully unpacked and stacked, then left for future placement inside the library. A set of new light-blocking curtains replaced the light airy ones over the library windows.

Nathan watched in awe as piece after piece of small furniture entered the house, was photographed where it was placed, and finally inspected. Nathan was expected to place his initials beside each item in turn.

It was nearly two in the afternoon when the perspiring driver handed him the pad for his signature. Great relief flooded his face when Nathan assumed final responsibility for the twenty some odd million dollars in inventory.

"Don't forget to fax this receipt to that number at the top or we don't get paid."

"I'll be sure and do it immediately," muttered Nathan, still looking at the different listed values.

The men left as quickly as they arrived.

Nathan walked through the house looking at each piece, frowning at some, grinning at the absurdity of others. The scant contents of the house were valued many times over the entire estate.

When the phone rang at precisely three that afternoon, Nathan wasn't surprised to hear the voice of Madeline on the line.

"Hello Nathan. I trust my first load of trinkets arrived in good order."

Nathan grinned at her attempt at trivializing the shipment.

"Everything arrived in good order, but I had no idea you wanted me to double as a museum curator."

She chuckled, "These were my random pieces. I needed to see if those hooligans could actually deliver everything without breaking something in the process."

"Well, it's all here. I assume you have the receipt."

"How are you doing Nathan?"

She actually sounded concerned, despite the bad crackling connection in their call.

He nodded at the phone, "Actually, I'm doing pretty well at the moment. How are you and your family?"

"Very well," she answered. "I apologize for the bad connection. The service here in Hong Kong is horrid. I'm going to have to break down and get one of those ugly satellite phones I so despise."

Nathan grinned. She was in Hong Kong? Not likely.

"There'll be another shipment arriving early Thursday if that's convenient for you?"

"Tell me when you need me here."

There was a hiss on the line and then the distinctive voices of a heated conversation in Mandarin Chinese arose in the background.

"I'll email you a schedule of the next deliveries. I apologize for not alerting you to today's shipment, but there was nowhere reliable to make a telephone call."

Maybe Madeline Stewart really was somewhere on the other side of the globe.

"Are the pieces I sent to your liking Mr. Heart?" she asked.

Did she just ask his opinion about her collectibles?

"I…, suppose so, yes. They're all very unique."

"Very good. You'll let me know if anything arrives that doesn't meet your approval?"

"My approval? I don't understand?"

Nathan could almost see her small shoulders shrug on the other side of the planet, "I trust your judgement. Otherwise, I'm going to have to rely entirely on my memory of the layout to situate the inventory. I'm not quite as sharp as I once was."

Nathan laughed before he could contain himself, "Somehow, I don't believe that for a moment."

"Flattery, Mr. Heart. It's a tool of the devil," she laughed.

The line crackled once again, "Nathan…, have you told your family about the sale yet?"

It was Nathan's turn to remain silent and in thought.

"Hello? This phone's gone dead again...," she grumbled to some unseen assistant.

"Madeline? Wait..., I'm here. No. I haven't told all of them just yet."

"It'll make you feel better if you just go ahead and do it. Snatch the bandage off that wound. I think you'll find it's already healed. Oh. I need to go Mr. Heart. We'll be in touch."

There was a loud snap and the call went dead.

CHAPTER SEVEN

As promised, Thursday morning an enormous orange moving van with 'air-ride suspension' stenciled on the side, inched slowly into the circle drive and carefully backed up toward the front door.

He was met by the same gruff fellow with his dull metallic clipboard, but there was a six-man team that exited the extended-cab truck behind him.

"Back again," he muttered anxiously.

Nathan nodded, "So I see."

"I'm Bob by the way. It looks like we'll be seeing a lot of each other the next few weeks."

"Hello Bob. I'll start something for lunch. It looks like you gentlemen will be here all day."

True enough, this shipment took until dark to unload. Each item meticulously placed according to a carefully thought out sketch of the house. The items from the previous shipment were the dark gray of a photocopy.

When the men were through, seated on the front porch, sweating in the cold evening air, Nathan walked out and sat beside Bob, handing him the signed document.

"Bob. Where did all this come from?" asked Nathan.

"You mean you don't know?"

"I'm just the caretaker. Didn't Ms. Stewart tell you?"

Bob shook his head and shrugged, "Don't know no Ms. Stewart. We get a contract with an address in Sacramento, we load up, we deliver. We get paid. It's none of our business."

Nathan looked at the manifest with a deeper frown. The origin of the shipment was "Secure Storage Services" with a Sacramento California address. How strange.

"What exactly is this place?" asked Nathan, pointing at the shipping document.

"You don't want to know. It takes an act of congress to get in and out of the place. All us guys had to get a top level security clearance just to get inside to the front desk."

Bob suddenly turned quiet and seemed as if his candor had overstepped a hidden boundary.

"Must be a stressful drive, knowing the value of what's in the cargo behind you," said Nathan, testing for more information.

Bob laughed and wiped his forehead, "Not nearly as bad as your job. Look…, when I get this stuff delivered here, I'm done with it. But you got this stuff around you all the time. I wouldn't trade jobs with you for no amount of money. You get me?"

Nathan's eyes were enlightened. He looked at the insured value of this shipment and cringed after adding it to the previous.

"Yeah, you get me," laughed Bob, "You ready boys? Let's start back. Mama's waiting on me at home."

This time when the truck drove away, Nathan watched it until it was completely out of sight.

When he turned around, the living room was now nearly full of well-matched, well-placed artifacts. Items you wouldn't bump a vacuum cleaner against and delicate carpets you wouldn't dare vacuum in the first place.

Again, he dutifully faxed the pages of the received inventory, then wandered back out to look at the oddities.

At the rate of deliveries on his weekly schedule, it wouldn't take long to furnish the entire household. With the combined value of the contents, he would have to leave his shoes by the front door to risk wandering through the house.

The clock in the vestibule began to bong the hour and Nathan wandered over and swiped a hand down its tall mahogany side like a pet. Its carnelian hue and the shiny brass detailing seemed to gleam in the warm recessed overhead lighting. His mother loved the old thing. The hourly chime finished with a muffled and contented tone, now that the adjoining room was full. According to his mother, the handcrafted clock hadn't been moved from where it was currently sitting since the house was first completed in 1902. Yet here it sat, a testament of time itself.

He carefully unlocked the clock's door with the tiny key mated with the gold chain around his neck and cranked the weights for another few weeks of service.

The ringing of the telephone usurped the silence and Nathan looked at his wristwatch for the time despite the vibrating chronometer beside him.

He barely beat the automated telephone system and expecting his caller to be Madeline Stewart, snatching up the receiver.

"Heart Realty."

"Nathan. Good. I just spoke with Charles' associates and I believe we've struck a deal to sell the Heart Estate, lock, stock, and barrel. We may not get the price we were hoping, but at least we'll be rid of it. I need you to send him a package of recent photos of the house and some brochures, especially that magazine write up from four or five years ago. You know the one that did a special on Historical Landmarks on the west coast. He needs this tonight or in the morning…, just as soon as you can…."

"Josie. Stop," said Nathan.

"No Nathan. I'm not willing to let you homestead there another year twiddling your thumbs like a vagrant, while the rest of us ignore the fact that you've done nothing for over a year.

"Not one more day Nathan. Do you hear me? Not one…, more…, day."

Nathan waited for her to run out of steam and catch her breath. Should he tell her? Should he just wait until she received her notice in the mail of her disbursement?

"Josie. You'll be receiving a certified notice of a bank draft tomorrow or the next day for your portion of the sale of the estate. The funds should be immediately available once…."

The phone made a loud tumbling ruckus and all Nathan could hear was a jumble of muffled voices.

"Josie?"

A high-pitched voice belted in his ear, "Nathan Heart. What in blazes did you say to my wife? Josephine has fainted. What scheme have you upset her with this time?"

"Charles? Is that you?" asked Nathan.

"Who the…. Who else would it be?" he barked, then held the phone away. "She's coming to? Josephine are you alright?"

The phone beeped in Nathan's ear; another call. It was probably the call he was expecting instead of his irate sister.

"Charles? I have another important call. I'm going to have to let you go."

The phone slammed down in Nathan's ear.

"Well…, that went better than planned," he grunted.

He hit the switch-hook and made another announcement.

"Hello Nathan."

"Ms. Stewart, so good to hear from you."

At least this voice was calm.

"You sound different Nathan. Oh my…. Did you snatch off that bandage as I suggested? You did, didn't you?"

"I believe I did," said Nathan.

"And you feel better now don't you?" she asked.

"I'll let you know in a few days," chuckled Nathan.

"Hmmm, apparently some hair came off with the adhesive. Just as well. I see you received my shipment today."

Nathan took a deep breath, "Yes and the house is filling up nicely. The front living area almost looks lived in as of about an hour ago."

"I'm glad you like it. Anything you want to rearrange, please feel free to do so. This next shipment will be much smaller, but please make sure that those ruffians are especially careful. Make them wear the gloves I've provided Nathan."

"Gloves?"

Nathan hurriedly looked at his next scheduled shipment..., books.

"Ah, I understand. You don't want gritty fingerprints on your books," he muttered, looking at the proposed list.

"Those books coming your way are all first editions. And no, I don't want any oils of any kind on them."

"Thus the darkroom?" prodded Nathan, remembering the vault like curtains from the first visit.

"Very astute of you Mr. Heart."

"Madeline, I already feel as if I'm going to break something if I walk through the house. Are you absolutely sure you want me living here after all your items arrive?"

"Don't worry about any of that old stuff. You just treat it as if it was yours and go about your business as usual. It's all insured, piece by piece. It's just stuff, Nathan, ...even if some of it isn't replaceable."

That didn't do much to soothe his worry, but he didn't want to argue the ever burgeoning value of everything around him.

"Well, if you've no more business at hand, I'm going to take off these heels and rest my feet. It feels good to be home Mr. Heart. You have a good evening."

Nathan bid her goodnight and toured the house, rechecking the items on the shipping manifest, then nervously checking the alarm system..., twice.

He flopped back down in the cushy chair in his office. The one piece of furniture he could relax in downstairs without fear of destroying some ancient artifact. He noticed the instant stain of perspiration on each of the leather chair arms. Bob was right about one thing, this was turning into far more than he anticipated.

Nathan pushed the worry aside..., it was time to call Jonas and Rachael, to clear the air before it was tainted with Josie's impending version.

He snatched up the phone and held it nervously before hitting the speed dial to his brother in Seattle Washington.

The call to Jonas Heart Jr. proved to be uneventful, anticlimactic, even cold and curt, lasting only about three minutes. Next was Rachael - Josie in training. He rarely heard from her or her family in Reno Nevada more than once or twice a year.

Strangely enough, her response almost mirrored the one to Jonas. Strange enough that Nathan could tell that they had been talking among themselves. But why? His imagination must be running wild. Any collusion at this point would serve no purpose whatsoever. The house was sold. They were getting their money. Wasn't that what they had been whining about all this time?

Nathan shook his head in awe and leaned back in the chair, closed his eyes, listening to the silence. Just as he let out a well deserved sigh....

"Nathan...," echoed from somewhere in the house..., or his head.

He leaned forward, suddenly alert. This time he wasn't dozing or nearly asleep, no phone calls, no storms..., no excuses. He was instantly standing at his office door, almost dizzy from the rush of motion.

"Hello?"

He didn't expect an answer, not that there was one. His mind instantly went back to the dark eyes of Madeline's niece, Lindsey Stewart. Her tightly crossed arms and adamant glare were etched in his memory. Even in memory, her honey brown eyes mesmerized him with their intensity. His head swam for a few moments until he relaxed.

The house was silent once again, all but the barely recognizable tock, tock, tock, of the grandfather clock far in the front of the house.

Surely, his problems with the nausea and dizziness would go away now that the stress of all the family problems was quieted. Then he remembered that he hadn't eaten more than a few bites of a sandwich all day, after following the movers in and out, inspecting each piece brought inside.

He looked at the time once again. It was getting late and he needed to call and make sure that Josie had recovered from her blight of shock. He'd hate to find out that she'd suffered some other serious malady.

After a deep breath, he pressed the number and waited.

"Charles?"

"Nathan." The man's voice was hard, cold, full of hidden emotion.

"How is Josie?"

"She's upstairs resting. I gave her a sedative."

Great. Dr. Charles Clarion would never let him live this down. Yet another mark against him.

"What's this business about the estate? She mumbled something on the order of it being sold already. Is that true?" he asked, with slow deliberate enunciation.

"Yes, it's true. I was trying to explain that to her when she had her sudden spell."

"Well. I suppose its all for the best then," he mumbled.

"What? I don't understand. I thought Josie would be thrilled. Wasn't that what everyone wanted?" asked Nathan, immediately wishing he'd kept his mouth tightly shut.

"Yes, of course…, and it was good of you to call. I'm sure Josephine will be fine after a night's rest. Thank you for concern, Nathan."

The phone went dead before Nathan could utter another breath.

Something was afoot or foiled, he couldn't tell which.

CHAPTER EIGHT

EARLY that next morning, Nathan had decided to enjoy some of the spoils of war and spend the day perusing the coastal towns. The sky was clear, the air fresh; a perfect day to wallow in self-indulgent activities for someone with a fresh deposit of liquid assets in his account.

He was barely out of the drive when his cell phone chirped. This time he was more cautious and identified the caller before answering.

"Caroline! How are you this beautiful Wednesday morning?"

"Nathan. You sound much better. Can I ask a favor of you?"

"The sky's the limit, Caroline."

"Can I meet you somewhere today, for a talk?"

"Meet me today?" Nathan felt his heart drop. "Are you alright? Is there something wrong? Please tell me."

"I'm driving to the coast as we speak," she said. "Allie's in school until three this afternoon. I thought we could catch a bite to eat in Tillamook. That little cove where we used to meet when Marion..., when mother was feeling spry."

Nathan was determined to keep this day free of depressing conversations and liaisons.

"You caught me on a perfect day for visiting. I was planning to drive south along the coast to California until my wanderlust had its fill, but I'd love to have an early dinner or brunch or any label you'd like to give it. Care to tell me what shook you out of your nest so early this morning?"

"I would have called you last night, but I wasn't sure where you'd be staying now that the estate is sold."

It was then he remembered that none of them knew about his future living arrangements.

"Actually, I'm still living at the estate. In fact, it looks as if I'll be there for at least another twelve months."

"You're still in that empty old house? I don't understand."

A horn blared so close it obliterated her next few words.

"Nathan, I'm crossing the bridge into Old Town and everything is backing up. I hate trying to sift through my thoughts while I drive in this crazy traffic."

She grunted a few choice words and he heard the distinctive sound of her car horn.

This was ridiculous, something had her disturbed.

"Did Josie call you? Or was it Jonas or Rachael?"

All Nathan could hear was the muffled sounds of traffic over Caroline's phone, then another blaring horn. She must be dead serious to be driving through Seattle this time of the morning.

"Can we talk later? I…, I'm a little distracted at the moment Nathan."

"See you in an hour, Sis."

Now what? Would he have to cut all ties to his family to get some modicum of peace in his life? Certainly not with Caroline, but what about the others? The unknown began to eat his reserve as his car lurched anxiously forward onto the interstate, headed north.

Caroline's chocolate colored Audi Spyder was already parked outside the waterside restaurant when Nathan arrived. His sister was seated facing him, cell phone plastered to her head as he parked beside her.

Her cell dropped immediately and she rolled out of her car to greet him with a blazing smile. She rarely drove the little two-seater unless she was looking for a change of mood or wanting to relive happy memories.

"Nathan!" she squealed, hugging his neck enthusiastically. "How's my little brother? Is that a touch of gray I see?"

Her contagious smile had him grinning in an instant as she fingered through the sandy brown hair at his temples.

"You had me worried. Why were you being so mysterious over the phone?"

"Let's go inside and order some food. It's chilly out here."

He felt his head droop at yet another postponement. Caroline grabbed his hand and yanked him into motion, her smile radiating once again.

He immediately noticed that Caroline had bobbed her tawny-brown hair off since he'd seen her last; she looked five years younger than him. Her thick gray sweater drooped merrily in the front, the collar swaying with her movements. Nathan grinned when he remembered that she'd turned down a career in modeling at seventeen. That's what love had done to her and Chris.

The breakfast crowd was clearing out and she asked for a seaside table with a view of the docks, where they used to meet every few weeks with

Marion. Most of the slips at Tillamook Bay were vacant, the fishing boats out for their second run of the day.

"Now. Tell me what all the mystery is about?" said Nathan, as he slid into the booth. "You're driving me absolutely insane."

Caroline tightened her lips, her eyes piercing Nathan as she accumulated her first thoughts.

"It's Josie," she said finally. She made their elder sister's name sound like a curse word.

After gazing into the mirror image of her brown eyes, trying to contain his emotion, he looked away.

"I knew it," gritted Nathan. "What's she chosen to berate me about now?"

"The estate Nathan. It's always about the estate. You should know that," she hissed.

"But it's sold? She should be thrilled. What could she possibly be irate about now?"

Caroline shook her springy hair from side to side, "I'm not supposed to know about this, so you didn't hear it from me, okay?"

Nathan rolled his eyes and nodded his agreement, attempting to wave the words from her mouth with his hands.

"The *Big Three* were planning a coup," she began, her voice barely above a whisper. "The three of them signed a contract to sell mother's estate to a developer. Some bigwig wanted to turn it into an exclusive B & B for the rich and famous. Put in tennis courts and a spa and gym out back. They were going to sell it for four and a half million, then fix it all so it looked like it went for a loss at one and a half."

Nathan felt himself wilt.

"Let me guess, I was going to get the short end of the straw?" he asked.

Caroline nodded slowly, her eyes forlorn, "Both of us actually. I wasn't supposed to know either. They know you and I talk. I can't tell you how I found out or my family mole would get in big trouble."

It was one of Josie's children. It had to be. Caroline was their favorite aunt, despite the continued tension between the families.

"Well…," whispered Nathan, when the storm in his mind settled. "Why didn't they just tell me? It's not like I was trying to monopolize the sale of the property for my own gain."

"That's not the way Josie has been playing it up to Jonas and Rachael. She's had them believing that you were trying to manipulate the whole thing in your favor, ever since the reading of the Will."

"Unbelievable. So she convinced them to agree to do exactly what she was accusing me of doing?"

Caroline nodded. It didn't make any sense. Well, maybe Rachael, but Jonas? Jonas Jr. was almost forty years old. Surely he could see through his sister's cunning avarice.

"Have you received your certified letter over the sale yet?" asked Nathan.

Caroline grinned and nodded, "Yesterday. Allie's college fund. I could just kiss you."

"What about the contract they signed?" asked Nathan.

Her face quickly turned into a grimace, "That's what has them all in a stir. There was a default clause in the contract. If for some reason the sale didn't mature as planned, each of them would have to pay ten thousand dollars in damages."

"That's extortion," hissed Nathan. "Who is this collaborator?"

Caroline shook her head, "I don't have a clue. Kate didn't...."

She suddenly cupped her mouth, her secret floating in the sudden silence.

Nathan grinned. It was Josie's daughter Kathryn, exactly as he suspected.

"Don't you dare ever, ever let them know it was Kate that spilled the beans. Nathan, please promise me?"

Nathan laughed at her innate inability to keep a secret from him.

"I promise. Not a soul. Now, if you manage to find out who was trying to undermine the sale will you let me know? I'd like to place them on my blacklist of all blacklists."

With that off Caroline's chest, she visibly relaxed, letting the conversation drift into the mundane trinkets of their lives.

Caroline made him promise to visit her family as soon as possible, to catch up, to relax, and to lock back into being a family. He eventually agreed to help with their Halloween festivities in the coming few weeks.

♥

The rest of that day was spent in the suburbs of Portland, trekking from shop to shop after deciding on another excursion the coming weekend. With the pressure from his last obligation relieved, his mind was finally opening up to the possibilities of life around him.

When he arrived back at the estate, a moving van was sitting parked in his driveway. Two irritated men were sitting on the front porch steps drinking coffee from a thermos. Evidently, the two stone lions hadn't bluffed them away by their angry stares.

"Bob? What are you doing here?"

"We got a call; told us to speed up our schedule. Nobody called you?" he asked Nathan.

"How long have you been here waiting?"

"Two hours," he answered. "This trip."

Inside, there was a message on his answering machine, informing him of the changes. His sudden guilt forced him to don a pair of white gloves and help the two men populate the shelves in the library.

"Make sure you look at the layout if you're going to help. They have to go on the shelves in a certain order," gritted Bob.

He may have been tired and angry, but he was right. Each ancient volume was pre-labeled in a version of the Dewey Decimal System and assigned to specific shelves. The process was as tedious as the idea compulsive and obtuse.

When the last book was removed from the meticulous wrapping and placed on the shelf, the library was full, hundreds of them. Every shelf, every last space filled with odd-looking rare editions from every place imaginable.

Bob handed Nathan a small metal cabinet, "Now. It's yours."

Nathan flipped open the gray top with a frown.

"A card catalogue?" he muttered.

This topped all the strange he'd seen so far. It was old school, which pretty much summed up his idea of Madeline Stewart.

CHAPTER NINE

TWO more weeks of shipments and the entire downstairs of the estate was completely settled with antiquities from around the world.

The most elaborate - a long ebony black dining table, inlaid with ornate Indonesian patterns of solid gold. The reflective glow from the two dining room chandeliers hovering above it was enough to mesmerize even the most jaded connoisseur.

Pictographs, lithographs, statues, busts, carvings, littered every available corner and wall space, all carefully located and arranged for their best preservation from daylight.

There were threadbare tapestries from most every known country, some encased within elaborate shadowboxes, others carefully displayed in dark regions of hallways.

Nathan couldn't help feeling a blanket of uncertainty about the unknown, hovering like a fog throughout the house.

At first he dismissed these feelings as remnants of the ignominious psychological war he'd just endured, just as he dismissed the sudden increase of ill mannered noises inside the old Heart Manor.

Creaks or groans, sometimes little pops would echo from a disgruntled room causing him to startle or spin a glance in their direction. Eyes seemed to be following his every footstep, listening to his very thoughts until he began to shy away from certain unused portions of the house.

This new opaque dread was definitely not the feeling of home he loved to reminisce about.

♥

On a Friday, the second week of October he received an eloquently handwritten card from Madeline Stewart:

Dear Mr. Heart,

This communication is to announce the arrival of myself and a few select family members on the 12th of November for the duration of the month.

I would also like to formally invite you to join with us in celebration of the Thanksgiving Holiday. To make your commitment worthwhile, I intend to extend to you a business proposition that I believe will be in your interests.

Dress will be formal.

Madeline Stewart

RSVP

p.s. A few of my staff will arrive on the 8th to prepare for our arrival.

How completely and utterly strange. Why so formal? Why didn't she just call? Surely she knew he had plans with his own family.

Or did he?

Nathan plowed back in his office chair and reread the stiff white card with its gilt edges, even sniffed the honeysuckle fragrance of the black ink, delicately swirled with some sort of fountain pen.

A formal invitation to spend Thanksgiving with strangers shrouded in a mystery of some sort of business proposition.

As if to reassure himself, Nathan snatched up the telephone and dialed the only family member that was communicating with him at the moment.

"Caroline?"

"Uncle Nate!" chirped a small voice.

"Allie, is that you? How is my favorite niece in the whole world today?"

"I'm quite fine, thank you," she giggled. "Are you still coming here for Halloween?"

"I wouldn't miss it."

Before he could ask her a dozen questions, someone took the telephone, "Hello?"

From the tone in the voice, it was Chris, Caroline's husband since college.

Nathan grunted and attempted to change his voice, "Hello? Yeah, I'm working my way through school and I was wondering if you'd be interested in buying some magazines to help me out."

There was a short chuckle, "No wonder it took you so long to sell that big boat. How are you Nathan?"

"Fine, really good. Allie sounds so grown. How's the family?"

"We're great. You're not calling to bail on the visit are you? It's all Allie's talked about," said Chris.

"Not at all. Actually, I was calling about Thanksgiving. I was wondering if Caroline had heard from any of the family."

Chris laughed into Nathan's ear, "I take it you're still on the excommunicated list?"

"Not a peep out of the lot of them," sighed Nathan.

"So you're really calling here for an invitation to our turkey and dressing?" asked Chris, a grin in his voice.

"You always know how to cut me to the quick, but I suppose I was trying to Jonesy for an invitation."

"Well you're out of luck this year buddy. We're all going on a cruise that entire week," he chirped happily.

Nathan felt his heart sink.

"You know how Callie is always entering those contests and drawings on her shopping sprees? Well this time she won. We received a notice a few days ago. All expenses paid. What can I say?"

Nathan heard another familiar voice take over the call, "Nathan? Why don't you come with us? Spend some of that money you're hoarding and come with us, please? We'd love to have you."

"Hey Caroline. Actually, I can't take off the entire week. I'm sort of obligated."

"You finally asked one of those local girls out?" teased Chris.

"You're ganging up on me? No, it's nothing like that. It's..., work related," said Nathan.

"You won't get a better offer than this," sang Caroline.

When Nathan was done with his quest, he was even more crestfallen than before. Fate was steadily pounding a wedge between him and his entire family.

He picked up the invitation and once again appreciated the practiced artistic handwritten scrolls.

"Looks like I'll be eating turkey here."

Nathan felt a warm sigh of breath over his shoulder, past his ear. He jumped from his chair and spun, eyes blinking around the small office.

When his heart stopped hammering in his chest, he picked up the chair he'd toppled.

"I'm losing it."

He grabbed his jacket and keys in a steady pace to the garage. It was Saturday after all; he had no obligations to anyone. Work was done for the day; he'd advertised four more slow properties through the capable Mr. Renaldo Lucas. It barely eased his conscience for not putting in his usual hours at Heart Realty, but wasn't the entire purpose of earning money to spend a little before you die?

The Cadillac XLR's engine galloped under the hood yanking the car sideways as he spun out the drive through the open front gate. He needed a drink and some friendly conversation.

The Blind Pirate, situated a short walk from the pier of Crab Cove, was packed. Nathan had to park around back in the owner's private parking area before walking through the cold evening air to the side entrance.

It was the only dive in fifty miles that had good food, good music, and an atmosphere.

"Nathan! Where have you been hiding, my boy?"

Troy smacked his big palm on the bar with a pop. He seemed to be a little too free with his own liquor tonight.

"Busy night?" Nathan yelled.

"It's the new band. I hope I can talk'em into staying another week," he blurted over the noise. "What'll you have?"

Right to business, "The usual. How's the grill tonight?"

"A new catch of fresh shrimp this morning, but you'll have to wait for a table like the rest tonight. We're bulging at the seams."

"I'm not in any hurry," answered Nathan, as Troy slid him a cold mug.

Troy was about to turn and walk to the other end of the bar, some yuppie waving him down, "You look like you're in the mood for a good talking to, am I right?"

Nathan shook his head, "Nope. I just needed to get away from that house tonight. It's driving me crazy Troy."

"Still living in your past. Drive any good man insane."

He finally turned around, "Hold your horses, I'm coming."

A small table soon opened and Troy forgot his earlier warning and gave it to Nathan, ahead of several others. Troy usually blundered over and sat to talk, but with all the excitement, the music and bustle, he was hard pressed to leave from behind the bar.

Troy's favorite waitress, Lisa came by and took his order, dropping down a full mug. Minutes later she returned, untying her apron and stood by the chair across from him with a grin.

"Troy says I should keep you company for awhile. Do you mind?"

She smiled when Nathan waved her into the other seat.

The old buzzard was trying to play matchmaker again, shoving Lisa his direction…, not that he was going to protest by any means. It didn't have anything to do with Lisa, she was very attractive, chatty, attentive, but he could tell she wasn't too sure about the arrangement either. Troy didn't understand anything other than she was a single gal, he was a single man, and that should be all that mattered.

"Thanks, Troy said I could take my break early. My feet were killing me."

Nathan couldn't help but smile. She had a schoolgirl innocence and a natural gift to serve those around her.

"How long have you been here?" asked Nathan.

"Six hours, just as busy as this," she answered with a huff.

"Actually…, I was wondering how long you'd worked for Troy," grinned Nathan.

"Now you're going to hurt my feelings," she grinned.

"Strike one," he frowned.

She laughed softly, "Off and on for…, almost four years I think." Her hand nervously pushed a length of light brown hair behind an ear.

No wonder she looked familiar.

"He's a good guy. Troy that is," Nathan commented, watching her closely. Her eyes seemed to be searching him every time he lifted his gaze her direction.

"Yeah," she smiled; her wondering expression seemed to soften a little.

A waiter dropped several platters of food on the table and grunted, "Your break ain't for another half hour."

"She's with me," said Nathan. "Lisa, what did you say you wanted to drink?"

Lisa grinned, "Just some tea."

"Lisa wants some tea and we need another plate and some silver for her."

Nathan watched the teenaged boy grit his crooked teeth before walking away.

"Nice co-workers you have here," said Nathan.

"Aw, he don't mean anything by it. He's just a kid," she answered.

It appeared Lisa was innocent to a fault.

"Just the same, I'd check my iced tea before I took a sip…, if it was me," said Nathan.

When the extra plate and tea arrived, Lisa stared at it for several seconds while the waiter was setting her silver.

"You know? I think I'd rather have one of those bottled teas in the cooler."

Her co-worker seemed more than just a little put out as he walked away.

Lisa scooted the glass of frothy iced tea away to the border of the table as if it was a dead cricket. Nathan pretended not to notice and shoveled a generous portion of grilled shrimp onto her plate and arranged the side dishes closer between them. He wasn't that hungry and she seemed more in need of a friend than he did tonight.

She didn't protest the food, and as Troy had recommended she made interesting company while the other waiter hovered past as a constant reminder of her neglected duties.

About an hour later, they were picking at crumbs and still chatting when Troy wandered over.

"Dearie, could you do me a favor and take over the bar while I cool my heels here with Nathan?"

Lisa thanked Nathan and hurried off while tying the ribbon of her apron behind her back. It was only then that Nathan noticed the music had ceased, but the noise was still one continuous clamor. His eyes seemed to follow Lisa of their own accord until she was out of sight.

Apparently, Troy had slowed down on his intake of alcohol, even seemed a little melancholy.

"Did ya enjoy your company?"

"Lisa's a very nice young lady," said Nathan. "You should have four more like her here and you wouldn't need a band to keep your business humming."

"Ah, now that's what I like to hear," he cheered.

"Now some of your other help is a different story."

"Young Bart? He's a real pisser of a waiter," said Troy.

Nathan waited for some type of hint if that was supposed to be a compliment or an insult.

"Yeah, well he's alright if you like spit in your tea," grunted Nathan.

Troy laughed and slapped the table, "The young swagger reminds me of myself when I was about his age. I don't use him much around people, mostly for maintenance.

"He's bunking in a back room while he earns his keep here. When I found him, he was nothing but skin and bones. Orphaned, he was. System spat him out. He'd a probably ended up in jail. Still might," Troy shrugged.

When Nathan refused to comment, Troy leaned over toward him, "So tell me what's got ya all topsy-turvy this fine evening."

"I've already told you. The walls were squeezing in as usual," said Nathan. He felt bad for lying even though there was truth mixed in.

"Ah, stir crazy," he nodded. "You'll tell me if you start a hearing them voices your old mom went on about, won't ya? It'd make for good conversation here on the slow nights."

Nathan glared at Troy for a second or two, then shook his head. That was something that he would never share with Troy if it ever happened.

"I just need to get out more," said Nathan finally. "I'm thinking about taking a few trips down the coast over the next few weeks. That ought to get me back in the groove again."

"Any of them plans include little Lisa over there by any chance?" he muttered, hardly the whisper he intended.

Nathan grinned, "Lisa's a wonderful lady."

"But?" he scowled, "You ain't interested?"

Troy didn't wait for an answer, "I'm telling ya, you're gonna end up an old hermit Nathan Heart. She's almost twenty six, just right for a man such as yourself. Make ya a good woman, even pop out a few kids for ya given a little time."

Nathan couldn't help but laugh at the raw sincerity of his gruff friend. To him, Lisa Evans was a shiny car sitting on a lot.

"I'll keep that in mind Troy. If I change my mind you'll be the first to know."

CHAPTER TEN

Monday rolled around quickly, met with another early delivery of furniture. Bob and his crew had to work doubly hard, carrying piece after piece of furniture up the sweeping staircase and down the long halls.

Nathan pitied their backbreaking labor, even overlooked a few bumps up the stairs with all the heavy solid wood pieces. More than once he saw Bob take a bottle of brown shoe polish from his jacket pocket and swipe the lip of a stair step.

Late that afternoon, two of the men were walking tiredly down the stairs, talking quietly.

"...if the money weren't so good, I know I wouldn't be coming back this week."

"Me neither, the place gives me the willies."

"Feels like a pair of eyes watching everywhere I go."

"My dad used to say...."

One of the men abruptly stopped his discourse when they passed the open door of the office where Nathan was seated, listening.

"Now that's a queer fellow if I every saw one," whispered one as they almost passed out of earshot. "Have to be, to live in this place all alone."

Wednesday, the truck returned, the huge trailer packed as tightly as a suitcase before an overnight trip. Friday was the same. By the time both cargos were unloaded, the upstairs was fully furnished.

The only bedroom untouched was Nathan's.

Nathan looked at the two previous shipping manifests, twenty-two pages..., and he didn't dare tally the collective value of it all.

On today's shipment, one item was left unchecked. A clock, and a large one by the dimensions listed.

Despite Bob's meticulous rigor, he had left the one item unchecked as delivered and placed where it belonged. Nathan almost checked the box for him, almost initialed the delivery, but his hand seemed to refuse.

Nathan walked the rooms for hours well into the night, one by one, placing a mark by each item listed and another on the sketch where the item was placed. After verifying hundreds of items, the only one left on the sketch unchecked was in the vestibule..., where his grandfather clock was sitting.

Nathan drew a single line through the item and wrote in, "undelivered" and placed his initials beside it. It was then he noticed that the value of this item was left blank.

Was this some sly attempt at theft by the delivery people? Bob was probably several things, but he didn't seem to be a thief. Then again the most trusted of people could surprise you, even family it seemed.

Surely this was only a test to make sure he was overseeing the deliveries as he'd agreed. Surely it wasn't some sly attempt at claiming his clock as part of the Stewart inventory? Surely.

"Now who's being naïve?" mumbled Nathan.

He hurried to his office to fax the pages to Ms. Stewart's number in North Carolina.

His thoughts torrid, he fed one page after another into the disgruntled machine. Nothing Ms. Stewart had shipped to this address was cheap; very few items were valued under ten thousand dollars and those were usually small items. He had no desire to be responsible for some stolen item of unknown value that could potentially be worth more than the price of the estate he'd just sold.

Nothing in his verbal agreement with Ms. Stewart covered this type of incident and he'd seen the other side of her personality. The unpleasant side of her business personality wasn't one he'd want to visit in a courtroom.

To his chagrin, the last few pages of the transaction failed.

Nathan slumped down in his chair, tried to relax, then picked up the telephone to call North Carolina. Then he noticed the time..., one-fifteen a.m. and set the receiver back down; far later in the Eastern Time zone.

Surely their fax machine was only out of paper or maybe it was simply a paper jam. Maybe there was a storm. Maybe the phone line was down in Charlotte North Carolina.

He redialed the fax number and stuffed a page into the document feeder. It failed to send, error unspecified.

Nathan nervously stacked the unsent portion on top of the fax machine; tomorrow was another day. Surely someone would go to their office tomorrow morning and fix their equipment.

Then he looked at the planner on his desktop. Tomorrow was Saturday.

He hammered his fist down on his desk in frustration, stormed out of the office and shut off the light.

Why was he wound so tight? If it wasn't so late, he'd grab his keys and head to Crab Cove, to the Blind Pirate Diner and let a mug of beer settle his nerves. But of course he never kept alcohol in the house. With that temptation constantly available, he'd be an alcoholic in no time.

Instead, he showered and fell into bed, then lay there until pre-dawn light before finally falling asleep.

Just before eleven, Nathan woke from a horrid stream of dreams and stumbled out of bed, forcing himself down the stairs. There was one message on his machine. Thankfully he'd slept through the process. He ignored the undelivered stack of paper on the fax machine and scooted zombie-like into the kitchen.

He noticed an odd stale scent, then traced the source to the large rectangular kitchen table. At least twelve inches of thick solid wood, the dark stains and gouges gave it the feel of a market place, probably a butcher block. His hand almost reached out to feel the rough texture and he quickly dismissed the whole matter.

With a fresh pot of coffee brewing, he stepped out onto the front porch and let the chill autumn air beat some sense into his lungs.

Today would be better. Even if he didn't get the early start he'd purposed, it was still a weekend with no obligations. He had to somehow enlarge his circle of friends. That last year of tending to his mother had decimated every phone call and invitation to the usual parties and get-togethers' of everyone he ever knew.

Now, only fair weather friends and short-term business acquaintances smoogeing for a cut in some business deal gave him a passing call.

At least he had a relaxing visit planned with his niece this coming Friday, with his sister and brother-in-law.

The coffeemaker gurgled happily as he hurried into the kitchen, shivering off the chill clinging to his arms from outside. He threw together a quick belated breakfast, stuffing it in just as quickly, planning his escape to somewhere…, anywhere besides this house.

He scooted into his office, held his breath, and redialed the fax number to North Carolina, stuffing the first of the remaining pages into the document feeder.

It went through…, then one by one each itemized list disappeared from the tray.

Blissful relief! Now he was sure it was going to be a good day. Nothing could go wrong now that he wasn't responsible for some extravagant missing entity, or a misprint on a piece of paper.

He flopped down in his chair and tapped play on his answering machine. The one message only regurgitated a name and a return number.

It wasn't an area code he recognized. Against his better judgment, he hurriedly dialed the number. It was an inquiry about one of his newly advertised properties through Lucas. They wanted to meet - today - adamantly insisting on viewing the property at two p.m. that very afternoon.

Nathan had one hour to get ready and an hour's drive ahead of that, to show the listed property. Where he should have been elated at the prospect of selling an overpriced, hard to dump property, he felt the chain tighten one more link closer to his anchor.

After refusing to let this spoil his day, Nathan jogged up stairs, noting a small-unmended jag on one of the stair steps along the way. The third from the top, he noted for future reference. He had some brown shoe polish to hide the scuff that 'Bob the mover' had missed.

In minutes, he was out of the shower when he heard what sounded like a low whistle. It didn't sound like any of the usual snaps and pops; unlike the creaks where the old house was angrily supporting new weight.

He quickly threw a towel around his bare waist and stepped into the wide hallway. The low moaning whistle obliged him with a repeat performance from down at the west end of the hall, the last bedroom at the end.

His damp feet made a dash down the long trek and he hurried inside, if only to prove to himself nothing was out of order. The room was detailed immaculately. A huge circular Oriental rug, probably from some Dynasty, rich in burgundy hues, covered one end of the expanse. The bed, some odd affair, with hand carved murals on both headboard and footboard, with a new bare mattress and box springs. Paintings of some unknown nobles, yet to be placed on the walls in several places, were all staring back at him. The closet was standing open; stacked inside were unopened clear packages of varied linens, towels, and bedding. His head spun, searching past all the furniture, but the source of the sound wasn't readily evident.

The time; he needed to hurry and get dressed, then if he had any time to spare he'd look for the source.

The farthest window curtain twitched and the wind whistled and moaned loudly through a slit in an open window.

His fist tightened on the towel at his waist and he hurried to the last of three large windows on that end of the house and threw back the heavy sash and billowing curtain. The window was raised just enough to allow in the frigid air blustering in from the northwest.

How did it get raised?

Why hadn't it set off the alarm for this segment of the house?

Nathan looked at the two sets of sensors. The first was an epoxy dabbed wafer on the thick glass pane, another was screwed onto the slide near the bottom of the sill. It was clearly askew, yet the alarm was still a sleeping dog.

He thrust the window down and slapped both slide locks in place, only to be greeted by the loud blast of a horn downstairs.

He stood there motionless for at least ten seconds in shock and unbelief, waiting for the system to reset itself.

It clearly didn't.

"Crap...," hissed Nathan, as he ran to shut off the alarm.

The main control panel was located downstairs inside the kitchen walk-in pantry. Its seven-digit code was the only way to abort the three phases of the elaborate security system.

First came the blast of alarm, good to thwart most novice intruders. The second - silence accompanied by a retrace of entry breaches, along with a text message to Nathan's cell phone.

The intelligent systems sensors -heat, motion, moisture- would isolate the emergency, be it burglary, water, or fire.

The third phase was a series of predefined phone calls to the Sheriff's Department and Morris County Fire department. A plethora of emergency services were listed in the event of some predefined disaster.

Nathan's bare feet were slapping down the hallway as he counted down the last sixty seconds he had to get to the security panel downstairs before all hell broke loose.

Thank God, he hadn't had time to add the State Police to the dialing sequence. He had no time to stop and catch his breath at the bottom of the stairs. His feet squeaked on the hardwood floor as he spun around the bottom stair post, when suddenly his bath towel snatched away, snagged on some unseen obstacle at the turn of the landing. With the last several feet toward the pantry insight through the nearby kitchen door, "...nine, eight, seven...," he gasped out the remaining few seconds. There was no time to reattach his only covering.

The pantry door flew open with a mad yank and he stationed one hand on the wall for support as he nervously punched in the code on the touch screen.

The seven digits beeped slowly, the panel flashed, then waited for the same digits to be entered in reverse order.

His hand shaking, he punched them in and the panel displayed - *Operation Cancelled.*

Now he could catch his breath. He'd intercepted the potential blunder, but how did the alarm system go off the rail? There would have been huge fees for a false alarm. He'd call the security company as soon as he returned and have the entire system rechecked.

He had only a few minutes to get back upstairs and get ready. Clinging to the post was his treacherous towel, still snagged on the bottom post of the stairway and....

"Well..., Mr. Heart. It appears I should have tarried a little longer at the front door."

Nathan cupped both hands below in a sad attempt at delayed modesty. Madeline Stewart turned her back to Nathan as he hurried to gather the towel, his closest available covering, when he heard another gasp.

"Lindsey dear, would you be so kind as to tell Lester to help Henry with our things?"

Nathan felt his face flame like a torch as he snatched the towel around his waist. Madeline's niece walked past him, her hand cupped against the side of her face, feet clicking in a fast pace towards the front door.

CHAPTER ELEVEN

"**P**LEASE don't apologize again. It was entirely my fault, Mr. Heart. Besides..., I was raised with six brothers and a slew of male cousins and I assure you, you have nothing to apologize for. We're all adults here."

Nathan blushed once again as he slipped on his blazer, "No, this is your house, but I would like you to have my cell number so in the future you can give me a little advance warning..., now that we're more..., familiar with each other."

Madeline Stewart chuckled, eyes glistening, and was about to fire another fringe comment when Henry walked into the living room.

"Aunt Madey, where would you like us to put your luggage?"

His deep voice resonated throughout the room like a wave.

"Any one of the downstairs bedrooms will be just fine. Thank you dear."

Henry caught Nathan's quick glance and smiled a crooked grin his direction before he walked away.

'Great..., just great,' thought Nathan. His sister must have filled him in on every embarrassing detail.

Nathan looked at his wristwatch, "I have to leave for an appointment, but I'll be back later this evening. You have the security codes where you can find them?"

"I don't see any reason to bother with all that while we're here. You go and have a good time. Take care of your business and we'll see you later."

Nathan nodded and hurried to the front door.

"Oh..., and Nathan? If by chance you return before seven, would you please join us for supper?" she asked.

Nathan nodded again and hurried out the door before something else could happen.

When he arrived in the little suburb north of Salem, fifteen minutes late for his appointment, his anxious client was about to drive away. It was the honking of his horn and meandering arm out the Yukon's window that convinced them to turn around.

Surprisingly enough they were actually interested and wrote a check for the minimum deposit to hold the property. Mr. Renaldo Lucas was proving to be an invaluable asset to Heart Realty. If he managed to open an office some place nearby, maybe here in Salem, not Lumberton, and list half his properties through this new Real Estate Directory, it could eliminate half his grunt work and most of his cost of advertising. It might even prove to be his first step back into the real world he enjoyed.

The euphoria quickly faded when it was time to start back home.

Nathan tried to think of every excuse available to drive beyond Lumberton, on to Crab Cove, or farther. The events earlier that day had his mind in a spin. The more he thought about it, the more confusing the whole scenario was becoming. It wasn't just the memory of flashing Ms. Stewart and her niece; that he would get past eventually. The culmination of events, all within minutes of each other bothered him. Of course it was coincidence, but tell that to his wounded pride.

Nathan passed every pleading road sign begging him down the coastline highway while an internal argument decided his final course of action.

By default, his Yukon crawled into its regular stable just before sunset. He was back at the estate, as if on automatic, sitting in his silent SUV in deliberation.

He had arrived, the Stewart's knew it, of that much he was certain. He doubted that much of anything passed their arduous attention.

With a deep sigh, he walked to the front of the house, just as the outdoor lighting automatically blinked on. Nathan turned and walked away to the rim of the circle drive for a moment's reflection on the estate, maybe to pay some ineluctable last respect.

Several curtains were coiffed and tied away from the windows, with almost every room warmly lit on the first floor. The picture window in front was uncovered, exposing the picturesque interior with all its new elaborate furnishings and decorations.

The place had a renewed warmth and charm that yanked emotion from his childhood memories. There was a time when this house was a home, much like this, back during an era when he was on speaking terms with all his siblings; back when Marion was still alive. She had been the cohesive force that bound them all together..., and now?

Sunset caused a distinct drop in temperature and he stepped forward to face whatever awaited him inside.

As soon as the door opened, the smell of woodsmoke and the crackle of fire in the fireplace honed even more memories.

"Nathan..., you're back early," said Madeline.

She was seated in an ornate divan of Egyptian origins, linen white patterned with rich blue orchids and much stronger than it's spindly legs suggested. The cup of tea in hand eased onto a close setting. Someone had shifted the divan closer to the open hearth along with two other cushioned chairs forming an amiable seating arrangement.

"Please, come have a seat with me. Supper is almost ready," she said, patting the seat beside her as if calling a favorite pet.

Nathan decided to play along with whatever ruse she was up to. Instantly he scourged himself; maybe there was no game afoot. Maybe this was just her usual demeanor and she thought nothing of the condescending offering. He sat in the closest chair near her and let out a comfortable sigh at the feel of the cushion beneath and the warmth of the glowing fire beside him.

"I trust your negotiations went well this afternoon," she said, reaching for her cup once again.

He nodded, "Another property in the hands of someone to care for it."

"Well put Mr. Heart. At least we understand each other better," she said, sipping her tea.

"Excuse me?" said Nathan.

She smiled. It was disarming; almost comforting, "The reason I like having you living here while we're traipsing all over Lord knows where. I know you care about the place."

Nathan smelled something wonderful drifting through the house from the kitchen and smiled.

"I hope you're hungry Mr. Heart. Lindsey probably cooked enough for a dozen people."

Her niece cooked? Then Nathan felt stupid at the thought of it. Who else would be in the kitchen? The chauffeur?

"I think I remember having a few bites of breakfast today," said Nathan.

She sipped her tea once again and set it back down. She had a specific thoughtful stare he'd seen once or twice before.

"Tell me Nathan..., what are your plans this next year?" she asked, cupping her hands in her lap.

He immediately felt like the child being interrogated by the parent over their choice of the next seasons courses at college.

"You'll have to forgive me for being unsure, but I've just been released from two major obligations that had me bound for several years. I'm still feeling my way out of the dark."

How did she do that, he wondered? He had no intentions of opening up his personal vault to a perfect stranger.

"I applaud your honesty," she said with a tilt of the head. "Do you enjoy your vocation? Private Realty must be very restricting on your social life."

"It wasn't restrictive until…," he stopped himself, letting his thought die.

"Forgive me," she muttered. "I've overstepped my boundaries. After raising three children of my own as well as my niece and nephew, I'm pretty good at that."

"No, I suppose I don't mind," he grunted. "I've managed to keep Heart Realty solvent for seven years. Even though these last three didn't bode well for any sort of social life."

"Tell me about your mother," she said.

Nathan stood and walked closer to the fireplace, "I'd rather not if you don't mind."

"You didn't get along with your mother?" she asked.

"Yes of course," he grunted, turning to face his inquisitor. "It's nothing at all like that."

She had ignored his refusal of the subject, but somehow he didn't mind.

"You're still going through the grieving process," she mumbled.

"No. Its been a year. I've made my peace. What exactly is it that you want to know Ms. Stewart?" he blurted.

She stretched like a feline and took up her empty teacup and saucer, "I like knowing the mechanics of my business associates, Mr. Heart. I've grown quite fond of our chats over the last few weeks and you *are* living in my new house."

Nathan felt somewhat scolded. Maybe she was innocent. He took a deep breath, "It was difficult to let go, of course. It's been my other relationships forcing me to relive it all. Surely you can see that."

"Your siblings, of course," she frowned and nodded. Madeline Stewart seemed pleased that she'd reached the root of her true quest.

She stood and motioned for Nathan to follow her.

"I can usually tell when the dinner bell is about to ring. Let's you and I wash up and check the dining room shall we?"

Nathan excused himself and trotted upstairs. The hallway was warmly lit and smelled of fresh linen. As he opened his bedroom door, immediately he noticed the change. His bed was made to perfection, the morning's discarded clothes picked up, with a scented votive candle flickering on his chifforobe. Why had they taken the liberty to invade his one private reserve? He certainly intended to find out and fully intended to enforce some boundaries.

He hurried into the restroom, raked a comb through his sandy brown hair, flicked at the few strands of gray his sister discovered, then stared into the reflection of his own dark brown eyes.

"Nathan, you're being an ogre again."

Why should he care about whomever straightening his room? No wonder Troy was so worried about him becoming a hermit. He hadn't felt this displeased with himself in a very long time.

"Nathan...," swam in from the hallway.

"Coming," he called out.

He dried his hands and hurried down the stairs and into the dining room.

Four place settings were carefully arranged at the very end of the long ebony dining table, two candles lit, and a horde of wonderful smelling food.

"Oh good," said Madeline. "We were about to call you."

"About to...," he muttered, then silenced himself.

Madeline, Lindsey and Henry were already seated, with the last place available directly across from Madeline's niece. The only thing Nathan could envision was Lindsey's cupped hand beside her face as she rushed away from him earlier that day.

Then he felt it. Lindsey. Madeline wasn't the garish open swale that Troy was, she was ambrosia on a silver platter.

With as much grace as he could muster, he sat down.

"Nathan, would you care to say grace?" asked Madeline.

"What...?" he stammered.

"Grace? A quick prayer..., before this wonderful food jelly's over?" she said with a grin.

He hadn't said grace over a meal since he was twelve, but at least he did remember how that prayer went and hurried through it.

"Is Lester not eating with us?" asked Nathan, as the food began to swirl across the table.

"He's at the kitchen table," said Madeline. "He always claims he's a bit of a loner, but in all honesty, he's just closer to the food."

"And the desert," said Henry.

"You cooked all this?" grunted Nathan, looking at Lindsey.

Her eyes swam beside her, "I had some help."

"Don't let her fool you, she cooked," said Madeline. "Henry and I only put away the groceries. Your pantry looked like an Ethiopian famine had stricken the place, so we took the liberty of running to town and getting a few things delivered."

Madeline queen of diversion. If he didn't know what she was up to, he would have missed it outright. Lindsey seemed a little off as well.

He picked slower at his food, thinking. Then he noticed something else. Even if they did straighten up some of the rooms and stock the pantry in the last five or six hours, now he was ingratiated to her for something else.

Subtle.

He'd pay her for the food in the pantry.

"I usually eat on the go, so I don't..., really..., cook that much," said Nathan, wondering how much stocking they really did. Madeline Stewart was known to be a little on the extravagant side.

"Now get that look out of your eyes," she scolded between a bite of roast beef. "We needed to get a few things for the Thanksgiving holiday anyway. Speaking of that, have you decided on whether or not you're going to spend the holiday with us?"

Immediately, Nathan felt a pair of eyes on him and looked up to see Lindsey staring at him, waiting for an answer. Surely, she wasn't in on this too.

"Only if someone else says grace," he said, forcing a grin.

"I think we can manage that," chuckled Madeline.

Nathan was beginning to eat as if it was his last meal until he understood it must be out of nervousness and pushed his plate away.

An elbow nudged him from the side, "Come help me."

Henry stood and Nathan followed him into the kitchen.

"Cream pudding or Custard Pie?" asked Henry.

"Do I have to choose?" asked Nathan.

Henry grinned, "Nope," then handed him a bowl from the refrigerator; he grabbed a pie cooling on the counter.

"Lester, you stay out of my cheesecake," he grunted.

"Ain't making no promises," said a voice from the corner.

Nathan looked at the source of the odd, almost hillbilly voice and had to force his jaw shut. Lester was talking to Henry, but only one of his eyes was trained on Henry, the other amblyopic orb was roving on him.

This one was quiet and creepy.

CHAPTER TWELVE

"TELL me Nathan, do you prefer the sunset or sunrise best on the west coast?" asked Madeline Stewart.

They were still seated around the end of the long sleek dining table, taking turns with light conversation until her question rolled out of the blue.

"Is this more of your mechanics?" he grunted.

"Maybe," she answered.

Fine, he'd play for a few more rounds, "It depends on who I'm with."

Henry laughed at this equally ambiguous answer.

"Don't mind Aunt Madey," said Henry. "She likes to figure people out. Everybody's a puzzle to her, especially people she finds interesting."

"Hush, Henry," Madeline scolded.

Her attack quickly turned to her left, "Lindsey you haven't uttered two whole sentences this evening. What's has you so deep in thought?"

"I think she's doing some figuring of her own," grunted Henry. Henry immediately rose from the table and began to gather dishes in an obvious attempt at penance.

Nathan followed suit, but not before noticing Lindsey's gaping jaw and burning eyes on her brother. Lindsey wouldn't have a snowflake's chance if both Madeline and her brother were playing matchmaker. Surely Henry wouldn't do that.

"Don't bother with those Nathan," ordered Madeline, somewhat harshly.

She was used to people snapping to her attention.

Nathan was considering ignoring her comment completely before he answered, "It's the least I can do after a five star meal with friends. I might not cook, but I do know how to do dishes. Thank you very much for dinner."

With both hands full, he hurried behind Henry to the kitchen.

As soon as they clattered onto the counter, "She'll get you for that," whispered Henry.

"I'm sure she will," grinned Nathan. "But it was worth it."

"Yeah," he chuckled. "It was."

Nathan took a very calculated chance, "Is your aunt always so…."

"Demanding? Conniving?" finished Henry, still keeping his voice down. "Of course, but she can't help it. In our family, it's survival of the fittest. Aunt Madeline is pretty much the matriarch of the North Carolina clan."

Henry's sly grin was amazingly friendly. Nathan heard the subtleties of his southern dialect surface, almost the southern gentleman. He was glad he'd taken the chance.

Henry quickly turned on the water in the sink and faced Nathan, "Don't judge her too harshly. Aunt Madey's good at heart. And I think she's taken an interest in you."

Great. Just perfect. The spider was playing with its food.

Suddenly, there was some muffled clamor from the dining room. The dishwater wasn't only being a subterfuge to keep their voices scrambled; it was drowning out another conversation.

"She's giving Lindsey another lecture," gritted Henry, shaking his head in disapproval.

Nathan frowned, "Another…. I know it's none of my business Henry, but is there something else going on I don't know about?"

He hoped Henry would continue to be as honest as he had before.

"You're right. It's none of your business. But it…, does concern you." He clanked at several plates, scraping off the food before he continued.

"Aunt Madey and I travel together, ever since Lindsey and I graduated from Duke University three years ago. I'm sort of the family protégé in training to take over Madeline's position.

"Lindsey…, took a fancy to this guy at college and Aunt Madey hates him. Well, so do I for that matter. So she's having Lindsey travel with us. She's calling it a 'cooling off' period, but she's actually giving this Jon Walthrop fellow time to pick someone else to mooch off of."

Nathan nodded and pushed Henry out of the way, rinsing the dishes and stuffing them into the dishwasher. He was right. Madeline was playing matchmaker, if only to redirect her niece's affections. How could she afford so much control over a grown woman such as Lindsey?

"Let's keep this between us if you don't mind. I've probably told you too much. I'll go get another load of dishes," whispered Henry.

Nathan rinsed a few more dishes, deep in thought, then felt a presence over his shoulder. He glanced back and staggered in shock at Lester standing barely a breath away. The tall gaunt man carefully placed his dishes on the counter by the sink and backed up a step.

"You should consider yourself lucky. Henry don't usually come right out and open up to strangers," said Lester.

Nathan watched him hurry back across the room, grab his jacket and pace his long thin legs out of the room.

"And you're a man of few words too," blared Nathan.

If he hadn't signed the one-year agreement with Madeline Stewart, he would be packing his things first thing Monday morning.

He heard footsteps plodding in with more dishes and turned to take them.

"I'll finish these, Mr. Heart," said Lindsey.

Her eyes were slightly puffy; her blond eyebrows barely hiding a pink hue. She'd been crying or something very near to it.

"I'm almost done here," said Nathan, taking the small stack of dishes from her hands. Lindsey didn't argue, only turned and left the kitchen.

When Nathan had put away the leftovers, he dried his hands and fully intended to go upstairs to his room to reassess his relationship with Ms. Stewart and her family.

"Won't you join us?"

Nathan's head stooped, tired of all the social games.

"For a few minutes," he replied, turning toward the living room.

A fresh stack of firewood was taking light in the fireplace and Madeline was already perched on her divan. Henry was stooped, busy poking at the glowing embers and humming some tune, while Lindsey had vanished to her privacy.

"Please have a seat."

'Said the cat to the canary,' thought Nathan.

"Do you stock any wine, Mr. Heart?" she asked.

"I'm afraid not, I haven't stocked any here in several years."

"That's too bad. A little after dinner burgundy would hit the spot. You know that some of the best piñot noir in the country comes out of Oregon vineyards. As a matter of fact, this place has a remarkably vast cellar; I'll put that on my list for the next shipment."

"Speaking of your shipments," said Nathan. "There was an item missing from the last one. A clock. I noted it on the manifest I faxed to your office."

Her face was fixed and expressionless, "I'm sure it was only a clerical error."

Nathan nodded, relieved to hear that this wouldn't become a point of contention, "I was a little concerned that your movers might have delivered it to some other location."

"Theft?" she laughed, "Hardly. I didn't hire that crew of workers just for their work ethic Mr. Heart. They signed a heavily binding contract with a confidentiality clause. If something goes missing or gets stolen from a delivery or from this house for instance, the authorities will look to them first. In fact, no one else knows the value of this house's contents except them and us. I made quite sure of that."

That was why she wasn't concerned with the security system, not to mention the fact that everything was heavily insured.

Nathan's clock chose that moment to sing its chime and sound off nine evenly spaced tones.

Madeline closed her eyes listening, as if appreciating a concert.

"Have you considered my offer?" she asked.

"Your offer?" he asked, somewhat confused.

"Yes, for your timepiece in the vestibule. I'm still very interested in it."

Nathan shook his head, "As I said before, I'd better hang onto it. It's been in the family for a long time. I can move it to storage if you need it out of the house."

If Madeline Stewart wanted that clock, there was no way he would sell it.

"Don't you dare," she scolded. "I'm quite fond of its tone."

"Just the same, not everything is for sale Ms. Stewart."

Henry coughed back a short laugh and shoved the firescreen in place, dusting his hands on his slacks.

Madeline never acknowledged Henry's insurrection or Nathan's challenge.

She smiled, "Well, if you don't want to sell it, perhaps we can make some sort of trade. After all, I do collect all sorts of items from most everywhere."

Was she showing some sort of desperation? Nathan felt a hint of embarrassment for Madeline.

"If I do ever decide to sell it, you'll have first bid."

Suddenly her smile turned genuine and all seemed forgiven.

"Don't you have a TV in this house?" asked Henry.

Nathan shook his head, "After the contents were divided and the house was up for sale I never replaced...."

"Not even in your room?" asked Henry.

"You can survive one night without watching college football Henry," said Madeline. "You and Lester can run to Salem tomorrow and pick something up if you must. I appreciate the fact that some men don't need to be entertained by violent sports."

Nathan caught her sad attempt at flattery, "I usually catch the games over at a place in Crab Cove. I'll be glad to take you over there sometime Henry."

She seemed a little more irritated at Nathan's confession.

"What about you Nathan? You look like you used to run around on the field," asked Henry.

"Linebacker for two years at Northwestern."

"Somehow I can't picture you as a knuckle-dragger," said Henry.

"I lost most of the weight right after I dropped the team."

Nathan patted his flat stomach, grinning at Henry. Henry shook his head with an almost panicked expression on his face. For a minute, he made Nathan feel like some type of traitor.

"You dropped the team?"

"I got tired of the coach yelling spit in my face, 'take out his knees', every time he stuck me in the game. We didn't exactly see eye to eye. What about you?"

Henry's chin rose almost imperceptibly when his teeth clenched, "Wide receiver. I was in line for an NFL pick before…, somebody with less of a conscience than you clipped me and ended my running career. I had 32 interceptions and 980 yards receiving that year before…."

Henry patted a knee and glanced almost angrily over at his aunt. There was definitely some muddy water in his memories of the event.

Nathan shook his head thoughtfully, not really knowing what to say as a consolation. It was Henry's turn to shrug the memories away and his playful smile crept back on his face.

"My career wasn't nearly as eventful. I'm better at watching the game," said Nathan.

Henry nodded with a grin, "No TV tonight. You do play poker don't you?"

CHAPTER THIRTEEN

LYING in bed, eyes wide, Nathan was mesmerized by the flicker of the little votive candle still forming shadows in his room.

Henry he liked, he felt sore empathy for Lindsey, but Madeline..., was a complete mystery. If he listened to Henry, he should somehow pity Ms. Stewart, even respect her for her accomplishments. Which overall from Henry's perspective was entirely valid. She'd been like a mother to him and his sister most of their lives.

Nathan never really liked playing all the social games, especially when the game board, the pieces, and the rules favored the other players. That didn't mean he didn't know how to play. He'd been trained by the best..., his own family.

Maybe it was time for him to step back in. Others usually misread his quiet demeanor as weakness, especially his family. He'd only deferred to them because of those last years with Marion Heart and her delusions. It had garnered him an entirely different perspective on life, being there with his mother as she slowly disappeared before his eyes. Maybe it was time for the bear to wake up and come out of hibernation.

He felt the grin on his face spread into a satisfied smile. Tomorrow was going to be different. He checked his alarm, made sure it was set.

As he finally began to drift off, his mind made plans, which eventually turned into vivid dreams.

♥

The two upward turned lamps in front of the house were causing a mellow glow in his bedroom as they did every night. Nights were always the worst for Marion. She dozed or napped off and on during the day and talked or mumbled all during the night to something..., someone..., from her past or in her mind. She always seemed to need a cool glass of water, always when the ice had completely melted from the covered carafe at her bedside. Tonight was no different.

He heard her mumbling and turned over, covering his ear with an arm, trying to ignore the sound. Just a few more minutes sleep and he knew she would be calling his name, Nathan. Over and over again, she'd moan out his name until he threw away the covers and walked across to the bedroom just down the hall. Her doctor had warned him against giving her any types of sedatives at this stage of dementia. This far progressed, she could wander out of the house, out onto the rural road near the house and get run over in the dark.

Then there were the days of perfect clarity, her mind sharp as a tack, begging to get out and go for drives, see old friends, eat at some café with him and Caroline.

"Nathan…, some water please?"

It had to be the third or forth time she'd called, it usually took that many times to wake him from his fitful nights of sleep.

"Nathan?" said the voice.

"Yes, I'm coming…," he heard himself say.

The bed was moving, someone gently shaking a shoulder.

"Nathan? Wake up."

He sat bolt upright with a gasp looking around in the dimly lit room. Next to his bed was a perfect oval face with a halo of blond hair dangling in soft wisps; this beautiful wraith was speaking to him.

"Nathan, it's me. You were talking in your sleep."

Nathan grabbed cover and turned, trying to focus, "Who?"

"Lindsey, Lindsey Stewart. I was afraid you'd wake Aunt Madey and Henry."

"Oh…, Lindsey."

His heart began to slow down beat by beat. He'd been in the house at night all alone for just over a year. The very thought of other people in the house had become foreign.

"I heard you from all the way downstairs. I was up reading. Are you alright?"

He nodded slowly, "I…, had no idea."

Of course he'd have no way of knowing that he talked in his sleep.

"I'm usually the only one here."

Lindsey stood up straight, "Try turning on your side…, that should help. I'm sure you were probably dreaming. I wouldn't doubt it after all that food you ate tonight."

She turned to walk out the door and paused, "By the way. Who is Marion?"

Nathan sighed deeply and turned to fully face her, "It was my mother."

It was her turn to nod, "Try to get some sleep."

"Lindsey?" he hissed, her feet already patting down the hall.

"Yes?"

"Thank you."

♥

The alarm clock beside Nathan's head hissed on, the radio set purposely between stations, white noise most people would ignore.

He tapped it off, remembering his last purposeful thoughts from the night before.

As he suspected, all the houseguests were still asleep at half past six on Sunday morning. He angrily choked on his own blunder - *he* was the houseguest.

After passing through his morning rigors he hurried down the stairs to his office, checked for messages, there were none, then to the kitchen.

The coffee grinder made far too much noise so he wrapped it in a thick towel until it decimated the coffee beans to perfection. Then he began breakfast, enough for..., five he presumed. These were southern farm raised heathen; they'd like farm foods, not his typical bagels and jam.

He was spilling pancake batter onto a griddle when Madeline walked in the kitchen about a quarter before eight.

"Up early for a Sunday."

Her voice had a tint of question to its inflection.

The coffee pot gurgled happily behind her and Nathan grinned.

"Breakfast is almost ready. Do you think the others would like breakfast, or would they rather sleep in?"

She sniffed, then looked at the bowls and watched the hiss of the batter as it hit the griddle, "They'll want breakfast."

Madeline watched him with a wary eye as she walked back out of the kitchen into the abyss of the house.

In a matter of minutes, Nathan had a dozen pancakes in a stack and a chorus of chatter began filtering into the spacious kitchen.

"I thought you didn't cook?" grunted Henry.

"Breakfast doesn't count," said Nathan, putting on his best cheerful voice.

"It does in my book," said Henry.

Nathan handed him a pair of mitts followed by a covered warming platter of scrambled eggs, crisp bacon, and corned beef hash, then turned to flip his pancakes.

Lindsey watched him with a small frown as he scraped up four more pancakes onto a serving platter.

"I scrambled the eggs, but I'll make something special. There's whipped cream and strawberries in the bottom of the refrigerator for the pancakes..." He droned on pointing to where all the accessories were stored in which cabinets.

Luckily, there were no special requests as he observed their interaction.

Nathan plucked a few bites onto his plate, watching what each of them preferred before mirroring his in exact birdlike proportions as Lindsey. Almost bite for bite, Nathan purposefully mimicked her intake, while he commented on Madeline's first love, her antiques. Henry needed no interaction, his plate was heaped and he was thoroughly occupied.

Lester..., well Lester he ignored.

Then it was time to step into his game.

"Tell me Madeline, how did you get started as a collector?" he asked.

"Oh, that's a long and drawn out tale."

Henry lifted his head from his plate, "One that she loves to go on about."

"Hold your tongue Henry. Our family has been dealing in antiquities since we first came to this country in the mid 1700's. We were mapmakers and importers from the very beginning. It was simply handed down from generation to generation."

"With a few bootleggers and slave traders along the way," chuckled Henry.

Madeline squinted his direction, "Yes..., well if you dig deep enough, every family has a few unlovely skeletons in their closet."

Henry was proving to be more help that originally anticipated and Nathan held his expression as neutral as a painting during each short discourse.

Lindsey was barely picking at her food and Nathan resumed his mirrored pace, "I'm sure you're right. But I was more interested in something you mentioned to me quite a while back. You said that you collected things which were important."

Madeline smiled, but was it from his remembering their conversation, or did she recognize the direction Nathan was heading?

"That I did Mr. Heart. Yes, I like to collect items which had some important event attached to them. Anyone can find an antique if you rummage through enough old barns or houses. Events, Mr. Heart, those are the things that make antiques interesting enough to be collectible."

"I agree. That would seem to make your antiques more desirable to your buyers as well."

Nathan had a sudden waver in his thoughts, "Tell me, what makes the divan in the living room so unique to you?"

It was almost her private perch ever since they had arrived and every time he'd seen her seated in the living room.

Madeline grinned and he thought he caught a hint of a blush, "It was Egyptian in original craftsmanship, but it once sat in the private quarters of one of the innumerable Mary's in Edinburgh Scotland. This particular

Mary was caught flagrante delicto, sporting with an Englishman, by her husband. He murdered her on the spot."

"On that very divan?" hissed Nathan, leaning forward.

"He got away Scot Free," she grinned at her own pun, then added. "It's been reupholstered since, which devaluated it somewhat, but I have its precise history on record."

Nathan never expected any sort of this type of an answer and he had to regroup his thoughts.

"Do all these pieces have similar histories?" he asked.

She nodded, "The breakfast table we're eating at was once used as a restraining block during the inquisition."

Nathan's hands slid away from the deeply stained and marred wood with an entirely different appreciation. Lindsey was no longer eating; her silver resting on her plate…, so was Nathan's.

"Honestly, Aunt Madey. Why do you have to be so morbid?" spat Lindsey. "I'll be in the library if anyone needs me."

She yanked up from her chair and hurriedly slipped around the table and Nathan wanted to follow her.

CHAPTER FOURTEEN

NATHAN Heart was standing on the verge of the front porch trying to revise his previous plans. Madeline Stewart, collector of death, had thrown him for a loop.

Somehow, she always managed to be two steps ahead and full of surprises. He was thankful that Lindsey hadn't told her aunt about his somnifacient chatter during the middle of the night.

Henry Stewart blustered through the door behind him, "Would you like to take a drive with us into Salem?"

"I have to get my schedule in order for next week. I guess I'd better stick close to the office," said Nathan, his arms folded tightly across his square chest.

Lester stalked past in silence and crawled into their limousine.

"Any particular brand of TV you like better than another?" he asked.

Nathan shook his head, but wanted to tell Henry that any brand would do as long as someone wasn't murdered during its manufacture.

"Oh, what kind of connection do you have here? Cable, Satellite?"

Henry drooped his head in defeat when Nathan didn't answer right away, then he snapped up with a smile, "Internet?"

"Broadband," said Nathan.

Henry snapped his fingers with a grin.

They drove away and Nathan decided to at least attempt the second part of his previous night's plan.

Madeline and Lindsey were having yet another one of their cold war conversations back in the library.

"I'm about to make some tea," said Nathan, intentionally barging in the room, and disrupting the uncomfortable conversation. "Any takers?"

"I believe I would," said Madeline, her previous sentence cut short.

Lindsey was standing in front of where Madeline was seated, her arms stiff at her sides.

"I'll make my own," she said, marching past Nathan.

Her somber eyes darted up at his, barely a flicker.

"Don't mind Lindsey, she's going through a troubled phase right now," Madeline muttered.

"I'm sorry to hear that," said Nathan. "Maybe she needs some time at home to think. You seem to be traveling quite a lot."

"Sitting at home is exactly what Lindsey does not need right now," she grunted. "I believe we picked up some Earl Grey yesterday. It should be in the pantry. Would you mind?"

Nathan turned, "Not at all," grinning to himself at her way of not just terminating, but controlling the conversation.

Madeline's niece looked frail and defeated, standing beside the largest of the two chef's ovens. The element on the stovetop began to glow as she placed a kettle of water on to boil.

"I'm sorry if I interrupted you earlier," said Nathan, pulling open the heavy pantry door.

His icebreaking comment was intended to open a different avenue into the psyche of Madeline Stewart, but that was quickly sidelined.

"Good heavens," he grunted.

Every shelf of the huge pantry was filled to capacity, with several boxes of goods stacked on the floor in the back. The security panel was completely obscured, barely accessible to anyone.

Nathan shifted the stack of boxes from in front of the panel, then noticed that the main key to disable the entire system was in place and switched to *OFF*. It would take a trained technician at least an hour to bring the entire system back online.

"My aunt rarely does anything half way," said Lindsey. Without a hint of movement she was standing uncomfortably close, staring over his shoulder.

"I see that," said Nathan.

Why didn't Lindsey have that same smarmy dialect of her aunt or her brother? In any case, it was time to make his ploy.

He hurriedly found the tea Madeline requested and followed Lindsey out of the confines of the crowded room.

When he was sure they weren't being eavesdropped on, "Lindsey, if I were to tell you something and ask you to promise not to be angry, could you do that?"

"It would depend on the question," she answered.

"That would be the entire purpose of the promise," grunted Nathan.

"Then we would be at an impasse, wouldn't we?" she sighed, carefully lifting the whistling kettle from the stovetop.

"What is it you want to tell me?" she grunted.

Nathan was taking a huge leap of faith, but plodded forward.

"Your brother Henry confided in me concerning a few details of your predicament..., between you and your aunt."

"That ass," she spat.

When she spun to face him, he was ever so glad she had already sat down the boiling water.

"You promised...."

Lindsey shook her head, "No I didn't."

Her blond eyebrows were beginning to infuse with hints of pink.

"Please hear me out. I think we can help each other. Please?" asked Nathan.

When her glare finally cooled to mere interest, Nathan continued, "Your aunt is obviously displeased with your choice of boyfriend, am I correct?"

She nodded stiffly, one quick little jerk.

Nathan found himself nodding, as if trying to prime her agreement, "I suppose you also noticed that your aunt has been trying to get me to take an interest in you."

"I thought it was my imagination," she sighed angrily, then she stiffened. "What exactly is it that you have in mind?"

"If we at least pretend to be interested in one another, for the sake of show, it might ease the tension between you and your Aunt Madeline. And..., stop her from trying to play matchmaker with me."

"She'll see right through it in a heartbeat," said Lindsey, shaking her head. "You don't know her like I do."

Nathan shrugged, "Alright then, it was worth a shot."

"Just how long does it take water to boil?" asked Madeline. Her voice arrived well before her feet clopped into the kitchen.

Lindsey looked at Nathan and their eyes locked for a defining moment.

"Nathan and I were..., having a private discussion," said Lindsey, turning away. Nathan noticed that she actually blushed, her cheeks showing high color.

"Oh...," said Madeline. "Oh..., well..., I'll let you two finish. I'll be in the living room when my tea is ready."

Nathan felt heat rise in his cheeks, causing no end of pleasure to Madeline as she turned and trod out of the kitchen.

Lindsey hurried over next to Nathan, "I don't believe it. It may actually work. You may be a genius after all Nathan Heart."

She jumped up and kissed Nathan's cheek and darted to her cup of tea.

"We'll have to play it by ear," whispered Nathan. "I'm not much of an actor."

She nodded, then an angelic smile spread across her face, "Neither was Ronald Reagan."

Lindsey balanced her tea and hurried from the room to parts unknown. Wait..., was that a compliment? Nathan felt himself smile as he poured hot water into two cups.

♥

Nathan parked himself on the grand sofa by the front picture window, watching as the sun tried to peek through the gloomy northwestern sky and brighten the day. The tea was chalky on his tongue, but it was helping him think.

He opened his planner, assembled several notes from a folder, and began to list the amenities of the one property he had scheduled to show next week. At least he hadn't completely lied to Henry about his need to stay behind.

His pen stopped as he thought; with Madeline sidetracked over her personal manipulations and since her impending shipments were almost complete, he could get back to planning his future with a clear mind. At least Ms. Stewart wasn't the antagonistic throng of the *Big Three*, as he and his sister Caroline liked to refer to their elder brother and sisters. And yes, the battle portion of that relationship was over. Maybe one day there would be peace between them as well.

The sofa suddenly shifted as Lindsey sank down with the dregs of her cup of tea and she sighed heavily, "Mind if I join you?"

Nathan stared for a moment as the sunlight flicked around her blond hair.

"I'm not interrupting anything am I?" she asked.

"Uh, no...," he said with a shake of the head, closing his heavy planner. "Not at all."

She turned and whispered clandestinely, "So far, so good. Aunt Madey's giving me some peace..., for the moment anyway."

Nathan felt his lips curl up slightly, "Good..., for both of us."

"So..., in the interest of keeping up our charade, what were you doing?" she asked.

"This? Oh, preparing to show a property, just boring details," he grunted.

"It must be nice," she sighed.

"Nice?" he frowned.

"I wish you wouldn't question everything I say...," she gritted, then shook her head. "I'm sorry, that was rude of me. What I meant was, it would be nice to relax and get to have your own thoughts without having to run here or there and back again."

Had he found another avenue into the mystery of Madeline Stewart?

"How was Hong Kong by the way?" he asked.

She spun her whole body around on the sofa to face him, "It was horrid. First, we had to land our jet in Bangkok Thailand, some airport clearance problem. The mosquitoes there this time of the year are absolute vampires. When we did get to Hong Kong there was an easterly breeze off the coast into the city and everything had this dead fish odor."

She gagged out her tongue with a nasty blah shiver.

So Madeline Stewart actually was in Hong Kong.

"Surely you get to travel to other places, some that you like?"

"When your heart wants to be home, every place looks the same," she sighed.

"It can't be all bad," he murmured, trying to cheer her.

She swallowed, "So then…, let's compare notes. What do you have planned for this week?"

He laughed, "Nothing as radical as you. A house to show, which you already know, two more properties to sign contracts over, then Halloween with my niece and sister this weekend."

Lindsey's face fell sharply, "How I envy you."

Her face snapped back into a painful looking faux smile, "Guess where I'll be by the end of next week. Bucharest."

"Bucharest?"

She rolled her eyes painfully; he'd done it again.

"Romania?"

"Yes, I'm well aware of where it's located," said Nathan.

"Aunt Madey and Henry are inspecting a spinet piano that was supposedly shuffled off from Germany during the war."

She leaned closer to Nathan, close enough for him to catch the soft fragrance of her perfume, even the freckles in her large honey colored eyes.

"Supposedly, it belonged to Adolf Hitler himself."

She glanced little daggers around Nathan's face and into his eyes before she sat back, "Luckily, I'll get to stay on the plane for that trip."

"You make Halloween with my niece sound almost boring," said Nathan.

"And I'd trade places with you in a heartbeat," she said as she stood. "Well, I'm sure Aunt Madey has seen us here talking long enough to satisfy her curiosity for now. Why don't you invite me for a walk this evening before we leave?"

Nathan stood up quickly. They were leaving? Of course they were. He felt a sudden unexpected drop, "Until this evening then."

Lindsey nodded curtly, too reminiscent of Madeline for Nathan's liking, before finally plodding off to disappear in the downstairs hallway.

CHAPTER FIFTEEN

"**I**T'S hideous…, put it on the bare wall in the den," scoffed Madeline. "I don't want to see it or hear it."

True to his word, Henry had purchased a television. A sixty-inch behemoth flat screen was waddling its way through the downstairs past the library to the den. If only to irritate Madeline further, Nathan hurried down the hall and slid open the double french doors for the odd pair.

Henry and his backwoods helper Lester, mounted the monstrosity on the wall, connected a plethora of electronics, and flipped it on.

The sound boomed throughout the entire lower west wing to the delight of Henry. Soon there was the roar of a live football game equal to any stadium.

Madeline shrank to the other end of the house to peruse the layout of her inventory, but not before announcing that their impending departure would be at precisely seven that evening.

The adjoining activities were at the very least interesting. At Ms. Stewart's insistence, the noise was off…, actually it was only muted; an amicable truce.

Nathan was watching the family's delicate balance of interaction, wandering between Henry's gleeful shouts at the silent screen and the dining room where Madeline and Lindsey were finishing up their meal. It was as if he was the invisible man for those few minutes of the evening. When he had absorbed what he wanted to see, he wandered in and sat at the end of the table where the two women were still picking at their plates.

"I hope you're satisfied," said Madeline, immediately glancing at Nathan.

Her scold didn't sound as angry as the actual words *and* the atmosphere was far more relaxed between her and Lindsey.

Nathan shrugged, "It's your house, your rules. I'm only the caretaker now, remember?"

"Once a caregiver, always a caregiver, Mr. Heart," said Madeline. "It's a curse and a gift."

Her eyes glanced toward Lindsey displaying some sort of repentant shadow that only appeared for a split second.

Nathan had braced himself for a longwinded discourse to end their evening together when Lindsey stood up.

"Mr. Heart, I believe you promised me a walk this evening," said Lindsey; she said it with a smile.

"Yes I did," he answered, standing back up.

"Don't be too long, we leave in an hour," said Madeline, quietly stacking their plates.

"I'm already packed," said Lindsey.

Both of them grabbed a heavy jacket to fight off a stiff evening breeze blowing in off the distant coastline. He flipped the heavy electrical switch at the back door. In the distance, the long stony path around the property lit up with small starlight near the ground. When the back door shut behind them, Lindsey seemed to relax, even against the night air.

"I can't thank you enough," she said.

"Just be careful when you call your real boyfriend."

"I've already called him twice today," she sighed.

Nathan couldn't think of anything clever and so accepted the silence, leading them along the path beside the burgeoning treeline.

"She's really not that bad when she's not trying to run my life," began Lindsey.

"I know," said Nathan. "I know how family can be. They treat you like a stranger when things don't go their way."

"Exactly."

She almost tripped on a jutting slick rock, then slipped a hand around his arm to brace herself.

"She really does like you, you know."

"Excuse me?" laughed Nathan.

She yanked his arm, gently scolding him, "My aunt seems to like you for some reason."

"So I've been told," he grinned.

He tried to find some sort of compliment to return, but at the moment all his beatitudes toward Madeline seemed like a lie.

"Henry does too. But I can't trust what he says. He'd say anything to get my mind off Jon."

Nathan grinned at her, "Even I can tell Henry only wants what's best for you."

"He wants whatever Aunt Madey wants for me," she countered.

Nathan shook his head, "Not according to him. Apparently he has his own reasons for disliking your friend Jon."

It was Lindsey's turn to fall into silence for several steps.

"I can't help but feel sorry for my brother," she said quietly.

Nathan laughed, "Henry's fine. He's at the last stages…, but he's fighting it."

Lindsey frowned, "What stages are you talking about?"

"Adulthood. Facing the responsibilities being handed to him."

She didn't seem to appreciate Nathan's opinion over the subject of her brother or maybe his remark fell into her own lap.

Eyes closed, Lindsey lifted her chin, as if testing the air, "The pines look the same here, but the sound is different…. They almost sound sad in the wind."

"It's the spruce behind them," said Nathan. Once again, he shirked his feelings of the past and lonely evenings spent jogging the trail they were on.

"I think I'm going to enjoy my visit's here," she said, with some hidden finality.

"Are you coming back for the Thanksgiving Holiday with your aunt?"

"It depends," she said, her head suddenly turned away.

"Ah, I think I understand. You're waiting for a better offer," said Nathan.

"Sure you're not psychic?" she grinned. "I'm waiting for…, several things right now. That's one of them."

"Didn't Jon ask you to Thanksgiving when you called him today?"

It took another three or four steps before Lindsey answered.

"I said I called Jon. I didn't say he answered."

Nathan suddenly wished he'd kept his mouth shut.

"I'm sorry; that was really none of my business."

Lindsey's hand slipped from his arm to his hand.

"We'd better turn back," she said with a shiver. "Aunt Madey will be spitting bricks if we're late to the airport."

When Nathan and Lindsey walked back through the house, there was nothing but silence. The kitchen was clean and bare and not a whisper of an echo from any direction.

Nathan was about to call out when the front door opened, "Let's go Lens! The car's running."

Had they been gone that long? It seemed like only a few minutes. They hurried through the house and out to the waiting limousine.

Henry was holding open one of the double side doors, shivering in his short sleeve shirt, "I already loaded your things."

He waved frantically at his sister, saluted Nathan with a grin, then slid inside the gaping cavern of the car.

Lindsey stopped short of climbing in, turned and hugged Nathan unexpectedly, "We have to keep up appearances."

When the door closed, Nathan tapped on one of the back windows and waited for it to slide down. He handed Ms. Stewart a card from his pocket.

"My cell number. Unless you enjoy being flashed."

Madeline chuckled, obviously stifling a naughty reply, then handed it across the lounge seat to Lindsey.

"Good night Mr. Heart. It's been a pleasure."

The dark window slid shut and the car drove away in silence.

Nathan hurried back up the porch steps, then turned to watch until it was out of sight.

"What...," he grumbled to himself.

The house was still warm with voices, still smelled of food, yet it was staring at him now, silent and empty. Silent as an early death sentence.

"Not tonight you don't," he grunted.

After a quick bathroom check, he switched jackets, grabbed his keys and rushed out the door. Suddenly, everything stopped inside him.

The security system was disabled.

Thoughts of being trapped for over a year, unable to go anywhere, do anything, have normal friends and acquaintances all rushed back in like a wave. He was still trapped. This house was going to be the death of him.

He hurried to his desk, called the emergency repair number to the security company and set up visit for the next morning.

'Now what?' he asked himself.

Should he sit here brooding in silence for the rest of the night or leave and risk something happening to the contents of the house?

He checked all the doors, locked the front deadbolt and headed to the garage at a trot. At this time of evening, he only had one choice of desirable destinations within driving distance. If only Troy would keep his matchmaking efforts to himself tonight.

CHAPTER SIXTEEN

THE Blind Pirate was quiet for a change, especially for eight thirty on a Sunday evening. Troy was busily wiping down the bar with some orange peel scented spray while Lisa carried a heavy looking platter of mugs through a swinging back door.

Nathan planted himself on one of the more comfortable bar seats and waited for Troy to wander over. He didn't seem his usual robust or half drunken happy self.

Troy turned and grabbed a bottle of black rum off the shelf and a couple of shot glasses before acknowledging Nathan's presence. The bottle clopped down, then the little glass jiggers. Troy poured them both full to the brim and drank one, shoving the other to Nathan.

"You look like you could use one of these as much as me," he grunted.

Nathan lifted the glass sniffing the sweet fragrance of the island rum.

"I don't know whether to wear it or drink it," he smiled.

"Therein lies your main problem," grunted Troy, refilling his shot glass. "You're either a partaker or a window gazer, you gotta choose which, Nathan my boy."

Nathan swallowed the sweet rum slowly, letting the sweet tingle settle against his tongue.

"What has you in such a melancholy mood?"

"Life…, my boy, life," he sighed.

It was twice he'd said 'my boy' within the last minute. Troy came around the bar and plopped into the swiveling seat beside Nathan, wiggling his ankles tiredly.

"Where's your band at tonight?" asked Nathan.

"Gone.... Poof.... They took off for greener pastures just after noon today."

Another round of rum for the both of them and Troy seemed to soften a little.

There was a loud clatter in the back and Troy bellowed like a foghorn toward the back door, "Lisa, leave it all be and come set a spell. That's an order."

"She's been at it all afternoon all by her lonesome. Working her legs off she has," he grunted.

Nathan was going to ask what happened to his 'pisser of a waiter' but if it was something Troy wanted to share he'd do it in his own time.

"I'm guessing the house weren't the only thing that ran you off this evening?" asked Troy.

How could this old drunken sailor be so dead-on all the time?

Nathan shook his head and slid his empty glass toward Troy and his black rum.

"You're right as usual," said Nathan. "It's been one of those weekends. I wouldn't even know where to begin, even if I felt like telling you about it."

Troy gave out a belly laugh, "Sounds like some woman were involved in the mix I'd guess..., if I were a guessing man."

Nathan shook his head in awe.

Lisa pushed through the squeaky swinging door from the back and plopped heavily into the chair on the other side of Nathan, then leaned over the bar and plucked an empty tumbler to slide to Troy.

"Troy, you know I like ya, but I gotta tell you," said Lisa, "...if we have many more like this one you'll have to do it yourself or you'll be scraping me up to throw in the dumpster."

"What happened to your other help?" asked Nathan, tired of waiting on Troy.

"One was sickly, the other already worked a double."

Troy had walked around his question, "What about that fellow?"

"Left with the band. Young Bart found out they was headed to Los Angeles and hitched a ride.... After he up and nabbed about a hundred dollars from my till."

"And all my tips," added Lisa.

She looked at the back of the restaurant where two tables were still occupied, "I just wish that bunch would leave so I could finish up and start the dishwasher."

"Has Eddie shut down the grill?" he asked.

As soon as Lisa nodded, Troy turned and belted, "Folks, we're closing in five minutes. Either eat it or get it t'go."

"I must have made twenty trips refilling their drinks and I bet I don't get a five dollar tip out of it," she sighed.

Apparently, listening to their day's problems, along with copious amounts of rum had eased the glum headache he'd walked in with.

"Me and Eddie can help Glen take care of loading the dishes tonight dearie," said Troy. "I don't need my only other reliable employee to head for parts unknown. By the way…, I'm sorry you had to cover the entire floor alone tonight. I know I weren't much help."

He gulped down another shot of rum and pushed the bottle to Nathan, "Gotta get busy. Keep your seat and we'll have ourselves a chat when I'm done for the evenin'."

He slid the bottle to Nathan, moving away with an ease no fellow his size should be able to negotiate.

Nathan glanced at Lisa and refilled their glasses, "I told you something wasn't right about your gritty little helper."

Lisa shrugged, "I always like to give people the benefit of the doubt."

In his mind, Nathan could hear Troy belch out one of his usual wise owl remarks on human nature and tried to stifle a grin.

"You think that's funny?" she asked. Her eyes were scolding him past some other mystery clinging in her voice.

"No, not at all," said Nathan quickly.

Before he had a chance to explain himself, the last noisy group of customers began to shuffle to the checkout and Lisa huffed a breath of air, walking their direction.

He suspected that Troy had left him and Lisa parked beside each other for more than just giving the girl a break, but tried to ignore the whole agenda.

He pushed away the rum that was already doing a fine job of calming his nerves and turned a gratuitous eye toward Lisa near the register. She smiled and chatted with each of the group as they finally walked out the door. Right on their heels, she turned the door latch then flipped the switch to the neon sign from 'open' to 'closed'.

The whole place was instantly muffled and silent and Nathan turned around before anyone noticed that he was stalking 'the help' with his eyes.

Lisa walked back where he was seated and dropped two crumpled one-dollar bills and a handful of change on the bar.

"Two sixty-five," she grinned. "Not exactly fifteen percent of ninety-six bucks is it?"

She smoothed out the two one-dollar bills and stuffed them in her apron and took her time dropping the change in some 'help the needy' box with the face of child on the front.

"I could tell you were mad at the kid. Don't be. If I had a chance to get out of here I'd probably do the same thing," said Lisa, her grin barely a twitch.

"It doesn't make it right," said Nathan.

"I never said it did," she sighed. "I'd better go help so we can all get out of here before midnight."

Nathan felt as if he should say something..., anything..., "I thought you were happy with life around here. From our last talk that is."

Lisa stopped at the end of the bar, "Don't mind my mood swings, tomorrow I'll be happy Lisa again."

"Can I ask you something?" blurted Nathan, when she'd turned to leave again.

"I don't see why not."

"What makes you feel trapped?"

Lisa finally smiled and let out a laugh as her answer, then turned and disappeared behind the squeaky swinging door.

Nathan looked at the mummified tarpon on the wall behind the bar, "Did I say something wrong?"

Eddie the cook and some short fellow he didn't recognize plowed through the door with a cart and bussed the two tables in the back of the restaurant as they blathered on about nothing.

With the speed of a hurricane, tables were swiped, chairs turned, and a push broom thrust into the hands of Nathan. It was his usual after-hours duty for the privilege of his hiding place. Ten minutes of walking with a broom seemed a fair price.

He sat back down and indulged in a few more quick tastes of sweet run, finally pushing the bottle away. The last thing he needed was a ticket for driving while under the influence.

He started to drop some money in the tip jar on the bar, to replace Lisa's losses for the day, but that would only hurt her pride. She didn't seem like the kind of person that would appreciate anyone feeling sorry for her. He pushed a fifty down its narrow throat just the same.

The photographs behind the bar caught his attention, some of the local fishermen, their boats, their catches. A few photos were of Troy when he was younger, at the helm of his own boat. Things looked different from the other side of the bar. The floor was raised a few inches, which explained why Troy always seemed to be hovering. Nathan ran his hands down the dark stained and scarred wood; it seemed to come alive against his bare skin. According to Troy, it was made from the salvaged deck of Blackbeard's Frigate.

With the peace and quiet of the friendly white noise, he had a chance to let the creative side of his mind catch up.

The sounds of chatter mingled with laughter started getting louder when the door from the back flapped open.

Troy turned, "Goodnight Eddie!"

He and Lisa walked past and sat down at a table in front of Nathan.

"Thanks for letting me hang out," said Nathan.

"Ya know I should charge you the same rates as a therapist," barked Troy.

"You're right about that," said Nathan. "This is a good place to think."

"How 'bout thinking a ride home for Lisa here?" asked Troy with a sly wink.

"I can walk. It's only a few blocks," said Lisa.

"I'd be glad to," said Nathan. "I need to get back early tonight."

"I'll walk," said Lisa. "Goodnight Troy."

She was already walking toward the side door when Troy began nodding his head her direction.

"Goodnight Troy," hissed Nathan, hurrying toward Lisa.

A blustery cold wind whipped both their faces just outside the door. There was a loud clack behind them and Nathan spun to see Troy locking the glass door with a big grin on his face.

Lisa turned her steps toward the front of the diner.

"My car's in the back," said Nathan.

"Goodnight Nathan," she said with a wave.

He hurried around back, jumped in his car and caught up to Lisa before she made it out of the parking lot. Lisa was fighting the violent wind, yanking at her long coat when the cherry red car door flew open beside her.

This time she didn't argue, but slipped inside as fast as she could.

She pointed which way, said thanks, then sat silently, waiting for some 'I told you so' from Nathan.

"It took me a few minutes to understand your answer," said Nathan.

Lisa strummed her wind whipped hair out of her face, "My answer?"

"About being trapped? It was a stupid question in the first place," he sighed.

She gave Nathan a little bit of a grin and turned.

"I'm at the end of the street, the duplex."

It was typical of all the houses in the Crab Cove community. Weathered gray by the brutal Oceanside wind and rain, very few renovations, a little on the bleak side.

Nathan parked in her empty driveway and at the same time, several of his recent ideas congealed.

"Do you have a few seconds?" he asked.

Lisa looked at him as a dozen thoughts filled her head. The insanely good-looking man she thought might turn out to be a gentleman was just like all the rest.

"Look, I appreciate the ride, but I really need to get some rest," she whined. "If this is about Troy and his...."

"It's not," grinned Nathan. "I just have a few questions."

Lisa sighed and took her hand off the door handle, "What?"

"Are you any good with a computer?" he asked.

"I..., suppose."

"What about a camera?"

She frowned and shook her head, "I'm really tired Nathan."

"I'm opening a small office in Salem and I need some part time help to answer the phone, do some filing, and place a few ads for me."

Lisa tilted her head up and laughed, "In Salem? Do you see a car in my driveway?"

Instantly, he thought of the Buick Special that had been parked in his garage unused for over a year. It made perfect sense.

"The job comes with a car. Well..., sort of. It's old but dependable," he offered.

"The job? Is this an interview?" she grinned.

She seemed more relieved than he expected about the offer, but she was actually relieved he wasn't trying to make the crude advances she had been preparing herself for.

"Yes..., I believe it is," said Nathan.

"Let me think about it?" she asked. "I can't leave Troy empty handed."

"Mornings, three days a week, nine to two. You can still keep your job at the Blind Pirate."

"And I can think about it?" she asked, popping the car door open.

Nathan nodded, then handed her one of his cards, "Don't take too long."

"I'll let you know."

CHAPTER SEVENTEEN

T HE tires on the cherry red XLR slid to a halt just inside his garage, but Nathan sat in the stillness for several minutes after the overhead door creaked to a close.

Had he actually let himself peep out of his shell?

Before he applied too much logic and talked himself out of his mood, he hurried and flipped on all the lights in the long, five stall garage.

The pistachio green Buick Special sat there in the third stall sleeping, awaiting its turn out of the chute. It needed a scouring bath and some basic maintenance, but mostly it needed to be driven before it turned into an unused heap of rust.

He pictured Lisa sitting behind the wheel and smiled. It would be freeing two birds with one snip, plus most would be a tax write off.

His mind was still whirring as he unlocked the front door to the quiet empty of the estate. He listened to the steady tock of the old clock as he slid out of his coat. Even it sounded happy for a change. The hands on the antique face told him that he'd been out longer than he realized and he hurried on inside, whipping off the red tie from around the neck of his navy oxford shirt.

With barely a concern, he checked the doors and rooms downstairs, cringing past a few pieces of odd humored furniture, then hurried up the stairs.

His bedroom seemed to welcome him and he let himself drift into an easy preoccupation of thought. Even if it was one tiny step at a time, he was inching out. Maybe there was hope for Nathan Heart after all.

It wasn't until he was in bed, thoughts still churning, that he finally relaxed. Still…, something was missing, holding his eyelids open as he stared into the mixed shadows of his bedroom.

The house was at its usual fervor, reenacting some unknown war with creaks and thumps every so often, along with the muffled sounds of the wind outside.

It was the quiet.

He found himself missing the noise of the past several hours of co-occupancy, human intersection, the juncture of humanity. He rolled onto his back and stared at the ceiling at the darkness, then something inside him smiled.

Quickly, he trotted down the stairs, to the fully stocked pantry and found one of the boxes he'd rearranged. With a satisfying jerk, it popped open and he took out one of the scented votive candles.

When it lit, with its satisfying little crackle, once he was back in his room, he mentally thanked Lindsey wherever she was for her gift.

The warm scent and the flicker of light filled the room with life, the memory of Lindsey's struggle as well as her genuine nature. She had a way of distracting him, even disarming him that he wasn't used to. Was there chemistry there? Time would tell.

♥

His alarm went off with only thirty minutes to spare before there was a knock at his front door. The security service took their emergency repairs seriously. The young technician was all smiles and relaxed confidence, carting in a two wheeler of equipment needed to reset all of the sensors, room to room, window by window, and door by door.

At nine a.m., Nathan was dressed to leave for his first appointment, leaving the repairman to his duties. He assured Nathan that he would be out of the house before noon and the system would send him a test message when he locked up the house.

Nathan almost felt guilty leaving a stranger all alone in the house, surrounded by so much ancient death.

That was his problem.

Time quickly slipped away; the first appointment let him clamp on a 'sold' addendum to the 'for sale' sign in front of the first property.

Two insurance inspections and one sales contract later, he found himself in downtown Salem, looking at several closet sized office spaces. Lumberton would have been far less expensive, maybe even a smirk in the face of his competition, but also practically invisible to potential clients. People from Portland rarely sought out suburbia properties in Lumberton; Salem was usually their maximum safety zone. With the price of gas inching up like a cancer, no one wanted to lock into a property that would stress that portion of their budget further than it already had.

He marked two little prospects and parked next to the closest one, right in front of a sandwich and coffee house, just before his cell phone rang.

"Heart Realty."

"Yes, I'm well aware who this is," said the gruff voice.

Nathan recognized the voice immediately.

"Troy? Is that you?"

"How long have we been friends, Nathan Heart?" he blurted angrily.

"What's wrong Troy?"

"You know full well what this is about you…, thievin' Judas. It's about Lisa. Is this how you intend to repay me? By stealing my best employee right from under my nose?"

"Troy, I have no intentions of stealing Lisa from you. I only mentioned that I was looking for some part time help."

"So she wasn't lying to me when she asked for three late shifts?"

"Monday, Wednesday, and Saturday, Troy. Nine 'til two. I didn't think Lisa was even interested."

The phone scrunched loudly against Troy's stubble before he continued, "Oh. Well then. That's a whole different ball of wax then, ain't it? Monday, Wednesday, and Saturday. Be seeing ya Nathan."

The phone clicked and went silent.

"Maybe that wasn't such a good idea," muttered Nathan.

The roast beef sandwich and double espresso revived his spirit as he took off to inspect the vacancy next door. The office was shaped like a tall shoebox; one glass paned door, one storefront window. It was stuffed like a sandwich between the coffee shop and another glamorous storefront, which sold homemade candles and crafts.

It was dark inside and as he twisted the handle, the door jumped open, jingling a little overhead bell. He liked it immediately, it was just the sort of small unassuming image he wanted for an office - Not some posh over-priced façade.

He peered inside cautiously, "Hello?"

His voice echoed blandly toward the back and he stepped inside. It was warm and smelled richly of coffee beans with a hint of pipe tobacco. It needed a little work and there was light peeking through around the rear entrance far to the back. It had the feeling of some dark narrow storybook alley converted into a building, but it was clean and dry.

With the right lighting, a little paint, a few partitions, it had the possibility of looking like a tiny office.

"Can I help you?"

A frail elderly lady, her gray streaked hair up in a beehive mound, was blocking the entrance. She was holding a broomstick in her hand as if it was a potential weapon, eyes flashing.

"I'm looking to rent," said Nathan, sticking out his hand.

"It's not ready just yet," she said, ignoring his hand.

"But the sign on the window...," he pointed.

She reached over, took the sign from the windowpane and set it on the floor without another word.

"When will it be ready?" he asked, refusing to give up.

"Don't know just yet. What are you wanting to put in here? We keep a clean group of stores on this street. No liquor stores, no magazines, none of them alternate lifestyle accessories...."

Nathan laughed before she could finish her list.

"I'm Nathan Heart from Heart Realty. I'd like to open a Real Estate office; that is if the price was right and the landlord wasn't too picky about my choice of paint colors."

She nodded, "I've seen a few of your signs, on those uppity properties out west of town."

"That would be me," he said, trying to smile.

She pushed a little stack of dirt away from the door with her broom and looked back up.

"I'm Gwen Helspeth. The place is too small for most businesses; just a narrow chute. I was considering renting it out as storage."

"I don't need much space," said Nathan. "A couple of desks and some filing cabinets."

She sighed and stared at her broom for several seconds.

"Two fifty a month, first month in advance..., and no black or red paint. My son is coming tomorrow to rip out this awful carpet and put down gray pile. It shares a restroom with the coffee shop as well as the heat and air. That suit you?" she asked.

It was theft at that price. Nathan picked up the 'for rent' sign from the floor and gave it a toss toward the empty floor behind him. He was surprised that the coffee shop hadn't annexed the space as storage or an internet café or extra seating.

"Gray carpet is fine. Who in their right mind would paint the walls black and red?"

"Tobacco accessory shop," she grunted. "At least that's what they said. Bunch of odd-looking contraptions if you ask me. Anyway, it took my son a week to get rid of it the last time."

Nathan handed her his business card, "I'd like to open the doors in two weeks. Is that agreeable?"

"I suppose you have references?" she asked.

CHAPTER EIGHTEEN

ANOTHER rung of the ladder was beginning to feel firm underfoot as Nathan hummed to a tune on the radio. When he returned home, the security technician's truck was still parked outside. He hadn't received his confirming text message from the system; this couldn't be good.

The front door was standing slightly ajar needing only a slight nudge to crest open.

"Hello?"

The otherwise confident young man walked quickly to Nathan, his face sallow and pale.

"I was about to call you. I'm having a problem getting the sensors to cooperate. Has the house been lightning struck recently?" he asked.

Nathan shook his head, "We've had a few storms, but wouldn't a direct strike set off the alarm system?"

"In theory," he mumbled. "I'm looking at replacing all the infrared sensors in two wings and some of the motion detectors. Don't worry, it's all under warranty."

"There didn't seem to be any problems until the system was keyed offline," said Nathan. "What do you suppose happened?"

"I sent in the data to be analyzed. I should know in an hour or so," he said, turning to go back to the pantry.

To Nathan, that was a technical term for 'I don't have a clue'.

He followed the repairman, saw a crumb littered plate on the counter by the sink where the fellow had made himself a sandwich, then decided to pull a chair close to the pantry door.

A mass of black cables were plugged into every orifice just below the touch screen panel.

The tech had resorted to scratching his head at a blinking yellow light and turned to look at Nathan.

"See? This says that someone is moving around in the upstairs west wing. But the house is empty. It is empty, isn't it?"

"All except for the furniture," grunted Nathan.

He didn't bother to explain his feelings over the macabre history of the inventory squatting in every room. It would have only served to agitate the technician's already distraught condition.

"Is there anything I can do to help?" asked Nathan.

"You want to watch this for me while I take a walk upstairs? These lights should come on one at a time as I make my way down the hall."

He sounded a little shy, even disturbed.

"Would you rather I walk upstairs while you watch the panel?" asked Nathan.

He held up a bulky test meter, while staring at the monitor once again, "I'd better do it. This one needs resetting again."

Nathan propped on one of the stacks of boxes inside the pantry, waiting. Moments later, like clockwork, six lights lit up in succession, but moments before he reached the end of the hall, that last yellow light went dark. It blinked back on for a moment and the entire procedure repeated in reverse, all of them finally going dark.

It was as if someone had hidden themselves in the room just before he arrived at the end of the hallway.

Then Nathan saw another sensor light up bright red on a different panel, just as he heard footsteps coming down the stairs.

"The sensor tested okay," he said. "I don't get it."

Nathan didn't feel the need to tell him about the odd activity of the yellow lights on the west wing.

"What does this red one mean?" asked Nathan.

The fellow uttered a curse and punched a button marked reset on the panel repeatedly, "Motion sensor on the far end of the upper East wing."

The red light went off, but only for a moment, then blinked back on.

"I'm going to order a complete upgrade to the entire system," he grunted as he indiscriminately snatched out wires from the panel.

Every light on the main security panel flashed on and off three times, then everything went dark. Only the faint glow of the LCD screen was blinking the words, 'System Online'.

"Huh. I don't believe it," he hissed. "That's what it should have done three hours ago. The system just reset itself."

He kicked the array of equipment on the cart in frustration. "It was probably something buggy with my test equipment all along," he gritted. "I'll get all my stuff loaded up and get out of your way."

Within minutes, he was pulling the cart behind him, stopping only to hand Nathan a card. "Now if it does anything crazy at all in the next thirty days, you call this number and we'll send a team to replace the whole system."

The entire scenario didn't incite much confidence in Nathan. He could picture a fire alarm going off ten minutes after the house was burning to the ground.

At least he was gone now.

His cell phone buzzed..., a text message, "System Online".

Nathan shook his head and went to pour something to drink, when he received another call.

"Heart Realty."

"Is that how I'm supposed to answer the phone for you?" asked a quiet female voice.

It had to be Lisa, but there was no caller identification.

"Hello Lisa?"

"Do you still need some part time help?" she asked, still not answering Nathan's question.

"I'll have an office ready in two weeks. Will that be enough time to adjust your schedule?" he asked.

"Troy was really upset with me," she sighed.

"He called me today," said Nathan. "I think he understands."

She was quiet for several moments.

"Is there going to be a problem with you working for me?" he asked.

"No. I guess I'm just nervous," she sighed again. "I'm not really good with change."

"Lisa?"

"Yes?"

"Does this mean you want the job?" he asked.

"I'd be crazy not to," she answered. "I guess that means yes."

Nathan could hear the sudden relief in her voice.

"You'll do just fine. I'll have your vehicle checked out in a day or two and we'll go look at the office together."

"Thanks Nathan."

Nathan explained as little as possible what he expected of her and her salary before ending the call. Where was the outgoing confidence he'd seen in her week after week at Troy's diner? She seemed almost afraid. Maybe it was as simple as she'd said..., it was the change itself that had her worried. Fear of the unknown could be a debilitating force.

He poured a glass of juice and sat down at the kitchen table, his hands hovering over the inquisitors refectory. It was unnerving as he slid his palm across the deep gouges and discolored wooden surface. Could this have really been a human butcher block for wild-eyed zealots? There were empty screw holes at regular intervals along the sides with circular rust stains, possibly where iron rings were used to lash a thrashing body to the top while unspeakable acts of torture were enacted. He looked closer at some of the scars, black with discoloration, letting his finger run lightly in their trough. His hand jerked back when he imagined the screams of some unlucky person as they lost a limb or tongue or their head.

Nathan stood away from the table, snatching up his glass, thrusting the chair back in its place. How had he allowed himself to be coerced into living in this house of horrors?

He hurried to his office, grabbing up a folder containing all the shipping manifests since the beginning, along with the final sketch of the house and each item's placement.

In the first downstairs bedroom was a large maroon prayer rug of Turkish origin. A dark faded stain saturated the fiber along one frayed end.

A white silk tapestry with Chinese Calligraphy covered a small spot in one corner - its origin claimed to be the Han Dynasty, acquired in Nanjing. It seemed innocuous enough, even though the ink used was a dark crimson red, and was entitled, 'Blood of a King'.

There were artifacts from various wars including the American Civil War, Plagues, Disasters, Famines, and upheavals between countries he'd never heard of.

Finally, he put away the manifests, deep in thought. Obviously these items were of tremendous historical and monetary value; not only to Madeline Stewart, but to historical societies, private collectors, or museums.

Why had she wanted the Heart Estate? Was it only needed as an innocuous storage facility? She already had one, somewhere in Sacramento. Why would she want to surround herself with death in a vacation home? None of it made any sense.

"Why do I care?" laughed Nathan.

His voice carried through the house and he laughed all the more. The house was sold, everyone received their share, everyone was happy. What did he care if the house was filled with coffins? Everything here was dead except him. He was still very much alive and all the more happy for it.

Tuesday morning a tow truck arrived and loaded the old Buick Special on its back for a thorough examination at a local mechanics shop.

Wednesday, he received an unexpected call from Lindsey Stewart, on the pretense of keeping up their charade. Nathan could still picture the freckles in her eyes and the way she shifted her blond hair when she spoke. When their conversation about nothing in general ended, he was left with an uncertain empty feeling he couldn't quite put a finger on. He couldn't allow himself to be attracted to someone already infatuated with another; that was heartbreak on a stick. He shook his head, quickly spinning his thoughts another direction.

Thursday, he spent eating like a pig while watching Henry's enormous flat-screen television in the den. That afternoon a trip to drop off all the laundry, that evening a trip to dinner at the Blind Pirate. He made amends with Troy and talked over some plans with his new secretary to be, Lisa Evans.

Friday morning, October 31st, Nathan was packed for an overnight trip to Caroline and Chris Masters. He was anxious to see his niece Allie and spend a fun evening with family. He locked the doors and set the alarm, thrilled that he wouldn't be staying in an empty tomb on All Hallows Eve.

Just before he drove out of the garage, he cast a warm smile over at the end stall where the old green relic was parked, fresh out of the hospital.

The 1958 Buick Special was back from the mechanic with a stamp of approval and a new set of tires, belts and hoses, among other upgrades. It was purring like a kitten when it arrived back in its stable at the estate. He felt further reassured of the shop's work when two of the mechanics offered to purchase the '58 Buick on the spot.

He couldn't wait to see Lisa's reaction to the relic, whether good or bad, it would still be amusing.

CHAPTER NINETEEN

THE long drive was cleansing. The air was still, cold and crisp with rare bright rays of morning sunshine following him the entire trip east of Portland. This time of year, the whole region of the northwest became one contiguous blanket of clouds, rain, mist, fog, or worse. Today was a welcome anomaly.

When he parked at the curb, Nathan noticed a small bicycle near the door of his sister's home, two yard gnomes, and rampant but neatly groomed colorful plants near the house, with more circling two huge trees in the front yard.

There was a note on the Masters' front door, from Caroline -

> Nathan,
> Please forgive me for running off.
> I had to make a last minute trip to the store.
> Ask Newton for the key and let yourself in.
> I'll see you soon.
> Caroline

Nathan tried unsuccessfully to subdue his laughter, for the sake of the neighbors, then scanned the yard.

The two yard gnomes were staring at him with cold unfeeling eyes, a silly smirk on their faces. He walked past both of them patting the crown of their pointy heads.

DAVID PYLE

On the closest tree was a giant green lizard with a pink tongue lolled out, frozen for eternity. With one hand propped against the slick bark of the tree, leaning carefully over his sister's circle of prized caladiums, he asked, "May I have the key please?"

His fingers tickled the underbelly of the ceramic lizard and felt the cold jagged cuts of a small key. The hidden magnet relented and it popped into his hand. He pushed away to regain his balance and looked at Newton's offering.

Of course, the key didn't go to the front door. It was a game he and his sister had played since they were teenagers.

He hurried over to one of the gnomes and pushed him over with his foot.

"Not you."

With a grunt, he stood the heavy creature back up and dusted the grass clippings from its face.

When the other tipped over, there was a square-hinged door on the bottom with a keyhole.

Nathan inserted the key and viola, one house key.

Suddenly, there was a sharp succession of clapping, then laughter behind him.

"Well... done... Nathan...," said Caroline. "And I have it all on camera for Allie. She'll love it."

Caroline's bright smile disentangled the last memory of Heart Manor from his mind.

"I should have known," he grunted.

They shared a quick hug and a playful shove.

"Go get your things and I'll pour you a cup of coffee."

Nathan brought in an overnight bag and a large sack of decorations for Allie.

Caroline was already dressed for the day, and knowing her, she had an agenda planned for the both of them until it was time to pick up Allie from her elementary school.

"Does it feel strange living in the old house now that it's sold?" asked Caroline as she sat down at the wrap-around bar.

"It's..., different," said Nathan. "You should come and see it soon."

"I'll pass," she grunted.

"I was being sarcastic," grinned Nathan. "The place is..., never mind."

He shook his head. It was better that he didn't tell his sister that their old childhood home was a house of macabre secrets. Why spoil her childhood memories to ease his own misery?

She nodded and poured herself a little more coffee from the carafe between them.

"Allie gets out early today. If the weather holds you'll get to do a little trick or treating through the neighborhood."

"How are you doing Caroline?" he asked.

"Me? I'm good," she smiled.

Not great, not wonderful, but good. Caroline was cradling some secret she didn't want to share and all the prying in the world wouldn't wrench it from her until she was ready.

"Heard from the *Big Three*?" he asked cautiously.

She grinned, then chuckled, covering her mouth, "You know we should probably stop calling them by that nickname."

"And spoil all the fun?" said Nathan. "There's no telling what they call us behind our backs."

"The Runts," she said, barking out a subdued laugh.

"*The Runts?*" he said, rolling his eyes. "Touché."

She sipped her coffee, gazing across the living room.

"Nice move Sis, but you still didn't answer my question. Unless you'd rather not talk about it?" he asked.

"They're still bitter," she shrugged. "So says Kate. She's such a sweetheart. She promised to drive down and see me as soon as she gets her permanent drivers license. I told her not to. Josie would probably take away her car keys if she found out."

"How's Chuck taking this ridiculous cold war?"

Chuck was Kathryn's younger brother by just over a year. Nathan hadn't been allowed to see either of them in almost three years. First, it was under the umbrella of protecting them from the bouts of dementia their grandmother Marion Heart suffered, then it all secretly became about the money.

"He's a follower. Kate says he'll come around as soon as he gets his head out of his butt."

Nathan laughed, "Have you sent them this month's message from me?"

Every four or five weeks, Nathan sent a card with a little cash for Caroline to relay to them.

Caroline nodded, her face falling a little serious, "She uh..., said to tell you she loves you and she read your email. She even talked with me about staying with you while she attended the University in Portland."

"Well..., I guess I threw the dishes out with the water on that one," sighed Nathan.

"Kate knew you wouldn't be living there forever. Are you looking for another place?"

"Oh, that reminds me. I'm opening an office in downtown Salem in a couple of weeks. Already hired myself a part-timer to man the phones."

Caroline grinned, "And what about someplace to call your own?"

Nathan shook his head, "Why would a confirmed bachelor like me need something permanent?"

She shook her head in frustration. There was no use reopening the same old conversation over again.

After setting their cups in the sink, she looked at her wristwatch, "Come on, we're meeting Chris for lunch and I have to be back in town before two."

♥

Downtown Portland traffic was a beehive, but Caroline managed to weave her way into a parking space only a block from her husbands little IT company.

Chris Masters was already standing outside on the sidewalk, his square jaw cast upward and glaring at the sun when they met. The blond fuzz of his military haircut gleamed like a halo over his head. When he looked down at the pedestrian traffic, he saw them coming and pointed at Nathan.

"Hey if it isn't the family outcast," grinned Chris.

"It's good to see you too," said Nathan.

Caroline glared almost angrily at her husband as the two men shook hands.

"Did you catch the Redskin's game this week?"

"Yeah, it was a slaughter," grunted Nathan.

Chris grinned even wider, "So how much do you owe me now?"

Caroline groaned and tugged them into motion toward their usual diner.

"Is this just lunch or are you really going to stick around so Allie can say hello?" asked Chris.

Nathan smiled, "You're not getting rid of me that easy. I'm here for the full experience with the Masters family."

"That'll be the day. Hey, I found…," began Chris.

Chris's voice faded into white noise as Caroline watched the two men carry on more like brothers than their blood family. She had something to tell Nathan, but it could wait until after their holiday together was over. Why should she spoil Nathan's few moments of normality with them and Allie? Besides, it was the same old story; another impending family storm.

"…so it can help you profile potential clients for future sales. It's better than the version you're using and the data is practically free," said Chris, as his voice faded back into Caroline's ears.

"Let me know when you get ready to beta test and I'll put it to use with my secretary," said Nathan.

"You have a secretary now?" blurted Chris, then nudged his wife. "See I told you he was working some angle Honey."

"You never told me her name," said Caroline, teasing her brother further.

The door to their café opened and they halted while a lively group exited. A few feet away, past the door, sat an aged scruffy man with his feet curled underneath his legs. Nathan quickly hurried over and emptied his pocket change and what little paper money he had into the cup beside the old fellow before he hurried in the restaurant behind his family.

As soon as they were seated, Nathan could tell that his sister Caroline was preoccupied by her uncommon silence.

Chris was scanning the menu up and down, then dropped it to the table with a flip.

"I don't know why I even bother to look at this. I already know what I'm going to order."

Chris looked at his wife, then at the somber expression on Nathan's face; he had been watching Caroline as well.

"I guess Callie has already told you about your family's latest scheme to...."

"Chris!" she blurted. "Not now."

Caroline's face paled, shoulders slumped and she dropped her menu to stare out the window of the café.

Nathan placed his hand on hers, "Hey Sis, don't sweat it. It can't be any worse than everything else they've done. Come on, relax. We can talk about it later, okay?"

Caroline turned and tried to smile and nod, noticing exactly how much alike she and her brother were in their reasoning.

Chris picked his menu back up and ducked his head, "Open mouth - insert foot."

CHAPTER TWENTY

TWO little legs spindled as fast as they could move through the obstacle course of elementary school children.

"Uncle Nate!"

"Hey Allie, how's my favorite niece?"

"Oh, you're just saying that to make me feel special," she grunted as Nathan squeezed her in a hug.

"That doesn't mean it's not true."

He held her in his arms for a few seconds longer, "I can't believe how much you've grown just in the last few weeks."

"It's been over a month," she smarted back, then stared angrily at the car-seat awaiting her. So small in stature that she still wasn't able to sit in a regular seat just yet.

Nathan put her down with a quick kiss on the cheek and let her climb in the back of Caroline's car. Had it really been that long? Of course it had.

"I brought a sack of decorations for tonight."

"Streamers? Orange and Black ones?"

He climbed in the front seat and spun around so they could talk.

"Black cats and ghosts too."

Allie grinned, "Did you make cookies mama?"

"We're making them together as soon as we get home," said Caroline.

The car swerved sharply around a corner and accelerated, "How was school today?"

"I'm not sure," said Allie.

"You're not sure? You were there, sweetheart," said Caroline.

"Ms. Cooper made me sit in the corner and read to myself," the little girl mumbled. "I don't think I was supposed to enjoy it."

The car braked hard and swung to the closest empty curb.

Caroline turned to face her little girl, "You were being punished?"

Allie struggled with the straps in her restrictive seat nervously, then looked up and nodded slowly.

"Tell me what happened," sighed Caroline.

"Do I have to?"

"I can turn around and go ask Ms. Cooper."

"Oh all right...," grunted Allie. "I was in trouble for talking in class."

"We've been over this before. You know better Allie," whined Caroline.

Allie rolled her eyes and sighed, "...and I... told her I thought the lesson was stupid. We were writing the first ten letters of the alphabet over and over and over for no good reason at all. I told her it was baby stuff."

Caroline turned forward in her seat and merged back into traffic, "I'll talk to Ms. Cooper next Monday."

Nathan gave his sister his best 'I told you so' smirk and glanced out at the neighborhood decorations.

Living only eight blocks from the elementary had its advantages. They were home only a couple of minutes later and Nathan remembered something very important; children rebound quickly from supposed problems.

Allie hurtled from the car, into the house, her school day forgotten.

♥

The scent of warm vanilla cookies was hovering in the air of his sister's house while Nathan and Allie sat on the living room floor and glued little ringlets of orange and black crepe paper. There were several chains stacked in a heap on the sofa ready to be draped under the tree limbs.

Strings of twirling silhouettes were already dangling in the breeze underneath the trees outside. Black cutouts of witches on broomsticks and white wispy ghosts flailed about, ready to entice the neighborhood children up to the door for candy treats.

The door opened with a grunt and Chris scrunched in carrying a bright orange pumpkin in each arm.

"A little help?" he grinned.

Nathan was already on his feet when Allie flew past him to greet her father.

Caroline peeked from the kitchen, "You're early. How did you manage that?"

Nathan took the larger of the two pumpkins just as Chris kneeled to pick up Allie as a replacement.

"Hey big girl," he said to Allie with a kiss. "I left an hour early to pick up a few things and managed to beat the traffic."

They all converged at the kitchen counter, with two pumpkins, Allie and a fresh batch of cookies filling all the available space at once.

Chris gave Caroline a quick kiss, "Glad to be home. I hate to be the bearer of bad news, but there's foul weather on the way."

"Then you'd better start the slaughter of the pumpkins while I get dinner going," sighed Caroline.

"Not tonight you're not...," said Chris. "I already called in pizza delivery for later."

"Hey you're ruining my reputation," said Nathan.

"I doubt that," laughed Chris. "Allie already thinks you hung the moon."

Allie's mouth was stuffed with a gooey cookie as her father lowered her from the tall counter to the floor.

"Let's gut the pumpkins," growled Chris, twiddling his fingers at his daughter.

"Yeah...," she growled back, "Brain surgery."

Caroline handed Chris a large butcher knife and a bowl for the seeds, "Take it outside. I don't want that sticky mess in my kitchen."

♥

Nathan thought his niece took just a little too much joy in watching the long blade of the knife plunge into the meat of the pumpkin. As soon as the 'hat' was off, her little arms thrust inside and grabbed handfuls of slimy strands of 'pumpkin guts'.

Caroline chirped a laugh from over Nathan's shoulder, trying to hold her video camera still.

"Ewww, nasty," grinned Allie, dropping the first scoop into the bowl. In minutes, she was sticky past her elbows with clingy goo and the first pumpkin was ready to put on a happy face.

Chris handed her a marker and she drew the traditional two eyes, nose, and large jagged mouthed face.

Nathan warily held it on its side as Chris carved out the face.

Caroline walked back inside the house with her video camera, shaking her head and grinning as she watched the little screen replay the ceremony.

"Hey Masters!" yelled a neighbor from across the street.

Chris waved in the air, still holding the orange stained butcher knife.

A family with three children was bustling out of an SUV, each carrying a sack of groceries, the youngest, probably three years old already dressed in a bright green pullover costume.

"That's Tony Vasquez and his crew," muttered Chris. "That's our cue to hurry up or they'll be over with their kids and we'll have a real mess on our hands."

The second pumpkin was carved and ready in record time, even with Allie ceremoniously pulling out the last of the Jack O' Lantern's stringy brains.

"Allison Marie? Come on. Let's get you dressed and ready," said Caroline, from the front door.

"Coming!" yelled Allie, her arms held up like a surgeon in scrubs before an operation.

The door opened for her and Caroline screeched.

"No! Don't you touch anything...," drifted outside where Chris and Nathan were situating the fresh yard art.

A gusty breeze was already making the decorations spin madly and Nathan saw the sun disappear behind a dark purple cloudbank.

"Are you ready to take her around to a few of the houses?" asked Chris.

"Aren't you coming?" asked Nathan.

"And spoil her memory with her favorite uncle?" he grinned. "Katy and Chuck came last year, but I don't see that happening again until Katy starts college."

"They're good kids," nodded Nathan.

"Their parents could learn a thing or two from them," grunted Chris. "By the way, has Caroline talked to you yet?"

Nathan shook his head, "I think she's waiting to build up her nerve or maybe she doesn't want to spoil the evening."

"Yeah, you're right. That sounds just like her," smiled Chris.

Nathan stared at his brother-in-law for a few bleak moments, "You want to fill me in? Maybe some highlights?"

"Are you kidding?" laughed Chris. "I'm not slipping that noose around my neck. That's your family business and I've seen how your family operates."

Nathan was about to argue the fact that Chris was part of their dysfunctional family if only by proxy of marriage. A muffled argument from inside the house caught their attention and both men wandered back inside the house.

"Oh Allie, you ruined one of my best pillowcases," whined Caroline.

"But I didn't want to be a fairy princess. It's Halloween!" chimed Allie. "Fairy princesses aren't scary."

"She has you there," said Nathan.

Allie turned around and both men laughed as soon as they received the full impact of Allie's self-administered costume. She was wearing the ruined white pillowcase like a shift, her head and arms poking through freshly cut holes. It was her face that caught them off guard. Her face was covered with a glob of white face cream with dark maroon lipstick under her eyes, on her nose, and around her lips.

"Isn't it perfect!" she shrilled, turning into a quick spin.

Neither Chris nor Nathan dared a comment, refusing to face the wrath of Caroline's scorn. The tight-lipped grin on their faces fueled Allie's fever to run out and terrify her neighbors.

The wind chimes whipped a bustling tune from the end of the porch outside, breaking the spell of the moment.

"Fine," hissed Caroline. "Here's your sack. You'd better hurry before the storm hits. OH..., let me get your picture."

"Just a few houses and get back before it gets dark," said Chris, kneeling in front of his daughter. "Don't run your Uncle Nate's legs off and stay close to him. Remember, safety first."

"I remember," she grinned. "I've seen Halloween."

Before Nathan could comment, a camera flashed and Allie grabbed his hand, pulling him out the door.

They were already to the curb and a bustle of other goblins were approaching in a small herd from up the street.

"Aren't you a little young to be watching movies like Halloween?" asked Nathan.

"Mom and dad didn't know it. They fell asleep on the couch and I switched channels."

"You're a little too smart for your own good sometimes aren't you?" asked Nathan.

Allie yanked his arm playfully, "So I've been told."

"You know you should probably take it easy on your mom. When we were little kids, she always talked about having a little girl like you one day. I'm not sure she expected one as..., challenging as you are."

Allie frowned just a little, "Mom always tells me that I'm just as bratty as you were."

Nathan nodded, "I was pretty hard headed too. But if somebody had pointed that out to me..., say..., when I was about your age, I might not have caused my mom so much grief."

The frown turned into a grin, "Sometimes mama tells me stories about how you and her were always outsmarting your brother and sisters."

"The point is..., you should learn from what your mom tells you, not use it against her. Trust me. You'll want her as your friend when you get a little older," he chuckled.

"I guess you're right," she grinned again, then made a sinister face at a group of other trick-or-treater's as they hurried past.

Allie seemed ultimately pleased at successfully scaring a couple of younger kids before she looked back up at her Uncle Nathan. "Mama said you always took up for her," she said with a quick squeeze of the hand.

Allie bolted up to the first house for her candy. She returned shaking her sack madly, listening to it rattle, her little legs suddenly fueled for half the neighborhood.

CHAPTER TWENTY-ONE

STREET lamps were glowing against an angry dark sky and huge drops of rain were pelting the sidewalk when Nathan and Allie hurried up the steps. The candles inside both grinning pumpkins' were whipping madly in the wind and most of the ornaments were either missing or wrapped in the tree limbs.

"Look!" Allie screeched, shaking her bulging sack of treats.

Caroline grinned at the smeared mess on her daughter's face, "Yep, and I bet you've been picking at it already. Come on young lady, let's get you cleaned up. Nathan, will you turn off the front lights? I don't think we'll have any more trick-or-treats tonight."

Hot pizza was on the counter and Nathan grabbed a piece before he sat down in the living room with Chris.

"I see you survived," said Chris, balancing a plate and drink on his knees while digging between two cushions in the sofa for the remote control.

"Allie's a real treasure," said Nathan. "You and Caroline are doing a great job raising her."

"So..., now that you're sold on the idea, when are you going to produce some offspring?" said Chris.

"Aren't we getting the cart before the horse?"

"Well..., what about this secretary you have lined up?" asked Chris.

Nathan almost choked on his bite of pizza, "She's my employee..., and a friend. She needed a break and I needed some help. It's as simple as that."

Chris grinned, "That's the way it always starts. What's she look like?"

"She's easy enough on the eyes," said Nathan, more thoughtfully than he intended.

Something about their conversation sounded more like college freshmen instead of adults with established lives and career's.

"See?" shrugged Chris. "You can run, but you can't hide."

Several more thoughts swirled through Nathan's mind as he stuffed the last bite of pizza in his mouth. Then it all congealed.

This..., this whole package. This was what he wanted; not just someone to cohabitate with. Now that he wasn't straddled with a mountain of obligations, it was something he felt he was ready for; maybe even deserved.

Caroline dropped a plate with another piece of pizza in Nathan's hands and sat down by Chris.

"She's in the bath. We're in for a long night. I think she must have sneaked a pound of candy from the bag on the way home."

"I only saw her take a couple," said Nathan in Allie's defense.

"Those were the ones you saw," said Caroline. "Trust me; my little girl's a tricky one."

"Just like her mother?" mumbled Nathan.

"What exactly does that mean?" grinned Caroline. "You were just as much of a brat as I was."

There it was..., straight from her own mouth. He wasn't about to tattle on Allie, especially when it was the truth.

"You set the example," shrugged Nathan. "I was only the impressionable little brother, remember?"

"I think you were both troublemakers," scoffed Chris.

Neither of them refuted his accusation, both for different reasons, laughing away the flashing memories.

"There's a marathon of all the old black and white monster movies on one of the networks tonight," said Chris, punching the menu on the television. "Allie's gonna love that."

"Nathan, thank you for coming," said Caroline. "It meant the world to Allison."

"It meant just as much to me," said Nathan.

There was a dull flash of lightning and low rumbling of thunder in the distance. The bulk of the storm was getting closer.

"I'd better get Allie out of the tub before she turns into a prune," said Caroline.

♥

True to Chris Masters' forecast, the bottom fell out of the sky with a torrent of rain and lightning. The remainder of the Halloween treats had been sequestered for the rest of the evening, well before Allison reappeared. She was now covered from head to toe in pink flannel and scrunched between her parents, while watching Lon Chaney grow elongated teeth and a mass of hair.

Caroline gathered a pallet of blankets and pillows for Allie to stay up late and watch more old movies after the exhausting romp throughout the neighborhood. At the rate her daughter's eyelids were drooping, even the child's preconceived ideas and sugar fed euphoria wouldn't be able to keep her awake.

Nathan's phone buzzed and began to circle the coffee table like a wounded beetle. He sighed. There were only a few people that knew his cell number.

He tapped the screen and read a text message.

"System Alert - UW7F."

"It's the security system," sighed Nathan. "The number seven window, upstairs on the front. I'm sure it's just the weather. Nobody in their right mind would climb the sheer face of the front of the house to break in."

Seconds later another text, "UW7F - System Reset."

Good. False alarm. He dropped the phone and went to refill his glass of soft drink.

"You aren't going to have to leave are you?" asked Caroline.

Nathan jumped at her sudden voice behind him and his sister covered up a laugh with her fingers.

"Trick or treat," she hissed.

"You Cretan..., no I think everything's okay."

She seemed to be lingering..., waiting.

"So..., when are you going to tell me what's bugging you?"

Caroline sat heavily on one of the barstools and tapped her fingernails on the countertop nervously.

"It's complicated Nathan," she whined. "I don't even know where to begin."

"When is it not complicated?" he groaned, then leaned over the counter to face his sister.

"Well, I can only tell you the bits and pieces I know about. First of all, the *Big Three* know that you're still living in mother's old house...."

Caroline shook her head, "No..., that's not it exactly, but.... Nathan, they've hired a lawyer to contest Marion's Will."

Nathan chuckled and shook his head, "That's ridiculous. We've already been through probate. All the proceeds were distributed. There's nothing left to give them."

Caroline's head bobbed, "I'm well aware of that, but..., they think that since you're still living in the house, rent free, that you made some underhanded bargain with whoever bought it. They intend to sue for damages based on the appraised value, the estimated rental value of you living there for the thirteen months before it was sold and the next twelve months you agreed to stay to watch the place. And that's just for starters.

They may even challenge Marion's mental state during the time she changed the executor of her Will."

Nathan scratched at his thick hair, resisting the urge to rip out a handful between his fingers.

"Who told them I agreed to stay there for twelve months?" he grunted.

"They hired some investigator that's digging into everything. Remember that bigwig investor that wanted to buy the property? Well Josie convinced Jonas and Rachael not to pay the money from their contract, so whoever this investor is was really pissed. They no longer want the property, but they're threatening to sue the Big Three for damages and breach of contract."

A total of thirty thousand dollars between his brother and two oldest sisters, plus court costs, plus reasonable damages; this could get ugly. With a suasible judge and an appraised property value of over five million dollars it could turn into an expensive circus.

"So it was cheaper for them to hire an investigator and sue me to pay off their debt," sighed Nathan.

He looked at Caroline with defeated eyes, "My own blood family."

"Of course none of them are speaking to me. It's the ripple effect," she shrugged.

Nathan's phone buzzed once again and started to dance. He hurried away to the coffee table and Chris held it up high for Nathan to grab.

Allie was already lying sprawled across the thick blankets on the floor, mouth open, fast asleep. She looked like an angel to Nathan. It took a little of the sting away from the knife blade he felt hanging from his back.

Why was his own family trying to gut him like one of Allie's Halloween pumpkins?

He sat back down beside Caroline before looking at his phone.

Another text, "System Alert - MB3U."

"Motion in upstairs bedroom three?" grunted Nathan with a frown. "That's my bedroom."

Then he began to receive a succession of alert messages; all upstairs, some windows, some movement. It was as if someone was running from one end of the upstairs hallway and back again.

"The systems on the blink again," sighed Nathan. "But I'd better go. I can't risk another lawsuit over all the museum pieces stored there."

'When it rains it pours', thought Nathan.

"Oh Nathan," said Caroline. "I'm so sorry. If I knew how to help you know I would."

She was clearly upset; silent tears streaming as she leaned tiredly into Nathan's shoulder. It had taken all she had to hold this information back, just so that he and Allie could have a good memory of his visit.

He hugged his sister and tried to calm her nerves.

"Will you please explain to Allie that I had to leave?" he whispered.

"It's getting so late. Can't you stay just until tomorrow morning?" she begged.

He had to choose, but the real choice was already made for him; he had to drive back to the Manor.

Once again, Nathan was ripped apart as he quietly gathered his things to leave. The torrent of rain had settled down to a bone chilling drizzle as the cold-front barreled past.

"You'll call me the minute you get home?" begged Caroline.

Nathan collectively hugged his family, then placed a kiss on Allie's warm cheek before he rushed out the front door of their home.

CHAPTER TWENTY-TWO

WHAT could possibly go wrong next?

Nathan set the cruise control just an inch above the speed limit and switched the radio onto one of the local jazz stations.

He saw only one way out of this and that was to break his agreement with Madeline Stewart and get out of the house. However, if he did, wouldn't it look like a last minute admission of guilt in the eyes of some eager prosecuting attorney?

His cell buzzed once again and he tossed it into the passenger seat out of disgust.

As he neared the front entrance to the old Heart Manor, a row of blistering red and blue lights were slicing through a thickening ground fog. A Morris County Sheriff's car was parked there at the entrance along with a tow truck, which was busily grinding an older model pickup truck behind it.

"Now what?" hissed Nathan.

Of course, the Security system had done its job and called the authorities.

Nathan parked as far off the shoulder as he could manage without getting stuck and climbed out of the little Cadillac.

The sheriff looked up at Nathan from a notepad while his partner clasped handcuffs on a stringy haired teenager and led him to the back seat of the cruiser.

"Nathan Heart?" he asked.

Nathan nodded and chanced a quick glance toward the front of the house in the distance.

"I called the number we have registered with your alarm system and left you a message," the sheriff grunted.

He didn't seem terribly pleased with Nathan about his lack of response.

"I made it here as quickly as I could. What happened?" asked Nathan.

The sheriff shook his head and thumbed over at the teenager, "When I arrived, Mr. Enterprise over there was parked out here by the gate selling admission to throw his truckload of pumpkins at the haunted house."

Nathan wiped his face with both hands in frustration.

"He even had a sign just up the road. There was a line of cars out here waiting to get in and three already parked in front of your house.

All I could do was issue citations for them, but this one will get a night in jail for drunk and disorderly. The criminal trespass and vandalism will be up to you if you press charges. I guess that all depends on what's broken or stolen up at the house. I was waiting on you to show up and take a look around."

All Nathan could feel was a deep tiredness in his soul.

He and the sheriff trudged up the long twisted drive stepping around pieces of pumpkin splatter as they went. One of the small evergreens near the front of the house was partially wrapped in toilet tissue, but otherwise unharmed. Several orange meaty chunks were stuck on the upstairs windows and the maroon front door was now an orange plastered mess. After circling the property, it was fairly evident that nothing was broken, only stained and bruised.

"I'll need you to come in and press charges tomorrow or the next day," said the sheriff, then handed the clipboard for Nathan to sign to verify his response to the call.

He scribbled his signature, "Did the kid say who rumored the house was haunted?"

"He hasn't said more than five words since we cuffed him. I think he's going to be a little embarrassed when he sobers up in the morning."

♥

It was almost midnight when Nathan walked through the door. The entry pad beside the front door was blinking madly, but no alarms were going off, thank God. He kicked a piece of pumpkin out of the doorway and locked the door.

Tomorrow was going to be a long day; starting with an early call to one of his cleaning crews.

He walked to the pantry and reset the system, then called Caroline as promised. The call lasted nearly an hour as she driveled on about nothing. Nathan let her, it seemed to calm her and it took his mind off tomorrow's decisions.

When Nathan reached the top of the stairs, he caught an unmistakable whiff of warm vanilla reminding him of the homemade cookies at his sister's house only hours ago.

The scent met him even stronger as he opened his bedroom door. On top of his chifforobe was one of the tiny votives, flame dancing happily in a circle at his entry. He was instantly angry with himself for leaving a lit candle in his room, even if it was housed in the auspices of safety glass. He removed a clothes hanger and slid out of his leather jacket, then dropped it on the floor as he looked at the candle. It was a new recently lit votive, with the little box of white tipped wooden matches sitting neatly a few inches away.

Nathan spun, suddenly feeling eyes on him from everywhere in his candlelit room.

His head swam, dizzy, "Who's there!"

He dove for the entry, slapped at the light switch, illuminating the huge cavity of his bedroom and with his back flat to the door, examined every silent inch around him.

Cautiously, he snatched open his walk-in closet and flooded it with light. It too was void of any intruder with a penchant for lighting candles. With more confidence, he circled the room, looking in, under, and behind every piece of furniture.

He turned and sucked in a quivering gasp of breath as he looked at the candle.

Then another unmentionable thought rocked his world, another alternative to his mystery. The candle was the type that would burn for twelve or more hours; could he have lit it and not remembered? It was unfathomable, but the only thing that made any logical sense. The dizzy spells, the odd dreams, the talking in his sleep, and the whispers..., it all suddenly made sense.

Alzheimer's was hereditary.

The stress of the familial attacks might have accelerated the inherited latent genome cowering in his body.

"Oh God. I'm going crazy," he whispered into the silence.

A dozen scenarios played on his mind as he quietly sat at the side of his bed. There would be no family caregiver to watch him circle the drain into insanity. No..., and after living through that awful experience, he would never expect any one of his siblings to endure it, not that they would.

Another doctor's visit was in order.

But then what? What if word leaked out that he was experiencing symptoms? What of his reputation; his livelihood? Doctor patient confidentiality meant absolutely zilch in a small town like Lumberton. Maybe there was a specialist in Portland that would see him on short notice?

Nathan kicked off his shoes and slid on top of his covers, barely remembering to roll the comforter on top of himself before he drifted to sleep.

MINUTES

♥

The nasty hissing of the alarm clock rattled Nathan awake at seven a.m. that next morning.

It was Saturday, November 1st, All Souls Day. His eyes were crusted shut and he was instantly reminded of his previous night's revelations. He remembered those mornings he had to use a warm washcloth to remove the crust from Marion's eyes, after a night of crying in her sleep.

The comforter went askew as he sat up, still fully dressed in last night's clothing. For now, he'd have to ignore it all and make the best of what was left of the life he had. There was no time for pity parties; he had to make arrangements for himself, make preparations.

After his morning ritual, he hurried downstairs to make his calls, first to his cleaning crew to remove all the debris before the front yard became a rotting stench.

After multiple assurances that they would come that very day, he thought of his list, called Gwen Helspeth to lock in his office rental, phone service, internet, then visions of Troy's waitress floated into view. He was going to need someone's assistance if…, he couldn't even finish the thought. The idea of relying on someone else to keep him on track was unthinkable.

Lisa Evans did seem reliable. Her raw innocence and integrity was the only resume she needed, but it didn't hurt that she had a winning smile and many other pleasing attributes. He hoped that that same integrity wouldn't make her back out on coming to work for him next week. Nathan decided to wait and talk to Lisa Evans in person that evening.

Now, he needed to make up his mind about how much of his dilemma to tell Madeline Stewart. He flipped through some photos of properties that he was under contract to sell in Salem. Only a few stood out as some place that he might consider calling home one day. His home office would be cleaned out next week, even the chair he was seated in would be gone. Another room for Ms. Stewart to fill with horror tainted furniture. Thoughts of his surroundings made him shiver once again. A break was in order.

He was making a late breakfast when he heard a vehicle rumble to a stop outside. It was the cleaning crew in a large truck with several trash containers and a power sprayer in the back. Evidently, they took his warning of the amount of carnage seriously.

No one bothered to knock as three men and a lady exited the cab and immediately busied themselves scooping and scrubbing away the mass of orange pulp.

Suddenly, Nathan remembered the veranda connecting the two middle upstairs rooms. He hurried to his bedroom and peered out through the drapes over the double doors. It too was harboring pulp and seeds.

Did he really want this cleaning crew upstairs in the house today? No one had been inside the house to so much as dust since Madeline Stewart had purchased the property and filled it with excess. That probably wasn't a good idea.

He hurried back with a dustpan and broom, shoveling and scraping the Halloween trick off onto the ground, after spouting several warnings to the workers down below.

The chill air was welcome in the bright warm sunshine, another blessed day without rain and he enjoyed the relief from his nausea inducing reminders just inside the doors behind him.

Once all the carnage was removed, he walked to the railing and looked out on the expanse of the front lawn with a sigh. Only a few weeks ago he'd been sitting here watching the sunset on the horizon. As jumbled as his life was then, it was no comparison to the web entangling him today. He had taken the time to forgive his family back then, and even now it was hard to point an angry finger their direction. Could someone want peace so desperately that they would continue to stand still and martyr themselves indefinitely? He wondered if his elder siblings would ever understand the reason for his complacency.

"Once a caregiver, always a caregiver," he muttered bitterly; the words of Madeline Stewart.

CHAPTER TWENTY-THREE

MADELINE Stewart was far more understanding than he had expected. There were no harsh comments or chides concerning his absence when the house was vandalized. No smart sarcasm that if he'd been present, the house wouldn't have been used as a Halloween carnival for miscreants.

"Now don't you fret yourself over those hoodlums Mr. Heart," said Madeline. "Not a peep, do you hear?"

"I understand," said Nathan. "The security system did its job just like it was supposed to and nothing was broken or stolen."

Ms. Stewart drew quiet on the phone for a few moments, as was her usual demeanor, then cleared her throat.

"What was the real reason you called, Nathan? I know you didn't call to tell me that a group of teenagers pulled some Halloween mischief."

"That actually was one of the reasons," he swallowed and continued. "Actually, it's more of a family matter I'm dealing with and I wouldn't even bring it up, but it presents a tangential connection on our arrangement."

Ms. Stewart chuckled, "Don't tell me..., your elder siblings finally found out about your habitation of their precious childhood home place and they want you out."

"I wish that was the end of the matter," sighed Nathan.

He felt sudden embarrassment and shame over the actions of his family, wishing it all away.

"They...," he breathed heavily, "It would take far too long to relate, but to give me some closure, it might be best if I move out of the house like I first suggested."

"Nonsense," she laughed. "I'm a well versed student of family rivalry, please continue. I'm all ears."

At the very least, he needed to explain the portion that involved the sale of Heart Manor.

"The most important part is that they are planning to sue me over the sale of the property," he blurted.

"Why that's ridiculous. I have a clear title deed including mineral rights to the property," she grunted. "They have no legal recourse whatsoever in the state of Oregon."

"That's what I believe too," he cut back in, "...however, they have hired an investigator to try and prove that you and I had some sort of under the table agreement about the sale, since the property was appraised at over twice the sale price. Part of that being the fact that I'm living here rent free while I watch over the estate."

Nathan could suddenly feel the air chill where he was seated.

"Ms. Stewart?" he prompted.

"Yes..., I'm still here," she mumbled. "They received their equal shares of the sale, did they not?"

"To the penny," said Nathan. "I paid most of the legal fees out of my own pocket."

"Hmm...," she muttered. "Then there has to be another player in the mix Mr. Heart. Can you, or rather..., are you willing to tell me more as to what prompted this barbarism?"

It was almost as embarrassing as being caught naked once again. Up until now, he'd managed to keep this entire matter away from her.

"Actually, this is very embarrassing for me to explain. The day after you and I went into escrow on this property, they...; they being my oldest brother and two sisters, made a deal with a developer to sell the property. But there was an indemnity clause in their contract...."

Madeline interrupted, "...and they intend to sue you to avoid paying this penalty and implicate wrong doing on our part."

It was actually very intuitive of her, Nathan thought.

"That..., pretty much sums it up."

"Nathan, you don't worry yourself one bit," she said quietly. "They've stepped barefoot in a bed of piss ants and don't even realize it yet. You don't happen to know the name of this other investor do you?"

"No. I wasn't even supposed to know about their contract or intent to sue."

"Alright then...," she said, the smile back in her voice. "I need to go for now, but I'll call you back tomorrow, if that's okay. Now you go play a round of golf or whatever it is you do to relax and let me handle this."

Nathan's internal alarm system began to flash a warning.

"Madeline..., as crazy as this all is, I can't find it in me to do something to hurt my family."

"Actually, I admire that quality in your personality Mr. Heart, but I know how to handle disgruntled family and your siblings are some real gems."

When the conversation ended, Nathan couldn't help the mixed feelings of relief and severe agitation. It was almost like drinking poison cool-aid as relief to a hot summer day.

A round of golf actually sounded good for a sunny day like today, but he had too many irons already in the fire to run off and play as Madeline had suggested.

It wasn't until that evening that he finally settled back down to the fundamentals of his life.

With the house secured and an envelope under his arm, he strolled into the garage, still intent with his plan for the evening. It was either a stroke of genius or the effects of his mental state, but he was certain that his plan was well thought out.

He walked to the third stall, slid into the pleated leather front seat of the 1958 Buick Special, and shut the door with a solid thunk. His hand instinctively slid along the soft leather ridges, then he gripped the huge steering wheel with both hands. It felt as sturdy as a battleship.

It cranked and idled with a deep purring rumble. The only reason the car was still around was because Marion refused to get rid of Jonas Heart Senior's pet project. There it sat for years except for the short drives to keep it from dilapidating.

The old Buick backed out smoothly from its stall, ready for a gallop or two across a few highways. The old vacuum tube AM radio took a few seconds to warm up, but played just as well as it did when the car first rolled off the showroom floor.

It not only handled the rural roads well, but managed to keep up with most of the traffic on the coast highway. The radio was crooning some old Patsy Cline melody when he turned into the Blind Pirate's parking lot. He drove past several empty slots out front and drove around back to park next to Troy's red Chevy truck.

There was the usual crowd inside plus a few newcomers filling an entire section with rumbling conversation.

"Well, look what the cat dragged in…," said Troy.

"…that the dogs wouldn't have," finished Nathan.

Troy stopped long enough to give Nathan a friendly slap on the shoulder before mixing several drinks for a stack of party happy yuppies crowding the other end of the bar.

When they slowed down with refills, Troy pushed a frosty mug in front of Nathan and propped up against the bar.

"Hmmm," he said with squinty eyes and a twist of the head. "I'd say…, you was a man that was up to something this evening."

"I'm as hungry as a bear," said Nathan. "Does that count?"

"That it does," he cheered.

Before he could turn around, Nathan noticed that there were two new faces serving tables that night.

"Is Lisa not working tonight?" asked Nathan.

"What? You keeping track of my waitstaff now are ya?" he grinned. "Not looking to hire out the whole lot of 'em?"

Nathan almost blushed, then took a quick drink from his glass to hide it.

"Just curious," he answered. "I need to talk to Lisa for a few seconds if her stingy boss will let me."

Troy laughed heartily, "I'd say the old laggard's been trying to get you to take an interest in Lisa for a while now. I guess he can spare her for a few minutes."

Troy waved over one of the new waitresses and told her to get Nathan away from the bar; he was attracting flies.

She laughed and directed Nathan toward his usual corner seat, then dropped off a menu.

A few minutes later Lisa strolled up and knocked on the table, "Mind if I have a seat?"

She looked almost as frazzled as usual, but a lot less melancholy than their last meeting.

Lisa quickly pushed stray strands of hair behind her ears and tried her best to smile, showing a favored dimple on one cheek.

"Busy night?" asked Nathan.

"Training two new recruits," she said with a toss of her chin. "It's twice as hard as doing the work yourself in the first place."

"Does that mean you can't take off a few minutes early tonight?" asked Nathan.

Lisa blushed and her eyes rounded, "I might be able to bluff my way free a few minutes early."

Nathan realized how his question sounded and grinned, "Have you eaten?"

"I could use a bite, but I only have about thirty minutes," she offered.

Nathan handed her his menu, "Here then, you know what I like. Would you order us both some food while I go wash my hands?"

Her face quizzed, but she agreed.

Nathan hurried up to the bar where Troy was still stranded, refilling tequila shots for the same group like a drunken mother hen.

"Troy," hissed Nathan. "I need to ask a big favor."

"I think the scale's already tipped my direction on the matter of favors at the moment," he grunted. "What is it that you need?"

"Is there any way that Lisa can get off work a little early this evening?" he asked.

Troy brightened to neon proportions, "Ah…, you sly dog. Did the fish scales finally fall off your eyelids?"

Nathan was extremely pleased with himself. So far his ploy was playing right in to Troy's misguided intentions. He only shrugged as his answer, which kept him from casting an outright lie in Troy's ear.

"I'll see what I can do for ya," nodded Troy, gazing over toward the table where Lisa was seated. Suddenly he grabbed Nathan's arm. "Don't ya go breakin' her heart now."

Nathan grinned and raised two fingers, "Scouts honor."

Troy grinned and nodded.

As soon as Nathan sat back down, Lisa leaned across the table, "What was that all about? Did you wash your hands in beer?"

"I had some business with Troy," shrugged Nathan.

"I ordered us the grilled flounder. What kind of business?" she asked.

"Troy business," said Nathan, trying his best to be secretive.

Lisa rolled her eyes, "That's not the way to start a…."

Nathan quickly leaned closer and stared into her eyes and she bit her bottom lip to keep herself from finishing the sentence. His sudden presence made her weak in the knees and she swallowed, wondering what was wrong with herself.

"You know what I mean," she mumbled, the flush back in her cheeks.

"I want you to go with me tomorrow morning to look at our new office in Salem," said Nathan, hiding his grin. "If your schedule is open that is."

"I don't work until four tomorrow. I guess I can take some time out of my schedule."

"Good. I need a woman's viewpoint on the colors and decorations. I want the office to have a…, cozy feel to it," he explained.

"Cozy…," she said, her eyes drawing to slits. "How cozy?"

Lisa felt a sudden anger at her own stupidity. So this was how he was going to make his play. The secretary with benefits.

Nathan shrugged, "You'll be the one occupying the space, but I want our visitors to feel at home as soon as they walk inside."

"Oh," she said, suddenly confused.

Nathan thought she almost looked disappointed, as if her mind had wandered onto a different subject.

One of the new waitresses appeared with drinks and several platters of food.

"I guess I'd better eat quick," said Lisa. "I only have about twelve more minutes for my dinner break."

"I think Troy will make an exception for you tonight," said Nathan. "I'd rather you get to enjoy your food."

She smiled the most disarming smile he'd ever seen and this time it was Nathan that had to reassess his intentions.

CHAPTER TWENTY-FOUR

LISA Evans tripped once again on the slick pavement as Nathan led her out the back door of the diner.

"Keep your eyes closed."

"I don't see what all the fuss is about," she whined, gripping Nathan's arm with both hands.

She suddenly felt that smothering feeling of fear and held her breath for several steps in the darkness. It was as if she'd instantly forgotten the grade of the parking lot and where all the holes were located.

"Okay," said Nathan, waiting to see her reaction to the old relic. "You can open up now."

Lisa looked around, bleary eyed into the odd colored hue of the lamps above the parking lot.

"Well?" said Nathan. "What do you think?"

She looked around, right past the Buick, "About what?"

"The car," grunted Nathan. "The one we're standing beside."

"This car?" she stared intently. "It's nice. My grandma had one sort of like it when I was really little."

Nathan handed her the keys, "Good. Here you go then."

She stared for a moment, "This is the car you're letting me drive?"

Nathan nodded his head, still trying to ascertain what she was thinking.

"It's perfect," she said quietly.

'He has to be kidding,' she thought as her mind flashed back to a childhood ripped straight from her heart.

Her hands released Nathan's arm and slid along the car's body from front to back, as if it the old car needed comfort.

"Where did you find this?" she asked.

"In my garage," laughed Nathan. "It's been there a while, but don't worry. It just received a clean bill of health from my mechanic."

He opened the door and let her slide into the driver's seat.

"Leather," she cooed, bouncing on the springy seat.

She stuck the key into the ignition and it cranked with a steady rumble.

"I'll be the envy of everybody I know," she grinned.

Her mind suddenly went to that void she hated, that place where she wasn't in control and something dark was lurking behind the corner.

Nathan nodded and his gut told him he'd done the right thing.

"Here then," he said, handing her the envelope he'd had stuffed in his jacket.

She took it carefully, "What's this?"

"The title. All you need to do is sign it and carry it to the courthouse in Salem. You should have a new title in about a month."

She turned off the purring motor and slid quickly from the car seat. As soon as the door thunked shut, she handed the envelope back to Nathan.

"I can't accept this," she shook her head in little quivers.

"You have to," said Nathan. She did exactly as he had expected.

"I have to...?" she squinted. "No I don't."

"That was the condition of our agreement. You'd come to work and I'd provide the transportation. You already agreed."

If he'd learned anything from Madeline Stewart, it was how to turn a conversation into a contract.

"You won't let me work for you unless I take the car?" she whined. "But Troy's already hired an extra girl to take up my hours."

Nathan shrugged, "It's just a car, Lisa. It really suits you."

Her arms flew around his neck in a bone-crushing hug. Maybe Nathan Heart was an honest man..., a generous good looking....

She lingered a few seconds, then slid away, "Thank you Nathan."

His hands seemed to linger on her waist just a little longer than he intended, "Uh..., there's a spare tire, a few tools, and a flashlight in the trunk."

Lisa smiled and years fell from her young face in a moment.

"Okay..., well good," he sighed in relief. "For a minute there I was afraid I was going to have to find you a different car."

"You really know how to show a girl a good time," she said with a chuckle.

"There's one more condition," grunted Nathan. "I need a ride back home."

♥

Nathan did his best to explain a few of the quirks associated with most vehicles from a different era. Lisa didn't seem to mind the fact that the radio only picked up static riddled AM stations, or that she had to count to ten before it actually came on. The bench seats were bigger than most modern sofa's, but were plush and comfortable.

"I had the safety straps updated so you won't get pulled over for a ticket, brighter headlamps and running lights," he droned on. "You're named on the Realty Insurance Policy…. Have I forgotten anything?" he asked.

"Only which exit I'm supposed to take to get to your house," said Lisa.

She seemed to take pleasure in the huge steering wheel, the way the car lulled around corners and even the musty smell of the seats.

"Up the curve on the right," said Nathan.

She turned through the stone gates of Heart Manor and slowed to a stop far from the house.

"You can drive on up to the front," said Nathan.

Lisa stalled out, observing the lighted trail of the driveway and the small flood lamps illuminating the circumference of the enormous house. It seemed a little intimidating, considering the six hundred square feet of apartment she'd lived in for the last several years.

"You live here?" she asked quietly.

"Temporarily. I grew up here…, with my brother and three sisters."

Marion…, why didn't he mention his mother, he wondered. Perhaps because it was a given? Perhaps he didn't want to tell Lisa Evans about…, the last three years of that life…, his life.

Lisa was staring lifelessly, waiting for him to continue.

"Temporarily?" she asked, prodding.

"It's a very long story," he laughed nervously. "I'm its caretaker for the next few months. At least until I can find someplace to call my own."

The car began to roll forward slowly until it halted just out of reach of the twin stone lions, mouth's open, teeth bared, guarding the entrance.

"You're more than welcome to take the fifty cent tour…, if you're not in a hurry," said Nathan.

Somehow, his offer seemed more than just an innocent invitation, but he had no idea how to rectify the situation.

She pushed the huge chrome lever on the steering column into park and turned off the ignition.

"Where do I pay?" she asked.

Nathan shook his head in a frown…, "Oh. For the tour. It's free tonight."

He slid out and rounded the car while Lisa stuffed the envelope with the title into her purse. She smiled when he opened her door.

Lisa stood quietly out front for a few moments, leaning against the car, looking up at the two tall columns supporting both the oval porch and veranda above.

"It's big."

"It was endless until I hit my teenage years," grinned Nathan. "It started to shrink every year after that."

Lisa seemed to be frozen in thought, immovable.

"Well, come on. I'll make us some coffee," said Nathan.

She stopped beside one of the huge roaring lions and slapped its stone head noisily, "Nice kitty."

Nathan vaguely remembered someone from his childhood offering the same affection, just beyond the tip of his recall. Then he felt that dizzy sinking sensation for a moment and shivered as it slowly faded. Now wasn't the time for another one of his strange unexplainable episodes.

They walked up the steps and when Lisa reached the top she stopped, "Seven."

She turned and grinned, "It's a silly habit..., seven steps?"

His head swam once again and he halted with her for an instant.

"Are you okay?" asked Lisa.

He nodded and smiled, shaking off the fading sensation as quickly as possible.

When the front door opened all Lisa could manage was, "Wow."

She was standing, arms clutched tightly across her chest just past the vestibule, looking into the main cavern of the house. He flipped on the main lighting along with the multi-tiered chandelier and the place took on a life of its own.

"Take your time and look around," said Nathan, turning off the alarm. "You'll need to get used to old houses this size. It's the bulk of what you're going to be working with at our office."

The grandfather clock chimed directly behind her and she chirped in fright, hurrying over to where Nathan was standing.

"It's a clock," laughed Nathan.

She held up her wrist in front of her face, "This is a clock..., that..., that's a monstrosity."

The nearly eight-foot tall chronometer finished gonging out ten solid strokes and fell silent as she stared its direction in awe. When she turned to comment, Nathan had disappeared from behind her.

"Hey! Hello? Where did you go?" she asked.

Lisa was frozen in place, her legs refusing to move.

"Kitchen..., remember? Coffee?" he laughed, his voice somewhere in the unseen distance.

"Yeah, well..., isn't there some rule about the tour guide staying with his tour?"

When he reappeared, Lisa was seated in the exact spot that Madeline favored, the divan of death, near the wide hearth of the fireplace.

She stood back up as Nathan approached and shivered visibly.

"I'm sorry if it's chilly," said Nathan. "I'll turn up the heat but it takes six or eight hours for the temperature to regulate through the house. It's kind of like steering a battleship instead of a speedboat."

"I just had a chill, I'm fine," she said quietly.

She looked around, then up at the huge staircase, "It's too quiet. It feels like a funeral parlor."

Nathan laughed, then had to stifle it. If he were forced to explain his sudden burst of insanity, she'd likely leave and never return.

"Oh. I'm sorry," she said, clearly embarrassed. "I didn't mean it as an insult to your home."

"It's no longer my home," said Nathan. "And you're right, it does have a solemn atmosphere. Personally, I hate it."

Lisa smiled and seemed to relax, as if she was afraid of something lingering in the back of her thoughts and it had suddenly settled.

Nathan wandered across the expanse to the vestibule, took the tiny brass key from around his neck and opened the casket-sized front door of the clock.

He cranked the weights up higher and relocked the door.

"You keep the key around your neck?" asked Lisa, suddenly standing against his side. She was staring at the gold linked necklace with the tiny key floating around its length.

He nodded thoughtfully, "My mother kept the key on her. The old clock was like her pet. It was one of the few things she never forgot after...."

Lisa's eyes were fixed on his as his voice trailed off. He never intended to bring any of that up, yet there it was.

He chuckled at the intensity of her interest.

"Lisa, meet my inheritance," he laughed with a mock bow. "Old clock, meet Lisa."

She grinned and tugged him back into the living room playfully.

"Do you want coffee before or after your tour?" he asked.

♥

When the pistachio green Buick Special drove out of sight, Nathan felt an emptiness fill the air around him. Talking with Lisa, roaming the halls, flipping on the lights to each room as they went along, was more emotionally engulfing than he could have ever expected.

By the time they descended from upstairs, where Lisa seemed most interested, she was comfortably clinging to his arm.

Nathan chalked it up to all the excitement of the evening, even the comfortable way she leaned into their conversation over coffee, just before she left.

He didn't let himself linger on the whole of the moment, lingering might produce a false positive of emotions he wasn't sure he was ready for, now that he was unsure of so many things.

CHAPTER TWENTY-FIVE

DAYBREAK came as harsh as a dagger, particularly after a night filled with fitful dreams. Confrontations, courtroom dramas, along with oddly secret conversations, but the most alarming were the ones reliving unheld conversations with a faceless woman. Both alluring and disturbing, unseen hands tendered his brow and cheeks with warm soft fingers.

Nathan sat up with a gasp of breath, as if surfacing from deep waters. Moments later, his alarm clock began hissing its white noise and he lay back down, trying to recapture those last moments of imagined intimacy.

Afraid to fall back asleep, he sat up on the edge of his bed, angry at the daylight, angry at it all.

He raked his fingers through his hair, didn't bother to shave, then trudged downstairs to finish packing his office. Somewhere in the mix of time, there was coffee and a few doughnuts that offset his fervor.

He settled back on the floor of his office more than once, worried that one of the gears in his head might slip. Worried that he might forget some detail of the move, then finally gave in to jotting down detailed notes in an open journal.

It wasn't just his memory that worried him, it was the fear of losing everything that was left of himself. There were certain things, even people he certainly wouldn't miss, but what of Caroline and Chris…, Allie. He remembered the vacant look in Marion's eyes the first time she didn't recognize him, calling him by his father's name, Jonas.

He was still recovering from one of his fearful musings when the phone rang, startling him to his senses, "Heart Realty."

"Nathan? You don't sound like yourself," said Madeline Stewart.

He sat up and cleared his throat, "I was sorting papers here on the floor."

She took a moment to assess him further before continuing.

"I've spoken to my lawyers and you can feel free to relax over the entire situation concerning any lawsuit from your family or anyone else for that matter."

Nathan felt the tension in his body melt away, "So they don't have any grounds to sue."

"Oh, they can open their can of worms, but they won't be able to put them all back inside," she whined sweetly.

Nathan felt the tension building once again.

"Nathan, now you stop that. I've been dealing with people like this ever since I was fifteen years old, following my Daddy around and learning the business. I can assure you, you'll never get a phone call or a summons over any of this."

"But how…," mumbled Nathan.

"I'm sending each of them a certified letter by courier next week," she began, shuffling some paper in the background. "Basically, it says that if they so much as smudge the Stewart family name or Heart Realty, I intend to pursue legal action in retaliation to the full extend of the law. It mentions a much larger figure in punitive damages than the indemnity they agreed upon. They just needed to see that I'm a bigger bully than Bogart Investments."

"Bogart Investments?" grunted Nathan.

"That's the two-bit outfit that's putting pressure on them at the moment," she continued. "While I do regret that they'll have to end up paying the indemnity of their contract, those are the risks you take when you deal with someone with a F credit rating."

Nathan was glad that he didn't tell Madeline of his family's intent to use Bogart Investments to defraud him of his portion of inheritance. That would have been a disaster. Bogart Investments would have quickly dumped the blame on his family.

"I'm sorry you were dragged into all of this," said Nathan.

"Pfff, this is trivial. Nathan…, our family owns the mineral rights to half the eastern seaboard. Did you think that my affinity for antiquities was a business? It's only a penchant of mine."

This time he felt genuine relief coupled with a few other irrelevant questions.

"Thank you Ms. Stewart. This is one item off my checklist," said Nathan.

"Good. Now, don't forget. My staff will be arriving on the eighth to get the house in order for the Thanksgiving holiday."

As her voice trailed off, Nathan made more notes in the open journal as his constant reminder of other duties…, and a possible failing memory.

He sat back down on the floor to continue his filing.

"Bogart Investments…," whispered Nathan, frowning.

Then…, his stomach clenched, "Oh my God!"

His face flushed with burning heat as he lurched into his chair and snatched up the telephone and dialed his sister's number in haste.

"Caroline?"

"Hi Nathan, I didn't expect to hear from…."

"Caroline listen, please. Is Kate the only person that you've spoken with about Josie's intent to sue?"

"Well, yes," she grunted. "Why?"

"She's your sole source of information?"

"Nathan, what's wrong?" she asked, her voice unsteady.

"Then we have a problem. The *Big Three* are going to receive a certified letter in a few days warning them to back off or face losing everything they own from a potential countersuit."

"Oh, Nathan," she whispered. "That'll just devastate Katy."

"I realize that. What we need to do is somehow get them to admit their intentions to one of us and close the loop so that Kate doesn't catch the fallout."

"But how do we do that?" she asked. "They won't even take my phone calls right now."

"Maybe they'll take mine," mumbled Nathan. "Maybe I can upset Josie enough to get her to admit her intentions. But I'd have to do it today. Right now. Think Nathan…, think!" he grunted angrily.

"What if I…," sighed Caroline.

"I have it," hissed Nathan. "I'll call you back and let you know if it works."

He hung up the phone and jotted down some prompts on his journal to keep him focused before he dialed Josie Clarion. Rachael wouldn't work as his target, she was too even keeled, while unemotional Jonas would see right through him and hang up. Josie on the other hand was a veritable powder keg with a short fuse and had been ever since they were children.

He took two deep breaths to still his nerves and dialed the number.

A quiet voice answered the phone.

"Hello?" said Nathan.

"Uncle Nate," the voice whispered. "You shouldn't be calling here."

"Kate? Is that you?" he cheered, surprised by his own excitement. "It's so good to hear your voice."

"Uncle Nate, you don't understand," she hissed. "My parents…, they're on the warpath."

"It's going to be okay," he said calmly. "Can you get your mother to the phone?"

"Yeah…, I guess," she whispered.

"Oh…, and Kate? I love you sweetheart. It was good to hear your voice."

"I love you too," she sighed.

The phone clopped down and Nathan heard, "Mom! Telephone."

Nathan punched another button on his answering machine and waited patiently.

"Hello?"

"Josie, this is Nathan."

She snorted a laugh into the air, "What do you want?"

"I'm just calling to check in. See how you're doing," said Nathan.

"We're doing peachy. If that's all you wanted, then…," she spat.

"I only called to let you know that I'm still living here at Marion's for the moment and I was wondering," said Nathan. "Thanksgiving is coming up and I thought it might be nice to get one last group photo of all our family…, you know, together. In front of the place."

"Is this some publicity stunt for your Real Estate business?" she asked.

Nathan noticed immediately that she wasn't surprised that he was still occupying the house.

"Why would you think that? Besides I'm opening an office in Salem soon."

"In Salem. Really…," she mumbled thoughtfully. "Why not the house? I heard that you've already refurnished it."

"Not personally, but that's mostly true; the new owners have filled the house from top to bottom. You should see the place. It's amazing. I'll give you a tour if you drop by," he teased.

"So you admit that you're living in the place?" she hissed angrily.

"Of course," he added glibly. "Why wouldn't I? I'm only acting as caretaker until they occupy it permanently."

"Caretaker?" she laughed. "You mean freeloader don't you?"

"Freeloader?" said Nathan, trying to sound hurt. "It seemed fair to me. I'm keeping away the vandals just like I did before I sold the place."

"Ha!" she laughed, "How is that working out for you?"

She knew about the vandalism? So it was true. They had someone watching the house and his every move. That made sense. Some snoop must have peered through the windows and seen all the furniture in place, maybe even when it was being moved inside.

Ignoring her incisive remark, "Actually, it's really good. It looks as if I'll be here for at least another ten or eleven months."

That should light the short fuse to Josie's powder-keg temper.

"Another year? Rent free?" she gritted.

Nathan waited in silence.

"We'll just see about that, won't we?" she grunted.

"I don't understand why you're so upset. Is there some reason you wouldn't want me to be here?"

Nathan could hear the explosion building in the silence.

"How dare you," she hissed. "You..., thief. I know all about your little underhanded deal with that buyer. What did they do, give you the extra money in cash? Was the living arrangement part of the deal also?"

"Josie, you should be careful who you're accusing," said Nathan.

"I'm not afraid of you..., you..., you Runt!" she yelled.

"I'm not talking about me," said Nathan.

"Josie? Hang up," said a commanding male voice in the background.

It was likely her husband Charles.

"I will not," she grunted as someone tried to wrest the phone from her hand. "You hear me Nathan Heart, you'll be hearing from our lawyer within the week..., you and your partner will be sorry."

"Josie, I wish you'd reconsider," begged Nathan.

This time he was sincere with his plea.

"I'll bet you do," she grunted, just as the line went dead.

Nathan sighed and clicked his phone recorder off.

That was so much easier than he expected that he felt guilty. Then the next stack of bricks fell on his shoulders. Why?

Yet he knew that once hatred had its grip on someone's mind it rarely let go until it destroyed everything in its path.

Nathan dialed another number.

Caroline answered immediately, "What happened?"

"Kate's off the hook," said Nathan.

His words fell as dead as he felt inside.

"Oh, thank God," she whined.

He could tell she'd been crying.

"Hey, try not to worry. It should all be over in a few days, unless Josie gets them in even deeper water."

"You know she'll try," said Caroline. "She has absolutely no control over her pride."

"I pray that Kate won't hate me for sending her mother into a tailspin," mumbled Nathan. "I don't think I could handle losing her trust."

"I'll do my best to smooth it over," said Caroline. "When I explain that they stand to lose everything including their home over it. Surely she'll understand that."

"I noticed something else, Caroline. Charles sounded like he was tired of the whole mess as well. The last time we spoke, he was almost civil to me over the phone," said Nathan.

"Charles was against the deal from the very beginning. I thought you knew that."

"Okay then, we're both going to agree not to worry. We'll know one way or the other by the middle of next week."

CHAPTER TWENTY-SIX

EMOTIONALLY drained and blank, Nathan mechanically stacked the last of the boxes from his office in the vestibule and went to get his Yukon and load it all up.

Despite his lack of zeal, he did manage to catch a glance at his distraught appearance and chose to clean up before driving to Salem with his first load of cargo. Should he chance upon the glowering Gwen Helspeth, she would have likely revoked their rental agreement at the mere sight of him.

No sooner than he had inched past the front gate onto the northbound rural road, he noticed a glint of reflection behind him, far into the distance. He came within an ace of ignoring it, changed his mind and turned the heavy-laden beast of a vehicle around to investigate.

Southbound, barely up the road towards Lumberton, sat an abandoned dusky blue vehicle. An older model he didn't readily recognize, with its driver side window slightly lowered.

Evidently, someone had problems or ran out of gasoline. He didn't see anyone walking, which was a good sign. Whomever it was, no doubt called for a ride back into town and with no face to attach to it, he dismissed the whole matter.

The half hour drive into Salem seemed mere seconds, his mind locked on the Sunday morning whirlwind of events. He backed into the angle-parking slot in front of the door to his new office. The coffee shop next door was a bustle of business and he immediately made up his mind to be a regular patron.

The rental space was dark and smelled of fresh formaldehyde from the new dark gray carpet, with the warm aroma of coffee fighting to hide it. Instead of paint, he'd asked to leave the bare red bricks exposed on the wall space, enhancing the 'alley' atmosphere. Lisa's desk was already in place near the front window, with a gray-carpeted partition standing just behind it. Phone and electrical cables dangled like precarious cobwebs from the ceiling, waiting for their final destinations. It was already looking like an office.

Box after box soon lined one of the walls from midway to the back, next to a stack of Heart Realty signs. Nathan stretched his shoulders, wandered next door for coffee, then headed back for another smaller load. He'd have to hire someone to move the heavy desk, filing cabinets, printers, fax machine, and other incidentals. Monday would be another busy day.

Nathan's mind was finally getting some peace; the very purpose of work always seemed to occupy and cancel out anything negative. That was how he survived through Monday, Tuesday, and Wednesday.

By Thursday morning, there was no more moving to be done; no more distractions. Even the grunts and complaints from the house, which were now so commonplace, weren't enough to help him veer from worry.

Noon Thursday, Caroline called. She confessed her own concerns. Neither of them had heard from their older brother or two sisters, but more importantly, Caroline hadn't heard from their niece Kate. Nathan knew for certain that each of them had received their certified deliveries. Madeline Stewart did not seem the type to offer idle promises or threats.

Was it possible that Josie was having problems keeping her other two partners committed to her hate? Maybe they were regrouping, circling their wagons, plotting further mischief.

A thousand scenarios were racing through Nathan's thoughts all that day, stretching his mind on a tortuous rack.

By Friday, he was a nervous wreck. His old home office was completely bare and swept clean. All his business calls were forwarded to a new number at the office in Salem and Heart Manor now had a new private telephone number; the last tie to be cut from its previous life. This new refuge would also conveniently serve as an excuse to afford him time away from another unknown; the imminent arrival of Ms. Stewart's staff members.

After an entire morning with no breakfast and mindless pacing of the halls, his cell phone rang.

A number he didn't immediately recognize until he'd already answered.

"Nathan? This is Charles. Did I catch you at a good time to talk?"

"Yes…, yes of course," he jabbered almost incoherently.

"I'm with Josephine at the hospital here in Seattle. I just thought you should know."

His cell phone began to beep incessantly with another incoming call.

"In the hospital? Is it serious?" asked Nathan. "I can be there by this evening if you need me."

"No..., that won't be necessary," sighed Charles. "She's..., well..., it might be a nervous breakdown of some sort or even a mild stroke. We don't really know anything for sure at the moment."

Nathan shrank inside. Had he caused this with his astucious phone call? He'd never forgive himself. His cell beeped again.

"I'm so sorry Charles. Are the children there with you?"

"We're all here, waiting for some test results," he grunted.

"What do you need me to do? Just name it. Anything."

Dr. Charles Clarion sighed heavily, "Just keep us in your thoughts."

They'd already been in Nathan's thoughts for the last several days without a moment's pause.

"Are you sure you don't need me there Charles? I don't mind helping with Chuck and Kate."

"Caroline is already on her way to pick them up. She was the closest..., and I'm not sure how long Josephine is going to be here."

"Charles, I'm only a phone call away. Whatever you need."

"Thanks Nathan, for everything. I know that, really...," he sighed. "I need to go..., one of the nurses is heading my way. I'll keep you posted."

Charles ended the call and Nathan's cell chirped immediately.

"Nathan?"

It sounded like he was about to repeat the past conversation with Caroline.

"Charles just called, I know...," he answered.

"Oh good. I wanted you to know what was going on. It's going to take me a couple of hours to get to Seattle. Did Charles tell you what brought all this on?" she asked.

"No, he didn't. I can only imagine that Josie received that blasted notice. Caroline I feel so guilty. What if I caused this? I was the one that stirred her up. I'd rather paid their debt and...."

"Nathan..., Nathan stop it," barked Caroline. "Josie brought this on herself."

Nathan took a deep breath to consider his next words, "What if she didn't?"

"What do you mean?"

"What if she's..., what if she isn't responsible for her actions?" he asked.

"You mean like mother..., don't you?"

"That would explain why Charles called me.... I believe he might suspect something, maybe he has for some time now."

"Nathan, wait until the test results come back. Quit jumping to conclusions."

Her voice was sharp, correcting, but she wasn't able to hide the tinge of fear in her voice.

"I'll call you after I pick up their kids. I'll know more then. Quit worrying and most of all, quit blaming yourself. I'll talk to you in the morning."

Nevertheless, he didn't feel better. As soon as Nathan ended the call, he resumed his slow methodical pacing from one room to the other.

When he believed his head would finally explode, he snatched his coat and rushed out of the house.

The tires on the XLR convertible screamed for purchase on every turn of the cold pavement. With no destination in mind, he and the car ended up at Crab Cove. He parked in back of the Blind Pirate and shut off the engine.

What was he doing here? The last thing he wanted to do was assuage Troy's inherent need to analyze his psyche or skirt the big man's efforts at matchmaking. The last thing he needed was to sit at the bar and get blitzed on alcohol, which at the moment was very likely and appealing. His hand was already on the ignition, ready to crank the car and leave to parts unknown when a familiar pistachio green vehicle drove in beside him in the employee parking.

The young lady behind the wheel took her time to adjust the rearview mirror as soon as the engine died. She ran a brush through her light brown hair, checked her makeup, then carefully slid her hands across the curves of the dashboard. Nathan felt something stir unexpectedly inside him.

Lisa Evans turned her head his direction and smiled in recognition.

That was when Nathan saw that he'd been staring at her the entire time. It was too late to snap his head away and feign ignorance; he was already caught in her snare.

He did his best to smile back as Lisa slid out of her car and then jiggled at his passenger door until he let her inside.

"Are you checking up on me?" she asked with a grin.

Her eyes had a light in them that he hadn't seen before.

"I'm not really sure how I ended up here. I think I must have been hungry and my vehicle decided for me," he answered.

It was the closest thing to the truth he could muster at that exact moment.

"I thought you might be here to remind me that tomorrow was my first day at the new office. I'm really looking forward to it."

"Oh, that reminds me…," said Nathan, as he reached for a folder on the floor near her feet.

"I'll get it."

As she reached down, they brushed hands for only a moment. It was as if the entire last weeks worry and panic began to drain from his body. Some invisible cord connected to an evil outlet was snatched from the source and everything went quiet inside him.

His mind was suddenly clear.

How could something as simple as a touch from another human being cause such a drastic effect?

She handed the leather folder to Nathan, eyes wide.

Had he just jumped back like some repellent fool?

"Thank you," he rushed, then forced a smile.

Lisa seemed worried for a moment as he scrambled, "Here it is. It's only an employee questionnaire. Just basic stuff really. Name, address, emergency contacts, that sort of thing. I have to have it on file for legal reasons. You do want to get paid after all."

She took the paper carefully from his hands, not glancing at the information at all, cautious not to touch him. Lisa froze as if wondering what had just happened. There had been some sort of static shock when he touched her.

"I tried to call you…, a couple of times yesterday," she said quickly. He was staring at her now and she tried her best to stop her usual melting into a puddle of goo inside. "I…, there was some weird automated message that died before it finished."

Lisa pinched her leg to force herself to focus.

Nathan noticed her voice seemed a little strained and wondered exactly what happened. Regaining control of his own stupid reactions, he tried desperately to correct the situation.

"Oh, that. The office number. It used to go to my home, now it ends up at the office in Salem. You should have called my private number."

He held up his cell.

"I lost your card somehow," she said, anxiously looking at the time on her wrist, late for work again.

Nathan nodded, Troy had probably thrown his business card away the day he called to 'bless him out' about hiring Lisa.

"Well, here then. Add my number to your cell phone," he said quickly, handing her his phone.

She took it numbly, looked at it as if it were a dead gerbil, and handed it right back, her cheeks suddenly flushed.

"I…, uh. I don't have a cell phone," she grinned, shaking her head in embarrassment.

"Oh. Well, we'll remedy that first thing tomorrow," he shrugged. "You'll need one if you're onsite with a client and have to contact me."

"Nathan, you've already given me a car," she grunted, shaking her head.

Lisa was relieved that the uncomfortable moment had somehow passed, but now he was trying to give her something else. What was wrong with him?

"Consider it a signing bonus," laughed Nathan. "And the phone is a tax write off, so…."

He didn't want to tell her that everything concerning her employment was a tax write off for fear it would cheapen their working relationship.

Lisa had never felt this uncomfortable in years. Did he know how much the car he'd given her was worth? She felt horribly guilty, thinking of a way to tell him.

"I've had a dozen offers to buy my green baby," she said with a long glance outside. "You'd be surprised what I've turned down."

"The old thing's really good on the road with foul weather, especially ice and snow," said Nathan, trying to divert the strange turn in conversation. He was glad now that he'd given her the vehicle. Marion would have been pleased.

Lisa turned back around quickly and placed her hand on his, "It's the first car I've ever owned outright. It means a lot to me, so don't you dare try to devalue it."

All Nathan heard was something about it being her first car…, because once again that strange feeling from the touch of her hand had him peacefully mesmerized.

There was a hard rap of knuckles on his window, "Would ya mind letting my hired help come inside now? I have hungry customers waiting in line t'be seated."

The bulk of Troy was blocking the entire view from his driver side window, then a glaring burly face peered down inside to meet Nathan eye to eye.

"Lisa happens to be on my clock at the moment," grunted Troy, uttering a few other unintelligible words off into space.

Lisa jumped and hurried out of the Cadillac, "I'm…," she blurted, considered a string of apologies; but instead, she turned and clopped hurriedly inside the Blind Pirate, retying her apron behind her back as she went.

Nathan eased out of his door, pushing Troy back as he stood up, "Slave driver."

Troy bowed slightly, "At your service."

"It was my fault she was late," said Nathan. "I was giving her some forms to fill out."

"Uh huh," he grunted. "And I suppose it required the holding of hands during this little exchange?"

"That was incidental," said Nathan, a little too defensively.

"You have heard about sexual harassment in the workplace, haven't you?" he mused.

Nathan felt a little resentment flush his face.

"I consider it a requirement for all my workers," laughed Troy.

CHAPTER TWENTY-SEVEN

SATURDAY morning, Nathan was up with the crows, shoveling down a quick breakfast and furiously making notes for his first official day at the office.

Caroline had called late the previous night while on her way back home with Kate and Chuck. Josie was stable and resting, but still no word as to her health, just more tests. At the very least, she wasn't in any danger.

He heard what sounded like echoing footsteps in the upstairs hallway, glanced up, then back down at his notepad in deference. Noises were such a commonplace now, he'd come to ignore..., even expect them.

A few minutes later, the front door chime sounded and he looked at his watch..., only a little after seven.

After a quick peek, there were three forlorn faces standing at attention on the front porch and an odd-looking rental car in the drive.

He eased the front door open and peered at the somber expressions.

"Mr. Heart? We're here to prepare the house," said the man.

His dialect was definitely tainted southern and his tanned skin spoke of something akin to an islander.

"You're really early. Please..., come inside. Didn't Ms. Stewart give you a key to the house?" asked Nathan.

The fellow had a pleasant smile as he stepped past Nathan, closely followed by two very quiet ladies.

"Yes, but we were instructed not to barge in on your privacy," he answered, his smile widening.

'Great, just great', thought Nathan, shaking his head in dismay. There was no guessing what rumors had reached their ears.

"My name is Bolton, this is Sara..., and Annie," he said, making introductions.

Each of them was standing in a line as if waiting for inspection or some sort of approval. It was..., strange.

Nathan shook each of their hands, "I'm Nathan."

Bolton looked to be in his early forties, built like a tank, Sara maybe a little older, with soft eyes and a kind, almost motherly face. Annie barely looked twenty, eyes downcast and shy to the point of perpetual embarrassment.

"Is there anything you need from me?" asked Nathan.

"No thank you. We'll do our best not to get in your way," said Bolton.

Nathan laughed, "Are you kidding? As big as this house is, we'll be lucky to cross paths during the day. Besides, I'll be spending most of the day at my office, so you'll have the entire place to yourselves."

Bolton frowned, "I'm sorry to hear that. Will you be home this evening? Ms. Stewart specifically asked us to make sure you were taken care of."

Taken care of? He'd seen the way she took care of people. Then he repented of the ill judgment, Madeline was only trying to look out after their best interests.

"That was nice of her, but honestly I can't answer. It's the first day at my office and I have a new employee to train before I open my doors to the public Monday. I might be late."

Bolton nodded, "Then we'll be about our business."

Nathan turned to leave, "Feel free to make all the noise you like. There's plenty of breakfast and a fresh pot of coffee on the counter."

The two ladies smiled and headed in the direction where Nathan had pointed.

"Mr. Heart, is there an outside entrance to the cellar?" asked Bolton.

"Around back, you can't miss it. It's where the firewood is delivered too, so it might be a little congested near the entrance. The key is hanging on a hoop by the back door."

Nathan spun back around, "Oh, and please, don't use the key to disable the security system. It's in the pantry. Just press the screen and enter the code. It was a real nightmare getting it back online after Madeline..., I mean Ms. Stewart..., left the last time."

♥

Nathan had to park several spaces down from his office and hurried to the coffee shop to start their first morning off on the right foot.

He stopped to gander at his office window where a large red heart logo was painted and stenciled with Heart Realty.

Gwen Helspeth was seated near the coffee shop's front counter and waved him a good morning without dragging him into some dutiful conversation. He nodded back at her unreadable expression and hurried to his office with two hot cups of eye openers.

Lisa was standing at the door, rubbing her hands and dancing at the chill morning air.

"Are you trying for boss of the year award?" she asked, taking the two cups of coffee.

"If that's all it takes," he grinned.

Nathan shifted the strap of the heavy bag on his shoulder and opened the door.

Lisa quickly bumped the door closed with her hip and sat down the coffee, carefully looking the place over.

The phone lines were latticed and attached with anchors down the brick wall. Nathan checked to make sure there was a dial tone and dropped the receiver back down. There were no messages on the machine. Then there was awkward silence for a few moments, after he handed her a door key.

"Well," said Lisa finally. "What do you want me to do?"

Nathan switched on the warm floor lamp behind her desk, then walked around the partition to his desk.

"Your first official duty is to make this place look a little less creepy," he frowned, looking toward the long dark cavity of the back. "Maybe a few plants, a radio, another lamp..., or six. Something besides all the hard fluorescent lights."

That was when he turned and noticed Lisa. Her long coat was hanging on a rack anchored to the brick wall and she looked different - Very different.

Her hair was clipped back, a nice blue pullover sweater and slacks that accented several of her best features. Nathan had never seen her wearing anything except the frumpy knee length dress and apron at the Blind Pirate.

"What?" she asked.

Nathan's eyes snapped to attention, "Uh..., you..., look nice."

Lisa rolled her eyes, "Troy said you'd do that. I hate that man sometimes."

"Exactly what else did Troy say?" asked Nathan, heavy resentment in his voice.

Lisa ripped open a package of notepads sitting on her desk and yanked a new pen out of a box, "What else do you want besides plants and pictures?"

Apparently, both questions were best left unanswered. Nathan quickly fought for purchase in his mind. Back to business.

"We need to cull last year's sales from the filing cabinets and stuff them in filing boxes and label them by date...."

The list went on until noon as Nathan read from his own prescribed itinerary.

"Time for lunch and I promised you a phone. That reminds me. I'd rather you either lock up your laptop in the small safe at night or take it home with you. There's no reason to dangle temptation in front of anyone willing to break in."

"My laptop...," she squinted.

"Oh, I forgot. It's on my desk under the clutter. We'll spend next Monday getting you acquainted with the software. Wednesday, we'll work with the camera. And hopefully by next Saturday we'll be settled in enough to take you on a few viewings. Make sure you keep track of your hours."

Lisa shook her head, "You need someone that can work full time, Nathan. I don't see how we'll be ready for anything by next Saturday."

Nathan laughed at her terrorized expression, "I work full time. This is the way I brainstorm. We'll take your list and mine and work together, alright? I hired you to help me, not do everything."

♥

Lisa was busily tapping at the screen of her cell phone while Nathan finished the last bit of his sandwich.

Then his phone rang and he cringed. None of his expected phone calls were likely to be good news of any sort. It was Madeline Stewart's number.

"Heart Realty."

His voice echoed blandly off the back wall, giving it a haunted sound.

"Hello Nathan," chirped a happy voice.

"Yes..., who..., Oh, Lindsey. I was expecting your aunt," he guttered.

"I thought I'd call to let you know we made it back from Bucharest."

Nathan picked up on her tone immediately. Lindsey had an audience and she was performing.

"I'm glad to hear it. How is your family?"

"Henry ate something that didn't agree with him, but other than that everybody's fine. Aunt Madey wants to know if you've met the staff yet."

"Yes, they arrived early this morning. I'm sure they're buzzing around the place somewhere."

"Okay..., okay..., Aunt Madey wants the phone. I guess I'll see you in a couple of weeks then..., Thanksgiving?"

Nathan felt that caving feeling for Lindsey. She hadn't received the offer she'd been waiting for from her boyfriend. Or some other blockade was preventing their union, namely Madeline Stewart. Otherwise, why would she still be playing their ruse?

"I look forward to seeing you," he said. "Bye Lindsey."

"Mr. Heart...."

There was the smarmy voice he'd been expecting. It always caught him off guard somehow.

"Ms. Stewart, I'm glad you called," said Nathan.

"I would have called earlier, but I was out of the country as you well know. I wanted to update you on our last conversation."

"That's what I needed to talk to you about also…," he began.

Madeline Stewart cut him off mid sentence.

"Well, after you and I spoke, I rethought the whole 'teach them a lesson' idea I had concerning your family. I could tell that you were a little worried about them, even though I still think my first plan would have been the better option. Anyway, instead of sending my big bully notice to them, I decided on a different tact and took the bull by the horns so to speak."

"I don't understand…," he grunted.

"Well, let me finish…. After my own investigator spent a day snooping, he found that there were several other similar people in the same predicament as your brother and two sisters. My lawyers sent a nice little letter to Bogart Investments instead, explaining what was going to happen if they didn't tear up that contract and apologize. It's amazing how the threat of a class action lawsuit can turn the tide on some people's thinking."

Nathan felt the air melt from his lungs, "So you didn't send anything to my family after all?"

"Not a bully notice. There was no need," she chuckled. "The fellow our lawyers spoke to at Bogart Investments buckled like a hen with a rooster on its back. He faxed a copy of his apology letter to my lawyers as a sort of promissory note just to keep the whole situation honest."

It was over. Finally.

"You never cease to amaze me Madeline Stewart," said Nathan, barely hiding his relief.

"I'm glad you approve," she chortled. "Well…, I do hate to run, but I have an appointment with the devil in about an hour. But I believe Lindsey wants to say something else…. You take care now Mr. Heart, we'll see you soon."

Nathan nearly choked with relief.

"Nathan?"

"Yes Lindsey…, I…."

"Thank you," she whispered. "I think Aunt Madey was getting suspicious. You're a lifesaver. I owe you a hug and a kiss. I'll see you soon."

"Glad to be of service," said Nathan.

Nathan hung up the phone and slumped against the warm brick wall with mind-altering relief. The self-imposed guilt over his sister's sudden collapse shredded off his shoulders. Now he needed to call his sister Caroline with the good news, but decided to finish as much organizing as possible before the afternoon at the office slipped away.

He turned to see Lisa, holding a stack of papers against her chest, glaring at him strangely.

"Who's Lindsey?"

CHAPTER TWENTY-EIGHT

HIS drive home that evening was filled with grievous thoughts. No matter how succinctly, how carefully he had crafted his explanation about Lindsey Stewart to Lisa, it grew worse each time. Finally, he gave up, trying his best to understand why she was so curious in the first place.

When Nathan arrived at Heart Manor, every light inside the place was on and Nathan could see movement everywhere. Even the lights in the two small cottages beside the garage were lit and all their windows were raised to the elements.

Inside, the main house was warm. Evidently, the maids were not as acquainted to the northwest temperatures and the thermostat was twisted to a balmy 78 degrees. Nathan shrugged. It was their money and apparently, there was plenty of it.

His stomach growled the very instant he inhaled the aroma drifting throughout the house and he decided to investigate before retreating to his room.

Sara, the elder of the two ladies, was pulling out two heavenly scented pies from one of the oven's open doors. As soon as they slid onto the countertop, she shut everything off and turned.

"Oh, Mr. Heart, I didn't hear you come in," she smiled, "Your food is in the other oven and there's fresh tea in the pitcher."

Her voice had a distinct splash of Irish that agreed with the flash in her green eyes. She nodded and quickly walked out of the kitchen.

"Thank you," said Nathan, thrusting his head out the door behind her.

The kitchen was spotless. Nathan eased quietly back into the living room. All the furniture was rearranged into groups of amiable little settee's, worthy of a social club. There was a short stack of firewood beside the

147

unlit fireplace, no doubt matching the one in the den and formal dining room.

This trio was as industrious as any people he'd ever seen. He took a walk down the east hallway, where all the downstairs bedrooms were located and found everything freshly arranged to equal any five star suite he'd ever visited. All the stacks of bedding that had been stored in each of the closets were now arranged in proper order in each room.

He heard blundering footsteps upstairs as the work continued and shook his head in awe. They were tireless workers.

Nathan heard a screech from upstairs, or actually a succession of chirps coming down the hall, then down the stairs.

Sara appeared at the foot of the stairs about the same time as Nathan, watching the younger Annie hurriedly trotting down.

"I heard it again," she warbled, her voice bouncing with each jaunty step downward. "Right in my ear this time."

She landed against Sara, who wrapped her in her arms, patting her back soothingly.

"You know nothing up there can harm you dear," she whispered. "You should know that by now."

Sara caught Nathan's furrowed brow, "Why don't you go get yourself something to drink and I'll help you with the rest of the upstairs? Go on now. Come fetch me when you're ready."

Annie looked shyly over at Nathan and turned quickly to rush into the kitchen.

"She'll be just fine," said Sara, turning to go.

"Wait," grunted Nathan. "What the blazes is she talking about?"

It was Sara's turn to shy away, "You'll have to excuse her. This is the first house Annie's worked in that had a restless spirit. She'll be fine in a couple of days."

Nathan shook his head as if clearing water from his ears, "What?"

"Oh my...," said Sara, before she turned and walked away quickly, leaving Nathan to his unanswered questions.

♥

Spirits? Hauntings? It was ludicrous. However capable the two ladies were at their chosen profession, they were as off their rockers as Ms. Stewart and her clan.

Still disgruntled, Nathan finally forced himself away from the table. If he ate like this every evening, his flat stomach would be as round as a toad. After watching the two women bustling about, it was obvious that they would have no problem burning away any amount of calories they might ingest.

"Restless spirit," hissed Nathan, scraping off his plate.

He cleaned up his mess and trudged upstairs.

He could hear the two women chatting softly from the west end and not being the type to eavesdrop, headed directly to his room.

His bedroom door was propped open and smelled warmly of vanilla. His bed had been remade, fresh sheets, fresh everything. New towels replaced all the shelves and displays, mirrors spotless, again everything to perfection.

He felt the slightest bit displeased with himself for his prejudice concerning their superstitious beliefs. Surely, they knew they didn't have to be his personal maid service.

After a shower and change, he felt almost compelled to take a look at the work they'd done throughout the house.

The drapes in every room looked vacuumed and pressed, again all the linen and bedding in their places to perfection. The paintings and mirrors that were previously propped against the walls were hanging in their designated spots. Each room on the upper wing was detailed immaculately.

Heart Manor had been converted into a pristine, yet macabre he reminded himself, bed and breakfast for the Stewart family.

Nathan chanced to peer outside through one of the upstairs windows in the end of the house.

He could see movement in and out of the two cottages down below, their lights still on, windows raised. It was probably Bolton airing them out. They hadn't been used in nearly a half dozen years and then only for storage. There hadn't been any reason for Nathan to visit them for more than a quick check for maintenance and repairs after the family had emptied them of their nineteenth century relics.

Curiosity began to pluck the strings in his mind and he walked back downstairs, leather jacket in hand, then out the front door.

The chill mist of rain made him shiver and he snatched on his coat letting his feet beat a quick path to the cottages. He noticed how quickly the small increase of warmth inside the house had affected his tolerance for the falling autumn temperatures outside.

As he approached the duplex arrangement, a silhouette appeared against the light inside and one by one the windows began to slide shut and latch.

Nathan knocked on the open door and peered inside.

"Come in."

Bolton was dressed in heavy coveralls with a cap on his head turned backwards.

He grinned at Nathan, "Watch the floor, it might still be slick."

Bolton had scrubbed the walls and floors and mopped everything clean of the slightest bit of dust. There was a fire crackling in the shared hearth between the two units, already drying out the cold dampness. It smelled fresh, not chemically caustic like it usually did when his cleaning crew drove away.

"Looks good, smells good," said Nathan. "You could teach my usual cleaners a thing or two."

"It's a special mix," said Bolton, pointing to the mop bucket. "Sibyl makes it up for us. Secret ingredients," he grinned.

"Sibyl?" asked Nathan.

"One of Ms. Stewart's sisters. Sibyl Bale. She's the family apothecary," he explained.

Nathan wasn't about to ask for yet another explanation for that answer.

"I'll have to get her recipe. Speaking of…, have you eaten?" asked Nathan, looking for conversation.

"Before you arrived," he answered.

That was ambiguous. For all Nathan knew it meant he'd eaten breakfast.

Bolton finished shutting the windows and stoked the fire quickly, then spun out the door to the adjoining unit.

It too was unblemished and the windows quickly slid shut and latched. Apparently, they intended to make this their living quarters while the Stewart family visited their vacation home.

"You three make an amazing team," said Nathan, still struggling to open a line of conversation.

"I've worked with Sara for several years and Annie for the last two. She fit right in as soon as she was hired. If you'll excuse me I need to get busy and bring in the furniture and bedding."

Nathan was about to ask his usual question, but instead jumped in behind Bolton and followed him to the first stall in the garage.

"Let me help you," said Nathan. "I've been sitting on my keister most of the day."

Bolton turned his head, "Ms. Stewart wouldn't like that."

"What Ms. Stewart doesn't know, can't hurt her," said Nathan.

Bolton chuckled, "Actually, you sound just like her."

The garage stall on the end was stock full of plastic wrapped furniture and bedding. A two-wheel cart and a furniture mover was shoved neatly against it all.

"Where did all this come from?" asked Nathan.

"One of today's shipments," grunted Bolton, lifting out a large mattress.

Nathan quickly grabbed the other end. Despite his smaller stature, Bolton had to be as strong as an ox as easily as he lifted his end of the bulk.

"One of today's shipments? How many shipments came today?" asked Nathan as they hurried toward the first cottage.

"Just two. Our furniture and the wine shipment," he answered, dropping the plastic wrapped mattress against the wall inside the first cottage.

That was why he asked about the cellar entrance that morning. Nathan felt as stupid as Watson in one of Sherlock Holmes' mysteries.

Trip after trip ensued and at one point, Nathan wondered how Bolton had originally intended to get all of this done by himself. Finally, it was all delivered, beds assembled, spartan chairs and furniture arranged and neat stacks of sealed linen and bedding in the center of each bed.

"Thank you Mr. Heart," said Bolton with a heavy sigh. "That went much faster than I'd expected."

He threw in a few more sticks of firewood and shut up the doors. Nathan happened to look down at the threshold as they were shutting up to leave. There was a line of dark red sand forming a line across the doorway outside.

"Is this for rodents?" asked Nathan.

"You could say that," grinned Bolton. "Its brick dust. Another one of Sibyl's recipes."

Nathan opened his mouth to ask, then shook his head as the two of them hurried back through a steady drizzle. It was a quarter past ten when they walked through the door and the warmth actually felt good.

Both women were seated in the kitchen, drinking hot tea and finishing the last crumbs of a slice of cherry pie. Both looked tired and weathered.

"The cottages are cleaned and ready," announced Bolton, digging a coffee cup out of the cabinet.

Both women thanked him and rose from their seats, headed toward the back door. It looked as though they took the delineation of their duties seriously. Bolton was muscle and scrub, while the ladies took care of all the niceties.

Nathan poured himself some coffee and against his better judgment cut a slim slice of the pie to go with it.

With a little idle chatter, Nathan managed to get Bolton to share a sparse outline of his history, which was surprisingly interesting. His family had known the Stewart family for several generations in North Carolina. After an undefined tour in the military, he'd been called upon by the Stewart family for a wide variety of duties. This was the end of Bolton's candid tale and although he was somewhat of a jack-of-all-trades, it was likely that he'd left out the majority of his true worth. After all, Madeline collected things which were important; that likely included anyone she employed.

With the snack consumed, as if a switch flipped, Bolton stood to put away his dishes and said goodnight.

CHAPTER TWENTY-NINE

NATHAN heard bells ringing in his head, then they congealed into frantic chimes just as he jostled awake.

His room was dark except for the flickering candle he'd grown accustomed to.

Someone was punching the front door chime with repeated urgency. Nathan threw on some pants and rushed downstairs and flung open the door.

"Would you mind calling the authorities?" grunted Bolton angrily.

He was holding a frail man about Nathan's age, down on his knees, with one tight hand sunken into the man's clavicle and a thumb shoved deeply into the socket beside his wry neck.

The mudsill fellow glowered at Nathan through wet stringy hair with an undiluted hatred in his eyes he'd only seen on some of the wild animals that drifted through.

"Who in blazes is this?" asked Nathan.

"It's a rat that was peeping in on the ladies from behind the garage. I came around the other side and caught him with a camera taking pictures," gritted Bolton.

"Well, bring him in and I'll call the sheriff," said Nathan.

"No Sir," said Bolton. "You should never invite evil into your home. I'll keep him right where he is until the authorities get here."

Nathan nodded at Bolton's unusual wisdom and ran to the telephone.

With the sheriff on the way, Nathan hurried back out, carrying an old pistol that hadn't been used in years. It wasn't loaded, but it might provide a healthy bluff for the intruder.

Bolton still had the fellow resting uncomfortably on his knees, while scolding him like an errant child.

"What were you doing here?" asked Nathan, leaning closer to the man's bruised face.

The man only winced in pain, still sporting his angry scowl of death toward Nathan.

Apparently, Bolton had done a lot more than just scold him.

Bolton reached in his pocket and handed Nathan a small digital camera and a thick worn notepad, filled with mostly illegible scribbling.

"The camera was in his hands when I caught him and the notepad was in his pocket," said Bolton. "If you hadn't opened the door when you did I was going to take him up the road a bit and leave him for the crows."

Still the man remained silent. Nathan hoped that Bolton was trying to scare the fellow into talking.

"There's an old water well around the middle of the property," said Nathan. "We could say he escaped."

Bolton grinned and lifted the groaning man by his collarbone, then he shrugged, "You're the boss."

"No...," hissed the man.

"Then who are you?" asked Nathan.

He ducked his head, then shook it.

Bolton began to drag him down the steps, arms flailing as he yelled obscenities at both of his captors.

"I'll get the cart," bluffed Nathan. "It's too far to walk in the dark."

He handed Bolton the empty gun, first showing him the empty cylinder, just so there wouldn't be any mistakes. Bolton grimaced and made a show of the weapon to the silent vagrant.

Then all the lights came on inside Nathan's mind.

"I know who you are, by the way," said Nathan, as he spun on his heel, still walking to the garage. "You're the snitch that was hired to spy on me and this house."

Immediately, the man stood and took a swing at Bolton. It was a very bad mistake on his part. One quick jab of Bolton's fist and he was unconscious on the ground.

"Oh well," grunted Nathan. "He probably wouldn't have talked anyway."

Bolton nodded, rubbing his fist, "Next time when you bring an antique, at least bring it loaded."

He handed the pistol back to Nathan only moments before bright red and blue lights flickered in through the gate.

♥

Nathan held the camera up, slowly scrolling through the last few images of Sara and Annie in various stages of undress.

"That's enough for me," said the sheriff.

"The other pictures are of the inside of the house through the windows," said Nathan. "I think he was planning a theft. The photos of the ladies were probably a crime of opportunity."

"If we find out anything from him, I'll be sure and let you know. In the mean time, I'd keep my eyes open. This type rarely works alone," said the sheriff.

"I suppose you need me to come down again and press charges," said Nathan.

The sheriff grinned, "Ask for Ben Kern."

He thumped at his nametag, "Keep this up and my office will think you're on the payroll. Oh and by the way, thanks for not breaking anything on him. Otherwise, he might be the one pressing charges."

The sheriff's car drove away with the two men standing outside in a cold drizzle.

"Is there really an old well on the property?" asked Bolton.

Nathan nodded, "It was filled up years ago. I never said it was empty."

Bolton grinned, "We should play cards sometime."

Nathan laughed, "We should never get in a fight. You have one mean left jab."

"Was he really hired to snoop on you?" asked Bolton.

Nathan shrugged, "I was told there was someone looking into my livelihood. In any case, it certainly struck a nerve when I confronted him."

"I hate snoops, but I hate Peeping Toms even more," he grunted.

Nathan took out the notepad and flipped through a few of the pages shaking his head.

"I'll have to get this under a bright lamp and see if I can make any sense out of this."

Bolton squinted at it in the dim porch light, "I was wondering if you were going to give that up. Looks like a three year old wrote it."

Nathan stuck out his hand, "Thank you Bolton, it appears that your little trio not only cleaned the house, but rid us of all our pests. What do you do for an encore?"

"I can play a little Harp," laughed Bolton.

♥

Sunday morning there was a soft tap, tapping on Nathan's door.

"Would you like breakfast Sir?" asked the muffled voice.

Nathan yawned painfully, throwing back the covers, "Yes, thank you. I'll be right down."

He hurried to dress with the full intent to have breakfast with the hired help. He'd learned through the years that most people were more likely to open up to personal information early in the morning. Probably something to do with their natural defense mechanism coming to life as the day drew on.

There was a place already set at the table; juice, coffee, and a few small items to choose from. He almost expected a menu to appear beside his plate. Much to his dismay, the hired help were nowhere to be seen. He'd already taken a few bites when he noticed that there was soft music playing from somewhere in the den. It was offsetting and relaxing at the same time. Even if he didn't have a human being present at the table, knowing that there was someone else in the house was comforting.

A face peered into the kitchen door from the dining room.

"Sir, you have visitors," said Sara.

"I have visitors?" said Nathan.

Sara grinned, then disappeared once again.

Why hadn't he heard the door chime?

Just inside the vestibule, stood Caroline, Kate, Chuck and Allie.

"Uncle Nate!" yelled Allie.

"Well look at you, my...," he began his usual greeting.

"Ssshh," hissed Allie, as she grabbed him around the neck. "It might hurt Katie's feelings if she knew I was your favorite."

Nathan laughed, then kissed her warm cheek.

Kate was next with a tight hug that was better than the breath she was squeezing out of him.

Chuck grinned and shook hands, just as Caroline made her greetings.

"Come in..., please," said Nathan.

"Who was the nice lady?" asked Allie.

"She works for the new owner of the house," said Nathan. "There are three of them here. That was probably Sara."

Caroline's eyes widened, "You weren't kidding when you said the place was refurnished."

He laughed, "Don't be too cheery, it's a very long story."

Nathan urged them into the kitchen for something to snack on and a private place to talk.

When they sat around the table, Caroline asked, "Are you sure it's okay for us to be here?"

"I don't remember any restrictions in my contract," he shrugged. "Coffee? Homemade pie?"

"How is Josie?" asked Nathan as he delved out pie and juices.

"She comes home from the hospital next Friday," said Caroline.

"So they didn't find anything wrong?"

She didn't answer, but looked over at Kate.

"It was a small lump on her brain," Kate said quietly. "They removed it last night, emergency surgery. She's going to be fine."

Nathan's eyes locked on each of them, "It wasn't...."

"No, it wasn't cancer," said Caroline. "Just a growth putting pressure on the side of her brain."

"Then we all have something to be thankful for," said Nathan.

Kate put down her glass of orange juice, "Uncle Nate, thank you for everything you did. After everything mom was doing, you still helped her."

Nathan looked puzzled, "It could have been the pressure from the growth causing her to act out. I didn't do anything."

Kate shook her head, "I'm talking about the letter those people sent."

Nathan sat down, "Letter?"

"Those people, BI, Incorporated. They sent a letter apologizing for scamming mama along with the contract torn in half. I saw the letter myself. It mentioned your name, that you'd warned them to drop the whole thing."

Madeline Stewart sent that letter. Why would she make it look as if it was Nathan that forced Bogart Investments to concede?

He suddenly heard Charles telling him thank you and it made more sense.

"I only played a small part in that," said Nathan. "I'd like to see a copy of that letter sometime."

"Daddy put it in the safe," she grimaced. "I'm just glad they're not fighting any more. Daddy said what you did was the way families were supposed to act."

Caroline saw Nathan's confusion and changed the subject, "You said you were going to tell us about the furniture?"

Nathan choked on a bit of bagel he was nibbling on and looked carefully toward both doors to make sure no one was listening. The music was still playing, hopefully loud enough to drown him out.

"Remember, I told you they were a strange bunch? Well, every piece of furniture you see in this house is worth a small fortune in itself," he whispered. "The place is like a museum."

"Cool," said Allie.

"What about this table?" grunted Chuck.

He had been looking at it the entire time, brushing at the gouges in the wood with his fingertips.

Nathan grinned, "Ah…, a disbeliever. It was imported from Europe. It was used during the Inquisition."

Both Caroline and Kate slid away from the huge block of wood, while Chuck slid his hands over the marred surface in admiration.

"And the entire house is filled with stuff like that?" asked Caroline.

Nathan nodded grimly.

"Can I take pictures?" asked Chuck.

CHAPTER THIRTY

THEY visited well into the afternoon, while crouched in the back recess of the den. It seemed the safest place away from potentially damaging something Nathan couldn't afford to replace. The massive television kept Allie mesmerized, while Kate and Caroline downloaded compounded pieces of the last year to Nathan's eager ears. Chuck roamed about the house with his camera until he became bored with photographing the different bedroom suites.

Caroline hinted that they needed to begin their long drive back home, when Nathan offered to show them his office in Salem.

It was on the way and after he further bribed them with flavored coffee they agreed.

Once they were outside on the front steps, Kate asked Nathan for a group picture of all of them in front of the old house and Chuck propped his camera on top of Caroline's sedan. He set the timer and shrouded the camera with the bill of his cap, then ran to stand beside their little huddle in the mist of rain.

It hadn't stopped raining all day, which was perfectly normal for anyone living west of the Cascades. Webbed feet and rain slickers were a common sight during the rainy seasons.

When they reached Salem, the angle parking in front of the strip of businesses where Heart Realty was located was quiet for a Sunday afternoon. Directly in front of the office was the old 1958 Buick Special patiently awaiting the return of its owner.

"Isn't that the old Buick?" asked Caroline.

Nathan nodded, "My new employee needed transportation and it was just sitting there turning to rust."

"Well, aren't you the sudden philanthropist?" cheered Caroline. "Bravo."

The tiny bell above the office door jingled happily as Nathan entered. "Hello?"

"Back here," answered a small muted voice.

There was another tall lamp-stand glowing warmly behind his desk as well as three new pictures and a mirror hanging along the stark red brick wall. A large potted vine was on a stand beside the front window, deep green heart shaped leaves winding their way around the inside rim of the glass.

"Lisa?"

"You were expecting the tooth fairy," she grunted as she stood up from behind some boxes.

The bell jingled several more times and Lisa stared incoherently, "Oh, I didn't realize you had company."

Nathan grinned uncontrollably at her, especially at a long swipe of dark smudge trailing from the side of her nose to her chin. Her navy blue sweat pants and top bagged crookedly, but didn't take away any of her schoolgirl charm.

"What in the world are you doing here today?" he asked.

"Trying to get a head start. I still work here don't I?" she grunted.

Nathan laughed, "Everyone, this is Lisa Evans, my new assistant."

The group introduced themselves, but not before Caroline gave Nathan a sisterly nudge in the ribs. His nephew Chuck began to stare like most sixteen-year-old boys when confronted with something shiny.

"I was about to get us all some coffee. Would you care to join us?" asked Nathan.

Lisa fought an unruly strand of hair behind an ear and sighed, "If you're buying."

Nathan cringed. She'd obviously purchased all the new things with her own money; which was probably exhausted from the looks of everything.

They began to exit single file when Allie dropped back to stand near Lisa, tugging on her sleeve.

Lisa bent down and Allie whispered in her ear and Nathan heard her gasp. She stood up and stared into the new picture-framed mirror on the brick wall.

Lisa knelt down to Allie, "Thanks. I think I'm going to like you best of all." Then stared up at Nathan, "Maybe even better than my boss."

She yanked on Lisa's arm until she leaned closer, then whispered something else in her ear and Lisa blushed bright red and glared at Nathan.

"Come on Allie…," said Nathan. "Before you get me in even more hot water."

Lisa met them a few minutes later, sans smudge, with a bit of mischievous grin on her face. She let her hand rest on Allie's shoulder in a perpetual hug until everyone crowded around a table for a few minutes.

Kate and Caroline spoke at the same instant with Kate winning the battle.

"So Lisa…, how long have you known Uncle Nate?"

That quirky grin was back on Lisa's face, with a dimple creasing one cheek.

"For a while…, but I'm not sure he knows that," grinned Lisa.

Nathan tightened, "We were just introduced a few weeks ago. Lisa works at the Blind Pirate down the coast at Crab Cove."

"Blind Pirate…, that explains a lot," laughed Kate.

Lisa gave her a scornful look and swiped at the clean side of her face once again in horror, however it wasn't the traces of soot on Lisa's face she was referring to.

"He usually comes into the restaurant about three times a week…, Mondays, Fridays and Sundays, for a couple of years now," said Lisa, subconsciously daubing a napkin on her cheek.

Nathan ducked his head in frustration after receiving a stiff infantile kick on the shin from Caroline. This was not going well.

"I hope you can overlook his peculiarities," sighed Caroline. "He really is a pretty good brother…."

Caroline shrugged away the last of her dying comment.

Nathan stood, "Well, I know you have a long drive ahead of you. I'm glad you came to visit me, but I won't keep you."

No one else stood, leaving Nathan glancing around at the table of smiling faces. Finally, defeated by the sudden collusion, he sat back down.

Nathan endured another twenty minutes of chatter between the ladies, unsuccessfully dodging every bullet, when Caroline finally looked at the time, "Lisa it really was a pleasure to meet you."

Kate and the others agreed as everyone hurried out to the darkening evening.

Allie jumped in Nathan's arms with a quick 'I love you' and then managed to steal a hug from Lisa, whispering something quick in her ear.

He stood outside under the street awning as they drove away, wondering what kind of damage control was awaiting him. Now it wasn't just Troy pushing him Lisa's direction, it was his family.

And Lisa seemed to be enjoying every minute of the attention.

He sighed and went inside his office.

Lisa was already busy behind the stack of boxes, stuffing last year's records into a box.

He began to straighten the stacks of confusion on his desk when Lisa stepped past the cubicle wall in front of him.

"Your family is nice. Make sure you tell them I said so," she said quietly. "I need to leave. I have a short shift that starts in an hour."

"Lisa wait...," sighed Nathan.

She stared at him for several seconds, "Did you keep your receipts for everything you bought for the office?"

It wasn't the original question that was on the cusp of his lips, but for her sake he was glad he remembered.

Lisa rolled her eyes, walked to her desk and came back with a stack of little slips of paper. She dropped them in his hand and turned to leave.

"Just a second," he grunted.

She wasn't making this easy for him.

Lisa took a deep breath and turned to stand back in front of his cluttered desk.

"What?" she asked glumly.

He looked at the receipts and quickly tallied the amount and scribbled out a check with extra for gasoline.

"I'll set us up a petty cash box with a ledger next week. If you need to buy anything else, just..., you know what to do."

He suddenly knew what he wanted to say, yet the entire complexity had him baffled. He had spent most of his time avoiding the complications thrust at him by Lisa's other employer. Almost resented these new insistent prods from his sister Caroline, then..., his niece Allie had taken an interest in Lisa Evans. Everyone else surely had their own misguided agenda's, but not Allie.

If her innocent eyes recognized something his didn't, then it was entirely possible that he was missing something obvious.

"Thank you," she said, then turned to leave again.

"Lisa?"

"What?" she grunted. "You're going to make me late..., again."

Nathan closed his eyes for a moment then looked at her, "Would you like to join me some evening..., maybe for a movie and some decent food? Somewhere..., anywhere other than where you work? A date?"

Lisa squinted her eyes and shook her head, "No. I don't think that's a good idea. You have too many conflicts and you're obviously not interested."

Her answer was quick and sharp as a knife.

Nathan shook his head, "Not interested?"

"I'll see you Monday at nine a.m.," she sighed.

Nathan was about to ask her to wait once again, but his opportunity disappeared with the jingling bell over the front door. Instead, he sat there at his desk stupefied, trying to understand what just happened.

"Not interested?" he hissed. "What in blazes does that mean, not interested?"

By the time he turned off the office lights and left, Lisa had been gone at least a half hour. That entire half hour was filled with noisy grumbling and arguing with himself into the echoing empty office.

Angry with himself, miffed at Lisa, he sped away directly to the Blind Pirate in pretense of his usual Sunday evening meal, to confront his accuser.

Had he really been eating at the Blind Pirate that long and never noticed her? Of course he had. Most of those times he'd been there as a service to Marion, to get her out of the house to someplace safe enough that she would feel comfortable.

Afterward, after she died, he was consumed by guilt, work, worry, and his own private cold war. But of course Lisa Evans would have never known what was going on inside his thimble sized brain. It was only by chance that he formed a friendship with Troy as he stood behind his bar shoving drinks in front of Nathan. Of course, Troy seemed to enjoy analyzing his every thought and motive as if it were all a game.

Nathan slid to a stop out in the front parking lot, taking up two empty slots, then hurried inside without a single plan of action.

As soon as he stepped inside, Troy waved him over to the bar.

"You'd better let me find ya a sittin' place tonight," he grunted. "Lisa's in a terrible mood this evenin' the likes I ain't never seen."

"She is?" grinned Nathan.

"Now wait just a cross-eyed minute," barked Troy. "You ain't the reason for little Lisa's foul mood are ya?"

Nathan shrugged innocently, "How would I know? Maybe it's just a woman thing."

Troy frowned at Nathan for a second…, thinking, "That could be true, but I still think you had a hand in whatever's ailing her. There ain't but one good way to find out."

Troy rounded the bar and grabbed Nathan by the sleeve of his leather jacket, pulling him to a familiar booth in the corner.

"Don't ya get up or move. I'm going to have my eye on you the whole time, ya hear?"

"Does this mean I can have my beer now?" asked Nathan.

"I'll get ya your beer. Now you just stay put," he grunted, his head nodding in exaggerated motions.

Lisa shot out of the noisy swinging door with several platters of food, serving a group a few tables away. She glanced up and spun to hand her new customer a menu, saw it was Nathan, then threw it on the table and walked away.

Troy was pointing his direction, an angry scowl on his face.

Before Nathan could get up and slip out the side exit, Lisa was in front of him blocking his path.

"Go sit down," she grunted angrily.

Nathan looked over her shoulder; Troy was barreling their direction.

She tilted her head in one of those motions that meant 'do it or else'.

Lisa followed him to his seat and took out her order pad.

"What are you hungry for tonight?" she asked sweetly, just as Troy slid into the chair across from Nathan.

"Why don't you pick for me?" asked Nathan.

Troy was still giving him a steady glare.

"That's probably not a good idea, unless you want spit in your beer," she said sweetly.

"Just bring him a beer for now," said Troy, waving her away from the table.

Lisa grinned in belated satisfaction as she walked away.

Troy sighed, "Now do you want to tell me what happened?"

"Family," laughed Nathan. "It's always about family."

"Your family gave Lisa grief and you didn't defend her!" spat Troy.

Nathan shook his head, "Are you kidding? They love her. They think she's Miss Perfect."

Troy leaned over with that scowl back on his face.

"Then what is it that ya did?" asked Troy, trying to control his words.

Only the truth would set things right.

"I asked Lisa if she'd like to go on a date with me," said Nathan.

"And...?" asked Troy.

"She said no."

Nathan carefully neglected to add that she believed he 'wasn't interested'.

Troy nodded..., then nodded again..., his eyes going glazed.

Suddenly, he stood and stomped toward the bar, "Lisa! I need to see you in my office."

Nathan watched Lisa turn and toss black daggers his direction before following Troy through the creaky swinging door.

CHAPTER THIRTY-ONE

T ROY O'Bannon shuffled back to the end of the polished bar, squinting out of the sides of his eyes at Nathan.

"You have to understand," said Troy. "I been working on you for months so's I could get you and little Lisa together."

Nathan sat at the bar, taking his medicine like a man, one shot glass at a time.

"Lisa gets lambasted for dates on a regular basis here at the Pirate. She swats 'em down like flies, but I always end up havin' to run defense for her. Nathan, I'm an old fisherman by trade. I know which ones to keep and which to throw back in the drink. I figgered you for a keeper."

Nathan had been sitting there long enough to begin feeling the alcohol, long enough to loosen his tongue.

"Troy...," he began, "I'm old enough to go fishing on my own. I did ask Lisa out. She told me she didn't think I was interested. What exactly is that supposed to mean? You tell me."

Troy grinned and leaned away from the bar.

"Did she now? Aye..., its true love in the makin'," he laughed, shoving a fresh bottle of black label rum in front of Nathan. "It's on the house tonight, Nathan my boy." Troy seemed overly pleased with himself, humming a tune as he walked away.

♥

The last thing Nathan remembered was tipping the bottle upside down, shaking it to get the last drop into his shot glass. Then cold drizzling rain was pelting his face, shocking him alive.

"What the blazes!" he groaned, swatting the raindrops as if they were a swarm of gnats.

"Calm down," said Lisa. "You're drunk. I'm taking you home."

Nathan began to sober quickly, "I can get home myself. Lisa, I'm so sorry. My car's right out…, it's…, out front."

"Troy parked your car in his spot for the night," she grunted, shoving his tall wobbly bulk against her car. Lisa was thankful that he could walk at least, but if he fell…, all she would be able to do is get out of the way.

He dropped heavily into the passenger seat of the old Buick and Lisa shut the door before he could slide back out. Lisa wondered how she was going to navigate him inside his house.

"I don't know what came over me," grunted Nathan, suddenly propped against the door.

Lisa latched his seat belt and cranked the car.

"Troy and his free liquor is what came over you. Now shut up and let me drive you home."

"You don't understand," said Nathan. "I hate being drunk. I haven't been drunk since I turned twenty-one."

"Well, you're good and soaked now, so just shut up and sit there."

Lisa turned on the radio, which took an eternity to warm up.

"You should've had Troy take me home," said Nathan. "It's all his fault I'm in this condition."

"We'll be at your front door in about ten minutes, just sit there and keep quiet. And don't you dare throw up in my baby."

The radio began to blare out some hissing static riddled tune and Lisa punched several of the buttons until one station came in clearer.

The sound of the engine, the road, and the windshield wipers seemed to lull her passenger into a calmer mode.

"Did you know you have really pretty eyes?" whined Nathan. "And…, the reason I never paid attention to you wasn't personal. Not at all. It was because I was dealing with so…, much…, sh…."

"I know! I get it. Now will you please be quiet?" barked Lisa.

Nathan thought he heard her muffled laughter, but the radio crackled with static and drowned it all out.

"We're here," she sighed. "Thank God."

The car went silent and she hurried around to the passenger door. Stuffing his wobbly body inside was difficult, but dragging him out was going to be impossible without his help.

"Can I help you?" boomed a voice from behind her.

Lisa screamed and spun, falling backward into Nathan's lap.

"I didn't mean to scare you," laughed Bolton. "I'm living right over there." He pointed toward the brightly lit cottage that Lisa hadn't noticed on her first visit to Heart Manor.

She cautiously sat up, just as Nathan's arms wrapped tightly around her waist, holding her down.

"Wait," he grunted. "I was only going to ask you for a date."

Bolton offered her a hand, pulling her free from Nathan's grip with a huge grin on his face.

"Is he often like this?" asked Bolton.

"Never...," said Lisa somewhat shyly, "I've never seen him drunk before. It was my..., employer's fault."

Bolton laughed, "I'll help you get him up to his room. Then you're on your own."

"Fair enough," she sighed.

♥

Nathan flopped onto his bed, then sat right back up near the side. His mind was slowly clearing itself from the black rum stupor.

Fading in and out before him was Lisa, talking to Ms. Stewart's helper Bolton.

"In the morning, tell Nathan that I'll be by to pick him up for work. Just in case he doesn't remember," said Lisa.

"I'll see that he's up and ready. Good night Miss," he said, shaking his head.

He heard Bolton's footsteps as they bumped down the hallway.

"Lisa I'm so sorry," whispered Nathan. "I can take care of myself now. Really I can. I feel really bad about this. You must think I'm some terrible lush."

Even with his head spinning, he could probably manage a shower and bedclothes in a few more minutes.

"That's right," chuckled Lisa. "Just keep talking Mr. Heart."

She yanked off his leather coat and draped it over a chair, then slid his huge leather oxfords from his feet.

"Please," whined Nathan, "You're making me feel like an invalid."

"Don't worry," said Lisa, "...this is as far as it goes, Mister."

Nathan slumped, "Thank goodness."

Lisa laughed quietly and sat beside him.

"You really know how to make a gal feel special," she sighed, then laughed at herself for talking to a drunk that probably wouldn't remember the ride home.

With a quick peck of a kiss on his cheek, she pushed him back as he drifted to sleep.

"Good night, Nathan."

"Good night, Lens."

Lisa shook her head, an odd grin on her face, then curled the neatly folded comforter at the foot of the bed up over his body.

♥

There was a pounding at the bedroom door Monday morning and Nathan lunged forward.

"Mr. Heart? Nathan? You need to come down for breakfast," said a small muffled voice.

The previous night came flooding back in and Nathan groaned, flopping back down on the bed. This was the exact reason he didn't keep alcohol available.

"Mr. Heart?"

The rapping was softer now he thought, but it was the pounding in his head he was hearing.

"I'm coming," hissed Nathan, then louder. "I'm coming."

He stripped, showered and dressed, mumbling angrily at himself the entire time. When he felt he was finally presentable, he hurried down the stairs.

Bolton was seated with a plate before him and another empty was waiting on Nathan to arrive.

"Mr. Heart...," said Bolton.

"I don't want to talk about it," mumbled Nathan, as he grabbed food for his plate.

Bolton almost grinned, then nodded.

Nathan swallowed and looked at his wristwatch; eight forty-five. He groaned and ate a few more bites. He intended to be at his office at eight thirty, before Lisa arrived. Lisa. His car was parked at the Blind Pirate. More memories flooded in, then everything all at once. What made matters even worse, he was going to have to relive the events at least once more with Lisa.

"Bolton..., I'm sorry about last night. It won't happen again," said Nathan.

"I thought you didn't want to talk about it," he said, his grin twitching.

"I don't. I just thought you should know," said Nathan.

"She's a nice lady," said Bolton. "Very pretty."

Nathan cringed and nodded, "She is."

'And look how I treated her', thought Nathan.

A very familiar car horn beeped outside and Nathan gulped his orange juice, hurrying to the door.

The '58 Buick was parked out front idling in anticipation. Clouds were lowering, threatening another deluge for the day, as Nathan ran down the steps.

He eased himself into the passenger seat and the car was moving by the time the door shut.

Lisa had her hands at ten and two on the steering wheel, fingers tapping and staring in silence at the driveway, then the gate, then the rural road.

"Lisa..., I...," began Nathan.

"You know you could have just told me," said Lisa.

"Told you what?" asked Nathan. "That I can't handle alcohol? At least let me say thank you and I promise it won't happen again."

Lisa's head spun in an angry glare, "That you weren't interested. That you were interested in someone else."

Nathan thought out his next words very carefully.

"What?" he squeaked.

"Don't play me for a fool," she spat.

This was her reward for trusting her instincts?

Nathan groaned miserably at his Monday morning. Oh God..., what had he said in his drunken stupor?

"Lisa, I'm not sure where all this is coming from, but I haven't so much as had a single date in nearly three years. If I offended you, or... or... assumed more than I should have, or...."

Her head snapped around to look at Nathan, suddenly curious, "That's fine. You're entitled to your privacy."

Suddenly Lisa looked embarrassed for her outburst, possibly mistrusting what she'd heard, the drunken slurred words he had mumbled.

"Let's just go to work. Go back to ground zero and keep it simple."

Her eyes darted back to the road..., and there was more silence. Nathan grilled his mind for relevance, trying to remember what it was that he must have said to bring on this hostility. Surely he hadn't made some crude physical advance, it was totally against his nature. But Troy's rum had his brain disengaged and his mouth running in neutral; there was no telling what his loose lips uttered last night. In any case, he had no one to blame but himself, certainly not Troy, and least of all Lisa.

"We're running a little late," he mumbled, searching for a hint of conversation.

"Well, I figured that since I was giving my boss a ride to work, that I should pick him up while I was on the clock."

Nathan's cell phone sang a tune and he looked at it dumbly; it was Caroline. He didn't answer, but put it back in his blazer pocket. This wasn't the time for family conversations.

"Your girlfriend?" asked Lisa.

"My sister..., Caroline," said Nathan.

Lisa shook her head, "I'm sorry Nathan; that was uncalled for. I just broke my own rule. You should probably call her back."

"It can wait. If it's an emergency she'll call back or text me."

A few minutes later, Lisa parked directly in front of their office. There were two messages inside, two meetings with potentials that afternoon that would likely be long drawn out affairs.

At least his headache had subsided to a dull reminder, with the aid of next door's caffeine laden coffee.

Nathan carefully placed a heavy unopened box on Lisa's desk, "I intended to open this up last night and install our software..., and let it charge the battery."

He dropped two plastic disks of software beside it and placed a plush leather carrying case on the floor by her desk.

Lisa was harboring sudden pangs of guilt. Instead of taking care of business, he'd chased her to the restaurant and ended up drunk as a sailor.

"Let me know if you have any problems. I need to clear my desk and get ready for this afternoon."

She slowly opened the box and set the new laptop on her desk, while listening to the sounds of shuffling, stacking, and clunky arranging going on behind her.

After returning the calls, Nathan mechanically spread out photos of three similar properties for the first buyer, noted their addresses and thrust them into a folder. He was in the middle of selecting three for the next client when Lisa appeared in front of his desk.

"I'm done."

Nathan tapped his desk nervously, "Why don't you test out our internet. We're supposed to share the WiFi from next door. See if Heart Realty's website is working and we'll set you up an email address before I leave."

He looked back down and pulled out four more photos as she disappeared once again. As soon as they were fanned out on his desk, he leaned back in his chair and sucked in a deep breath. If this was going to work, he couldn't have another cold war, this time with his employee. They had to communicate.

His cell phone fired again - Caroline.

"Hey Sis. Is everything okay?" he asked.

"You didn't listen to my message?"

"No, not yet," he mumbled.

"Oh, good. Just delete it. I have something you're going to want to see. I can't explain over the phone."

"What's this all about?"

"I don't want to tell you. I want your unbiased opinion. I want to send you something in the mail today. Just let me know what you think? You'll understand when you see it."

"Should I be worried?"

She sighed deeply into the phone, "No. It's..., you'll understand. What's your office address?"

Nathan spouted the information from memory and waited for something equally as cryptic.

"How's your first day going?" she asked.

"My...?"

"With Lisa. Your first official work day?" she asked.

"Oh. It got off to a late start," he grunted.

"Oh no, trouble in paradise?" she asked.

"You know me. Give me pudding mix and I'll make concrete."

Nathan thought he heard a stifled cough or a laugh, then the little bell over the front door jingled.

"Aw…, I'm sorry. Allie fell in love with her," said Caroline.

"So did…, Hey, it's a long story. Can we talk about it later?" he said, lowering his voice. "I think I have a visitor. Talk to you soon."

Nathan stood quickly to peer over the carpeted partition, but the office was empty.

CHAPTER THIRTY-TWO

A cup of hot coffee swam into Nathan's view, just short of his day planner.

"Truce?" asked Lisa.

"Truce," nodded Nathan. "Thanks."

Truce or not, even with the offering of hot coffee, the atmosphere felt much cooler in the office. After lunch, Nathan explained how the software worked, which his brother-in-law Chris had crafted for his business. How it matched and qualified buyers to properties based on their questionnaire on the website or in person. It was how he managed to operate a private realty all alone; one that normally would staff at least three people or more.

Lisa was walking out the door with the new laptop in her leather shoulder bag when his first client arrived.

The couple was smiling and eager, which was a good indicator, then sat and talked with Nathan for at least an hour while Nathan pitched three potential photo spreads.

As predicted, they wanted to see each one.

Nathan grabbed his blazer, reached in his pocket for his keys....

"No," he sighed.

He reached in his pocket for his cell phone and came to the cold realization that there wasn't a single solitary soul that he could call.

Lisa was probably at work, his closest family member was at least an hour's drive away. Yet here he stood, with close to nine hundred thousand dollars in semi-liquid assets and a steadily growing business, but not a soul to rely on in a pinch. Money was truly not everything.

It was shoring up to be a great day for a pity party.

His first official day at the new office and he had to lie through his teeth about his car being in the shop. All he had to do was hop in the Yukon this morning. Once again, he had let his emotions dictate his reasoning. The entire rationale for Lisa coming by that morning was to drop him off to get his car at the Blind Pirate. Even that would have been fruitless; the little Cadillac was built for two, not escorting clients to view homes.

Surprisingly enough, viewings with both clients turned out well.

At seven that evening, he flipped the 'open' sign around and walked down the street to a little bistro still serving Italian food.

A merciless wind was whipping the green and white striped awning above the door even though the threatening clouds hadn't produced more than a few sprinkles all day.

He was seated just long enough to open a menu when he received a text message:

> Coming to get you. There in 30 minutes.

It was from Lisa. She'd finally realized what happened or maybe she was through punishing him for whatever evil he'd thrust upon her.

Nathan ordered something to drink, then walked back to the office. True to her word, Lisa arrived a little later and sat there still as a statue inside her car. He turned off all the lights except for the one over the front window, streaming with its thick green vine, before locking the door.

Without a word, he slipped inside the old Buick.

Lisa was in her dowdy uniform, apron still attached, order pad dangling out of one of the pockets. Even her ponytail was hipshot with stray strands of soft brunette hair dangling over her ears.

"Say something," she whispered.

"Thanks?" he mumbled, then shrugged.

"That's all? I'd be so..., so..., mad," she grunted.

'What brought on this change of heart?' he wondered.

"I just want to get my car and go home."

The Buick cranked immediately and she backed out.

"Just out of curiosity; when did you realize I was without transportation?"

She couldn't look him in the eye.

"Troy asked me where you were when you didn't show up at your usual time," she confessed. "I know he's pissed. I left in the middle of my shift."

"Next time just call. I could have stayed here until you were off work," he said.

"Next time? You're not going to fire me?" she whined.

"No. I'm not going to fire you," sighed Nathan.

There was a lengthy silence as she navigated out of town.

"Troy was right after all," she muttered.

Nathan was so tired of Troy but at the risk of saying something else he would regret, he only grunted.

"You are different," she said, turning her head to glance at him.

"That's nice to know," he chuckled. "I hope that was a compliment."

He leaned back in the seat and closed his eyes, wishing the last two days away.

"It was. Can we start all over?" asked Lisa. "Not just a truce."

"Sure," mumbled Nathan. He was used to hitting the reset button with his family on a daily basis. Why should she be any different? He sat there on the brink of dozing, wondering if all his personal relationships were doomed to failure.

Lisa stared at the highway for another ten minutes, almost to Crab Cove when she noticed that Nathan was asleep.

It was probably one of the few times she could openly stare at him without him knowing. His sandy brown hair was in bad need of a barber, his jaw hard and set. At least his heavy seven o'clock shadow had finally covered the two places he'd missed shaving that morning. If only she had thought to get a picture with her phone. She smiled. It was only fair after all; he'd let her stand and greet his family for the first time with black war paint covering half her face.

She exited at Crab Cove, turned in the entrance to the diner and parked in back.

Now it was time to go inside and face the music. She shook Nathan's arm, noticing immediately how solid it felt under his perpetual choice of long sleeve dress shirts. Somehow she'd been too preoccupied with getting him home the night before to notice these interesting details.

"Nathan," she tried again. Pushing against the firmness of his chest with her palm only caused his head to loll away from her. Her hand took it's time sliding across the top of his button down oxford shirt, then guiltily snatched away as he shifted.

"Nathan," she hissed louder, gripping his bicep.

Her hand slid back in surprise at the solid mass. There was a lot more than met the eye with Nathan Heart.

His eyes popped open as he gasped in a breath.

"Where are we?" he mumbled.

She swallowed when he turned to look at her. Why did she have to turn to goo every time he looked at her that way?

"The Pirate," she managed.

"Good. I'm starving," he said with a long stretch.

♥

Nathan was almost finished eating when he heard his car keys jingle across the table. Troy stood there staring for a few seconds, but Nathan didn't bother to acknowledge him. He picked up his glass of iced tea to emphasize his alcohol free status.

"Are ya just gonna sit there like a wife holding a grudge?" asked Troy.

Nathan looked up, "Yep."

"I see you and Lisa made up with each…."

"Troy. Stop. No more matchmaking. No more schemes. No more plots or hints. Lisa and I are just now back on speaking terms and I'd like to keep it that way," said Nathan.

Troy grunted, nodded thoughtfully, then walked away.

"Well, that was a first," smiled Nathan.

He took his keys, paid his way out, and made it all the way to his car, when Lisa came bustling out the back door. She skidded to a stop a few feet away looking like someone that had forgotten what they were after.

"I guess I'll see you Wednesday?" she asked.

"Nine sharp," he grinned.

"Call if you need a ride," she chuckled. Lisa wiped her hands down the front of her apron, smiled and hurried back inside.

One of the cottages beside the Manor was lit, the other dark when Nathan parked in the garage. He carefully inspected all the stalls for more surprises before going inside.

Bolton was seated in the living room waiting. It was late.

"I see you made the trip alone tonight," said Bolton.

"Were you actually waiting up for me?" asked Nathan.

"These things have a way of repeating themselves."

"True, but I made you a promise."

"You did. Ms. Stewart said you were a man of your word."

"You talked to Madeline today?" asked Nathan.

Bolton stood and stretched, "For a few minutes."

"You didn't happen to mention…, my little incident last night did you?" said Nathan, shaking his head hopefully.

"No, only about the intruder and how helpful you were," he grinned.

"How's the hand?" asked Nathan.

Bolton made a fist a few times, "Same as always."

He was becoming the king of ambiguity.

"Ms. Stewart asked me to remind you that she and her party will be arriving Wednesday. She also suggested that you might want to invite a guest for the Thanksgiving Dinner with her family."

Madeline Stewart was at it again. She wasn't only suspicious of Lindsey's act, she was going to find a way to rout her out. If he invited a lady as a dinner companion, the cat would be out of the bag, claws extended.

"I suppose you mentioned that my family visited," hinted Nathan.

DAVID PYLE

Bolton chuckled, "…and a certain young lady."

"My assistant and secretary," said Nathan.

"She seemed…, a little more intrigued by you to only be an employee."

Bolton was instantly elevated in status, from handyman, to spy.

Denial would only bring further suspicion on his relationship with Lisa and more suspicion on Lindsey and whatever scheme she was perpetrating to her Aunt Madeline.

"There might be some underlying feelings. We've known each other for some time now," said Nathan. "My closest family is going to be on a cruise that week. I suppose Lisa would make a good plus one if she doesn't already have plans."

Bolton suddenly looked brighter. Maybe he was feeling out their relationship for more selfish reasons. If he spent any time with her last night, he was no doubt attracted to her. He'd be a fool not to. Despite that, Nathan didn't feel it was right for this stranger to be referring to Lisa as if she were a pawn to push around on a chessboard.

"I think she would be a very good choice," said Bolton.

Nathan grinned inside.

"That might be true. Maybe I've been so close to Lisa I've overlooked her true feelings for me," he nodded, thoughtfully. "Thanks Bolton. I'll see if she's game."

Bolton's light went out. He was suddenly tired and ready to trot out to his private quarters.

Nathan couldn't help but laugh when the front door closed behind him.

CHAPTER THIRTY-THREE

TUESDAY seemed to inch by, deluged by rain, cooped up in the Heart Realty office alone. Nathan finished sorting and filing, shifting all the previous years' sales to the back of the office. Later, it could all be used as data for Chris Masters to manipulate and massage. For now, it was heavy, ugly, and taking up space.

Lisa called and checked in, mostly to find another excuse to use her elaborate cell phone. At least she was in a good humor.

Caroline was silent and no mystery mail had arrived through the office door's mail slot.

Wednesday morning it was as if someone had lit a fire under three house elves. Food was already in the oven when he walked in the kitchen, yet none of the usual breakfast assortment. He made his own coffee, which he actually missed doing, then grabbed a bagel with some strawberry cream cheese. The front curtains were letting in the first morning rays of light as he sat on the grand sofa with his breakfast and notes.

Not a soul appeared or spoke a word, but he could hear them bustling from here to there. If Madeline Stewart and her bunch were on their way, if they arrived before he left, he would be late once again to his own personal responsibilities.

He stuffed the last two bites of bagel down, drank half the cup of coffee in a gulp and hurried to get his blazer and office gear.

When he was only a quarter mile up the road, two long black limousines passed him in some sort of funeralistic entourage. Nathan blessed himself a dozen times for his stroke of genius.

DAVID PYLE

Maybe it was a little antisocial, but the last thing he wanted was to play the role of blushing suitor to Lindsey and witty conversationalist to Madeline Stewart until ten that morning.

If not for his empathetic feelings for Lindsey, he would have never allowed himself to be trapped in that role in the first place. He determined to find a way to end that charade and give Lindsey what she wanted, whether it be right or wrong. She was old enough to make her own life choices.

He was surprised, relieved, even pleased to see Lisa Evans park beside him moments after he arrived in Salem.

He hurried out and unlocked the office and she rushed in behind him out of a misting rain.

"Is this sharp enough for you?" she asked.

"Couldn't be better," he said catching his breath.

It was almost impossible for him to take his eyes off her for those first few moments. When he did manage to look away, he remembered last night's conversation with Bolton.

The only problem with the plan he was conceiving was the fact that Lisa had already turned him down for a date and the infamous brick wall was in place.

"Had breakfast yet?" he asked.

She shook her head shyly.

He fingered some cash out of his wallet and forced her next door with a promise to bring him something with mass amounts of espresso when she was finished.

Lisa was becoming his personal enigma. She wasn't only shy to his advances, he hardly knew anything about her. She wasn't the sort to readily open up and share little bits and pieces of herself to anyone.

He unpacked his older model Digital SLR camera, cleaned the lenses, and removed all the old photos from memory. One of the legs to the tripod was hinky, but still usable for training. Nathan was wrapping the unruly joint with duct tape when Lisa returned with his large cappuccino drizzled with caramel.

"It must be camera day."

"There's not a lot to it if you develop an eye for what people want to see," said Nathan, tearing off the end of the tape.

He handed her a couple of dozen eight by ten photos, both color and black and white.

"Take a look at these and tell me what you see," he grinned, "...besides houses."

"You know how to take all the fun out of the morning."

Nevertheless, she skipped through the stack and waited.

"Well?" he asked.

"I'm not sure what you want me to say."

"Look outside, tell me what you see," he grunted, as he tightened the camera to the top of the tripod.

She shrugged, "The usual dreary day."

He set the ensemble up and tested its stability, "Very good. Now look at the photos again."

"Sunshine, blue skies, glitter?" she asked.

Nathan nodded and fiddled with the Nikon's controls, "Blast. The batteries went dead."

He slid a chair closer and motioned for her to sit.

"Okay. When we take a photo spread, it needs to look like the all-American dream. That's what we're selling. Do you see any small three or four-bedroom starter homes in the mix?"

Lisa stared, "They're all monstrous."

"And that's because we don't contract to small houses or even larger ones that are in a depreciated neighborhood."

"Uppity houses?"

Nathan laughed at the same reference his landlord had used.

"When you take a photo spread, make sure you can see the neighborhood around it. If you take a picture of just the front and sides like some catalog selling a car part, our customers will skip right past. And they won't even realize why they did."

"Wait. You're not planning on getting me in a swimsuit to stand out in front of these are you?" she grinned.

"If it would help sell it I might," he chuckled, "...I'll keep that in mind."

"Don't get your hopes up," she grunted. "So we're selling the pretty car..., parked in front of a beach..., with a hunk standing in the background."

"If we're selling to that target audience. You're catching on."

"Then what's the big deal?" she asked.

"The big deal is, its going to be your responsibility to take the photos we're going to use and I want you to get an eye for it," he tapped his head. "Up here."

She dropped the pictures on the desk, "Some of these don't look much like a dream to me."

"That's because it's always cloudy or raining. If by some miracle the sun shines, I try to rush out and update the ones with bad photos. But I can't always do that if I'm busy trying to sell to a client or bogged down at the title company, the finance company, the court house; you get the idea."

"You want to pay me to get out in the sunshine and take pictures...," she grinned. "I'm liking this job more every day."

Nathan shook his head, "It'll get old."

Explaining the camera only took ten minutes, everything on it was automatic, which pleased Lisa to no end.

She rushed out, bought batteries, and began to take pictures of everything in sight for over an hour.

When she had finally run aground, bored with her new toy, she came back and plopped down in one of the chairs in front of his desk.

"That wasn't so difficult, was it?" he asked.

"Okay, you made your point smart guy. What's next?"

"The next sunny afternoon I'd like for you to be ready to take a photo of the both of us, standing in front of our office for a local Ad."

"Our picture? In the Salem paper?"

Lisa's eyes drew large and fearful.

"Take the camera, practice with the timer and get used to it. You'll do just fine."

He handed her the camera's hard shell case.

"As a matter of fact, why don't you take it with you during the Thanksgiving holiday and get pictures of your family?"

Her practiced gleeful expression went blank.

"You mean while I'm eating turkey and dressing at the Pirate, don't you?"

"You're not going to visit your parents or relatives?" he prodded.

"Ha!" she spat. "My foster parents kicked me out when I turned seventeen. It's a miracle I finished school. I'm not taking a bus all the way back to Michigan to see them."

"I'm...," he began.

Her hand flew up, "Don't..., dare..., say you're sorry."

This wasn't what Nathan expected at all. Evidently, Troy made a habit of salvaging every hard luck traveler that passed his way as an employee.

"Alright, I won't," he said. "My family aren't exactly model citizens most of the time."

"You're kidding me right?" she grinned. "The ones I met were like the Cleaver's."

Nathan grinned, "You and Allie seemed to hit it off right away. She's really fascinated with you for some reason."

"The little one. Yeah, she's a real cutie," said Lisa, ignoring his jab. "And the older girl..., she's beautiful."

"Kate," said Nathan. "And my sister's name is...."

"Caroline..., yeah I remember. You're..., you're all like carbon copies of each other."

Lisa's comment almost sounded sad. She stared blankly into space until Nathan pushed for a little more information.

"Actually, I'm in kind of a similar situation; about the holiday. Caroline and her family are going...," he stammered for the right words. "They're taking a weeks vacation during Thanksgiving. I've been invited to spend the holiday with the people that own the house where I'm living and listen to a business proposition of some sort."

Lisa chuckled, "How is that similar?"

"Well..., I won't get to see my family either. As a matter of fact," he added cautiously. "I was just informed that I was expected to bring along someone else."

"Like a date," she said, her eyes arching suspiciously.

"I suppose. Since you're not obligated, why don't you come along as my...."

"Date?" she finished, her body stiffening.

"Well..., as my executive assistant," said Nathan.

"Your secretary, you mean," she corrected.

Nathan grinned, "You're a lot more than a secretary and we both know it. I could make it a condition for your employment. After all it is business related."

Lisa smiled back, "I can quit."

"I think it would be a good way to introduce you to the type of people that spend...."

"Yeah, yeah, big spenders," she grunted, shaking her head.

"...people that spend a lot of time traveling the world," he corrected. "These people don't assert themselves as better than anyone else, but they have experiences that you seem intelligent enough to absorb without them knowing. More importantly, these are the kind of people that we work for, the ones that buy our properties..., and pay your salary. And I'd like you to be there."

Lisa twitched at the hidden compliment, then received it quietly.

"And just how is this supposed to be anything more than a slick way for you to get a date with me?" she asked.

Nathan shrugged, "I guess it's not."

Lisa laughed and stared up at the ceiling for a second.

"I know I'm going to regret this," she sighed, shaking her head. "I can feel it already."

"Does that mean you'll join me?" he asked.

"I'll give you an 'E' for effort Nathan Heart. I guess I'll join you."

"Oh, there's one more thing you should know. Dress is formal."

CHAPTER THIRTY-FOUR

DESPITE Lisa's instant about-face, Nathan managed to calm her down before her two o'clock departure. Her new objection was using the last of her savings to purchase an expensive dress that she would likely only wear once, then hang in her closet for the moths to eat.

Nathan quickly explained that since it was a business related venture, that he could take care of the expense and write off most of it on his taxes. It probably wasn't entirely true, but it seemed to calm some sudden fear of Lisa's, which Nathan didn't understand, until he probed deeper.

During the process of spooning out information, he learned much more about Troy than he did Lisa.

All but one of Troy's employees were either transients, vagrants, or lost people looking for a place to survive.

Troy owned three of the waterfront duplexes, one of which Lisa currently lived in. For the employees Troy believed had 'potential', he would front them money for their first months rent and let them pay it out in half their weekly salary. That was where his altruistic nature dimmed.

He was also a convenient payday loan shark to those same people that relied on him for food and a dry place to lay their heads. Lisa had been fortunate enough, a penny pincher by nature, not to get into the perpetual debt cycle dangled in front of her nose month after month. She was in effect the only employee that wasn't an indentured slave to the borrow-pay-borrow cycle.

Nathan stood staring out his front window, remembering the little skip in Lisa's step as she hurried to her car and the way she'd childishly stuck out her tongue at him when she caught him watching. He admired her stamina and resourcefulness, her willingness to learn and her refusal to alter her standards. He silently hoped her character would be strong enough to withstand meeting Madeline Stewart.

After checking his watch, he felt it was time to see if his character was strong enough for what was facing him back home. It seemed that the longer he was acquainted with Ms. Stewart, the more obligated he was becoming. She was well versed in the subtleties of duty bindings.

♥

Nathan stopped just short of the front steps and affectionately slapped the gargantuan head of one of the guardian stone lions.

"Nice kitty," he smiled and chuckled, his thoughts drifting to Lisa.

Through the large picture window, he saw a blurred glimpse of blond hair disappear just before the front door opened.

"Hello, Mr. Heart," said Lindsey.

"Hello to you," he nodded. "May I come in?"

She stepped aside and helped him off with his blazer. Nathan's eyes were instantly magnetized to her chocolate hued dress; while modestly tailored it still accented her petite frame as well as every curve.

He leaned closer to ask her if they had an audience when she tiptoed and kissed his cheek. Her warm cinnamon fragrance crashed his senses forcing him to relive some fringe memory he couldn't quite recall. Thankfully, Lindsey didn't notice how distracting she had become.

"Didn't see that coming," he grinned, then whispered. "Are we alone?"

"It's good to see you too," she cheered a little louder, which meant they were both under a microscope at that moment.

She placed his blazer on a newly positioned coat rack just past the vestibule and hooked a hand on his arm to draw him inside.

Two of the several small conversation pits were occupied with family members in some sort of didactic mumbling convention. The closest was a pair of older gentlemen dressed for the theater. If not for his tie and starched oxford shirt, Nathan would have felt completely out of place.

"Nathan these are a few of my Uncles..., Albert and George. This is Nathan Heart."

Albert was portly, but had a brilliance in his eyes..., that of a snake. George was thin and tall and seemed oblivious; an ornate black cane with a heavy silver head hooked over his thigh.

The two men stood stiffly, shook his hand and grunted something that sounded like, "A pleasure."

Both instantly dropped back into their seats and began where they left off with their conversation.

Before Nathan could formulate an opinion, Lindsey was pulling him to the next pit of vipers. Vipers because all four ladies had the patented Madeline Stewart stare on their faces, trained exclusively on him and Lindsey.

DAVID PYLE

"Everyone, this is Nathan," she chirped, then pointed in succession around at the group. "Adelaide, Percy, Yvonne, and Carmen; a few of my aunts."

Nathan nodded, tried to smile, while the women perused him from nose to wingtip. All four ladies were in detailed dress, pearls, glittering broaches, and hinted strongly of rose balm and jasmine.

Finally, the first, Adelaide, tilted her head, "Madeline has spoken very highly of you Mr. Heart. Something she rarely does…, it's a pleasure."

Her inflection hinged on gelid, but was softened somehow by her unusual dialect. The other ladies then spoke in turn and it was impossible to miss that Adelaide was the leader of this hens nest and there was a pecking order being observed.

It was incredibly disconcerting how each of their eyes seemed to dart and plunge into his like soft daggers. Flattery and accusation glittered from their twitching smiles and short conversation.

Nathan was in the middle of attempting small talk when Lindsey tugged him away, "I'll let you all talk to Nathan later."

Nathan scanned the room quickly and noticed the white floral divan where Madeline always frequented was empty. There was no doubt in his mind that it had something to do with an invisible hierarchy in the seating arrangement.

Two of the ladies smiles followed him, containing something secret as he was quickly led down the hall toward the library. A young lady dressed in black slacks and white blouse bustled past balancing a tray of cups and a silver carafe. Another house swain no doubt; he was surprised she wasn't wearing a bonnet and apron.

Lindsey ignored her as if she were a specter and stepped even faster until she reached a hall cubby just outside the den.

Lindsey snatched him to the wall, looked both directions, before she whispered, "You passed the first inspection, but be careful around my Aunt Sibyl. She's…, well…, different and Aunt Madey trusts her judgment on almost everything."

"Wait…," he grunted.

"We'll talk later. I promise I'll explain everything."

"Lindsey dear?"

Nathan needed no introductions to the familiarity of that voice.

"Coming!" chirped Lindsey, while facing the opposite direction.

"Now just remember, try to relax and be yourself. You'll do fine," she hissed, pulling Nathan back into motion.

Instead of finding closure with his entanglement, the ball of yarn was getting more tangled by the second.

MINUTES

Madeline was seated under a drooping umbrella lamp, next to a short squat lady at least ten years her senior. Both were leaning over a leather bound book in this new relative's lap.

"Mr. Heart, good of you to join us," smiled Madeline.

Her hand made an unconscious swipe to a glittering broach on the lapel of her jacket; something akin to petting the back of a child's head.

"Has the situation with your family resolved itself?" she asked.

Nathan nodded, "I believe it has, but I should know more in a few weeks. I appreciate your insight and the way you diffused the matter."

Madeline, flicked a hand, "It was the least I could do."

The other lady, sat with kind expressionless eyes, gazing up at Nathan, supposedly waiting for an introduction.

"Aunt Sibyl, this is Nathan," said Lindsey, with a gentle push on his arm toward her.

Nathan put out a hand and she took it..., and held on.

Instead of the usual hello, she reached up and sandwiched his hand between her soft wrinkled palms, delicately testing some unknown.

"I see Lindsey has made you welcome," said Madeline, while Sibyl continued to pet his hand.

Lindsey blushed, then snatched a little kerchief from her waist and wiped away a trace of pink lipstick from Nathan's cheek.

Sibyl patted, then released his hand with a smile.

He felt Lindsey's grip on his other arm suddenly relax. He hadn't even noticed her grip had tightened almost uncomfortably.

"It's a pleasure to meet you, Mr. Heart," Sibyl wheezed. "I'm Sibyl Bale."

It was obviously a struggle for her to speak, but her voice was the only pleasant one he'd experienced from the lot of them.

"Likewise," he answered. "Were you reading one of the relics from your library?"

Madeline answered for Sibyl with a chuckle, "*Reading...*, yes..., Sibyl was reading this one for me. It has quite an interesting history."

When she didn't elaborate on her odd insinuation, Nathan felt sudden relief and backed away closer to Lindsey.

"Did Henry make the trip with you?" asked Nathan, hurrying to divert the sudden silence.

"Henry will be joining us this weekend. He's busy tending to a few last minute acquisitions," said Madeline.

"He's in Panama," grunted Lindsey, her inflection cold. "Another artifact."

"I'm surprised you didn't go there with him," said Nathan. He knew Lindsey hated to travel.

183

"The sunshine there is a little toasty for my pale complexion," she answered, a little too quickly.

It seemed that there was some new contention gnawing between Lindsey and Madeline's already fragile relationship. Either that or the ruse simply wasn't working. They had only spoken to each other a handful of times on the phone and Lindsey was always the one that called.

"I promised Henry a trip to a few of my haunts the next time he visited," said Nathan. "I'm glad he'll be coming."

Madeline held her relaxed expression without fault, but Nathan knew she remembered his offer to take Henry to the Blind Pirate, a local bar; something she considered a crass establishment.

"I'm sure Henry will be ready for some relaxation when he arrives," she smiled.

"Well…, if you ladies will excuse me. It's been a long day and I need to shed my baggage and change."

"I'll go with you," said Lindsey.

"Do you need to help Nathan change?" asked Madeline, coldly.

Nathan expected Lindsey to slash back, but instead, "I thought I'd walk Nathan back to his room and allow us a chance to get reacquainted for a few moments Aunt Madey."

Lindsey had far more restraint than he gave her credit for. He wondered if he should push the unknown boundaries of his relationship and step in for her defense. Absolutely not, this was a family matter; the sharp words were only symptoms of some unspoken deeper problem.

"As long as its only talk," she grunted, then turned her attention back to the book in Sibyl's lap.

"What else would it be?" Lindsey muttered, turning quickly.

Nathan felt his arm gently twist as Lindsey escorted him out of the room. He was glad to be free from the sudden oppression he felt lingering in the air.

CHAPTER THIRTY-FIVE

WHEN they traversed the living room, Lindsey made a grand spectacle of slowly parading Nathan up the gently curving stairs. It was yet another performance of some sort that he was getting more and more uncomfortable with.

Two more ladies in black slacks and white blouses swept past them as they hurried to Nathan's room.

Lindsey shoved the bedroom door open and flopped into one of his dressing chairs.

"Oh God she makes me so angry," blurted Lindsey.

Nathan perched against his door facing in thought, "Lindsey, why don't you just come out and remind your aunt that you're a grown woman. You have a right to make decisions for yourself. It's the only way you and your friend Jon will ever survive."

"If only it were that easy," she laughed quietly.

"I know it's none of my business, but why can't it be that easy?" he shrugged.

"Money. If Aunt Madey doesn't approve of my choice in friends, as my sole guardian she can withhold my Trust until I'm an old maid," she answered, her voice fading to barely a whisper.

"Lindsey, money isn't everything. What about this Jon? Surely he has resources."

She shook her head, "No..., bless his heart, he's a mooch, just like Henry says he is."

Tears were welling in her eyes about to spill down her cheeks.

Nathan picked up a small mirror from his dresser and held it up to her face.

"Lindsey…, have you taken a good look at your reflection lately?" he asked. "You could have your choice of suitors."

She slapped it away, "What does it matter?"

Lindsey was in love. Nothing would do except this Jon person, that everyone except her hated.

"Then I'm afraid you'll have to choose," said Nathan.

She looked up at him with her freckled irises, her round eyes spilling tears, "I think Jon may have already made that decision for me."

♥

Nathan showered and changed, then sat in the privacy of his room deliberating. No matter how much his heart broke for Lindsey, he couldn't keep up this act much longer.

Her friend Jon the Moocher had asked Lindsey for a reprieve. Bluntly put, he'd asked her if they shouldn't see other people, which according to Lindsey had something to do with a young rival named Judith Hammersfield. A young lady with looks and a free spending legacy to go with it… - And it undoubtedly had something to do with her Aunt Madey.

A very simple choice to Nathan, yet it was a desperate situation in Lindsey's mind. He had to place some sort of a time limit on this charade before it negatively impacted his relationship with Ms. Stewart.

Before Lindsey left the room, he stressed to her that they couldn't keep up pretenses much longer, to which Lindsey begged him for a few more days…, a week at the most.

Three soft raps on his latched bedroom door and a muffled voice announced dinner. Without a viable excuse, he was practically obligated to join his host on their first night in the Manor. Again, it would look strange not to attend and at least converse with Madeline's niece.

"Blast," he whispered, snatching his dinner jacket off a hanger.

He wrenched his bedroom door open and almost ran full steam into Annie.

Nathan saved both of them from colliding, "I'm so sorry, I hope I didn't hurt you."

She smiled shyly, "No Sir. I was about to announce dinner."

"Someone already beat you to it," he said, while slipping into his jacket. He realized at that moment, he hadn't seen anything of her or Sara or Bolton the entire evening.

"I don't know how that's possible Sir. All the staff are serving downstairs at the moment."

There was no use arguing, Nathan let it drop, and offering his arm her direction, "Alright, why don't you join me then?"

She ducked her head and retreated a step, "Oh no sir, I couldn't be seen escorting one of the house guests, especially you. Miss Stewart wouldn't like that at all."

"Then we can simply walk together," he shrugged. "No harm in that."

What strange Elizabethan rules were leaking into the air?

"Thank you Sir, but I'd better not," she mumbled, then turned back the other direction.

Nathan shook his head dismally, "It'll be a miracle if I survive the evening."

Lindsey's eyes were the first to set on his, the ones to follow him to the only unclaimed place setting on her left at the dining table. His first internal question was..., who engineered the seating arrangement? At least he was the last on that side and mostly invisible.

The others were already eating some unknown bisque in small cups and mumbling amongst each other, hardly acknowledging him.

There was another new face addressing the table and no one bothered to make introductions. A slim elderly gentleman with graying hair was seated next to Sibyl, most likely her husband. He could have easily been upstairs or wandering the house when he arrived. It was just as well, the whole group seemed quiet and friendly, more like a board meeting of slight acquaintances.

A server stepped up, turned over the cup in front of him and filled it with a creamy broth, maybe split pea soup.

An empty wine glass was perched at the ready by his place setting and a server was making the rounds with an open bottle of deep hued burgundy. Its rich aroma was swimming around the table; that was the last thing he could afford to allow pass his lips this evening. Just looking at the empty glass caused the previous bout of vertigo to clench his gut. He hadn't had that sensation since..., since Lindsey opened the front door. Something like hope sprang up; hope that these episodes weren't entirely the encroaching fringe of mental void.

The lady leaned closer and repeated, "Would you like steak tartare or filet mignon this evening?"

Of course, they had a chef or maybe Sara was more diverse than he first believed.

"Steak tartare," answered. "And could I have tea instead?"

She nodded and left without another word.

"You're late...," breathed Lindsey, barely tilting her head.

Before Nathan could respond, she placed a hand on his arm and forced a careful smile.

"How is your new office?" she asked, her voice was increased to that same reserved utterance as the rest of the solemn assembly.

Office? Nathan hadn't spoken to anyone present regarding his office or any relevant events.

'Ah..., Bolton, the spy', he remembered suddenly.

"As a matter of fact, it's looking promising," he answered. "It's not much to see, but it is in an excellent location."

In his peripheral vision, he saw a glimmer of interest from Madeline, pretending not to notice. It was either lead the conversation or become subjected to an evening of interrogation.

"Please, I'd like to hear more about your life in North Carolina. I haven't traveled much along the east coast," he asked.

He emphasized the 'more' to imply an earlier conversation. And thus, the exchange shifted away from his personal life for the rest of the dinner.

Given a subject, Lindsey was entirely comfortable with face value facts about her childhood and home life. For the most part she and her brother Henry lived an extremely sheltered childhood.

With tutors and private schools, most of their social interaction was restricted to regular church attendance accompanied by the massive family of Uncles, Aunts, and a throng of resultant cousins.

Lindsey played her part perfectly with subtle but continual physical contact; a touch of the hand, turn of the head, playful smile.

College was the first freedom that either of the two siblings had experienced in their first eighteen years..., and then it was time for a subject change. Lindsey grew uncomfortable explaining her newfound freedoms in near proximity to the one person holding a short leash on her present life.

Nathan easily diverted Lindsey's stream of consciousness toward her studies at the exclusive Duke University and her discourse relaxed once again.

Soon their performance was complete and Nathan was able to escape once again, unscathed and unscrutinized by the growing list of questions on Madeline Stewart's face. Their game of chess was still in play and Nathan sensed this was the calm before some well-directed analysis.

Before they left the table, he thought back on the events that started this game of deceit, frustrated that he had initiated the concept, and even moved the first game piece. He grunted to himself, wondering how his cleverly conceived ingenuity would conclude.

CHAPTER THIRTY-SIX

NATHAN dissolved onto his bed, flat of his back, trying not to think…, about anything. He was going to have to plan better, make himself less available and more invisible; after all, he wasn't the host to this gathering. In fact, he'd only agreed to be present for the Thanksgiving Day festivities.

Then there was Lindsey. She was a sweet girl, attractive, and if he allowed himself to dwell on it, precariously desirable.

Another rap on his door caused him to groan and look at the late hour on his watch.

With great effort, he sat up and strolled to the bedroom door. One of the cloned staff members was standing at the door with downcast eyes, "Mr. Heart, Ms. Stewart wishes to speak to you in the library."

She nodded her head and walked away before Nathan could respond.

"Now what?" sighed Nathan.

He didn't bother stepping back in his room, but took off toward the stairs. Avoiding the expanse of the heavily occupied living room, he chose the west hallway and cut through the den into the library.

Madeline was standing at a shelf, perusing the card catalog and Sibyl was seated in the same spot as when they first met. Sibyl placed a book carefully on the table, while there were a half dozen tossed to a heap on the floor beside her chair.

Madeline snatched out a card from the file, tore it in half, then walked back to sit beside Sibyl, only glancing at Nathan.

She sat down and tossed the torn card on the heap of books, "Hello Nathan. Would you please have a seat?"

Her air of command was becoming sickening.

"Mr. Heart, I'll come right to the point. What are your intentions with my niece, Lindsey?"

She propped her elbows on the arms of the wing back chair and laced her spindly fingers waiting for his reply.

Nathan leaned back in his chair and thought, 'Rook takes Pawn'.

"I barely know Lindsey, Ms. Stewart. I'm not sure I understand."

She sighed and closed her eyes, "I think you know exactly what I mean Nathan."

"We have a few common interests…, I find Lindsey interesting."

Her eyes were as piercing as a hawk for several moments.

"I suppose it's possible that you haven't noticed. A man with your upbringing, your stature, your looks; I can see you overlooking the obvious."

Nathan sat quietly, weeding through the compliments, holding back the fumes building inside. She was waiting for a response, waiting for another pawn to steal from this ethereal game.

"Women may fawn over you on a regular basis and you never pay it the least attention," she nodded to herself.

Nathan noticed her pry bar, her 'tool' of flattery pressing at him, "Madeline, I'm not sure where you're going with our conversation. Are you suggesting that something improper is taking place between Lindsey and I?"

Her eyes hooded slightly, "I've only recently had to deal with a bawdy attachment Lindsey formed. I believe Henry explained that situation to you?"

"He did. Madeline, I truly believe you have Lindsey's best interests at heart, but don't you think you should ask Lindsey what she wants?"

"She's too young and impressionable to know what she wants," chuffed Madeline. "Haven't you noticed that my niece has phoned you several times since you first met? She seems to have taken an interest in you."

Nathan shook his head, "And you believe that because our friendship is so comfortable and easy that there must be something more to it. You think she's rebounding?"

"Lindsey is at a vulnerable state and it would be easy for someone to take advantage of her, Nathan. I don't want to believe that you are that sort, but as you so deftly put it, I am in a position of responsibility for her livelihood."

Nathan sat back in his chair, trying to relax. Maybe this was his chance to unleash himself from the game of pretense between him and Lindsey.

"I assure you I have no intentions of causing Lindsey any grief. However, I still believe that you should take into account Lindsey's opinion. In fact, you should probably be having this conversation with her. Personally, I think you've underestimated your niece."

There was a slight grin on Madeline's lips and Nathan wondered what the devil he'd overlooked.

"As a matter of fact..., I have spoken with Lindsey. It seems you've come to understand my niece better than I originally believed. Am I to understand you're considering courting Lindsey?"

Nathan felt his head shake and his mouth opened before he could rein it in, "Is this the dark ages? Do I need permission to be friends with Lindsey?"

"From what I see, your mutual interests have already stepped just beyond mere friendship, Mr. Heart."

What in blazes had Lindsey said? He was suddenly stepping through a minefield. How could he keep Madeline from winning this round?

"Is this your way of asking me to back away?"

"Actually, Mr. Heart, we've come full circle and once again I'm asking you what your intentions are with my niece."

Nathan jumped in immediately, "Certainly nothing disreputable."

Madeline folded her fingers once again, thoughtfully, "I see. So you don't consider Lindsey someone you wish to continue to pursue?"

Continue to pursue? Maybe Madeline did believe their act and this was her way of flushing out the truth! There were too many maybes to make a decision.

"That's not entirely true," said Nathan, carefully weighing his words. "Lindsey and I seem to enjoy each other's company. I don't see any reason to abort our friendship for no good reason at all."

Madeline leaned forward, "I wasn't suggesting that you abort anything Mr. Heart and I see now that you don't intend her any harm. I only want to make sure she doesn't end up even more confused with her current infatuation over you."

Infatuation? Is that what Lindsey said? Or was it Madeline's interpretation? Surely Lindsey hadn't..., she couldn't have.

"I'd have to speak with Lindsey," said Nathan. "In fact I think I should speak with her as soon as possible."

♥

"How do I always manage to do this to myself?" whispered Nathan. His eyes didn't seem to be able to close as he lay in bed staring at dancing shadows of candlelight.

"Every time I try to do the right thing, something always disconnects."

What made matters worse; he could see no malice in Madeline Stewart's intentions. It was likely, actually very likely, that she had something to do with ridding Lindsey of her notorious freeloading suitor, but could he honestly blame her? Perhaps he had misread Madeline and Lindsey's hushed confrontations as a continual carping into Lindsey's personal affairs.

His true error was placing himself in the mix with his innocent proposal to help Lindsey past her distresses concerning her aunt and guardian.

Of course, Lindsey was already tucked away in her room across the hall from him, unavailable after his jousting match with Madeline. He couldn't exactly go beating on her door and demanding answers, at least not until in the morning.

Actually, the entire day wasn't a total wash. He had coerced Lisa into accepting his invitation and tomorrow he'd find a way to have dinner in Crab Cove away from all the confusion. Tomorrow was without obligation to anyone inside this household, except himself.

Nathan heard more mumbling and shuffling down the hallway, back and forth. Did these people never sleep? Of course he had no idea if it was the Stewart family or the helpers transversing the halls.

With all the older Stewart family member's arrival, the eldest and least mobile had occupied all four of the downstairs bedrooms, forcing Lindsey to the upstairs quarters with a few of the other family.

Sleep graced him without the slightest hint, then hurled him into some transfixed dreamscape which occluded all reasoning. One flicker of light opened his dreamer's eyes to a lingering conversation with Lindsey; the next twitch of candlelight was accompanied with the brush of her lips on his. Every force of his will was suddenly freefalling, Lindsey's hands sliding along his bare chest.

As quickly as it seemed it had started, he awoke with a gasp, throwing away the covers to assure himself that he was both awake and in *his* bed.

His breath came in gulps, trying to clear his mind, to regain some sort of control.

Moments later, he heard a quick chirp, a muffled sound of fright, then footsteps coming down the hall outside his door. Muffled voices, female, frightened, were a rapid-fire conversation just across the hallway.

"Come down here sweetheart, you can stay in my room tonight," said a voice that sounded very much like the tranquil Sibyl.

He heard a solitary soft whimper as the mumbling retreated and the house once again became silent. Carefully, he leaned his ear away from the bedroom door, not realizing that he'd even rushed over to press against it.

Once Nathan's heartbeat had slowed to something just short of a stroke, he sat back down into the comfort of his bed. He'd never felt such a loss of control either awake or while sleeping. He'd never experienced such vivid emotions sweeping him away and in that moment he'd never wanted it so badly.

He ran his fingers through his hair, tugging carefully, felt the heated blush on his cheeks while trying to make sense of it all. What had prompted such a vivid escapade? Did he have some sort of repressed subconscious desire for Lindsey Stewart? Was this all the result of the building scenario brokered between himself and Madeline Stewart? It seemed so real…, it had to be more than just dreamscape.

Just before he allowed himself to inch toward that horror he'd been ignoring, that possibility of mental instability, he remembered that he wasn't the only one affected by the house phantasm.

What had awakened the occupant in the bedroom across the hall…, most likely Lindsey herself? Why was she frightened? Could Madeline Stewart actually be correct?

Was the old Heart Manor haunted?

CHAPTER THIRTY-SEVEN

WARM inviting lights were flowing out the front glass panes of the coffee shop as Nathan arrived in Salem. Traffic would soon be streaming inside, as soon as all the chairs finished turning onto the freshly mopped floor.

His abrupt exit of the old Manor shocked even himself. With only a few hours of torrid sleep, he'd showered and dressed, hurrying out the door at barely five in the morning.

Maddening silence greeted him as he situated his desk for the upcoming day's business. Silence that lent purchase to a repeating of the previous nights questions.

As soon as there was an influx of traffic next door, he exited his office and hurried for some breakfast. He tried to sit there, nibbling, sipping hot coffee, staring out the coffee shop window into the bleak drizzly morning. Instead, he threw away the remains of his half-eaten breakfast sandwich, asked for more dark roast coffee and hurried next door.

The tiny bell above his door made him shiver and he quickly turned and locked the door behind himself. He left the room in near darkness as he sank into his chair, propping his feet on the cluttered desk.

It was just a dream, he kept repeating to himself as he slowly dozed off into oblivion.

The blaring of a car horn in the street awakened him at nearly ten a.m. and he sat up slowly, still gripping the unspilled cup of coffee resting on his chest.

His hand was sorely stiff as he wiggled his fingers back to life, amazed that he hadn't given himself a lukewarm java bath.

When he stood, he noticed immediately that all the traffic in the street had their headlights on in the gloomy day, with wind sprayed mist covering the foggy glass window.

Nathan flipped on the all the lights, blinding himself in the process, then hurried back behind the front partition to crunch into his chair. It was while he was clearing his desk that he noticed three photos printed with their own laser printer, sitting in his inbox.

One was the front of the Heart Realty office, the other was of the statue in the town square, the last one of him busy at his desk. Sometime during the previous evening, Lisa had dropped by and left them, he supposed to show off her increasing talents with the digital camera. Something about it brought an immediate smile.

The loud clank of brass on the front door grabbed his attention, then a single tap on the door. The mailman waved an unseen salute in the front window, making his rounds downtown at just before noon.

He took one more look at Lisa's handiwork and grunted his way to the mail-trap on the door. Inside it was the usual flyers, their first official bill, and a large manilla envelope from Caroline Masters. Finally, he would get to see what had caused all the excitement from his sister's phone call.

He tossed the extemporaneous mail in Lisa's inbox and slid open the large envelope.

It was several copies of the photo of himself, Caroline, Allie, Kate and Chuck standing in the mist of rain in front of the old Manor. An immediate smile creased his face as he warmed to each of their faces. They looked so happy all together. Caroline was in true form, Allie hugged close to her front. Then he remembered Lisa's comment about how beautiful Kate was…, and of course, Chuck had on his usual mischievous grin.

He picked up his phone to call Caroline, looking for a place on the wall to mount the eight by ten landscape photo. What could possibly have been so blustering and mysterious about this? He dropped the first picture on his desk, then looked at the next. It was a closer cropped photo of their collective smiling faces, even more reason for the happy swelling inside him. The third photo was another close up, another cropped section of the front of the house, with someone standing in one of the tall window panels beside the front door.

It seemed a little out of focus and he held the picture up against the lamp behind his desk for a better look. Nathan's stomach tightened and he slowly dropped his cell phone back to his desk and held the photograph with shaky hands. He swallowed and inhaled slowly, then saw there was another photo beneath the one he was viewing. It too slipped to his desk and he was now viewing a close up of just the window panel and the blurred but unmistakable image…, of Marion Heart.

Nathan fell into his chair with a chunk and felt that horrible swimming of his consciousness once again. Attached to the top of the photo was a note from Caroline; Call Me.

He stared at the image of his deceased mother for several minutes, at the shape of the grandfather clock in the background.

Marion Heart was standing there, translucent, a distant gaze in her eyes, turned toward the group of them in the middle of the circle drive.

Was this some sort of prank, perpetrated by his nephew Chuck? Surely he wouldn't be that calloused. Surely Chuck would know how horribly this might affect him, knowing all that had transpired over the last few years.

Surely.

Nathan dropped the picture and wiped his jittery hands on his trousers, then snatched up his cell phone.

Caroline answered after the first ring, "Nathan?"

He felt his breath hiss, "I'm here."

"You received my envelope."

"I'm looking at it now."

Caroline breathed deeply, "Do you need a moment?"

"Is this a prank Caroline? Because if it is I don't see the humor…."

"It's not a prank, Nathan," she answered. "I was the one that carried the camera to get the pictures printed at the photo store. Allie's the one that asked me who the lady by door was. That's when I enlarged that section. Nathan? What does this mean?"

"Mean?" he heard himself answer. "Maybe there was someone standing by the window when the picture was taken…."

Out of the three advance visitors, neither Sara nor Allie looked anything like the person standing there; even if it was one of them, there was no way they could make themselves transparent.

"No Nathan…, that's Marion. I'd bet all I possess on it."

"What do you want me to say Caroline? That the house I'm living in is haunted by our deceased mother?"

The very words from his mouth awakened memories of conversations not too distant; of Madeline Stewart's accusations, Lindsey's frightful announcement, and even Annie, the shy young lady almost in tears rushing down the staircase. The voices.

"Nathan? Are you still there?" asked Caroline.

She'd been talking, but there was only a dull echo in his mind.

"Y…, yes…, I'm here. I don't have an answer for you, Caroline. But it might actually mean that I'm not losing my mind."

♥

Nathan asked his sister to keep the entire incident a secret for the time being. Although she pressed him for an explanation for his sudden admission, he put her off, with promises of future clarity. There was no way that he could toss such a basket of the ethereal at her. Maybe there was a logical explanation.

He stacked the photos on his desk, opting for a walk to lunch in the misting cold rain to clear his head. It was just then he remembered that he hadn't even asked how Josie was doing or when she'd get to go home from the hospital. He still hadn't heard a peep out of Jonas or Rachael, but that wasn't anything out of the ordinary. Hell hadn't frozen over quite yet.

His back was turned when he heard a tap tapping on the glass paned door.

The wispy slim figure of a blond lady was cupping her hands against the foggy glass peering inside. He rushed and turned the latch and Lindsey Stewart rushed inside.

"Nathan," she smiled. "About to go eat..., I hope?"

She gave him a quick hug and turned to gently shake away the water droplets rolling off her cape.

"Lindsey. Yes I was. How did you find my office?" he asked.

"Downtown's not that big. I stopped and asked," she shrugged. "Everyone pointed across the street and..., here I am."

She looked around at the walls, the pictures, eyeing the decorative front desk with increased scrutiny.

"So this is your office," she said. There was no hint of disdain or sarcasm, as he would have expected from her aunt.

She hurried past him and peered down the long chute toward the unlit back area. Her smile brightened his mood until visions of Lindsey in the previous nights dream invaded his thoughts. That was when he felt her hand resting lightly on his arm, as if holding on while peeking over a tall cliff.

"A little spooky back there, don't you think?" she grinned.

"We just moved in. I have partitions yet to put up," said Nathan nervously.

"You were gone when I woke up this morning and I wanted to see you. I need to thank you for going out on a limb for me Nathan.

And..., I want you to know that you don't have to pretend any longer. I confessed that our show of affection wasn't real."

Nathan stared in shock for a moment, amazed at her sudden admission of bravery.

"Don't worry. I told Aunt Madey that it was all my idea," she continued. "There was no reason to get you in dutch with her."

Madeline was bluffing last night? Or worse..., Madeline didn't believe her niece at all. Her denial may have been viewed no differently than when she'd refused to admit the boyfriend she truly cared for.

"Are you sure she believed you?" asked Nathan.

Lindsey's eyes squinted, "Is there some reason why she wouldn't?"

"I spoke with your aunt last night in the library. She asked me point blank what my intentions were concerning you."

Lindsey's eyes widened, the overhead florescent light causing her iris' to glitter like diamonds.

"And what did you say to her?" she asked quietly.

"That I saw no good reason why we shouldn't be friends," he answered, "…and that I had no intentions of causing you any grief."

She nodded quietly, suddenly nibbling at her bottom lip, "Then there's no more reason to worry. We can just be ourselves around each other."

Her voice seemed a little sad. "Did I say something wrong…, to your aunt?" asked Nathan.

Lindsey smiled and shrugged, "Would it matter? Why don't you take me out for lunch?"

Nathan grabbed his phone from his desk just as Lindsey reached for something out of the corner of his eye.

"What a sweet picture," she sighed, looking at the group photograph. "When did you take this?"

Nathan tried to hide his nervousness, tried to take it from her hands, but her catlike reaction shifted at the waist causing his body to collide with hers.

"Who are they?" she asked cheerfully.

Nathan sighed, hoping that she wouldn't see the other photos.

"My nephew took the picture a day or so before you arrived," he answered, then pointed and gave each face a name and relation.

Even quicker, she flipped through the stack, ending with the closeup of the wispy image of Marion Heart.

Lindsey stopped, stared, then shivered and chirped, that same chirp he'd heard last night through his door.

"Jesus!"

She tossed the stack of photos on Nathan's desk as if the paper burned her hand.

She spun and looked up at Nathan, "That's the lady I saw in my dream last night."

CHAPTER THIRTY-EIGHT

NATHAN feigned ignorance of the entire ordeal from the previous night while Lindsey poured out the last of some dream she'd experienced. There was no way that he could hint any reciprocating portion of his dream, consisting entirely of vivid emotions and tactile urges that included Lindsey.

"I..., was with someone..., someone that I know," stuttered Lindsey. "And this older woman..., that woman in the picture, just appeared like she was watching me..., glaring at me. She didn't seem angry, but it scared me, her being there all of a sudden, watching me. It felt so real that it woke me up."

Nathan listened carefully, waiting for her to finish, "Do you remember who you were with?"

Her eyes flicked to his, then away, shaking her head, "Not really...," she said, "...but almost. You know how dreams can be."

Her answer was far too shy, maybe even an outright lie. Could she have been having the same sort of dream as his? It would explain her reluctance to tell more of her dream. Could he expect her to divulge the very thing that he was unwilling to share?

Nathan took her hand, "I think it was just a dream. We should forget it and hurry down to the corner bistro before it starts to pour again."

They both stood and Lindsey's arms instantly wrapped around him sliding up his back, "Maybe you're right. I should try and forget it all."

The front door flew open, sending the tiny bell above it into a tinkling spasm, as someone backed in the door, shaking an umbrella.

"I feel like a drowned rat," barked the muffled voice. "I had to park a block away. Somebody's hearse has all the good spots blocked. I hope you haven't eaten yet."

Lisa turned around grappling two large sacks with colorful labels advertising The Blind Pirate, her keys clenched jingling between her teeth.

Her smiling face froze in place as she slowly closed the miniature watershed.

"Well," Lisa grinned, spitting the keys onto her desk. "We obviously haven't got around to this part of my training yet."

Nathan felt his face flush with heat, just as Lindsey's arms snatched away, brushing down her disheveled blouse.

"Don't let me interrupt anything," said Lisa, waddling past the narrow opening to set down the sacks. She had been right. Nathan Heart was playing both sides of the street just as she had suspected.

"You didn't interrupt…," grunted Nathan. "Lisa Evans, this is Lindsey Stewart. Her Aunt Madeline is the new owner of…."

Lisa grinned slyly, "Oh, so *you're* Lens. I've heard so much about you and your family. It's a pleasure."

Nathan cut in quickly, "Lisa is my new executive…."

Lisa stuck out her hand, "I'm Mr. Heart's… secretary."

Lindsey shook her hand quickly and drew away, "It's nice to meet you too. Uh…, I should probably let you get back to work, Nathan. Will I see you this evening at dinner?"

Lindsey was hurrying toward the door, shaking her cape back around her shoulders in a swirl.

"I'm not sure I'll be there in time…," he began.

"I'm sure I can get Mr. Heart out of here in plenty of time," said Lisa, donning a bright smile. "Have you had lunch? Why don't you stay and eat? There's more than enough for three people."

"I'm not much of a seafood person," she said, with a crinkle of her slightly freckled nose. "Maybe next time."

Lindsey's eyes darted at Lisa from nose to toes, while fastening her cape at the neck.

"I'd better be going," said Lindsey. "Nice meeting you Miss Evans. Maybe we'll see each other again soon."

Lisa nodded, "I'm sure we will. Nathan invited me to your family's Thanksgiving Feast. We'll probably have a chance to get to know each other better then."

"Oh…, well…, then I'll see you soon," she said, with a strange uncertainty. "Bye then."

Lindsey hurried out the door in a flurry. Nathan stood in stunned silence leaning against the brick wall until the jingling of the tiny bell over the door quit echoing in his head.

It was the rustling of soggy paper sacks that yanked him from his stupor.

"Are you going to eat?" asked Lisa. "I brought grilled shrimp and baked whitefish. Troy threw in a basket of his spicy fries you like."

"Lisa, what was all that about?" asked Nathan quietly.

She shrugged and continued to divvy the steaming food out of thickly foiled containers, "You said I should get to know these people."

"That's not what I meant and you know it," grunted Nathan.

She popped the crust off a shrimp and plopped it in her mouth, "Was I supposed to offer Lens a hug too?" she asked, chewing noisily.

"No..., of course not," he said, shaking his head angrily. "What I meant...."

"She is really pretty, but I'm not that good with affectionate women," said Lisa, hiding a scowl.

"Lisa..., stop."

"Look..., boss. I only dropped by to bring you some food and let you know that I found a dress to wear on our date. I have to be at work in a little over an hour so why don't we eat and then I'll let you know how much our costume party is going to set you back."

Nathan slowly closed his mouth. All amorous hopes of Lisa were drifting out to sea in a thickening fog. He was outgunned on all fronts and slowly backing into a corner. It was time to regroup.

When Lisa Evans bustled out the door, Nathan wished himself to be lying on a warm sandy beach where a stranger in a bikini delivered an endless stream of fruity alcoholic drinks capped with tiny umbrellas. Maybe it wasn't too late to purchase a ticket on the cruise with his sister Caroline and her family.

"Blast it all," hissed Nathan, thumping his head on his desk.

When he arose with a sigh, he noticed that the photos from Caroline were missing off his desk.

♥

By the time Nathan left the city limits of Salem, he had burned every scenario through his mind, trying to figure out which one of the ladies had taken the ghostly images of Marion off his desk. If it were Lindsey, it would explain her sudden immediate hurry to leave. He could already imagine the barrage of questions awaiting him as soon as he arrived at the Manor, especially from the strange family with a predisposition to the supernatural. Lisa on the other hand, would have had no valid reason to take them beyond curiosity.

If the photos were already in the hands of Madeline Stewart, the hurrying home to enact some feeble attempt at damage control was needless.

If there was any damage he needed to avert, it was awaiting him at the Blind Pirate. Besides, he had something to prove now. Lisa couldn't just cast him away, making promises to scuttle him into the clutches of Lindsey's dinner plans.

By the time he parked in back of the Pirate, next to the pistachio green Buick, he was almost in a fit.

♥

"Nathan! Not your usual night. To what do we owe this pleasure?" asked Troy.

"I need to talk to Lisa," grunted Nathan, flopping into a bar seat.

"I'm afraid you'll have to wait your turn. She's a little busy at the moment; her section is full. Did ya enjoy today's catch she brought by?"

Troy slid a cold mug of beer in front of Nathan, but he was already looking around trying to see where Lisa was working.

"Yeah, sure. The food's always good Troy," mumbled Nathan.

Where was she?

Then he spotted her, seated in a table across from some customer, a man in a suit, tapping her finger on the table, talking and laughing.

"Nathan, why don't you let me order you up some food here at the bar...."

The voice of Troy faded into the surrounding din of piped in music and restaurant chatter. Nathan's calculated footsteps were rattling his empty head.

Lisa stood up and patted the stranger's hand, then turned to walk away, when she ran head on into Nathan.

Her smile faded in an instant, "I'm working, Nathan."

She seemed surprised to see him as she spun past, staring him in the eyes.

Nathan followed right on her heels up to the bar, where she dropped down an order for the cook.

"Lisa I only want a few seconds of your time, maybe when you get a break?" he asked.

"I just took my break," she grunted.

"But...."

"Nathan..., I'm working," she sighed. "Call me after I get off this evening."

She spun quickly and disappeared back into the mass of movement.

Nathan glanced back over at the table where she'd been seated and the table was now empty. He slowly made his way back to the bar and took a meager sip of his beer.

"Steak..., I'll have a steak," he stuttered, as Troy closed the distance behind the bar.

Why wouldn't Lisa let him at least talk to her?

Troy's hand nudged Nathan's shoulder and repeated, "You want it medium or burned tonight?"

"Uh..., burned. I mean, medium is fine," said Nathan.

Troy wasn't the usual chatterbox he'd come to know.

"You want to tell me about it?" asked Troy.

Nathan had been staring down at the bar in a trance just long enough for Troy to lean over his direction undetected.

"No," mumbled Nathan, shaking his head.

"I'm a little disappointed in you, if you really want to know," said Troy.

"Disappointed? In me?" said Nathan, suddenly interested.

"If ya were already sparkin' with another young lady, all ya had t'do was tell me and I'd pointed little Lisa in another direction. There would'a been no hard feelin's," said Troy. "But now..., well she's all sullied up. She ain't a listening to anything I have to say."

"Sparking with someone else? I'm not sparking with anybody. What exactly did Lisa tell you?" spat Nathan.

Evidently, Lisa had shared everything she'd seen at noon that day. In which case, no amount of explaining could correct it. But why should he care unless he actually was developing something genuine toward Lisa?

"Never mind," grunted Nathan, raising the flat of his hand to Troy. "If Lisa's already made up her mind and you've already made up your mind, I'll just eat my steak and be on my way."

"Are ya sayin' there's another side to this story?" asked Troy.

"There's another side to every story Troy. You were the one that taught me that..., more than once if I remember," said Nathan, pushing away his half-empty mug of beer.

Troy walked away quietly contemplating, "That I did."

CHAPTER THIRTY-NINE

TRUE to his word, Nathan ate and left without speaking to Lisa.

What amazed him more than her shunning him…, was the unexpected empty feeling when he drove away. It had been years since he'd let anyone into his life and that had turned south when she moved to Antigua immediately upon graduation. Even that harsh turn of events hadn't affected him quite like this and Lisa was only a friend.

The Manor was quiet and solemn; the cottages showing only dim light when the Yukon settled into its slot in the garage. Nathan sat there in the dim silence until the overhead garage light timed out.

Moping produced nothing and rarely prevented facing the inevitable. He threw the door open and stalked the long trail into the house. Nathan paused only for a moment to peer in through one of the tall windowpanes by the door, into the vestibule where the image of his mother had appeared in the photograph. He was too tired to give it more than a passing thought tonight and hurried on inside.

As soon as the door shut, Madeline called to him. Nathan slid a hand along the side of the old grandfather clock as he passed; his only friend left in the world.

"Good evening Mr. Heart. We missed you at dinner."

"I apologize. I tried to explain to your niece that I had a heavy schedule today and I might not make it here on time."

Nathan shifted the uncomfortable strap on his shoulder while still walking, heading toward the staircase.

"I see. Sara set aside something for you if you're hungry."

"I've already eaten," said Nathan, still moving. "But I'll make sure to thank her personally."

He breathed a sigh of relief when he reached the bottom stair.

"I'd like to have a word with you when you get settled in."

There it was; the expected demand, "Can I take a rain check? It's been a trying day."

"It's rather important…, I don't mind waiting up," she countered.

Nathan felt his shoulders tense, trying to measure his words.

"If you'll give me a few minutes, I shouldn't be long."

"Good. I'll ask Sara to make us both some tea," she smiled. "I'll be in the library when you're ready."

The stairs took forever to climb and the hallway echoed his footsteps right up to his bedroom door.

"Nathan?"

He turned tiredly, "Hello Lindsey."

She was standing at her door across the hall, lips spread in a thin smile. Her robe was lashed tightly around her waist and she looked as though she'd been waiting up to speak to him.

"Hey," she sighed. "Have you talked to Aunt Madey yet?"

Nathan shook his head and opened his bedroom door, "I'm supposed to have a word with her in a few minutes. Is there something I should know before I see her?"

"No. She only asked me if I knew when you'd get here."

Another prod?

"Lindsey, I'm sorry I missed dinner. I had a full day today, it didn't work out."

He slid his satchel off his shoulder and set it just inside his bedroom.

"I hope I didn't cause any trouble for you at work…, with your friend."

"Miss Evans? Lisa is my employee. She's new…, and she hasn't quite learned the art of tact."

"She seemed…, well…, maybe a little protective I suppose," said Lindsey. "She *was* friendly and…. Are you sure she knows she's only an employee?"

"She knows," grunted Nathan. "I hate to do this, but I need to get downstairs before…."

Lindsey smiled, "Go. Don't keep my aunt waiting. I'll be awake for awhile if you want to talk later."

Nathan grinned, "Only if your aunt gets through with me before midnight."

Lindsey giggled, "Good luck with that."

♥

"Please come in," said Madeline.

Once again, she was standing at the little metal card catalogue rifling through the mass of cards.

Sibyl was seated in the same chair as if she'd never left it, contentedly perusing a rough leather-bound book in her lap.

Nathan chose a seat inches closer to Madeline, just out of reach of Sibyl's powdery soft palms.

"Good evening Mr. Heart," she smiled.

Nathan nodded to her as Madeline walked between them and dropped a torn index card on the heap of tossed books.

Curiosity ate at him until he had to ask, "Won't that damage your collection?"

He'd seen the appraised value of some of these and most any library would love to have them sitting in their collectible shelves.

Madeline looked up, then at Sibyl, "They're worthless forgeries. I bought them with the first lot I had delivered to the house, Mr. Heart. I didn't get to authenticate them before I made my bid. Haste makes waste. Needless to say, I removed that auction from my normal circuit."

Nathan looked at Sibyl, carefully gliding her hands on the pages and instantly had a new respect for her. She was the one that was authenticating each volume.

"That's amazing," said Nathan, looking at Sibyl. "Do you test the quality of the paper or have you seen so many of these that you just know by inspecting them?"

Sibyl smiled and looked over at Madeline, actually deferring to her, "Sibyl is…, the family *Sensitive*, Mr. Heart. She's been authenticating all my purchases…, since I can remember."

Nathan frowned at both of them and heard Lindsey scold him for his patented response, "Sensitive?"

Madeline sighed, "Every few generations one seems to appear in certain families and most don't even recognize the telltale signs, much less utilize them."

That wasn't an answer; it was another one of Madeline Stewart's rabbit trails. Madeline seemed reluctant to continue for a moment or two.

"Sibyl can touch things and feel their history, see where they've been, know their origins. In the case of these books…, she can eventually tell you which forest the paper was milled from."

Nathan grinned at the lunacy. Most people believed in ghosts from one varying degree to another, but this was more hillbilly magic than he could digest in one sitting.

"For instance…," she continued, somewhat perturbed, "The day you met Sibyl was when I knew all about your little plot with Lindsey to hide her true feelings about that awful Jon Walthrop."

Her deep hazel eyes were piercing now, watching Nathan's expressions, "Oh…, Lindsey was holding your arm like a June-bug on a window screen, but it didn't keep Sibyl from telling me the truth."

He remembered that much was true, but that only meant Madeline was extremely observant.

"If you knew all along, then why all the questions and pretense?" grunted Nathan, his skepticism turning into a grin.

Madeline smiled back, "When you get to be as old as I am Mr. Heart you'll understand. I simply enjoy the game. Lindsey should have known better, the little scamp."

Nathan sat back in his chair, preparing to test this fallacy, "Yet you purchased this estate without Sibyl's authentication."

Madeline laughed and clapped her hands on her knees, "Sibyl was seated in the limousine while you were giving us your dog and pony show, Mr. Heart. I knew the moment we drove through the stone gates that I was going to buy this place. And incidentally? I would have paid you a lot more than the asking price."

Nathan's gut clenched, a little from anger, a little from how foolish he felt. He was stunned into silence.

"Don't get your feelings all in an uproar, Nathan. You'd have been sitting on this property at least another year before someone else offered you even less than I did. Unless you consider what your siblings were collaborating an alternative."

She was probably right. She was right about everything else.

"What made the estate so special?" asked Nathan.

He didn't really want the answer. It would probably make him even sicker inside. It was as if she had something to prove now, as if his skepticism over her announcement was fueling her barbed tongue.

"Its history of course," she frowned. "You gave me a detailed outline of the house as a historical landmark." Then she smiled, "But what you didn't know was that the very back of the property was once a sacred Klamath Indian burial ground. I know at least four historical societies that will be thrilled when I offer them access; and that tiny portion of land can easily be pruned from the rest of the property."

"And you know this how?" said Nathan, leaning forward on the verge of his seat. He was feeling all the more a fool.

Madeline waved a hand toward Sibyl.

"Meet the family treasure."

Nathan stood and began to pace the room, "I don't believe you."

"Yes you do," she said soothingly. "Deep down inside you know its all true."

Nathan turned around to face them, "And I suppose you're going to tell me that's how your family amassed all it's wealth over the last century?"

"Far, far longer than that. Since we learned how to recognize the traits and utilize our family talents...."

Nathan felt heat flush his cheeks as he slowly sat back down in his chair.

"Mr. Heart?" rasped Sibyl. "Have you been experiencing some slight dizzy spells? Nausea? Or maybe you've been hearing things you can't quite explain."

Nathan tried to swallow the dry lump that had formed in his throat.

"No…, of course not. Why would you think that?" he lied.

"Strange dreams maybe…?" she asked.

Sibyl turned and nodded to Madeline and went back to sliding her palms down the pages of her open book.

Nathan stood once again, angered by their odd collusion, "Is this all you needed me for or do you have more carnival tricks you'd like to share?"

His head was attacked with that wretched vertigo even as he was denying the accusations of these two plotting women. All his other woes paled in comparison to this new blasphemy.

Madeline turned toward Sibyl and the older lady shook her head slowly, "He's not ready just yet."

"I suppose it can wait, Nathan," said Madeline. "Don't be distressed. I never meant to upset you."

"It's a little too late for that," he said, inching backwards toward the door.

"If you do experience something out of the ordinary, please feel free to come speak with Sibyl. People have paid small fortunes to spend a few minutes with my sister."

CHAPTER FORTY

JUST short of jogging, Nathan hurried to his bedroom. What sort of witchcraft was this? What did the old woman mean; he wasn't ready? Ready for what? The insane asylum?

Lindsey's door opened just as he neared his door and poked her head into the hallway.

"Nathan?"

"Not tonight Lindsey," said Nathan.

He hurried inside his bedroom and suppressed the urge to slam the door. His fingers fidgeted with the lock and after scanning the room, he grabbed a chair, pushing the back underneath the doorknob.

"I've been reduced to idiocy," he hissed, pulling at his hair.

How did Sibyl know about his dizziness, or the voices? He had told no one.

Were they drugging him somehow?

He paced the room in madness. Of course not, he was having those symptoms for almost three months before he even met the Stewarts. The doctor explained them away as stress related.

He wrenched off his jacket and tossed it across the footboard of his bed. It slid to the floor with a thunk just as his cell phone blazed in its pocket.

"Blast," he hissed, almost tearing the cloth pocket to force it open.

He gazed angrily at the caller ID and tossed the ringing phone onto the bed; it was Lisa Evans. Now she wanted to talk? He was in no frame of mind for her moodiness, not this late at night.

It was a bitter pill to swallow, knowing that he could have sold the estate for probably twice what he had; all for the joy of his ungrateful siblings. And what about the supposed burial ground?

There was a bare knoll at the very back of the property surrounded by trees; it always made him uneasy to play there as a child.

"Ridiculous…," he spat. "It's all a mind game."

The phone beeped, announcing a new voice message, which he cheerfully ignored.

Madeline hadn't mentioned the photograph, the one with the spectral image of his deceased mother staring out through the glass. Maybe Lindsey hadn't told her. Maybe she had told Madeline everything; about her dream and the photo and that was the 'thing' he wasn't ready for.

When his adrenaline began to sour, he sat heavily in his favorite chair by the veranda door; the one where he used to spend hours driveling away in contemplation.

If Madeline was right, then the answers he was desperate for were waiting downstairs, in the form of an elderly lady seated in the library.

His cell phone sang its tune once again. He'd come full circle, once again seated in his wingback chair, mindlessly ignoring the telephone.

It seemed mere seconds later it beeped again, another voice message, also ignored.

He was content to throw on a wrap and sleep where he was; where he could see the lights glowing out on the front lawn, circling the drive.

A soft rapping on his door stirred him, only barely.

"Mr. Heart?"

It wasn't Lindsey or any voice he recognized.

Nathan scooted the chair from the door and turned the latch, peering through a thin opening.

It was one of the house staff, standing to attention just outside in the hallway.

"Sir, you have a telephone call," she said.

Nathan expelled the last of his heavy breath in a sigh, "Where can I take the call?"

She handed him a wireless handset and stepped back, "You can leave it in the hallway when you're through."

"Hello, this is…," he started to say Heart Realty, "Nathan."

"Why didn't you answer your cell phone?" whispered Lisa.

"Because it's almost midnight, Lisa. It's late and I'm in no mood for more drama."

"Drama? You arrogant…," she hissed. "I need your help."

"Why don't you call Troy?" he grunted.

He could hear her angry breath stabbing at his eardrum.

"Nathan…, please?" she begged, barely a whisper.

"What?" he grunted. "I can barely hear you. Why are you whispering?"

"Because, they might hear me," she whined. "I'm at Black Shoals Beach, about ten miles north of Crab Cove."

"I know where it is," he sighed. "What are you doing out there?"

"This..., this car you gave me won't crank and there's a bunch of people out here in the dark," she hissed.

"Did you call the auto service number on your insurance card?" he asked. "Towing is free."

"Nathan..., please don't argue with me. I'm...," she let all her breath out. "I'm scared."

"Fine. I'm on my way," he grunted angrily. "I'll phone you when I get close."

He kicked the chair away from the door in a tantrum, then fished through his closet for his trench coat.

The house downstairs was already dark and quiet as he hurried out to the garage. Now he was reduced to roadside service for his belligerent employee.

He was barely out of the garage when his cell phone rang again.

"Lisa I'm on my way this very second," he blurted.

"Nathan...," she whispered. "They're just outside my car. I'm afraid they saw me hiding in here."

"Stay on the phone with me," he yawned. "The Buick is built like a tank."

"They're..., touching stuff," she whimpered, "...on the car."

Nathan could hear deep muffled voices in the background.

"Honk the horn," said Nathan. "That ought to run them back a few steps."

"Were you not listening?" she whined. "The battery is dead. Just get your ass here and help me."

Nathan had to suppress a laugh, despite the serious situation.

"Alright, I just jumped on the shortcut to the 101. Black Shoals is closer to me than Crab Cove, I should be there in ten minutes or so."

The phone was silent except for what sounded like sobbing.

"Lisa?"

"They..., they're..., stealing my baby's hubcaps...," she warbled.

Nathan stomped the gas pedal and the Yukon roared to life underneath him. Whoever it was, wasn't just admiring the car like he'd assumed.

"Oh..., no...," she whined. "My cell phone is going...."

"Lisa?"

He looked at his phone, the call was lost and he was still another five minutes away.

Nathan made another quick call, then dropped the phone in the other seat, both hands forcing the big SUV onto the coast highway. The exit was only a few miles ahead, but the road seemed to be expanding underneath him, slowing him down.

When the exit arrived, he barely had time to slow his vehicle down, just enough to make the exit ramp, just enough not to roll his Yukon.

Glowing white letters, Black Shoals Beach, flared on the black exit sign and he could faintly see silhouettes of two older trucks parked near the pistachio green Buick. Lisa had driven the car past the paved parking lot onto the restricted area of the dark gritty beach.

He slapped the switch on the Yukon's dash to all wheel drive; flipped on his over-the-cab lamps and the beach became daylight.

Three men covered in gray hoodies fled like cockroaches across the hard packed gritty beach, pieces of glaring chrome in their hands.

Another car raced into the parking entrance, bright lights bouncing as it neared, blocking the vandals exit.

A slim-jim was still wobbling, suspended upward from the driver's side window where they'd tried to unlock the car door. That would have taken them all night considering the car had old style electric locks.

The two hooligan filled trucks accelerated down the beach, but Nathan could already see red and blue lights coming from the opposite direction.

The other vehicle with blinding red and blue strobes, drove up and parked facing the opposite side of Lisa's car, just as Nathan was tapping on the Buick's window.

"Lisa?"

"Lisa. You can come out. You're safe now."

A stark white mascara streaked face that would have made Alice Cooper proud slowly emerged into the glaring lights. Nathan was already kicking himself for not answering his phone, angry at his selfishness, and scared at what might have happened.

The door clicked open and Lisa climbed onto Nathan like a scared kitten.

A flashlight glared in both their faces, "Nathan Heart?"

Nathan nodded, "I think she's alright. Thank you for getting here so quickly."

"I was handling an accident just up the highway. You know, we're going to have to stop meeting like this," grunted the sheriff. "What is it with you and vandals?"

"It's a new talent," grunted Nathan.

A quick silent interchange took place between Nathan and the sheriff as he shifted the weight of Lisa Evans in his arms.

"Did you ever get a name out of the one you arrested at my house?"

The sheriff flicked his light back on Lisa Evans, watching her carefully, "Yeah, but he jumped bail…, disappeared; we have a warrant out."

The patrol car's radio hissed loudly and announced that the other officer had cornered the other two vehicles, asking for assistance.

"Ma'am, do you need medical?" he asked, trotting back to his car.

Lisa's head leaned away from Nathan's chest long enough to wiggle side to side.

"Alright, stay here," he barked. "I won't be long."

The sheriff's car took off spitting a trail of grit behind it.

"What were you doing out here this late?" he whispered in her ear.

He hugged her closer and felt her shiver against him.

"I..., needed to be alone," she sobbed.

Her ice-cold fingers were still digging into his back, underneath Nathan's coat. There was no telling how long she'd been hiding in the floorboard of the car with no heat. There was no telling how long it took her to void her pride and call Nathan.

"Come on, get in over here where it's warm."

He carried her to his SUV, setting her into the passenger seat. As soon as he shut the door, he hurried to the other side.

"What possessed you to come out here alone?" he asked, covering her with his thick trench coat.

"I already told you," she sniffled, covering her face up to the nose with Nathan's warm coat. She kicked off her flats and stuffed her bare feet next to the Yukon's heater vent, curling her toes.

"Troy could have been here in five minutes Lisa."

She shook her head, her eyes glazed, "I tried. Troy was already drunk. I didn't have..., there was no one else I knew to call."

Nathan remembered the feeling, standing in front of his office, not a soul to rely on.

"Next time at least call me with a flight plan, okay?" he chuckled.

"There won't be a next time," she snubbed. "I'll stay where I belong."

"Lisa, you belong wherever you want to be. What happened?"

He'd never seen this side of her before; almost broken.

"I was having a pity party okay? It was my birthday. I drove out here to celebrate. I guess I left the radio on too long and..., you know the rest."

Nathan groaned, "Why didn't you tell me it was your birthday?"

Her eyes glittered and darted, as if she was deciding whether or not to get angry all over again.

"I filled out your stupid employee form. I figured you could read," she grunted.

Confident Lisa was still in there somewhere.

"Well, considering you're my first employee, you should be happy if I remember to pay you."

Lisa giggled past her snubs and almost smiled.

"I guess I forgot to tell you. Those old tube radios really suck the life out of a battery. It's just as much my fault."

"Well my car is ruined…, happy birthday Lisa," she whined.

Nathan slid over closer, offering her an arm.

"We'll fix your car. I'm happy you're all right."

For a moment, he felt pure empathy for Lisa and slowly breathed through what was becoming a normal occurrence of vertigo. He finally felt himself relax when Lisa slumped into the seat, "I guess it was the picture of your mother that set me off. It sort of put things into perspective, you know?"

He withdrew slowly back to his seat, "My mother?"

"The pictures on your desk. I grabbed them by mistake. I thought it was the ones I left for you to look at."

"You saw…, how did you know that was Marion?" he whispered.

"Because I used to talk to her when you brought her into the restaurant, while you and Troy were at the bar arguing," she frowned. "Wow. You don't remember. Troy was right. You were really messed up back then."

CHAPTER FORTY-ONE

IT was the first peaceful morning Nathan had enjoyed in several weeks. No one bothered to wake him and he slept in until nearly eight that Friday morning. Lisa Evans would have to do without her car until the following week. It would take at least that long for the shop to straighten and replace all the chrome trim yanked off the sides of the 1958 Buick Special. One of the hood ornaments was forever lost to the waves of the chilly pacific coast.

Madeline Stewart was seated quietly at the human chopping block in the kitchen, looking over a portfolio of photographs and sipping at a cup of coffee. Even she couldn't ruin his mood this morning, now that he knew there might be another explanation for his strange episodes; if he chose to believe Madeline and Sibyl.

"Sleep well?" she asked, baiting Nathan into conversation.

"Like the dead," he smirked. Of course, she knew it was after two a.m. when he made it back to the house last night.

There were several fresh homemade pastries on a platter by the coffee and he took his time choosing a few.

"I'm surprised you're up this early," she muttered.

"Me too. I apologize for the late phone call last night. It was an emergency."

Nathan sat across the table from Madeline; his plate made an odd clacking sound against the thickness of the wooden table.

"Family?" she asked.

"Employee," he answered.

Her eyes glittered upward for only a moment.

Nathan grinned at her interest, "It's a very long story. I was a last resort."

215

She smiled without looking up, "Once a caregiver, always a caregiver, Mr. Heart."

"I believe you're right," said Nathan. "A gift and a curse."

"Depending on how you perceive the two," she added.

He was learning to appreciate the way she never actually came right out and spoke what was on her mind. Her conjecture always left room for interpretation on his part.

"I have something I want to show you later," said Nathan. "A photograph."

This piqued her interest enough for a quick glance away from her folder.

"Something I'd rather we kept between us," he continued.

"And Lindsey?" she asked.

Nathan nodded, "As few eyes as possible."

So Lindsey had told her about the photograph.

"I'd be glad to help you find some answers," she said, rustling through another page. "There it is," she grunted, tearing the page from the folder. "The price is ridiculous."

"Shopping?" asked Nathan.

"Repopulating your old office," she answered. "I despise vacancies. You should understand that more than I, Mr. Heart."

Nathan grimaced uncontrollably for a fraction of a second, "That I do."

She slapped down the discarded page in front of Nathan, displaying a worn roll-top desk, with assorted built-in mail slots and an inkwell holder. Her finger tapped the black and white image almost hatefully.

"The curator states that this desk was once used by the late Edgar Allan Poe. It's highly unlikely he ever graced his ass to even lean against it, but…, it would go perfect with the mahogany desk and lamp I've acquired."

Nathan didn't dare ask about their unique histories as he took a closer look at the image on the auction sheet. It looked a shambles, with the pull down cover stuck at an odd angle high in its track.

"Looks a little worse for wear if you ask me," he grinned.

"Maybe. With a little careful cleaning and teakwood oil, it might turn out alright."

"You won't have it restored?" he asked.

"It would lose all its value. The human interaction and even the abuse is what interests me."

Nathan couldn't look up into her eyes as he replayed her sentence. There was some morbid truth hovering just beneath the surface. It wasn't so much the deaths surrounding the pieces of collectibles in the house that held Madeline's interest; it was the vivid lives that surrounded all the tragedies. He heard her voice in his head repeating, 'hot or cold - things that are important'.

Suddenly, the table he was eating at took on an entirely different perspective. He felt the passion of those lives, not only the ones that died torturous deaths while lashed to the unforgiving wood, but also the interrogators hell bent on destroying something that they couldn't understand. It was almost as if he could see the victims faces contorted in pain, the screams, begging for understanding while the irrational fear of their tormentors compelled their destruction.

Nathan's head was swimming as his palms slid from the surface of the table and the images slowly faded from his vision.

"Sibyl says it can be a little disconcerting the first few times."

♥

Nathan managed to make his way out the back door and was still bracing his hands on his knees, when he heard the voice behind him.

"Nathan? Are you going to be okay?" asked Lindsey.

Nathan nodded, but waved for her to go away as another wave of nausea clenched his stomach. Despite his tall frame, for the first time in his life he felt very small.

Now he knew for certain that 'thing' he wasn't ready for.

"Aunt Madey said to tell you it helps if you walk around some," she offered, before she disappeared back inside the house.

Nathan spit the bitter retch from his mouth and drew in the cold morning air. He looked up at a few stray streaks of early sunshine filtering through dark puffy clouds and ground fog.

He was afraid to think, afraid to recall those invasive, unwelcome thoughts, perilously close to actual relived memories. Sibyl..., poor Sibyl. A life lived with these horrors was no life at all..., yet she seemed in her right mind. In fact, she seemed the most normal out of the entire bunch.

Nathan hurried back in the house, to the sink, splashing cold water on his face. Madeline was where he left her..., waiting.

"I'd like to speak to your sister now, I think?" he asked.

"I'll arrange some time with her before lunch, unless your schedule has you somewhere else today."

Surely she was joking. There was no place on earth more important than a few minutes with Sibyl. Hopefully she could explain what was happening to him.

"I think all my appointments have just been cleared for the day," he sighed.

"Then you should go lie down and rest. I'll send someone up to wake you when Sibyl is ready."

♥

Nathan didn't believe he'd be able to sleep for the rest of the week, but as soon as his head touched his pillow, he was out.

It was three hours later that a tapping on his veranda door stirred him awake. Miracles of sunshine were filtering down instead of the mixed morning fog from earlier. He did feel better even with the new void he had discovered inside himself.

Nathan pushed the wispy white curtain aside and saw an elderly face smiling back at him.

"Better bring a wrap, it's cool out here," said Sibyl Bale.

Lunch came in the form of two bowls of steaming soup as they sat in the first few minutes of silence on the veranda. The two white wrought iron chairs grunted underneath them and the table screeched as Nathan pulled it closer to Sibyl's reach.

"I don't know where to begin," said Nathan. "My questions don't seem to intersect the way I thought they would."

"It's best to take one at a time, think it through, let everything ferment for awhile," she nodded, sipping slowly at her broth.

Sibyl was cuddling the bowl, warming her hands and gazing across the lawn. A colorful wool blanket was wrapped around her like a cocoon.

"Well then..., what exactly happened to me this morning?" he asked.

She nodded, then chuckled, "Madeline told me she led you into your first *Awakening*. She can be crafty like that. Madeline has always had a gift for stirring up the true potential in people."

Something in her voice, her manner caused him to relax.

"Then I have a confession. I have been experiencing some vertigo..., at random times."

He wasn't quite ready to admit to hearing his name called, or other things.

"They aren't as random as you think. You only get the spins around vivid objects or people you're most drawn to..., and of course others like us."

Nathan shook his head, then when he noticed Sibyl was watching, he felt as if he was obligated to explain himself, "I've had them around people..., a few times. But not always."

He remembered several times in and around the house he'd felt those sudden sinking feelings.

"When the time comes I'll help you understand what's happening," she answered. "It'll help if you take these things slowly. Not like what happened this morning with my sister."

It would have been just like Madeline to force him to acknowledge something he didn't want.

"Don't be too upset with Madeline, she means well. In her defense, most *Sensitives* never know what's happening to them. They go to their doctors, get their MRI's and CAT scans, take their Zoloft or Lithium, or get misdiagnosed with something even more horrible."

Sibyl suddenly cut her explanation short and stared at Nathan, "There's a lot I'd like to tell you, even ask you, but I don't want to upset you more than you already are."

Nathan hadn't realized that he was now perched on the brink of his wobbly seat, hanging on her every word.

"Madeline told me a little about your mother," she said quietly, carefully. "You seem like such a nice young man. I'd rather that not happen to you."

Nathan put down his bowl of soup and sat back a little, the chill air starting to seep into his body.

"Is that what you think happened to my mother?" he asked.

She shrugged, "There's no way I could know that, but it is very likely. If a person doesn't learn how to turn it all off...."

She sighed deeply and closed her eyes, "Sometimes..., when we touch things..., we see or even hear those that were attached to it in life. Those voices seem as real as you and I talking to each other. It's hard to know the difference and it can be very confusing, even maddening; especially when they don't answer us back."

He sat all the way back in his chair, his thoughts spinning. Was that what happened to Marion Heart? Were those her unseen associates she held endless conversations with?

That was near what happened to him at the breakfast table, but it was as if he'd been dropped head first into a murky pond of confusion as face after face swam by.

"Why does this all seem so dark, so strange, if it's supposed to be natural?" he asked.

"Because, you're accustomed to looking at the world with your natural eyes. What we do, what you'll have to learn to do, is feel around in the dark and see things with the light that's inside you."

The mere thought of that sent chills up and down his back that had nothing to do with the temperature.

"How do I block it all out?"

"Oh..., that takes time," she chuckled. "The easiest way is to concentrate on someone that you care for deeply. That seems to work like an emergency shut off."

Marion Heart had those days of perfect clarity, when she came to herself and seemed as normal as the next person. It was those days when she was reminiscing over his father, Jonas Heart Senior. Those were the days she enjoyed their long rides along the coast and their visits with Caroline. If only he'd known then..., if only she'd known.

Maybe it had already been too late for her.

CHAPTER FORTY-TWO

"**A**ND you're sure this is your mother standing by the door?" asked Madeline, looking carefully at the photograph.

Nathan nodded, worried that he was assuming too much about their sudden openness, maybe even friendship. Sibyl had grown tired and cold, even with the sun's rays blessing their conversation. Madeline had been patiently waiting her turn for a few moments with Nathan.

"My sister Caroline recognized her too. She was the one that had it printed. She has lots of questions too."

"There are no easy answers," she muttered. "You should realize that by now."

Madeline shuffled in her seat, contemplating something, "A ghost? Possibly. But that's such a bland answer. A part of your mother; her living memories most likely. She was fractured during the last years of her life, pieces of her clung to what was most familiar to her, things she loved."

"I don't understand. Is she trying to reach out to me?" he asked, looking at the wispy image of Marion Heart.

All Madeline could do was shrug, and out poured her lazy southern drawl, "You tell me. You see all the antiquities around you in this house. The easiest ones to authenticate are the ones where there was an extreme tragedy, where pieces of the living became attached."

She was talking in circles again. At least Sibyl tried to speak English.

"I know you think I'm being evasive, Nathan. And I am…, simply because I don't understand everything I know. Every time I think I've wrapped up all my explanations in a nice neat box, the pretty little ribbon always slides off the top. And here we go again."

Madeline stood and stretched, "But I do love old houses like this. There are times that I'd gladly trade places with people like Sibyl..., like you. Just to be able to hear the conversations, the hopes, the joys, the laughter of all those past lives. Then, there are these moments. The ones that make me question the sanity of that desire."

Nathan felt himself drop, sink just a little, then stood up quickly to quash Madeline's attempt at leading him back down the rabbit hole.

Walking helps. That's what Lindsey had told him that morning as he was puking up his breakfast on the back lawn.

He caught a quick grin on Madeline's face, then he reached in his pocket and pulled out a notepad. After flipping through a few pages, he snapped it shut and handed it to her.

"There's something else. I'd like for you to give this to Sibyl. I'd like to know the truth about the person this belonged to."

It was the notepad taken from the intruder Bolton had surprised behind the garage.

She took it carefully, scanning several pages, "Not a very educated person, unless it isn't what it seems. Deep gouges in the handwriting though..., a lot of anger or passion for whatever his purpose was. Where did you get it?"

Nathan shook his head, "I'll tell you after Sibyl has had a chance to look at it."

"Ah..., a test," she smiled. "Still not completely convinced of this new world you've discovered."

She nodded and glanced up from the little pad, "Then we'll find out its origins together. Perhaps you'll want to be there? Maybe learn what's available to you someday if you let Sibyl point you in the right directions?"

Nathan had no desire to follow in his mother's footsteps. Marion Heart's life had dwindled into darkness and insanity. If Sibyl could teach him to step around the edges of that darkness, he'd take advantage of every opportunity available.

Nathan nodded, "I'd like that."

"We'll do it together then..., tomorrow," she nodded.

♥

Nathan was glad for the intermission. He wasted no time in climbing in the cherry red Cadillac, looking forward to doing something normal, something grounding.

After a quick telephone call to Troy O'Bannon, a conversation in which he negotiated a reasonable dollar value; he then rushed into Lumberton to test a few theories.

His first stop was the Courthouse Annex and Sheriff's Office to make a few inquiries. He was met by a barrage of smiles and teases about his recent encounters with the gamier crowd he was suddenly attracting.

Nathan went along with their lighthearted fun until the clerk finally asked him what he needed.

She gave him the name of the person Bolton and he had apprehended and informed him that a local bail bondsman had been involved with getting him released. That was a disappointment. He was hoping that the person responsible for the Peeping Tom or someone complicit in his actions had made an appearance. There was no way that a bondsman would release that same information to him, so all he had was a name..., John Smith. There were probably ten million John Smith's in the directories of every state. A needle in a haystack even for a well versed private investigator.

When he stepped outside the Annex, a bewildering cloud of disappointment trickled down like a mist over his soul. His one grasp at getting to the root of the responsible party was gone.

Across the street at a small strip mall, he noticed a metal sign carefully erected out front; an advertisement by his one major competitor in the private realty sector, adding insult to his misery. When had Eben shifted to selling commercial properties?

"Pick your battles," he whispered to himself.

After two more quick stops in Lumberton, his vehicle full of assortments, he took off for Crab Cove. Arriving a few minutes before six o'clock, with time to spare, he parked in back of the Blind Pirate as usual.

Eddie Cole, Troy's full time cook, met Nathan at the back door and ushered him inside, gathering several items from his hands.

"The front parking lot is still full," grunted Nathan, carefully setting down a birthday cake.

"Troy locked the front door right at five. They'll all be clearing out a few minutes after the hour," he said with a grin.

"Lisa doesn't know does she?"

"Nah, she thinks we're having a health code inspector dropping in," grinned Eddie. "You should'a heard her griping about Troy cuttin' her hours back tonight. Whew! She was fit to be tied."

'The tightwad', thought Nathan. Troy wasn't going to pay her for the time that Nathan had negotiated for the restaurant.

"I was just glad that I'd get to eat with the rest of ya tonight instead of slaving over that damned grill," grunted Eddie.

Nathan chuckled, "Don't forget you still have to cook for us."

Eddie chunked him a menu, "Better order up then. I'm going to shut this beast down as soon as the clock ticks seven."

Nathan sat crunched in Troy's tiny cluttered office until a huge bearded face poked through the door.

"The last customer's leavin' out the door," said Troy. "I got little Lisa scheduled to clean up the stock room for the inspector that's comin'." Troy grinned and chuckled, "She don't have a clue."

With Lisa behind closed doors, the small group scurried out into the main court with the balloons and streamers from Nathan's car, sat out the cake and setup a table where they could all congregate together.

Troy flipped the breakers for the back rooms and dining area. Now all they had to do was wait for Lisa to come scratching out of the stock room in the back.

They waited for several minutes, expecting her to come out spitting, until Eddie nudged Troy.

"Hey, something's wrong."

"Hmm. She could'a found her way out'a there with her eyes closed," grunted Troy.

"I'll go look," said one of the other waitresses. "She won't think anything about me coming to get her."

She flicked a lighter that was stuffed in her apron as she wandered back down the stockroom hallway.

Seconds later, she came back in the main room, "Lisa's not there, not in the back either."

Troy flipped on the emergency lights behind the bar and took off like a tumbleweed in a breeze.

He came back a few minutes later scratching his head, "She couldn't a got far. She's afoot with her car out'a sorts."

Nathan was already out the back door, scanning the road in the growing twilight. There was a sole pedestrian, fighting a long coat in the usual whipping breeze near the waterfront.

He quietly drove around the loop, onto the deserted road, inching behind the steady pace of Lisa's long slender legs.

"Excuse me, Ma'am. Can you tell me if there's a good restaurant around here?"

The grim stare on Lisa's face softened when she saw who was pacing her. She slowed down and ducked her head with a grin, peering in at Nathan.

"There aren't any good restaurants around here."

"Care for a ride?"

Lisa looked at the three blocks in front of her and let out a long breath. She opened the car door and slid inside.

"What's up with the Pirate tonight?" asked Nathan.

"Water bugs," she said with a grin. "Health inspector or who knows what; probably another one of Troy's schemes."

"Go with me then?" asked Nathan.

"Dressed like this? I wouldn't be caught dead in public wearing this."

She flashed open her coat to reveal her food and grease stained uniform from the Blind Pirate.

"I'll give you a few minutes to change," he offered.

"Is this your way of making up for not answering your phone last night?"

"No."

"Good, cause it wouldn't have worked."

He let her out in front of her apartment and called Troy to let him know the situation.

Lisa came back dressed in one of the three mix and match outfits she rotated through during the workweek at Heart Realty.

"I miss my baby," she sighed as she slid inside Nathan's Cadillac. "How long do you think it'll be before the Buick's out of the shop?"

Her eyes sparkled, dancing around his face in the dim light.

"You look nice," said Nathan.

He thought he saw her blush before she turned to look out the window.

"Is that your way of avoiding my question?"

"It's my way of offering a compliment," he grunted.

He stepped on the gas and spun to the intersection, whipping back into the Pirate's parking lot.

Lisa slid down low in the seat in a panic, only her eyes and nose visible from the outside.

"What..., what are you doing? Go! Get us out of here," she hissed.

"I have to drop off a check to Troy," said Nathan. "What's wrong with you?"

"I..., I skipped out on the cheapskate," she blurted. "He had me in the stockroom cleaning house for him, for free."

Nathan killed the engine right by the front door.

"Nathan Heart," she whined. "Don't do this to me."

"I won't let him put you back to work," said Nathan. "Why don't you come inside with me. Rub his nose in it a little?"

Her head shook violently, "No."

Both Troy and Eddie walked out the front restaurant door and leaned down, staring through the window at Lisa, tapping lightly on the glass. She spun angrily, her face beet red, "I'll never forgive you for this Nathan Heart."

CHAPTER FORTY-THREE

"**Y**OU might as well come in with me for a few seconds."

Lisa sputtered and grumbled every embarrassing step, the last one to venture back into the main dining room. When the lights came on, she was standing just inside the door with her arms crossed angrily across her chest.

Nathan shifted closer to her and lowered his voice, "Surprise."

The small group blurted 'Happy Birthday' while Eddie fidgeted to light the candles on her cake.

Lisa's feet didn't seem to want to move. Nathan had to take her arm and lead her toward the grinning faces of the group.

After gawking at the decorations, Lisa turned and punched Nathan on the arm and whispered, "I hate you."

His grin widened, "So now I'm forgiven?"

"We'll see," she said quietly.

An uncomfortable timidness seemed to shroud Lisa throughout the dinner, the cake, and the festivities. She made over the little gifts her half dozen co-workers gave her as if it was Christmas. Among the assorted last minute gifts, were two boxes labeled Glorious Vanities, which Lisa shoved to the side. They were obviously from the dress shop she had visited in Lumberton. Nathan had picked up her formal dress and some other oddity and presented it as her birthday gift; the duality left her feeling a little cold inside.

It felt like such a pretense that it was almost unbearable to open them. After all, she had spent two hours trying on a dozen dresses to pick out something affordable to wear; it wasn't much of a surprise. Lisa immediately scourged herself at the ungrateful idea, especially after all the trouble and expense Nathan had gone through to rent the Blind Pirate for a

Friday evening. Thus, a thousand troubled thoughts rumbled through her head.

It was one of the co-workers that finally scooted the longest cumbersome box toward her.

Lisa forced a smile, "I already know what this is."

"Well, we don't," grunted the others. "Give us a peek."

She looked up at Nathan with that same forced smile, but he only shrugged at her.

"As long as I don't have to model it for everybody."

She stretched out the long slim box and slowly removed the lid, then stood there staring down.

"They gave you the wrong one," she sighed.

Nathan frowned in disbelief, "This isn't the dress you liked?"

"No. The one I picked out was..., black," she whined.

She raised just the top of the gown, felt the cloth carefully and set it back down.

"Huh. The owner said that this was the one that fit you best," said Nathan.

Lisa gaped at it in sudden recognition. She replaced the lid.

"Take it back."

She blinked her eyes twice, forcing them to dry.

"I can't," grunted Nathan. "They already tailored the length."

"Quit yer whinin' at the gift horse and try it on for us," barked Troy.

Lisa swallowed the knot in her throat and looked at the potentially ruined face of Nathan Heart.

"Fine."

With a deep breath, "I knew this would happen," then grabbed the box and headed toward one of the back rooms.

Nathan handed the smaller box to one of the ladies, "She'll need these."

The older waitress hurried off behind Lisa while everyone stared at Nathan.

"It's for a formal dinner we have to attend," he explained, "...for business."

"Uh, huh," grunted Troy suspiciously.

With unsteady steps, Lisa finally emerged doddering on four-inch heels, with her helper holding a hand.

"You bought me heels," sighed Lisa happily. "The ones with the bows on the back. And they match the dress perfectly."

It was suddenly quiet as she held out a foot, twirling it from under the hem of the long formal dress.

Lisa's hair was down, out of its perpetual ponytail, draping just past her bare shoulders, covering the thin straps of the dress.

The midnight gown appeared royal blue underneath the harsh florescent lighting, but nothing seemed to distract from how perfectly it clung to the shape of her body.

"Blackbeard's balls," whispered Troy. "I ain't never seen nothing like that before."

Lisa ignored his off color remark and stared at Nathan - waiting. She had never seen him at a loss for words, but there he stood in some sort of trance, frozen as if in some strange daze.

Nathan placed one hand on the table beside him to steady himself as he looked at Lisa. The instant she stepped in the room, that damnable sinking feeling had caused the floor to drop away from underneath his feet. He would have loved to believe it was the transformation of the beautiful woman he was witnessing.

"Well..., say something," she frowned, looking down at the conservative plunge of her neckline, pinching it together over her cleavage. She fidgeted with an odd little gold-rimmed pendant that matched the dress perfectly, waiting for him to open his mouth.

"I always heard that the way to a woman's heart was through a nice pair of shoes," mumbled Nathan.

He was quickly getting his bearings and remembered to walk; hurrying over to stand where he could see Lisa better.

Even in her heels, she was still looking upward, waiting for some mysterious clue on his face.

"You're perfect."

Lisa finally smiled.

♥

Lisa Evans was deathly silent during the short trip to her apartment. Nathan parked in her empty driveway and killed the engine.

"Are you going to tell me what's bothering you?" he asked.

"Nathan..., I need to know why."

Her words were carefully metered, frightfully precise.

"After what happened yesterday..., I had to make it up to you somehow. I let my own problems interfere with my better judgement."

She shook her head slowly, "That's not what I mean."

Nathan saw this conversation developing into some sort of defining personal moment, something that wasn't his strong suit.

When he didn't answer..., "The job..., the car..., the phone..., and now this six hundred dollar dress. The shoes cost more than I make in a week, Nathan. Do I need to go on?"

He winced at her recollection of the prices. This looked bad for him. The last time he'd tried to urge their friendship into a relationship, she'd ran away in terror. Did he dare try again?

"I see great potential in you, Lisa," he said quietly. "I want you to believe in yourself as much as I do."

Lisa's eyes locked on his, as if looking somewhere deep inside him, until she slowly looked away.

"Potential...," she breathed, her expression suddenly unreadable.

"Did I... say something wrong?" he stuttered.

Her breathing was slow as she turned back around, "As long as you understand that you can't buy something that's not for sale."

'Blast', thought Nathan.

"Is that what you think? That I'm trying to buy your affection?" he wheezed, wishing instantly he'd kept his mouth shut.

"Then what is this?" asked Lisa, waving her hands at the boxes and presents behind the seat, the balloons. "You tell me."

Nathan closed his eyes and turned away; he'd heard that same phrase turned on him once before, that very same day.

"Why are you being so difficult Lisa? Is it so strange for somebody to take an interest in you?"

"It all depends on what kind of interest it is," she grunted.

If there was some secret code word or clandestine handshake, he wasn't privy to it. What was she asking for?

"Its late," she breathed finally, rushing the conversation to a conclusion. "We both have work in the morning."

Her door opened before Nathan could say anything else, which was probably for the best; at least until he figured out what was going on inside her head.

Lisa never turned on an inside light to her home during the entire time Nathan helped her relay in the remnants of the party. When the last of it was inside, Lisa stopped him at her door and looked at him cautiously. There was something weighing heavily on her.

Before he could try to examine her mood, she placed a hand to his cheek, then tiptoed up to brush a kiss across his lips.

"Thank you for the birthday party, Nathan," she said softly. "My last one was when I was five. This meant more to me than you could know..., even if it was a day late."

That simple kiss felt horribly familiar to goodbye.

She turned and stepped inside closing her door and he heard her growl like a child throwing a temper tantrum, just before it reopened to a sliver. Her face was reflecting a stream of tears in the ambient street light.

"Good night. Don't forget to pick me up in the morning."

Nathan stood quietly just outside her closed door for at least a full minute, a finger to his lips, before he could move.

♥

A light was on in the west end of the Manor as well as a few rooms upstairs when he arrived at his old home. In hopes of a moment alone with Sibyl, he hurried inside and down the hallway to the library.

Madeline Stewart was seated comfortably underneath a warm yellow lamp, reading one of her many books. The other stack of refused books was gone, and so was Sibyl.

"Please, come in Nathan," she said, closing the book.

He stood beside the hallway entrance for a moment, thinking of a dozen polite ways to excuse himself.

"I had it happen to me again this evening."

The words seemed to come out of his mouth of their own accord.

"That blasted sinking feeling sneaked up on me twice tonight and I almost made a complete fool of myself."

She motioned to one of the chairs beside her, a frown creasing her forehead for a moment.

"Why don't you have a seat and tell me more."

"Actually, I was hoping to speak with your sister. I didn't mean to disturb you."

She chuckled, "I'm not Sibyl Bale by any means, but I've had a few years experience with these things."

He hurried and sat down before he lost the opportunity to make sense of his personal madness. How would he be able to sleep tonight without some answers?

He explained about the birthday party for his employee, leaving out all the personal details, especially his mixed feelings for Lisa Evans.

Madeline seemed more interested than he had expected, hanging on every detail that he offered.

"If you're truly experiencing an *Awakening*, it could be any of several things. What did you touch just before you experienced the vertigo?"

He shook his head thinking carefully, "Nothing that I remember. I was standing beside an ordinary dining table."

"What were you focused on at that moment?" she asked.

He had no desire to open himself to her probes any more than necessary, "My secretary walked in. She'd tried on a dress to show her co-workers; one of her birthday presents."

All Nathan could remember in those first few moments was Lisa's expectant face and her darting eyes following his.

"And no one touched you?" she asked carefully.

Nathan shook his head in remembrance, "Not that I can recall."

Madeline's eyebrows arched slightly with interest, "Really. And when did you have your second experience?"

Nathan thought carefully, but something breached his filter of intent, "I dropped Lisa off at her apartment...."

"Your employee," she repeated back to him.

He nodded, angry at his sudden vulnerability, "Just as I was leaving."

"Well. I'd certainly like to meet this employee of yours," she said, with sudden piqued interest. "When you spoke with Sibyl, did she happen to explain some of the circumstances that can provoke a *Reading*?"

"A what?" he blurted.

"The vertigo..., the precursor to a *Reading*," she said hastily. "*Objects* you touch that have unusual history or..., others like yourself."

Suddenly he remembered verbatim what Sibyl had said, "The spins...."

"Yes..., the spins," grinned Madeline.

"You think my secretary was responsible?" he asked.

Madeline smiled and sat back in her chair smugly, "You certainly do..., and I'm starting to agree with you."

CHAPTER FORTY-FOUR

LINDSEY was blocking his doorway when Nathan arrived upstairs; her lovely face was unreadable. He wasn't sure if he could deal with another emotionally charged dilemma today, especially this late in the evening. But, he felt that he owed her some sort of an explanation.

"Lindsey..., I'm sorry I cut you short last night. It was rude."

"Yes it was...," she said, her head tilted up, a little off center, "...but."

Lindsey let out a thoughtful breath as Nathan watched her carefully, "I know a little about what you're going through. And..., I want to help. If you'll let me."

"You want to help?" asked Nathan cautiously, staying just out of her reach.

Lindsey chuckled at his endless quirky repetition, "That was why I wanted to talk to you last night."

Nathan urged her away from his bedroom door and pushed himself inside, "Last night wasn't a good time. Come to think of it, today was just as jumbled."

The warm scent of vanilla welcomed him inside, a newly lit candle on his chifforobe. Lindsey followed quickly behind him and sat in the closest chair, insinuating that she wouldn't stand for rejection again.

"My Aunt Madey has a way of twisting things to her advantage. You tried to help me so I thought I'd return the favor."

Nathan opened his mouth, thought twice, then rearranged his question, "You think Madeline is responsible for all that's screwed up with me right now? My sister Josephine was supposed to get out of the hospital today and I didn't even call to find out about her. Then there's my new office..., my personal business.... I'm just trying to juggle too many things at once, that's all. Not that your aunt is incapable of manipulating people by any means. It's in her very nature."

"Ha! You make her sound so saintly," she scoffed. "Why do you think she's been herding me so closely these last few years? Do you think it's all because she's being motherly? Did you assume it was because she doesn't want to see me hurt or see me squander my inheritance on some worthless lover? She's not worried about my money."

It was the first time he'd heard Lindsey freely acknowledge her feelings over her recently ruined relationship. Nathan threw his jacket on the bed and drew another chair closer to Lindsey, then sat down. He felt the tiredness in his body.

"Fine, you tell me then," said Nathan. "What is she up to?"

This sounded like another plea to hook him into helping her, not the other way around. Maybe Lindsey wanted revenge.

Lindsey's silk nightgown rose and fell heavily with a deep breath, settling herself.

"I was just a little thing when Aunt Madeline discovered that I had all the indications to be the one that could succeed Aunt Sibyl. I was also too young to realize that Aunt Madey wanted to groom me, as she likes to call it, to be Sibyl's replacement when she retires."

"What?" asked Nathan, leaning forward.

"You didn't know?" she grinned. "Good Lord you are so naïve. I can't believe you haven't put two and two together yet. Please tell me you didn't think there was something romantic going on between us. We're alike Nathan. All *Sensitives* have a proclivity to be attracted to one another. We all just seem to gravitate to one another over time. Or didn't Aunt Madeline tell you this?"

"She intends to have you replace Sibyl?" he scoffed. "But you have your entire life ahead of you. Why would she want to turn you into some sort of..., Archaists Tool?"

Lindsey visibly sank at how concise her future had been described to her in two single words. She jumped from her chair and shut Nathan's door, latching it.

"One of her spy's might hear us," she explained.

Nathan ignored the impropriety of them being locked in his bedroom together for the moment, "There's no way for you to get out of this? If it's not the money, then get yourself free."

Lindsey shook her head, "You don't understand anything about my family and I can't tell you. It's supposed to be some great honor to be the next *Sensitive* of the family, to carry us into the next generation."

"It's not just antiques we're talking about is it?" he whispered.

Lindsey looked toward the locked door and back, then shook her head, "No, it's not."

Something about her story was lacking, something he couldn't quite pin down.

"How does Henry fit into this picture then? I thought he was the one being groomed as you call it."

"My brother?" she grinned. "I love the big doofus, really, but he's all fine and dandy with his part in our family plans. He is being groomed..., to replace Aunt Madeline. Can't you see?"

"And the two of you, together, would be the family successors," he added.

Lindsey nodded, "That's the gist of it..., and all I can tell you."

Her insinuation carried something darker, some threat or maybe her knowledge of past repercussions, should more truth come to light. If all of this was true, then Lindsey was truly tangled in an inescapable web.

Nathan sat back, his body stiff from tension, "And how are you supposed to help me?"

Lindsey sat forward, "That's where it gets tricky."

"As in?" he shook his head.

She sighed, "Aunt Madey was ecstatic when Aunt Sibyl revealed her suspicions about you, that first day we showed up to view the property."

Then she leaned forward to whisper spitefully, "And Nathan..., whatever you do..., don't you dare sell your grandfather clock to Aunt Madey..., don't sell it to anyone."

Lindsey put up her hand to stop the inevitable question he would ask her about the clock.

"I'd never seen Aunt Madey or Aunt Sibyl so excited about discovering you. Nathan, she'll find a way to weave you into the family or lure you somehow. She's the most brilliantly divisive woman I've ever known."

Nathan couldn't help but notice a bit of admiration in her last admission.

Lindsey leaned forward and took his hands in hers.

"They can both help you with learning how to deal with what you are, but it will come at a price Nathan," she whined, shaking her head. "Please be very careful with anything she offers you and I mean any...thing."

Lindsey stood from her chair, urging Nathan to rise, "I have to go now. Someone will notice I'm not in my room."

Her arms went around him and she slid close against his body.

"Thank you for listening to me."

"But I have so many questions?" he whispered, suddenly feeling the softness of her blond hair against his cheek.

Yes..., he did feel that dizzy drawing of the two as she pushed away from him. Lindsey blushed and hurried to the door.

"Lindsey...."

She put up her hand to silence him as hurried footsteps clattered down the hall outside.

She waved him to her and opened the door, then spoke just loud enough for her voice to carry, "I enjoyed our chat Nathan. Maybe we can get away from the house soon. Henry will be here tomorrow; maybe you can show us some of the local interests?"

Lindsey rose up and kissed Nathan on the lips, his arms suddenly holding her in place.

"That part wasn't for show," she whispered.

She slid away slowly, when suddenly her eyes glittered with something forgotten, rushing back to add with barely a breath, "Oh..., one more thing Nathan. Your mother doesn't like Sibyl."

Lindsey grinned at the shocked expression on Nathan's face as she backed across the hall to her room.

When her door clicked shut, Nathan heard the soft steps of someone scurrying down the staircase in the distance. No doubt it was one of the cloned retainers constantly perusing every hallway.

He stood there in a daze, pushing away his feelings for Lindsey, with even more blazing questions to reconcile.

A new rule had possibly been thrust into the game between him and Madeline Stewart.

If what Lindsey told him was true and not just paranoia driven blather, it was possible that his very stay in this house had been pre-orchestrated by her. If Madeline already knew that he had the same potential as Lindsey or Sibyl, then filled his surroundings with objects of violent history..., my God! It could have been a full-fledged shove, instigating what she and Sibyl had admitted was an *Awakening*.

♥

Seven dream-scourged hours later, Nathan was walking down the stairs to catch whatever breakfast Sara had begun. She was indeed working on the meals for the entire upcoming day, and pointed toward the counter when he walked inside the kitchen.

"I figured you'd be up and at it before the rest...," she muttered. "There's also fresh coffee or tea, whichever you fancy."

Nathan had determined last night, to avail himself of every person in the house to get answers, hoping to sort out truth from fiction.

"I'll gain five pounds just from the scent of your food," he replied. "How long have you been the Stewart family chef?"

Her head twisted around with a squint of her green eyes, "Going on nigh ten years now. They've been good years though. No one's complained."

"I definitely haven't had any complaints," said Nathan.

She paused kneading her dough long enough to spite his pandering.

"Ooh, you're as bad as Henry," she huffed. "His flattering tongue usually ends with some special request..., usually my cheesecake. One of these days it's all going to catch up to him and he'll be the size of a cow."

Her hands were choking off pieces of rising dough onto a baking sheet, almost ready to stuff in the oven.

Nathan chuckled, "Guess I'll have to be careful how much I stack on my plate."

Sara turned again with a sly grin, "You look like a fella that can handle a full meal without that kind of worry."

Nathan pushed his luck a little further as he sat down at the table, "It certainly doesn't look as if your cooking has caught up to you. What's your secret?"

Sara spun, grabbed a small hand towel off the counter and threw it at Nathan, "You'll be watching your tongue in my kitchen, you sly devil..., and keeping your eyes on your breakfast."

She turned back around to hide the grin already on her face.

Nathan smiled to himself and began to eat in silence. A few minutes later, he refilled a cup of hot tea, just as Sara was stuffing a second large tray of dough in the oven.

"Could I ask you a question, Sara?" he muttered past a bite of food.

"I don't see why not, considering you just did," she spouted.

Nathan swallowed, "Well..., I'm just beginning to understand some things..., very recently in fact..., one of which you seem to have some experience with. It has to do with the restless spirits you mentioned right after you arrived here."

Sara shook her head slowly, "Such a heavy subject so early in the morning, but I supposed you'd get around to asking about it sooner or later."

"Annie hasn't had anything else happen..., to scare her I mean?"

"The *lady of the house*, you mean?" she whispered, looking around at the doors. "Not since all the family arrived. Quiet as a church mouse. Not so much as a whisper."

"I see," he muttered.

"It's nice that you'd be worried after Annie, but the *lady* doesn't seem to be a belligerent soul, if you don't mind my saying."

"The lady of the house you mean," he added.

Sara nodded and turned back to her duties.

The oddity of it all. An excellent chef by all rights, and an educated woman, speaking about ghosts and spirits as if it was as commonplace as the next day's menu.

She seemed quiet now, her chatty mood was blanched, but he couldn't blame her. There was one more thing he needed from Sara before the opportunity was lost.

He cleaned his plate and stuck it in the dishwasher, "Thanks Sara. The food hit the spot."

She nodded quietly once again, her hands busy shuffling vegetables under running water.

"If you do happen to hear…, or see anything out of the ordinary, would you please let me know?"

Sara continued working busily at first, as if she were going to ignore him, "I suppose I could do that…, but next time I'd rather you ask me to bake you one of my homemade apple pies."

CHAPTER FORTY-FIVE

NATHAN wanted to ask Sara what had become of Bolton these last few days, but he'd already used up all his conversational graces by the time he walked out of the kitchen that morning.

Lisa Evans was standing, peeking out her front window when Nathan arrived at her apartment. She scooted out her door and hurried through the dense morning fog, jumping inside Nathan's Yukon.

"Colder every day," she grunted.

"Yep."

"I see I still have a job."

"Yep," repeated Nathan.

"What are we doing today boss?"

"We're not on the clock yet," he answered. "And we need to leave an hour early today. I have some personal business."

Lisa fell into a quiet glare and Nathan knew immediately what was on her mind.

"Don't worry, I'll still pay you for your regular hours."

Nathan inched out of Crab Cove's fog-choked cul-de-sac onto the highway behind the train of several other drivers creeping along at barely 40 miles per hour.

Lisa stared out into the cold white blanket, chewing her bottom lip nervously.

"That doesn't mean we can't talk," he sighed.

When she continued to stare out the passenger window in silence, Nathan said, "Alright, I'll talk to you then."

His fingers danced on the steering wheel, "I need to explain something to you about our Thanksgiving obligations…."

"Nathan, I'm so over that," she whined. "If you want to spend a fortune on my costume, that's your business. It would have probably been cheaper for you to use an escort service if all you needed was some arm candy."

He gripped the steering wheel until his knuckles whitened before answering, "Lisa…, it, has, nothing, to, do…. Why would I want a bobble-headed call girl as a plus-one when you were available?"

She finally turned to face Nathan, "So I'm your bobble-head?!"

Oh…, that came out so wrong that he sucked in a gut full of air, willing the words back inside.

"What? No! Will you please stop jumping to conclusions?" he gritted.

"Sure, but I'm letting you know right now. I'm charging you a lot more than fourteen bucks an hour to be your plus-one!"

Nathan instantly felt fumes seeping from his ears. All he intended to do was forewarn Lisa about the people she would be meeting at their Thanksgiving Dinner. He felt it only right to prepare her for whatever Madeline Stewart might have up her sleeve.

"Well? What was it you wanted to talk about then?" she asked.

"Nothing. Not a damn thing," he grunted, slamming his hand on the horn at the two fog-hazed brake lights swerving in front of them. Lisa Evans could figure it out all on her own.

♥

Nathan sat at his desk for nearly a half hour in the quiet office, wishing that his morning vanilla latte were a full cup of Kentucky Bourbon.

Finally, Lisa stalked around the partition, arms crossed, "Are you going to sulk all day or give me something to do?"

He flopped open his planner and shuffled through some recent business cards and tossed one to edge of his desk.

"Give Renaldo Lucas a call and introduce yourself," he said, pointing at the card.

He wanted to tell her to use whatever moniker she preferred to go by at the moment, but closed his eyes with a slight wobble of the head.

"There's a manilla folder in your inbox with three sets of photographs and the descriptions of each estate. I need you to make sure he adds them to the Heart Realty account and double check the information on his website as soon as he calls you back."

She stared at the business card, then returned to her desk. Seconds later she was back, still looking at the card.

"You want to give me a clue who this is and what I'm doing?" she asked.

"You're a bright girl, you can…," he sighed, then clenched his teeth tight enough to hear them crackle in his head.

"Mr. Lucas is our advertising agency. You'll need to scan in each of the photos, name each one using our account number plus an alpha, then email the photos and descriptions to his address using the account number as the subject. Make sure you send three separate emails, one for each estate."

Once again, Lisa disappeared around the partition. Once again, she reappeared, still holding the card.

"What?" asked Nathan.

Lisa looked up, "I have this awful feeling that I should have let you explain about our mystery dinner."

"Yes, you should have," he answered, then pointed toward her desk. "Let me know when Mr. Lucas calls you back. I need to speak with him."

By the time one o'clock rolled around, Nathan had isolated four more slow moving properties for Lisa's Monday duties. Thus he kept his hired help too busy to incite any distracting drama for the rest of that day.

The two of them were just past the Salem city limits driving home when Lisa broke the stalemate of silence.

"Troy says I can be more trouble than I'm worth."

Nathan sat quietly, trying to find some encouraging rebuff, but drawing a blank.

"I'm not really going to charge you for the dinner date…, and I'm glad you asked me…. The dress is amazing by the way…, and the shoes."

Nathan focused on the highway onramp, merging into the weekend southbound traffic.

"Are you going to tell me about the dinner now?" she asked shyly.

Nathan glanced her direction, just as his cell phone rang. Their eyes met and Nathan's lips curled in an evil grin as he took the call, "Heart Realty."

"Caroline! I'm glad you called."

Lisa rolled her eyes angrily and turned to stare out her window.

Nathan listened for several minutes, "Then Josie is home and well now?"

He nodded with the phone, "And the kids are still with you?"

"Oh, I see, just until Monday."

Nathan's face froze as their conversation took a different bend, then his voice hushed as he switched the phone to his left side.

"Caro…, Caroline…, can we discuss this in about…, oh…, twenty minutes or so?" he mumbled into the phone.

Lisa was now biting at one of her cuticles, still staring into the distant scenery of the Cascade foothills.

"Yes…, I promise. Love you too."

The phone dropped carefully into the center console as Nathan stared at Highway 101. In another ten minutes, the exit sign to Crab Cove would pop up and Lisa would be delivered to her apartment.

"Want to tell me about your sister?" asked Lisa.

"You've met Caroline, remember?"

Exasperated, Lisa twisted around in her seat with a leg curled underneath her, facing him completely, "I wasn't talking about Caroline."

"Josephine," Nathan nodded. "Just released from the hospital. She's going to be fine."

"So there's five of you, right?"

"And a few distant relatives I hardly ever hear from."

He could feel her eyes probing into him.

"What was it like..., growing up with a big family?"

"Chaos," grinned Nathan, remembering the better moments of his childhood. Not all of his memories were bad, at least until adulthood set in.

"I've never heard you talk about anyone but Caroline, the one I met. Who did the other two younger kids belong to? Kate and..., Chuck?" she guessed, trying to remember his name.

"Kathryn and Chuck belong to Josie."

She was still staring at the side of his dense two o'clock shadow. Waiting for more information?

"Those are the ones in the picture I saw. All the ones I've met."

Nathan nodded quietly.

"Are the others as nice as Caroline?"

Finally, Nathan turned her direction and back, "No. They're not."

Lisa fidgeted in her seat, "So..., I probably won't ever meet them I'm guessing."

"Probably not," he chuckled.

"Do you have pictures of them?"

"None that are recent. What exactly is it you want to know?" he asked.

"If I'm going on a date with you, I'd at least like to know something about your family," she shot back.

Nathan glanced her way for a moment, feeling a little more anxious than he had expected, "We're not really close any more. We drifted apart a few years before Marion started having the first signs of her illness."

He squinted his eyes for a moment, "I'd really rather not talk about my family right now."

She slumped, but didn't turn away from him, "So what about you then? You know all about me..., at least you seem to think you do."

"What you see is what you get, Lisa."

She shook her head, getting frustrated, "So..., fat chance of getting to know anything about you either."

Nathan took the exit leading to Crab Cove and Lisa spun back around in a huff.

"Looks like you're off the hook again," she grunted.

He shrank inside. No one had made the slightest attempt to get to know him since college. Was he really that closed off?

Lisa was busy gathering her things when Nathan parked in Lisa's empty driveway. She was determined to jump out as soon as the Yukon began to slow down.

"Wait...," he said, leaning toward the steering wheel.

Lisa sat expecting some strange apology or rightful accusation against her as to why he shut her down.

He leaned back in his seat, took a deep breath and stared at the charcoal gray ceiling tack above him.

"My great-great-great grandfather's name was Phillipe Bearheart, half Yakama Indian. Our last name was shortened to Heart by my great grandfather Jonah, when he started a trading company on the Washington coast back in 1840 something. Right after Oregon became a legal territory. As I understand it, it wasn't popular to be a half-breed Frenchman back then if you intended to run a business. Anyway, Jonah Heart inherited a huge plot of forest along the coast and made a fortune from selling lumber to several logging companies. Somehow he fell in with the wrong people and most of his earnings disappeared, probably stolen. According to the stories my mother used to tell, that was some sort of big deal. Anyway, before he died..., that is, just before he was murdered..., Jonah and his sons built Heart Manor, right after the turn of the century. At one time, there were three generations of the Heart family living in the house you visited.

"One of his sons had opened a lumber mill, trying to cut out the middleman in the logging industry. That was my grandfather Jeremiah. He was the main supplier to all the shipyards on the west coast. My grandfather was the last owner of the Heart Lumber Mill in Astoria before it was shut down...."

By the time Nathan was through telling Lisa sketches of his family history, she was comfortably twenty minutes late for her shift at the restaurant.

He waited outside her apartment while she changed clothes and gave her a ride to keep her out of a steady misting rain that had begun to fall. It had felt good to share bits and pieces of his life while listening to her questions and comments. She didn't even complain about being late for work when he dropped her off.

Now, he was driving back to his other life, the one that made less sense every day.

♥

Nathan had just parked in the garage when his phone rang. It was Caroline. He glanced quickly at the time..., three fifteen. So much for his promise to call her right back.

"Caroline, I'm so sorry," he began. It seemed all he was doing lately was apologizing for something that was either beyond his control or forgotten.

"Its okay little brother," she answered. "I knew you had a good reason for making me wait."

He wanted to tell her that he had no good reasons for anything lately, let alone keeping her in the dark. But even his best explanations would have to be just as opaque for the time being.

"I know you want answers about the photograph, but all I can tell you at the moment is all speculation. Was it real? If you'd asked me that a year ago, or before that, I would have laughed at you."

Caroline jumped in before he could continue his discourse, "But now you do believe it's real. I can hear it in your voice."

Nathan sat in the stillness trying to mull through a response.

"Of course you do..., so do I," she said finally. "It's the only explanation Nathan. I played with the image on my computer so many different ways, even you would have been impressed. It's her, Nathan. It's Marion."

"I think so too," he muttered. "But I still don't know what it means Caroline. I'm looking for answers, even though there may never be any."

Caroline breathed heavily into the phone, "I know. I haven't even told Chris. He already thinks our family is a nightmare. This would drive him into a frenzy. And besides, he'd think you had something to do with it and you're the only one he even acknowledges out of the whole bunch, except for the little ones."

Did he dare tell her anything? Nathan shuddered at the very thought of revealing what was going on with him at that very moment. Of course not. There was no way on earth he would ever breathe a word about his recent experiences.

"I might know someone that can offer a little help," he hinted. "Even that's doubtful."

"You know some..., Ghostbuster?" she squeaked. "Exactly who have you been hanging around lately?"

Nathan suppressed a violent laugh that tried to erupt, "I sell a lot of old houses Caroline. I meet some very strange people with very strange ideas."

"Nathan, I don't need to know that badly. Don't get mixed up with some lunatic that talks to ghosts just because of a picture. I'm satisfied that it's an image of mother. Maybe we both should just leave it at that. Maybe it was her way of saying goodbye."

It was far, far too late for Caroline to offer him any common sense at this point in his life. Ghosts were the very least of his concern.

"Maybe you're right. We'll just leave it alone for now and if anything else happens, we'll deal with it then," he said as calmly as he could muster.

She had given him a way out. He couldn't have asked for anything more tidy.

"Nathan?" she muttered. "You didn't argue. Is there something going on that I need to know about?"

"Of course not," he chuckled nervously. "Why would you think that?"

"Nathan Heart, I know when you're lying," she gritted. "And you're lying to me right now."

He had no answer, no reply..., he was stunned at her sisterly accuracy.

"I'm sorry Nathan," she said suddenly. "I don't know what came over me. I know you'll tell me if you figure something out. I guess I forgot that you've been through a lot lately. I love you little brother."

CHAPTER FORTY-SIX

"**Y**OU have to trust someone eventually," said Sibyl.

Nathan gazed slowly around the library shelves and pushed his chair back a few inches, settling his focus on Madeline and Sibyl. She was holding the worn notepad taken from John Smith, carefully between her fingers.

"I don't mean you any disrespect, Ms. Stewart, but trust is something that is earned over time. Not with a quick handshake. At least that's the world I grew up in."

Madeline nodded appreciatively and thankfully didn't seem offended.

Sibyl handed the pad back to Nathan, "Not everyone is like your elder siblings, Mr. Heart. Take you for instance. You were the youngest of five, raised by the same parent, in the same household. You went to the same schools, ate together, argued together, and even laughed over the same mistakes together. Yet..., you turned out far..., far different than the others."

"Again, I mean no disrespect, but this is my very..., life..., I'm trying to protect. Sibyl..., I watched my mother transform from a healthy, active, caring woman into an empty shell of her former self before she died. If I'm to put my life in your hands and believe everything you're telling me, instead of seeking professional medical help for my symptoms, then I need to know more than you're telling me."

Sibyl sat bolt upright in her chair, then leaned forward and took Nathan's hands in hers.

"Good. Then let's take a little journey together, seated right here."

She had him place the notepad in both their hands and patted his wrist to make sure he was looking at her.

"Now what I'd like you to do, is follow me for a few moments. Experience is a good teacher, is it not?"

Nathan nodded slowly, carefully.

"Well then..., I want you to close your eyes and take a deep breath. When you start to feel that little trickle of dizzy, when the floor falls away beneath you, instead of fighting it, I want you to picture yourself the first time you went swimming. I want you to just jump right in as if it was a warm summer day without a care in the world. I'm going to be right here the entire time, holding your hands."

Nathan took a deep breath, his eyes already closed, listening to Sibyl's relaxing voice.

Despite her warning, despite her instructions, he gasped for breath when the earth disappeared from beneath his chair. He felt Sibyl's hands tighten on his and managed to relax.

"That's good. You're doing just fine," she whispered from somewhere far away. "Now..., feel the cover of the notepad we're holding together. As soon as you see it in your mind, you're going to drop one more time..., a little deeper this time."

He felt the slick texture of the wrinkled cover, then Sibyl opened it and guided his fingertips across the deep gouges, written on several of the pages. Without the warning, he might have fallen face first onto the floor that must still be only a few feet below his chair. Wasn't he still seated in a chair?

It was suddenly hazy daylight and he was standing behind a tree, looking toward a dark blue car that was parked on the side of a road. It looked very familiar somehow and he felt a few drops of rain pelting his shoulders. A red car was coming up the road, Marion's Cadillac..., and it slowed and stopped beside this older car. Nathan felt his world sink once more as he saw himself get out of the Cadillac and walk around this strange car.

He was viewing himself through the eyes of the owner of the notepad, quickly remembering the abandoned vehicle from weeks ago. This person had been watching him even then, for longer than he'd known. Quickly..., photographic flashes of the delivery trucks, peeks into his windows, repeated scribbles on the notepad's pages. Then he saw himself playing with a slanted door-lock, then the door opened and he recognized it as the external cellar door at the rear of the house. Even faster, he descended into the darkness of the cellar, then faster still..., hurried up the stairs to the washroom entry inside the very house. In seconds, he was peering into the kitchen, looking around, listening, then shuffling through papers and receipts in his office.

Nathan was faintly aware of Sibyl's voice whispering instructions from somewhere, not really cognizant of what she was saying.

Then the scene changed and he was seated in an ugly chair in a hotel room, with a phone receiver in hand, holding a conversation. The strong smell of cigarettes blanched his nostrils, almost making him cough.

Fistfuls of warbled sounds, distorted voices, echoed toward him. Whoever was on the other end of the telephone call was angry..., a man's voice with a strong accent.

It was just there..., recognition hovering on the rim of Nathan's consciousness.... He felt his fingers tighten the pages of the little notepad somewhere back in reality and his body quivered at the expense. He dropped..., deep, as his vision followed past the telephone line the horrible little man was holding in his vision.

The voice now had a face....

Nathan gasped as he felt dizzying heat flow into his body. This familiar face was barking threats at the terrified investigator until....

Nathan opened his eyes, blinking them furiously, forcing himself back from some depth and gasping for breath.

"Stäkkr."

He felt his lips move, but no sound seemed to emanate past them as if he were in a vacuum. His body lurched forward and found himself still planted in the chair, holding the notepad with both hands gripping a mutilated page of the notepad like steel.

Both Sibyl and Madeline were watching him carefully in silence as he reeled in his anger, back to the rollercoaster ride he'd been strapped in.

Nathan looked down at the notepad, then threw it onto the floor in unbridled anger.

He swallowed, "What just happened? How long was I gone?"

Sibyl smiled at him, then at Madeline before she answered, "You just experienced your first *Reading*. It only lasted about ten or fifteen seconds. You did quite well."

Nathan tried to stand, but sank right back down into his chair.

"You shouldn't move around for a few minutes after a *Reading* that intense, not until you get used to the spins and drops. After that..., it all becomes second nature."

"It felt like..., I was right there..., for hours," he whispered.

He looked down at his watch; practically no time had passed. He suddenly wanted to be somewhere else, throttling the face he'd seen back inside the tunnel.

"Once you acclimate yourself to the process, you just touch an *Object*, see where it's been, and eventually..., with practice..., you can steer your visions to only those things you wish to learn about."

Nathan's head spun once again, but his pulse was gradually slowing down.

"How accurate are the visions? Are they ever wrong?"

Once again, Sibyl gave Madeline a glance, deferring to her, "They only tell the raw truth, but you need to be careful with what you learn. Like all things in life, there is always more than one viewpoint. The information can easily be skewed by the eyes you're looking through and their emotions."

Sibyl spoke up once again, "Later on, you won't have to be limited to the owner's viewpoint, you'll see things from the *Object* itself. It gives new meaning to being a fly on the wall."

Hadn't he just done that? He'd somehow ripped himself free from the horrid owner of the notepad and....

"This is too much to wrap around all at once," he muttered. "I can see how knowledge like this might even get you killed."

Sibyl grinned, "And that is precisely why only those with the predisposition of our burden know about us. The only ones we can't completely hide from are others like ourselves."

"I'm not going to lie to you. I don't like it," said Nathan.

Two small warm hands slid on his shoulders from behind him.

"Neither did I at first," said Lindsey. "But it's much better than the alternative."

Nathan nodded thoughtfully. It was better than the insanity of misunderstanding what was going on inside his head, listening to the past, viewing the past, virtually reliving the past.

"Lindsey, this isn't a good time," said Madeline, her voice almost cold.

"I didn't mean to intrude, Aunt Madey," said Lindsey. "But you have a delivery truck waiting outside."

"Mr. Heart, who or what is Stocker?" asked Madeline, ignoring her niece. She had perfectly reproduced the pronunciation from the moment of recognition in his mind.

Nathan felt the same heat rise, flooding his face. It was too late to hide his emotions, too late to formulate some clever lie.

"An acquaintance," said Nathan. "I'd rather not share just yet. I want to verify my experience in my own way."

In truth, he'd been so happy that it wasn't Jonas or one of his other relatives on the other end of that telephone call that he almost dismissed the whole matter.

"Very wise," said Sibyl. "But share with someone..., someone you do trust in case...."

Madeline touched Sibyl's arm, interrupting her sister, "What Sibyl means is..., be very careful how you proceed so something dreadful doesn't happen to you. Outsiders will not understand the questions you ask."

Nathan's eyes glossed for a moment before he nodded, "Of course, you're absolutely right. Thank you. Thank you both."

Both of the elder women excused themselves and Lindsey sat down in the chair where Madeline Stewart observed his first training session.

"I hope you didn't mind me eavesdropping on your time with my Aunts," said Lindsey. "It was the only way I could know how to answer any of your questions, or know if they were trying to nudge you into something you might not want."

"It's too late for that," huffed Nathan.

He leaned forward to pick up the discarded notepad, then thought twice as he saw the familiar face in his mind once again.

He kicked it across the slick hardwood floor.

Even with Lindsey hovering close, a welcome distraction, he thought of how this experience might have been perceived if it happened to his mother. Marion would have been completely devoid of understanding without someone to take her hand and pull her from the mire.

Marion Heart..., she'd lived lifetimes inside herself, other people's lifetimes instead of her own, lost to reality. No wonder she would sit and talk for hours on end about the history of his family. The house or some of its objects had completely stolen her away from reality.

"Are you feeling alright?" asked Lindsey.

She was suddenly kneeling in front of him, staring up into his face..., and there were tears resting on his cheeks.

No longer was there a reason to keep a journal of his thoughts. His memories weren't being swept away down a drain as he'd suspected; quite the contrary. They were lying stagnant all around him.

♥

Lindsey had urged Nathan to sit outside in the fresh air for a few minutes, until the delivery truck drove away.

Nathan was coming to appreciate her kindness and acceptance as he braced himself for the impact these changes were going to have on his future. He had to remind himself that if he could somehow see past what others might think, the theater of his life might expand beyond his imagination. In fact, if he could learn to control the awkwardness of this *Awakening*, it could be a true benefit for him and those he cared for.

If he survived, he reminded himself.

For the rest of the afternoon, he found himself caught up in conversation, enjoying Lindsey's company, huddled away in the den together.

"You must have known Jon was only using you for your money," said Nathan.

She grinned, "I fought the knowledge with all my heart, wishing it not to be true. But..., when I accepted who he was, I found that he was a means to an end and I didn't care. We enjoyed each other's company and he was wonderfully reckless. When rebellion takes over you, sitting at home in front of the television for an evening is not on the menu. Jon was my escort into all things adventurous and exciting, even dangerous. My early life was so sheltered at home, so when I saw there was no one holding my reins, I wanted to run like the wind. That was all my entire second year at Duke University consisted of..., and why Henry finally felt duty bound to inform Aunt Madey of what was going on.

"I don't blame Jon..., not anymore. And of course I can't blame Henry, he was only trying to help. After all, he did cover for me for almost an entire year of missing classes, near failing grades, intercepting letters of reprimand from several of the University Staff. I think he might have eventually done some harm to Jon had I not come to my senses when I did. But by then..., I was already in love.

"I managed to right myself and repair my grades, but I never quite let go of my relationship with Jon. Then after graduation, Aunt Madey wanted me to concentrate my time with Aunt Sibyl..., training. That was when I chanced another unexpected meeting with Jon; everything rekindled and my personal war began."

"I can understand why you wanted your freedom," said Nathan. "It's too bad your friend Jon turned out to be less than you expected."

"Enough about me...," she grinned. "What about your love life?"

Nathan laughed, "My love life? Well..., when...."

"Lindsey, your brother is here," said a voice from the hallway.

"Mark your place, Nathan Heart," she smiled. "You're not getting off that easy."

CHAPTER FORTY-SEVEN

HENRY Stewart was parked out front, with his uncles surrounding a white vintage automobile. Each one was pointing to some item of glory on the extravagantly restored vehicle. Even Nathan ripped on a coat and thrust himself into the mix to get a closer look at Henry's new toy.

"Nathan Heart, good to see you," said Henry. "What do you think about my new Jag?"

His voice boomed as he shot out a hand with a quick violent clasp and shake. Henry welcomed him like some old well-acquainted friend.

"Good to see you too, Henry. I've never seen anything like it, especially up close. This didn't come from any dealership I've ever seen. Where did you find it?"

"At an auction in Vancouver, yesterday morning. I traded a nasty old piece of furniture for it, but don't tell Aunt Madey whatever you do. She probably wouldn't understand."

Nathan zipped his lips and grinned back at a younger version of himself. Madeline was already glaring through the front picture window, her face expressionless.

"I think it's too late for pretenses now," said Nathan.

"Why don't I say hello to everyone and we'll gather up Lindsey and take it for a drive?"

Nathan laughed outright, "You just made it here."

"And I can't imagine being cooped up inside with all the family elders for more than an hour at a time. You must be ready to crack your own skull by now," said Henry.

Nathan shrugged, "I've had some moments like that, but it hasn't been all bad."

Henry's smiling face spun and he waved at Madeline, "I don't suppose Lindsey had anything to do with that did she?"

Warning lights flared in Nathan's head, "We had a chance to talk for a few minutes."

"Talk..., a few minutes?" he spat a laugh. "Well..., my little sister's pretty good at spilling whatever's on her mind. Anyway, thanks for keeping her from killing Aunt Madey. The rest of the family might not have understood."

Did Henry know about what was going on? Or was Madeline keeping that information close to her chest? That would be impossible. He had to be privy to all their conversations; it was the nature of the beast.

"Lindsey's been helpful," said Nathan. "I've learned a few things about myself in the process."

Henry laughed, then shook his head, "Oh no. You must have met Aunt Sibyl. When those two Aunts of mine get their heads together, I try to run like hell. Those two are always plotting something."

Sure, Henry knew, and was trying to lighten the situation or maybe add perspective. He liked Henry all the more for it.

"Well..., let's get this over with," grunted Henry. "The sooner I go make peace with the family, the sooner we can get out of here."

♥

"You know how I despair at showy trinkets. Why would you purchase such an atrocity?" asked Madeline. "What do you intend to do with it?"

Nathan was standing far away, at the door to his old office, where a few pieces of plastic wrapped furniture were pushed to a corner. He was itching to take a look, but his ears were trained to the conversation out in the center of the living room.

"We have three empty stalls alongside this house to store it, and besides..., I like it," Henry balked. "It would have ended up in some snooty collectors archive if I hadn't saved its life. Besides, a 1960 Mark II will only appreciate in value. This one was used by Moore in one of the old Bond movies."

He was talking about the relic as if it were a discarded pup he'd salvaged from being euthanized.

"You'll learn someday that a mass of toys that need caring for on a regular basis soon become a boat anchor," she chided.

Henry's eyes rolled around at the insides of the living room, where all eyes were affixed on their controversy, "So that must mean I'm not allowed to get married either," he laughed.

Madeline's expression became her practiced frozen tilt up toward Henry's face.

Lindsey hurried up beside Henry, who was about to start a war he could not win, "Aunt Madey, can we have this conversation later? In private?"

Madeline's eyes darted about in little fractions of a second, "Of course. You're right dear. I let my emotions get the better of me. Consider the matter settled Henry," she sighed. Her hand waved him away. "Go. Go play with your toy."

Henry turned away without another word to Madeline Stewart, "Nathan! Grab your leathers and let's go. Are you coming with us Lens?"

Lindsey glanced back at Madeline through her lashes, possibly seeking some hint of approval, "I'll get my coat."

♥

"It looks like we're going to be too late to eat with the family. Isn't that too bad? Do you have any suggestions, Nathan?" asked Henry.

Lindsey squeaked, leaning in between the two front seats, as Henry took another curve a little too quickly for the vintage antique. They'd been driving around the hilly area like three teenagers, almost until dark, with Nathan as their tour guide.

It was their loops in and around Lumberton that had Nathan immersed in quiet speculation as once again, he glimpsed signs with Stäkkr Realty glaring back at him. He didn't want to believe that Eben M. Stäkkr was involved in anything so despicable as hiring an investigator to spy on him. They were by no means friends…, but enemies?

Nathan returned from his stupor moments before he would have received a nudge from either or both Henry and Lindsey.

"Turn west at the next intersection. I know just the place."

Nathan had deep reservations about taking this brother and sister combination to the Blind Pirate. Maybe he could solve two problems with one innocent evening meal. He had tried to explain the Stewart family to Lisa with no success. Even though these two were not a valid sample of the personalities of the elder Stewarts, they might serve to give her a glimpse of what to expect at their dinner party.

♥

"I love the cliffs," said Lindsey.

Although the sun had set and only twilit glimpses were visible, the wind was carrying up the sounds of the steady roar of crashing surf beyond the shelter of Crab Cove.

She curled against Nathan for warmth, "I never get tired of listening to what the ocean has to say."

The wind whistled loudly as it rushed past two strands of steel cables, protecting onlookers from a sudden perilous drop to the darkness below.

"The poet has spoken," grunted Henry. "Now can we go inside? It's too cold to stand out here and marvel at nature."

The three hurried back along a thin gravely path, following the cliffs suicidal escarpment to the restaurant parking lot.

♥

"Nathan!" said Troy, his bluster suddenly failing him. "I see you brought more happy customers with you tonight. And a mite better lookin' crowd as well."

Troy's eyes were bulging, staring at Lindsey.

Nathan made quick introductions, noting how strangely Troy was behaving. It didn't help that Lindsey had a hand draped around one of Nathan's arms.

"What's on the grill tonight?" asked Nathan. "We're starved."

"A tank of fresh lobster from up the coast and shark steaks that haven't even hit the freezer," said Troy. "You'll have to wait a spell here at the bar though."

True to his word, the waiting area was standing room only, so the three of them took a seat and Troy returned moments later, shoving mugs in front of Nathan and his company.

Troy was already glamoured by Lindsey, yet primed and cocked to try out his blustering style of bull on her brother Henry.

"Yer obviously not from these parts," he began. "Nobody has any color to their cheeks lest they've been standing out facing the wind for a spell."

"Is that your way of asking where we're from?" asked Henry.

"Watch your manners, Henry," said Lindsey, thumping at his arm. "We're from a little town on the east coast, where the beach is usually warm and sunny."

Henry slid away from his sister, "And it has sand, not the cold grit and rock that passes for a beach around here."

"Henry, stop it," hissed Lindsey.

She put down her drink and let her palms slide slowly across the scarred wood on the bar, then her glazed eyes looked at Nathan before she spoke again.

"What unusual wood to be on top of a bar," she mumbled.

Nathan followed her gaze and felt himself drop, as if his stool anchored on the floor, sank at least a foot. She was *Reading* the planks like he'd seen Sibyl do and with a simple meeting of their eyes, she was somehow taking him along for the ride.

With an inroad to impress Lindsey, Troy began his practiced dissertation explaining the origins of the planks. This time the boards not only came from the deck of one of Blackbeard's wrecked frigates, it came from inside the old pirate's private quarters.

"Interesting tale," said Henry, as soon as Troy's story ran to ground. "What do you think Lindsey?"

She felt the wood, then peered over at Nathan with a sly grin, "Portuguese pine, right Nathan?"

"James Cook," hissed out, just as his eyes met Lindsey's. "Captain Cook."

His chair felt as if it had suddenly righted itself, just as the feeling of cold hard waves were about to lash the storm tossed ship he'd seen in his mind. A ruddy faced man had been screaming out the captain's name through the dark sounds of splintering wood somewhere below deck.

Lindsey smiled, "I believe you're right."

Troy belly laughed, "Bosh. I know'ed the old salt that sold me these planks. Had 'em stored for years; I mounted 'em on this bar with my own two hands."

Lindsey ignored Troy as he stalked off in a bluster, "Aunt Madey would be interested in this, Henry."

Henry shook his head, upending his mug, "Whatever you say."

"What's bothering you tonight?" she asked. "You never let your feelings get in the way of business."

"I don't like the guy. He's full of himself," grunted Henry.

"And you're not?" she laughed.

CHAPTER FORTY-EIGHT

TROY eventually edged back to where Nathan and his companions were seated, then directed them to a table instead of calling for a waitress, which no doubt would have been Lisa. Nathan's forehead creased in wonder.

"Is this Lisa's section?" asked Nathan as they slid into a large booth at the far side of the restaurant.

"Her section is pretty well stuffed, but…, if that's what you'd rather. I can seat ya over by the corner."

Nathan stood back up from the booth, "That would be perfect. I'd like Lisa to have a chance to get to know my best client's. It was their family that purchased the old Heart Manor."

Troy mumbled something incoherent, bordering on a grumble as he led them over to an open corner table.

Lisa arrived in a flurry just as they were about to take a seat.

"Good evening…, we have fresh…," cheered Lisa, her voice stopping cold with surprise. "Nathan."

Her glittering eyes flicked between Lindsey and Henry, suddenly becoming dead and unreadable.

"Lisa, you remember Lindsey Stewart," he said. "This is her brother Henry Stewart. Henry, this is my new…, assistant at my Salem office, Lisa Evans."

Lisa unfroze just long enough to shake their hands and offer a smile.

"It's *very*…, nice to meet you, Miss Evans," said Henry, his voice suddenly a low rumble. "You let someone as lovely as this work another job? Shame on you Nathan."

Nathan froze for an instant, taken completely by surprise, "Well, I'm working on getting Lisa as a full time employee."

All the sincerity of his words turned to flotsam as soon as he noticed that Lisa was just as fixated on Henry.

The four of them were standing beside the awaiting table in an uncomfortable pause.

Lisa's head wobbled, "If you'll take a seat..., I'll be right back to uh..., get your drinks."

She disappeared in a flash, Nathan watching her retreat.

When he turned, Lindsey was seated on one side of the booth, Henry on the other. Suddenly, the whole idea of acclimating Lisa to the Stewart family turned sour in his gut.

Lindsey smiled, "Have a seat Nathan, she'll be back."

"You have a very attractive assistant," said Henry. "How do you get any work done at your office?"

Nathan slid in beside Lindsey, now scoffing at her brother as she peered over the menu, "Is there anything on here that isn't fishy?"

Of course..., Lindsey didn't like seafood; another blunder to add to his list of charms.

"Lens, it's a seafood restaurant," grunted Henry. "Deal with it."

"There's steak on the back of the menu," muttered Nathan.

Lisa walked back up, just this side of breathless, "Now, what can I get you to drink?"

Her chestnut hair was carefully rearranged in a loose ponytail, light blush on her cheeks and a fresh touch of rose lipstick. Her eyes trained on Henry as she waited for their order.

'Unbelievable', thought Nathan as an unexplainable jealous twinge twisted inside, constricting around his spine.

Lindsey leaned heavily across Nathan, draping an arm on his closest shoulder to place her order first. Lisa saw the display of comfortable familiarity and her Henry-trance shattered.

Lisa scribbled Lindsey's request on her order pad in jerky little strokes and glanced angrily at Nathan, "Troy said he needs to talk to you..., at the bar."

Nathan couldn't remember a time he felt so relieved for an excuse to get away from the quickly mounting tension. He glanced over his shoulder where Troy was standing behind the end of the bar, waiting impatiently.

Nathan excused himself, fighting off a heated glare from Lisa as he pushed past her to get out of the booth.

He hurried over to the bar and leaned closer to Troy, "Lisa said you wanted me. Can you make it quick?"

"Aye, if that's how you'd like it. What the devil were you thinking, bringing another woman the likes of her in here? Are ya trying to send Lisa packin'?"

Nathan stepped back in shock, "The likes of her...?"

For a split second, he was considering an end of their quasi-friendship, but this was the same Troy he'd come to expect.

"I need Lisa to get to know both of them."

"Well, it looks like yer gettin' yer wish," he nodded toward the table.

Nathan jerked back around to see Lisa seated next to Henry in the booth, holding up a menu and smiling..., laughing as she pointed to the list.

"She's just doing her job," said Nathan, although he didn't quite believe his own words.

"Well if you ask me, a man shouldn't piss in his own flower garden. It looks like ya introduced little Lisa to the devil himself."

Troy's myopic brain was still in matchmaker mode. Nathan shook his head in disgust, "Troy, just try to..., never mind. I have to get back."

Nathan walked away as quickly as possible without bowling someone down in his path. How could Troy get under his skin so quickly?

"Mark my words Nathan Heart...," grumbled on behind Nathan as he hurried back through the maze of busy tables.

By the time he arrived, Lisa was leaning over the end of table, her palms flat on its top, talking to both of his guests. Nathan laid his hand lightly on the flat of Lisa's back to prevent his usual train wreck as he shifted past.

"My shift ends at nine.... I don't see why not," she said, answering some unknown question.

"Good, we'll wait for you then," said Henry.

Lisa turned to walk away, speaking over her shoulder, "Oh..., I ordered you the smoked salmon, Mr. Heart."

She didn't wait for his reply, hurrying away with a mischievous grin on her face.

"I like her Henry," said Lindsey. "For once you actually might be showing some good taste."

Henry grinned and took out his cell phone to make a call just as Lindsey shuffled closer to Nathan, "Henry has a wonderful idea Nathan. Our jet is still docked at the airport and we want to make a quick trip to Ventura Beach tonight. Would you please come with us?"

Their private jet could probably make the trip in just over an hour..., then his head shook into gear, "Southern California? Tonight?"

Nathan listened quietly, his eyes blinking in thought, as Henry called their pilot and setup a flight schedule.

"Or would you rather go back to that dreadful house and listen to our Aunt Madey drone on about the benefits of being a *Sensitive*?"

Lindsey made the word sound like sour milk as it rolled off her tongue, yet she'd yanked him into a *Reading* with her hardly an hour ago.

Henry was suddenly off his phone, staring at Nathan, "Don't be noddy..., come with us Nathan. It'll do all of us some good."

Warning flags were raising their beacons but he couldn't tell if they were simply his own fears of stepping past his comfort zone.

"I don't see why not," Nathan said finally.

He wasn't about to let Lisa blaze off on some late night escapade with a virtual stranger. He owed her that much if only as her employer. He alone was responsible for dragging Lisa into this.

Lindsey hugged his arm in delight, "Good. Isn't it going to be too late when we get there?"

Henry tapped the table with his index, "There's an all night music festival along the beach and our regular suite is always available at the Hilton if we run out of steam."

"What kind of festival?" blurted Nathan.

Henry made an odd face at Lindsey before he answered Nathan, "Local bands…, all kinds of music. I promise you'll like it."

Lisa walked up carrying three fresh mugs and sat down across from Nathan, next to Henry.

"Troy's in a mood. What did you say to him Nathan?" asked Lisa.

"He was playing mother hen again and I sort of told him to back off," he answered.

It wasn't an exact interpretation, but it was close enough.

"Really…," said Lisa, her stare fixed on him. "Will wonders never cease."

Henry sat down his mug and turned to Lisa, "If he's that much trouble, why don't you quit?"

Lisa blushed just a tint and looked at Nathan for help before she answered, "Because I don't just work here, I rent an apartment from him."

Henry continued, "Let me guess…; if you quit, you'd have to find somewhere else to live?"

Lisa let out an uncomfortable chuckle, "That about sums it up."

Henry tapped his finger on the table in front of Nathan, "Don't you work in real estate? Why don't you find Lisa somewhere else to live…, close to your office, maybe in Salem?"

Nathan almost choked at the question. Lisa was already keeping him at arms length, "Because I assumed Miss Evans was happy where she is at the moment."

Lisa shook her head at Henry, "I think you're assuming too much, Mr. Stewart. Nathan's not responsible for where I live. This is my choice for now."

Nathan felt a palpable relief and pride at Lisa's reply as well as an admiration for her refusal to be belittled over her social status. Her declaration of independence seemed to have quieted Henry's air of judgment, at least for the moment.

She stood up after a quick glance at the bar, "Your food's up. I'll be back in a minute."

As soon as Lisa was out of earshot, Lindsey slapped Henry's arm angrily.

"What was that all about? You don't ever challenge a girl's independence. What were you thinking Henry?

"And shame on you too, Nathan…. A girl's never completely satisfied with where she lives. She makes the best of whatever situation she's in. You have to make her think it's her decision to better herself.

"I've never seen such incompetence in two men in my life."

Lindsey took in a deep breath and distanced herself from both men just as Lisa returned with their food.

CHAPTER FORTY-NINE

LISA Evans was trying unsuccessfully to hide her apprehensions as they stepped up the ramp into the Stewart's private jet.

"What do I do?" she whispered to Nathan.

Henry and Lindsey were arguing with the person about to drive away in Henry's restored Jaguar while Nathan escorted Lisa inside the aircraft.

"Sit and try to relax," he said with his best comforting grin.

Lisa frowned at him, "Don't be dense, Nathan. I've never even been inside an airplane. I'm scared to death. This is all your fault."

How was this his fault? She was the one that agreed to cavort off to parts unknown with perfect strangers.

"It's just like riding the bus," sighed Nathan.

"Buses can't fly!" she hissed angrily. "And I didn't get a chance to grab my emergency stuff before we left."

He looked her over quickly, considering some sort of a compliment. She had changed into a nice pair of jeans, a thick sweater; more than just mildly attractive.

Nathan closed his eyes feeling just a twinge of jealousy, "Next time don't be so quick to fall for some stranger's smile."

Lisa gasped and turned in the seat she'd just plopped down in.

"You..., you.... What did you expect me to do! Aren't these the people you wanted me to rub elbows with? You think I wanted to spend my only day off tomorrow babysitting some overgrown, pretty rich kid?"

Nathan looked stunned.

"I thought you were...," he began, just as Lisa stood from her seat to face him.

"You thought I was what?" she gasped, her eyes flaring. "You thought I had a personal interest in him?"

She looked back at the empty cabin to make sure they were still alone, then hissed at Nathan, "I hate you Nathan Heart."

Lisa hurried back down the aisle heading for the exit.

"Lisa. Where are you going?" he asked, trying to scramble out of his seat.

"Home. Anywhere away from you," she muttered, waving goodbye. "I'll remember to keep the receipt for the cab fare."

"Wait, Lisa, please...," said Nathan.

His heart was pounding once again, reminding him of the sudden angst of some childish game.

Henry and Lindsey stormed up the stairs into the cabin and the heavy door thumped closed behind them, cutting off Lisa's escape.

Nathan sat back down listening to the sudden hissing of air, pressurizing the cabin. Lisa was completely ignoring his existence, still looking for an escape as she wilted just out of their sight.

"That was ridiculous," laughed Henry. "We leased the hanger for the entire month of November and they couldn't park my car inside it for a few hours?"

The twin turbine engines whined a shrill pitch and the aircraft shuddered to life.

"Quit complaining Henry. You'll spoil our fun," Lindsey scolded her brother.

They met a very frustrated Lisa standing in the galley, realizing that her one mode of escape was long gone.

"Where is the ladies room?" she asked, before either of them could probe her with questions.

"Right behind you," said Henry. "But we're moving now..., I'm afraid you'll have to wait a few minutes until we're in the air."

Lindsey hurried down the oval cabin to sit beside Nathan, her eyes assessing the distance between him and Lisa.

She leaned over her armrest closer to Nathan, muttering quietly, "What did you do Nathan?"

Nathan was sporting a blank stare out the portside window, considering an exit strategy, "Besides get out of bed this morning?"

Her very presence against his shoulder settled his nerves like a tonic, so immediate that he had to take a deep breath before accepting it.

Lindsey laughed and hugged his arm, "Come on."

She stood up and yanked at Nathan's arm, "Lets all sit together, we're supposed to be having a good time, remember?"

They rounded the row of seats where both Lisa and Henry were both in a dead stare, Henry's brow developing tiny trenches.

"Let me guess…, you don't fly very often do you Miss Evans?" asked Lindsey with a sympathetic grin.

They took seats directly across from each other before Lisa responded.

"Not very."

"Well…, let me put you at ease then. Our family…, mechanics have a way of knowing if there's some issue with one of our aircraft. We've never lost one."

Lindsey gave Nathan a knowing look to bring him along with her explanation.

"Never?" mumbled Lisa.

"Ever," said Lindsey. "So try to relax and enjoy yourself. Think of this as a…."

"Please don't say bus ride," sighed Lisa, darting a harsh look toward Nathan.

"…mini vacation…," finished Lindsey, noting Lisa's every movement. "Henry, do you think the street vendors will be out tonight?"

Henry woke from his transfixed stare and began a steady, happy faced drone as the twin-engine Gulfstream whined and shivered, taxiing to the runway.

By the time the aircraft was at altitude, Henry had sold the relaxing time in Venice Beach to everyone in the group, including himself.

♥

Warm sultry air blasted their faces as they stepped down onto the tarmac. Lisa stopped on the last step lifting her face to a soft night breeze.

"It's warm. It's midnight in the middle of November and its warm," she sighed, hurrying down to stand by the others.

Henry looked at his watch, just as a short limo pulled up close by. "Don't be too impressed, the weather here is as fickle as a kite."

Lindsey had managed to knit their fellowship back into one happy cohesive group. At least everyone was speaking to each other in more than short sentences.

They all slid inside along the round lounge seat inside the car, with the two women suddenly seated next to each other.

Lisa looked uncomfortable once again, let out a deep breath and leaned toward Lindsey for a private conversation.

Henry tapped on the forward partition, "Venice Beach please."

The car had just begun to move when Lindsey blurted, "Stop the car."

She opened the door as soon as the bulky vehicle shook to a halt. Dragging Lisa by the hand, they hurried back to the aircraft without any explanation.

"What was that all about?" asked Henry.

"How am I supposed to know?" grunted Nathan.

"She works for you."

"For the last ten days. That doesn't make me an expert."

"You're right. Sorry Nathan. I've been around my sister all my life and I still don't understand her."

Both men laughed uncomfortably until Henry's phone rang.

"Aunt Madey..., sorry about supper, we...."

"Yes, we took the.... Just a short trip down the coast."

Henry glanced over at Nathan, his voice a low growl, "I'm well aware of.... Of course. I'll see to it. I understand. See you tomorrow." He yawned to tears and brushed them away, "You'd think I kidnapped the King and Queen of England."

The whole scenario couldn't have been more cryptic and there was no open context to ask Henry.

"Trouble?" pried Nathan.

Henry waved his hand, "Of course not. My aunt was worried about...," his eyes glittered as he sought an answer, "...some of our cargo. It doesn't matter."

Lindsey and Lisa opened the car door and stepped inside. Both were wearing matching Capri's, heels, and some sort of glittery indefinable camisole; very attractive and warm weather appropriate. Their smiles were infectious and they seemed extremely pleased with themselves as they slid across the lounge seat together.

"Very nice," said Nathan, trying to get first compliment. "Do you carry a magic wand?"

"Lisa's just about my size, even if she is a little taller. Since I've been forced to tag along on all our business trips, I made sure I had a few reserves onboard the plane."

"Reserves? Lens keeps half her closet back in the hold of the plane," argued Henry as he tapped a knuckle against the privacy window.

Lindsey opened a small bag and forced Lisa to spin and face her just as the car lurched forward once again.

The inside lamps came on while she applied makeup to Lisa and herself, and then began to fuss over each other's hair.

"You know we're going to the beach," grunted Henry.

His lighthearted and frivolous mood seemed bruised after the telephone conversation.

"A girl always has to be prepared," said Lindsey. "You do realize where you're taking us. You know perfectly well how snooty the locals will treat us if we're not in top form."

Henry sneezed when Lindsey spritzed hairspray over their heads.

"What's bothering you now Henry?" sighed Lindsey, as she strummed slim fingers through her blond hairdo.

"Besides your hairspray? Nothing really...."

Lindsey glanced at her brother, easily seeing past his lie, but Henry had already flipped his switch back to mischievous smile.

♥

The entire strip of beach had a carnival atmosphere, multicolored lights and a different local band playing every few hundred feet.

"Do you get away like this often?" asked Nathan.

Lindsey had claimed Nathan's arm as they strolled through a steady crowd of pedestrians.

It was Henry that answered, "Not really. But we're always bouncing around somewhere. I think we're supposed to believe it's all a grand adventure."

"Don't you?" asked Lisa.

Lindsey tilted her head back and offered up a soft laugh, "Henry, tell Lisa our itinerary for the first week of December."

"I don't want to talk about work, Lens," he sighed.

Lindsey leaned her head on Lisa's shoulder for a moment to get her attention, "First we drop off a couple of tidbits at the Museum of Arts and the Smithsonian in New York, which happens to be one of my favorite stops. Then we're off to Singapore, London, Naples, and Luxemburg," she chanted, counting off with her fingers. "Am I missing anything Henry?"

"You forgot Charlotte," grinned Henry.

"Home…, of course," said Lindsey throwing up both hands.

"Which is exactly my case in point. Now can we get back to the present?" asked Henry.

Lisa spun around, walking backwards in front of the group, "Why can't I feel sorry for you then? At least you're not fastened to the woodwork in some little town in the middle of nowhere."

"It's the little breaks like this and meeting new people like you that make it bearable," said Henry.

A band nearby began playing opening headliners from Bad Company and Lisa fell back into line, crunched between Lindsey and Henry.

"That and funnel cake," chirped Lindsey, pointing at a station donned with a string of bright yellow lights.

CHAPTER FIFTY

COOL surf rolled over their ankles along the beach as the two women washed the sticky residue of melted sugar off their fingers.

"This is heaven," sighed Lisa, her bare toes digging in the soft sand.

"Cabo San Lucas is heaven," giggled Lindsey. "This is just the weigh station."

The sounds of some musical group tuning up instruments, quavered in the far distance as a warm breeze wisped the varied notes away.

"Tell me what it's like...," said Lisa.

Henry overheard their conversation, carefully dangling a pair of red heels in one hand.

"We'll be going to Cabo in mid-January, for three days. Why don't you come with us?"

Nathan felt a sudden unexpected heat rise as he stood in the sand, arms crossed, holding another pair of heels tightly in his grip.

"Still trying to steal my best employee?" he asked, trying to make it sound a joke.

Henry laughed, "Why don't both of you come then?"

"Because some of us have to work," said Lisa. "I like my new job, but I'm not independently wealthy just yet."

Nathan heard her defense, despite their continual rift she'd bounced right back to his side of the fence.

"Maybe you should ask your new boss for a raise?" huffed Henry.

"Henry," grunted Lindsey, kicking water his direction. "Your manners."

Lisa put a hand on Lindsey's shoulder, partially for balance, "I already make more part time with Heart Realty than at my other job. Don't get me fired before I can buy my own private jet."

Lindsey swished up something from under the sand with her polished toes and leaned quickly to rinse it off.

"Oh look. It's still in one piece," she smiled. "Here Lisa, a souvenir of our trip."

She dropped a perfect bleached-white sand dollar in Lisa's palm.

Lisa held it up in the dusky light, "Well! My first raise!"

Nathan saw her childlike appraisal and decided to call Henry's bluff.

"I'll put your trip on my calendar Henry. I'm still not sure what Ms. Stewart has in mind at our dinner party, but if we aren't booked that week, we'll take you up on your offer."

Nathan was referring to Madeline's mysterious announcement on his formal invitation.

Henry gave a strange chuckle, "It's almost four a.m. Why don't we call it a night?"

Lindsey rushed through the surf and took her heels from Nathan's grip, "Yes, let's do. Maybe we can stop off for a nightcap before we go up to our suite."

"Sorry Lens, but we're going to the Villa," said Henry.

Nathan felt Lindsey stiffen as she shuffled barefoot against him, "Henry…, no. You know how I hate that place."

"I've already promised Aunt Madeline that I'd check on it and we won't have time tomorrow," he said sternly, offering a hand to Lisa.

Lisa took her heels from Henry and plodded barefoot through the sand beside him, suddenly interested in Lindsey's every move.

"Then I'm definitely going to need a nightcap," muttered Lindsey.

♥

Due south, the lights from the city faded from view, still polluting the night sky where they exited the main highway. The limousine stopped in front of a sprawling traditional Mexican Villa. Lights flowing around the edges of the adobe walls, obscured the tiled roof and anything that might be considered attractive. It rendered the whole atmosphere as glum as a long stretch of twenty dollar hotel rooms across the border.

At first sight of the place, Lindsey sat down her begrudged nightcap, consisting of some chilled white wine she and Lisa found inside the small cooler in the car.

The entire surroundings were dark and none of the internal house lights were on. When the car doors opened, a stray dog began barking in protest at their arrival.

"Can you say Hotel California?" whispered Lisa.

Lindsey fought back a chuckle and nudged Lisa, "Don't say that. This place already gives me the creeps."

Henry stalked up to the front door and rang the chime. After a few minutes, a portly Hispanic lady with a colorful shawl draped over her head opened the door and let them inside. Nathan thought she seemed unusually alert for five a.m., unless the woman was a naturally early riser.

Henry muttered something to her in Spanish and she nodded before walking away.

"All the north rooms are ready for us. Nathan, why don't you take the one on the right at the end. There's plenty of men's things in that room, if you don't mind the Hugh Hefner look. Lisa, the room across the hall from Nathan's has plenty of lady necessities in it."

The shocked look on Lindsey's face caught Nathan off guard, "Are you sure Henry? When did the north end get finished?"

"How should I know?" grinned Henry. "It was Aunt Madey's idea. You know her about as well as I do."

"I'm staying in my usual room," she muttered strangely. "If either of you need me, I'll be right through that door."

Lindsey pointed in the opposite direction toward an open door at the beginning of another sprawling hallway.

"Good! Brunch will be at eleven a.m.," said Henry. "Our flight back is around two."

He glanced at Nathan, then looked at Lisa, "And if anyone needs me for anything…, I'll be three doors down."

Lindsey rolled her eyes and walked away, "Good night all."

Lisa followed closely behind Nathan down the long dim hallway, looking at the haunted paintings along the walls.

She heard Nathan's door unlatch and hurried to catch up to where he was, as he fumbled for a light switch he incorrectly assumed would be near the door.

Lisa pushed him inside and closed the door just as he fumbled the lights to come on, "Nathan, this is creepy."

"It's just an old house on the beach," said Nathan. "Once you lie down, you'll think you're at home in your own bed."

Lisa was ignoring his pep talk, pacing around in his spacious room. With the low ceilings, it had the distinctive look of one of Madeline Stewart's European museum collections. The room had a definite man's air about the décor. The huge bed looked practically out of place with a colorful hand-stitched quilt stretched from top to bottom.

"At least come and check out my room for me?" she asked.

Lisa nervously took his hand and led him back across the hall, flipped on the light to reveal a stark white French provincial bedroom suite, complete with canopy bed.

Lisa gasped, "It's beautiful."

She ran her fingers along the cascading chiffon cloth gathered at the four corners of the bed.

"Does that mean you're not creepy anymore?" asked Nathan.

Lisa smiled, "I guess I'll be alright. You don't snore do you?"

Nathan laughed and shook his head, "I doubt you'd hear me through these walls if I did."

He walked to the door, ready for a shower and a few precious hours of sleep.

"Nathan?" hissed Lisa, waiting for him to turn around. "Thank you."

Nathan nodded, "I'm right there if you…."

Lisa raised her hand and grinned, "Please don't say those words."

Nathan could still hear her chuckling when he closed his bedroom door.

A blasting hot shower, one white linen t-shirt and black silk boxers later, and he was in bed, dragging the covers to his chin. Seconds more, he was asleep.

♥

"Look at me when I'm speaking to you!" growled an angry voice.

Nathan could feel both stain and sting of a young hyssop branch fresh on both his bare legs as he stood, suddenly wide-eyed, aback a strange barn. He was standing in the stead of a frail young boy, listening to the father's odd accent, barking orders his direction.

"Cry if you must, but keep your eyes open or I'll wear out another wisp on your legs."

The boy's father threw down the correcting rod and pointed to the vile work he was yet too young to perform. Huge gnarled trees were in every direction capturing a foul stench hovering in the air.

Two strong men hoisted another young boar up by its hind legs, which were splayed wide with an iron stock. Three thick quivering poles suspended the boar's heavy length as its front hooves fought the air for purchase.

Screams as fearful as a demon from the pit of hell pierced the child's ears. Then the horrible creature's eyes blazed with hatred right into the young boy's soul, while the rope was quickly cinched to the closest tree.

This man, this father, spun a gray millstone with a foot pedal and laid a straight edged steel blade to spark against it from end to end. He glanced at the boy once again, "Good. I'll make a man of you yet."

The suspended animal's red eyes bulged from its sockets, twisting violently to stare at the boy.

"He's four hundred pounds if he's an ounce," yelled one of the men, his voice barely above the hog's death knell.

The tripod and pulley shook violently as the demon bared young tusks in a snapping fury in all directions.

The father held the sharpened butcher's tool before the boy's eyes…, Nathan's eyes.

"Always start with a sharp blade and work it quick."

As soon as his father stepped closer to the boar, it's guttural screams doubled and the boy swore on his mother that it sounded like so many voices tormented in hell, cursing what was about to happen. The two men backed away and the air seemed to fall still as the boar emptied the stench from its bowels in protest.

One fast and practiced swipe and three things happened at once.

The screaming stopped, a foul gurgling stench of red sprayed the washtub just below the wrenching porcine body, and the boy puked.

♥

Nathan fell to his chest onto the bedroom floor, crawling as quickly toward the only dimly lit place within his immediate grasp.

The death gurgle of the dying boar was beginning to fade from his hearing as he tried to orient himself to these strange surroundings, finally remembering where he was, who he was with.

On his arms and elbows, he struggled the final few inches to the toilet, "What the he...." Nathan heaved violently, cutting off his intended rail.

After the third loud expulsion, the bathroom light flicked on and someone was instantly wiping his face with a warm washcloth while wetting another under the faucet.

"Are you okay?" asked Lisa. "You scared the crap out of me."

Nathan sat up and covered his face, shaking his head, "Must have been something I ate."

He hated lying to Lisa, but at least his reasoning was solid, then he realized he was sitting on the bathroom floor in borrowed black silk boxers. Nothing like a business trip to shatter all pretenses of modesty.

The toilet flushed once again as she smoothed his face with another warm clean cloth.

"I'm sorry I woke you up," he apologized, trying in vain to shift his body to the side.

Lisa tightened the belt around her robe and helped him closer to a vertical seat on the river stone floor, then rung out another cloth to wipe his face.

His whelkishly pale face was almost the face of death, retching up memories of her long ago past. Memories of death she hadn't seen since childhood, one she never expected to see again.

Nathan peered up past the glaring vanity lighting and mouthed an almost silent thank you.

"Here..., let me help you get that off," she grunted, pulling the puke-splattered linen shirt off over his head.

His gold necklace tried desperately to cling and ensnare itself in the damp clothing, garnering her attention as she loosed the little key from its grip.

Lisa tossed the shirt in the tub and turned on the shower to let it self-rinse before she hurried out of the room. Seconds later, she returned holding a clean white jersey, handing it to Nathan, but not after a long cautious glimpse at the expanse of his bare chest.

"What happened? Is everything alright?" asked a voice from just outside the bathroom door.

Lisa hurried over and eased the bathroom door partially shut as Lindsey tried to step inside.

"Bad food," said Lisa. "Probably the smoked salmon."

Nathan stood of his own accord and washed his face once again before turning off the shower as the two ladies continued to mumble just beyond the doorway.

"What's all the excitement?" boomed Henry from the open bedroom door. "Good God. Smells like a sick room in here."

"What did you expect, Henry? You put Nathan in the butcher's room," barked Lindsey angrily.

Henry chuckled sleepily, "It wasn't my idea, little sister."

He yawned slowly and peered between her and Lisa, "I'm going back to bed before the sun comes up."

CHAPTER FIFTY-ONE

"**W**HAT did she mean by that?" asked Lisa. "The butcher's room?"

Nathan looked down the quiet hallway, watching Lindsey step out of sight. Lindsey had stripped off the colorful quilt from Nathan's bed and replaced it with a comforter from somewhere in the closet. Evidently, that hand-sewn cloth was the closest culprit with attachments to violent past memories.

"It's a long story and we both need some sleep," said Nathan, grasping both her shoulders. "Thank you for everything, Lisa."

Lisa's eyes roamed his thick chest and shoulders for the umpteenth time before she answered.

"I'm ready for my bed…, in my apartment," she sighed. "I hope all our business trips aren't like this."

Lisa seemed to be inheriting Lindsey's strange calming effect. When her eyes met Nathan's, she softly cleared her throat, "Uh…, Lindsey told me she was the one that invited you to come, after the fact. I guess I assumed some things too. So…, it looks as if I'm the one that should say thank you."

It must have taken all Lisa's reserves to admit that she didn't know her invitation had initially been intended for her and Henry alone. It proved that there was not only more to Lisa than he'd expected, but that Lindsey was also full of surprises.

Nathan shook his head, "No you don't…, but we do need to discuss more and argue less from now on."

Lisa nodded and placed both warm palms on his chest, "Agreed."

She pushed away slowly; her eyes suddenly glazed and shy, as she slid quietly back across the dark hall to her room.

♥

The flight back to Salem was uneventful and no further mention of Nathan's sudden illness was made. Despite Lisa's initial beliefs, Nathan had no doubts that both he and Lisa were intended for a visit to the Villa. Especially after he caught a piece of another telephone conversation between Henry and Madeline Stewart.

More cryptic than the first one he'd overheard, this one seemed more troubled, "Nothing happened. No. I didn't ask her...," he'd muttered, before turning to walk away.

Nathan doubted that the 'her' Henry was referring to was his sister Lindsey. It must have had something to do with Lisa Evans.

After they'd dropped Lisa off at her apartment, Henry was more reserved than usual, not his typical boisterous flamboyance. With Henry's open-house personality, it was hard to assess any real damage. It was unlikely he was fully responsible for the weekend's activities.

As soon as they arrived back at the Manor, Nathan quickly excused himself to his room for a few hours of privacy.

Every event-filled day around the Stewart family seemed to be pulling him further and further away from the usual set routine of his life. There was always the option of retreating to a hotel, but there were only a few more days left in November. Then the entire troupe would pack up and leave for parts unknown, possibly for several months. Perhaps Ms. Stewart would set her sights on some other location and he could ride out his remaining twelve-month contract in peace.

Nathan stretched diagonally across his bed in a sprawl, reviewing a different dilemma other than all the odd exchanges.

For years he'd lived consumed by obligations and notably alone. Suddenly, he had not one, but two interesting women in his life. Two beautiful women vying for his time and attention. Each one with completely different attributes, yet both with enticements he could not ignore and either one was only a spark away from a fully engaged romance.

He had also been presented with an emotion he never expected..., jealousy. He fully intended to take his time, to date Lisa, find out who she was..., to go slow. He accepted her reluctance, even enjoyed the chase. It was her untamed, headstrong freshness he enjoyed. But when he felt the mere insinuation that she might have other interests or that someone else might have sights set on her, everything changed.

Then Lindsey entered the picture, almost absently offering herself as confidant, comforter, with her ability to completely disarm him at her whim. All she had to do was lay her hand on his arm, to gaze at him, to say a few words, then everyone and everything else dissipated from his mind. She could calm a torrent of worries in a single instant and have him willingly focused totally on her.

He'd never had anyone with that much power over his emotions, now there were two.

A gentle tap on his bedroom door woke Nathan from daydreams just this side of sleep.

"Mr. Heart?"

He sighed heavily and found his way to the door.

"There's someone at the front door that wishes to speak with you."

It was one of the house clones, with no indication as to who this visitor could be.

"Blast it all," whispered Nathan. "I'll be right down."

Nathan looked at his wrist for the time, then snatched his jacket off the back of a chair. Visitors this time of day on a Sunday rarely came to sit and talk over a cup of coffee. Lisa would have called first if only for the opportunity to use her cell phone, but it couldn't be her, she was likely asleep. Not to mention, she was without a vehicle until Wednesday. He had no client meetings until Tuesday, but again, they would have called first since his office was now in Salem.

He heard the faint familiar voice in the vestibule and hurried down the stairs.

"Ben..., what brings you out this way?" he asked.

The sheriff nodded after shifting past a small gathering just inside the door.

"Hello Nathan. Can I speak to you for a few minutes?"

Madeline Stewart waved an arm, "You're welcome to come inside and have your conversation."

The sheriff's eyes flickered up to Nathan, "It won't take that long, Ms. Stewart."

Nathan foresaw the upcoming volley of persuasion and stepped around the huddle onto the front porch.

The sheriff apologized and backed away, closing the door behind him.

"Sorry...," said Nathan, as he continued down the steps.

He leaned against one of the roaring lions as the sheriff made his way closer.

"I'm sure you remember our friend John Smith?" asked Ben, getting right to the point of his visit.

"Of course..., the Peeping Tom. Did you finally catch up to him?"

The sheriff nodded, "In a matter of speaking. Some hikers found his body at the bottom of The Falls early this morning."

Nathan's ears perked. The Falls were only ten or twelve miles outside of Lumberton.

"He's dead?" said Nathan, leaning closer.

"The coroner says it happened around midnight last night."

"That's awful..., even if he was a creeper," said Nathan.

"I guess I don't have to tell you we don't have a clue what happened to him as of yet. I was wondering if he might have come back around here or tried to make contact with you?"

"Not at all. So he drowned?"

Ben took a deep breath, "Funny you should ask that. No. His neck was broken. We're guessing he fell from the lookout at the top of The Falls."

"So somebody could have killed him," said Nathan.

"It's possible…. Which brings me to my next question…, and I have to ask, so don't get offended. Can you tell me where you were last night?"

"Midnight, I was listening to a tribute band to Bad Company on Ventura Beach. Before that I was at a restaurant over in Crab Cove."

"You weren't in Lumberton all day yesterday?" he asked.

Nathan explained his schedule in detail, including the extensive tour through Lumberton and how he ended up in southern California.

"Good," said the sheriff, looking somewhat relieved.

Nathan's mind drifted back to the notepad…, the conversation…, finally to Eben M. Stäkkr. Could he have done something so heinous? Before his experience with the *Reading*, he couldn't have even known that Stäkkr was the one employing the dead man. But in his vision, he'd seen the murderous anger in Stäkkr's face as he yelled into the telephone.

"Is there anything else you want to tell me?" asked Ben.

Nathan looked up from his musing and shook his head.

"What about the fellow that was here the night you caught him on your property?"

"Bolton? I don't have a clue. I suppose he was here. He works for the Stewart family."

"Hmm, well I'm already here," said Ben. "I suppose I'll take Ms. Stewart up on her invitation."

♥

Bolton stood calm and relaxed, coveralls covered in gray and dark red smut, while his advocates chattered on.

"I can assure you, Bolton hasn't left the premises in several days. As you can see, he's been completely occupied with revamping the free space down here in the basement."

Nathan stood in the distance, wanting to add his two cents, but he hadn't so much as seen Bolton in days. Now it appeared that he may have thrown him under the bus.

Sheriff Ben Kern finally nodded, took a few more notes, "I don't see any reason to bother you folks any more this evening."

Nathan stepped forward, "Ben…, did you try showing a picture of this fellow at any of the hotels in Lumberton?"

Ben looked up from his notes, "In town?"

Nathan shrugged, "He had to stay somewhere close while he was keeping tabs on this house. Unless he was living in that awful car of his."

"That's something else that's been bothering me," said the sheriff. "I looked through all the pictures on the digital camera Smith was carrying. Most of the pictures on it were of this house and the contents…, and a few of you."

Madeline Stewart immediately jumped back into the mix, "Sheriff, Nathan has been under my employ to safeguard the contents of this house. Every piece of furniture is worth a small fortune and I can assure you, only a handful of people outside this small circle are privy to that knowledge. I'd be glad to give you a list of those names if you'd like."

The sheriff shook his head, "I don't see any reason to take it that far. I've known the Heart family since before I became Sheriff. But…, just for the record, we did find the car. It was clean. Too clean in fact. Not a speck of trash or prints inside it."

Nathan stepped closer, "So you do believe he was murdered."

Sheriff Kern nodded apologetically, "I had to cross everyone here off the list before I started digging any deeper. I hope you understand."

Madeline led the sheriff back up the stairs into the house, followed closely by Sara and a few other members of the staff.

Nathan lingered behind, looking at the mass of framework and partitions erected around the previously unused portion of the basement.

"You've been a busy fellow," said Nathan, scooting his feet on some sort of gravely red grit covering the basement floor.

Bolton gave Nathan a wary eye, ignoring his comment.

"Bolton, I didn't mean to throw you to the dogs. The sheriff asked about you directly and I honestly haven't seen you in days," said Nathan. "What else was I supposed to do?"

Bolton waved a dusty hand, "Nothing, I suppose."

"How long have you been down here?"

Bolton grinned a little, "I only come up for air about twice a day. You keep pretty strange hours yourself."

"Only recently," laughed Nathan.

"Yeah…, the Stewarts have a way of stirring things up."

"What exactly is all this?"

Nathan scrunched a shoe on the strange grit on the floor and looked around at the mass of interconnected studs.

"More storage space," said Bolton, waving a hand around the framework. "A new cellar door that seals and locks from the inside. A dehumidification system…, and I'm having the security panel moved out of the pantry and relocated down here."

"You are a jack of all trades," said Nathan.

Bolton made a silly bow, "At your service."

CHAPTER FIFTY-TWO

WHEN Nathan passed through the kitchen, Sara nodded him over her direction.

"I have some fresh apple pie cooling on the shelf if you're interested."

She handed him a small platter and pointed him in the right direction.

As soon as Nathan was out of earshot of the main entrance, she followed to where he stood whittling at the open pie pan.

"There's been no more fuss in the house of the likes you asked about," she mumbled quietly. "But if I were of a curious sort, I'd be asking about that clock ticking away by the front door. Apparently, some of the folk around here have an unusual interest in its upbringing."

She nodded and walked quickly back to her business with the last of the evening meal she was at work with.

Nathan sauntered over to the open kitchen doorway, taking small bites of hot green apples, all the while observing new activity between Madeline and Sibyl.

With a few quick bites, he finished his desert, then flicked a look at his wristwatch and decided he'd forgo his visit to Crab Cove for one Sunday evening.

"Thank you Sara."

He caught her sly nod out of the corner of his eye as he walked into the almost deserted living room.

"Madeline, Sibyl, I'm glad I caught the two of you together. Could we talk for a few minutes?"

Madeline put down a thick ledger she'd been jotting in.

"Can it wait?" asked Madeline. "Supper is hardly an hour from now and I'd like to finish cataloging this half of the room."

"Why don't you let Nathan stay?" asked Sibyl. "Perhaps he might be of some assistance."

There was an exchange of glances and Madeline sighed, "Very well."

"What exactly are you cataloging?" asked Nathan.

Madeline pointed to her elder sister, "History. I would have thought you'd guessed that much on your own."

"I thought you authenticated your antiques before you coughed up money at your auctions."

She nodded, "And I do...."

Sibyl lifted her hands off an end table, "Why don't you tell him more? What can it hurt Madeline? You know he's trustworthy."

"Does that mean you're willing to tutor Mr. Heart the same as Lindsey?" she asked.

Sibyl looked carefully at Nathan. Her gaze was so incisive, he felt the small hairs on the back of his neck rise followed by the tiny follicles on his arms.

"Yes..., I suppose it does," said Sibyl finally. "But only if he's willing to submit himself my care."

A merry-go-round of questions began playing tag, just before he nodded, not fully realizing what he was agreeing to.

"Come sit then," said Sibyl.

He eased himself down on a small cushioned chair beside Sibyl, "What exactly is it that I've committed to?"

Sibyl smiled that suasible soft smile he'd seen on her face the first time they met, "Freedom."

He was smart enough not to ask the full meaning of her enigmatic answer, "Alright then. I'm all yours."

"You do realize you are going to owe me for this, Mr. Heart?" asked Madeline. "Sibyl is a force all her own, but she has her limitations. Some day I may need to call upon you. Do you understand?"

Nathan remembered the words of Lindsey..., how her aunt would try to draw him in..., that..., and the monition concerning his antique clock.

"Do I need to sign another contract?" he asked somewhat sarcastically.

"No. Your word of honor is good enough to send you deeper down the rabbit hole, Mr. Heart. I only wanted to make sure you knew the consequences of what you were asking for before I unleash Sibyl on your mind."

"Madeline, don't scare the poor boy," said Sibyl. "You know how rarely I get to tutor a natural born *Sensitive*."

Nathan took a deep breath, "And how many have there been before me?"

"Three, including Lindsey," she answered. "Now..., no more trivia. We need to get busy before all the others start filtering back in for supper."

Madeline picked her ledger back up and took a seat, "Let me know if you find anything of interest."

Sibyl nodded, "Alright Nathan, here is what we're going to do. I understand that you've had a few more vivid encounters since our last *Reading* together. We skimmed the surface of your little notepad and I have a feeling you actually went farther than I expected. I also heard that you suggested the sheriff look at hotel registrars to learn more about his mystery man. I happen to know where you ferreted that idea.

"You should be very cautious of any future hints or you'll become suspect in his investigations."

"But what if he's looking in the wrong places…, at the wrong people?" asked Nathan.

"Steps, Nathan. Take little steps. Let's focus on your kindergarten. Now…, did you happen to notice a little ebony statue on the mantle above the fireplace?"

Nathan shook his head no; a little put off at her diversion. There were so many little items like it everywhere in every room.

Sibyl pointed, "Run and get it for me, would you? Careful now."

Nathan handed her an effigy of some African descent, holding a long spear. It was highly polished; created from one single piece of ebony wood.

"Alright. Before we start, I'll tell you that this little monster was hand carved by an Arab prisoner for an African King over twelve hundred years ago. While the Chinese were learning how to print literature, this bloody little heathen was still running naked and eating the hearts of his enemies. But he's not the one we're interested in."

Sibyl handed Nathan back the statue.

"Now this king had a very powerful attachment to this *Object* and he likes to show up and dance around in your head. What we want to do is turn him off, then look at the *Object* itself and see where it's been all this time."

Nathan lifted it a few times, "It's heavy for its size."

She nodded, "For a very good reason. Now if you need to close your eyes so you aren't distracted, go ahead. Take a deep breath and prepare to meet King Oonfu."

As expected, two stark white eyes met Nathan after his first drop and he gasped as his eyes opened back up.

"Blast it all," hissed Nathan, swatting the air at some sharp-headed object poking at his mind.

Sibyl chuckled, "Yes, he surprised me too. Now again. Tell him to be quiet and sit down, you're not there to entertain him."

As Nathan sank back down into the statue's memories, the angry little ruler reappeared, his jagged teeth filed to points, leering at him. Nathan issued the stern order and his kingliness obeyed and disappeared into the shadows.

The statue began to move, first to an auction, then it was wrapped in brown paper, stuffed in a carefully packed wooden box, opened, inspected, handled by a dozen or so strange faces. After being stuffed in a primitive looking X-ray machine, it was stuffed in a safe with a multitude of other valuables.

Nathan waited until nothing else was happening and opened his eyes. The first thing he noticed was the lack of vertigo. He didn't feel as if he was going to hurl his last meal onto the floor.

"It stopped moving," he shrugged. "Now what?"

"Where did it stop?" she asked.

"I think it's in a safe somewhere."

Madeline sat back in her chair, "Amazing."

Sibyl nodded, "Good. Very good. Now that you've been there once, you don't have to travel that tunnel again. I want you to close your eyes again, then concentrate on the instant the statue was placed in the safe. That's where we're going to disconnect from the *Object* and look at where we are. Your quest is to get a physical location..., an address."

In the next few seconds his view turned to the insides of a plush home, furnished with dark rich colors..., an enormous fireplace, several carefully preserved trophy animals arranged on the walls.

It had the look and feel of some old big game hunter that had been everywhere and done everything imaginable.

The safe itself was behind a large hidden panel on one side of the stone hearth, unlocked by the pull of an iron rod, which was hidden in plain sight and dutifully supporting one end of an elaborate andiron in its hoop.

On the other side of the room was a writing desk with a stack of unopened mail..., all of which had one thing in common.

"43 Hennington Way, London," mumbled Nathan as he slowly opened his eyes.

Madeline Stewart was now seated, perched on the edge of her chair in fascination.

"Do you have the old photograph Madeline?"

Madeline quickly fumbled toward the back of the ledger and produced a faded five by seven photo, handing it to Nathan.

"That's the room, the very room," he exclaimed. "But how did you get this?"

"The house was vacant for fifteen years, until I purchased it back in 1987, sight unseen," said Madeline.

"And the safe?" asked Nathan.

Sibyl took the statue from Nathan's grip and set it on the floor, "You're the only other person that's ever seen the location of the safe..., besides us."

"I purchased the little warrior for five hundred dollars at an auction in Belgium, but the other contents of the safe it shared, more than paid for the abandoned estate itself and a dozen more just like it."

"You're thieves," whispered Nathan.

"It might seem that way at first glance, but..., think of us as treasure hunters. What do you think would have happened to the fortune hidden in the safe if we hadn't found it?"

"It could have sat there for another hundred years, but what about the family? Don't they have a right to it?" asked Nathan.

"Only if there's a survivorship clause in the original Will," said Madeline. "This particular old fellow was the last of his line. We're very cautious to keep everything perfectly legal."

Nathan looked carefully at the photograph once again. It was the very room he'd just envisioned down to the last detail.

"And this is just your hobby?" asked Nathan in amazement.

"Now do you understand my pension for passion and violence Mr. Heart? Abrupt endings usually leave untold stories as well as interesting hidden dividends."

"You have my undivided attention," said Nathan.

CHAPTER FIFTY-THREE

IT was near midnight by the time the three of them had tunneled into at least forty more *Objects*, three of which promised nice returns in a museum, one which might recover the investment for every other in the entire room.

All the other relatives had ignored them for all intents and purposes, sitting around in little huddles of conversation, moving when necessary. It seemed that all the family was attuned to the usual antics going on with Madeline and Sibyl.

Finally, the three of them were sitting alone in the quiet gloom, excited beyond their tired bodies, sharing a pot of hot tea when Nathan posed the question that had been burning in him for hours.

"Madeline, what prompted you to purchase Heart Manor?"

"Initially? It was one of the images from your advertisement," she began. "The picture of the entrance, the vestibule to be precise."

Nathan turned and looked back in memory of the photo's he'd taken himself, "The clock?"

"The clock was what brought me here," she continued. "But the Estate was far more exciting after Sibyl learned of the burial grounds. Then by complete surprise, a fellow by the name of Nathan Alexander Heart caught the attention of my sister Sibyl. The entire estate was worthless compared to this new discovery."

Nathan leaned forward tiredly, "Me? I don't understand."

Madeline laughed softly until it turned into a chuckle, "And that is exactly what made it all the more exciting. You have no clue as to how valuable you truly are."

"You bought the estate because of me?" grinned Nathan, remembering a previous conversation with her niece. Finally, Madeline was showing her hand, admitting what Lindsey had told him.

"On the whim that we'd get the chance to show you your potential and make a valuable ally in the process."

"Then what about the clock?" he asked.

Madeline shrugged and looked at Sibyl with a grin.

"You'll have to tell us, Nathan," said Sibyl. She seemed somewhat perturbed. "It won't let me near it. It's guarded by…."

Sibyl looked questioningly at Madeline before she continued, "It's seems to be guarded by your mother, Marion Heart. She won't let me near it."

Nathan laughed quietly, "I thought you told me these *Objects* only retained the memories of those in the past."

"And we told you the truth, but there are certain situations I've encountered over the years that leave me baffled," said Sibyl. "If I had to guess, it was either very sentimental to her or extremely valuable, maybe both. But again, I have no way of knowing. She's as present around that clock as you or I."

Nathan stood and walked the full length of the living room, out to where the old clock stood. Its mechanics gave a single loud clack, about to chime its midnight toll.

"Marion Heart…," he whispered.

He placed his hands on either of the mahogany hued sides and did exactly the same as he and Sibyl had done to a room full of other antiques.

In an instant, a harsh flash, the single frame of a projector, Nathan saw his mother's face looking sternly back at his mind's eye.

Nathan fell backwards, removing his hands as if shocked by some otherworldly power.

When he came to his senses, Sibyl was standing beside him laughing, "It looks like we're both on Marion Heart's bad list."

Nathan didn't utter a single word. It was definitely his mother he'd seen and felt propelling herself at him. But why? Why would his own mother be protecting this last piece from him? All the other household items were long gone; most had already been auctioned off by the eldest three siblings.

The grandfather clock began to hammer out the twelve blows of midnight as the three of them stood in question.

His eyes were suddenly drawn, then focused downward, to a hand carved indenture just above the large base and just below the casement of the clock's mechanics.

As he knelt closer, he looked at the spot and its detail. It was a perfectly oval recess, not quite the size of his thumbprint, and barely visible inside it was the silhouette of a woman's profile.

His head instantly swam and the floor seemed to drop away as he looked into the depth. Then he saw his mother's face smiling back at him and fell backward on his rear into a dead faint.

♥

"I think you've had enough for one day," said Madeline.

Nathan nodded as he gained his footing to walk upstairs. His blanked mind had only lasted a few moments and was more disconcerting than damaging.

"Are you sure you wouldn't like me to call someone to help?" she asked.

"I'm fine."

She accepted his answer and disappeared into the lower hallway as Nathan left off to his room. The first-floor lights went dim as soon as he turned toward his upstairs bedroom door..., and there stood Lindsey.

Propped against the wall, arms crossed, a bewildered expression on her face, Lindsey expelled a deep breath.

"I tried to warn you Nathan Heart," she shook her head.

"You did warn me," he agreed. "I remembered every word you said, but I had to have some answers."

Lindsey grinned pitifully, as she twiddled her long slim fingers, "And with every answer, there'll be ten more questions. Believe me, I understand. I was fifteen when I started getting the dreams and spins as Aunt Sybil affectionately refers to them. Welcome aboard, I hope you enjoy the ride."

Nathan eased her away from his door, "Where were you when I needed saving?"

"Ha! I was forbidden from interfering and Henry left me stranded here, the coward," she grunted.

She stood there transfixed, staring all the more at Nathan, "It's just as well. I'm starting to get used to you being around. We might even make a good team."

Her cattish grin and a sly wink was the last he saw of Lindsey before her bedroom door shut.

Without bothering to try to think anything through, he disrobed and climbed into bed. Every step he'd taken was through an array of carefully laid invisible snares. Each one luring him into an unknown and the only one with the answers seemed to be the one placing the bait.

Now he was committed, he had committed himself to find out as much as he could of this new domain locked away inside him. That last vision of his mother's face wasn't a warning; it was an invitation. Marion Heart had issued a challenge to her youngest son. The message had been clear, whatever this mystery was, it was for him alone. If only he could speak to her, wouldn't it make the entire process much simpler?

Nathan felt a warm hand on the side of his face as he drifted through the last walled vestiges of sleep.

♥

Monday breakfast with a few of the Stewart family was hurried, with promises that he'd return early that afternoon and continue listening to Sibyl's easy handed tutelage.

As much as he wanted to deny it, Nathan's mind was spinning endless daydreams of possibilities. With the right instructions and careful attention, he could see how knowing hidden things about the properties he was buying and selling could turn his meager career into an adventure. The money would be a nice side benefit, but his previous visions of a drear future were actually beginning to diminish.

Still…, something bothered him. With all the immense wealth at their disposal, why did Henry and Lindsey seem so resistant? Then he imagined being under the thumb of Madeline Stewart twenty-four hours a day, as well as the expectations of the entire Stewart family. That final thought sent a shudder through his shoulders as he parked in front of Lisa Evan's apartment.

Nathan was still filing away questions when the door to the Cadillac opened and Lisa slid inside.

"Good morning…, you look nice today," he said, throwing the car in gear.

Lisa smiled and slid her heavy shoulder bag between her feet.

"I've had some time to think Nathan," Lisa began. "About my job at Heart Realty."

Nathan's foot slid off the gas and he turned, "You're not thinking of quitting are you?"

"No…," she frowned. "No. Are you kidding?"

He let out a sigh of relief and the car thrust back into motion, "Good, because I'm having a new vision of where I want Heart Realty to go…, and I want you to be a part of it."

Lisa turned to stare at him, huge questions forming, "Really?"

He caught a glimpse of her out of the corner of his eye as he merged into a stream of traffic.

"I have a confession," she whispered. "And if I don't tell you now while I have my courage up, I know I'll chicken out."

"You have the floor," he said cautiously.

Lisa took a deep breath and pursed her lips, "I was going to leave."

She uttered those words in a huge exhale, then continued, "I'd planned it all. The morning of my birthday party, I already had my things packed into a suitcase. I tried to say goodbye to you that night. I wanted to tell you. You'd been so good to me, then I let the car you gave me get ruined and it felt like an omen. I knew it was time to leave."

Nathan nodded, "What changed your mind?"

She laughed softly, "You're not going to yell at me?"

"How could I possibly judge you? Lisa I've wanted to run away more times than I can count. Something always held me back; I'm sure my lists were as long as yours. When I recognized that what I was running from was myself and that I'd have to start all over wherever I stopped running, I decided to stay and work through my fears."

She slumped into her seat and remained quiet for the longest.

"I think you had something to do with it," she said finally. "You gave me something that I haven't had in a long time. Hope…, and it scared the crap out of me. It scared me so bad that I was willing to take the two hundred bucks I'd saved up and get on a bus to…, I don't even know where. I hadn't planned that far ahead."

Nathan took the exit heading to Salem and looked her direction, "I'm glad you stayed."

Lisa smiled and steadied her gaze out the front windshield.

"Me too."

CHAPTER FIFTY-FOUR

"**N**o Lisa, we can't put any more listings up until I finish the contracts on these four. There's only so many hours in a day."

Two more pre-qualified buyers had made appointments for Tuesday, a total of four viewings, four more rounds of escrow contracts. Six land plats were already en-route for delivery from the courthouse and two sets of records from Salem Title. At this rate, Renaldo Lucas would be increasing his take on sales in the near future.

Lisa threw up her hands in frustration, "But if we get these out there now, then we won't be sitting on our thumbs waiting for them to sell," she argued.

Nathan rocked in his chair angrily, "Pick two…, just two and put them on the listing. Then I want you to sign up for classes and get your Realtors License. I can't keep up with that kind of volume alone. I'll always be sitting here behind this desk until midnight."

"Classes?" she whined. "I thought I was supposed to answer the telephone and get coffee…, and look nice."

He laughed a little haughtily and smiled at her, "Congratulations. That's the price of being a decision maker. Take it or leave it."

He could tell she was thinking; she was desperately quiet.

"Unless you'd rather I place an Ad and hire someone else," he added. "Answering the telephone can get pretty boring after awhile."

Lisa hid behind their common divider nervously, "Alright…, alright, I'll do it. But you'll have to help me."

He couldn't believe she hadn't balked or argued the idea to the Nth degree.

"And where is my coffee?" he said jokingly.

Her head poked back around as she shuffled a stack of folders, "It's almost noon. You promised me lunch, remember?"

♥

They were becoming regulars at the cramped Italian bistro just up the street. For the second time that day, Nathan noticed the complete change in attitude of his new assistant.

She was quiet, her thoughts roving as quickly as her eyes, to and fro across the restaurant.

"Lisa, I'd like to make you an offer, but you don't have to make a decision right away."

"Why can't we just eat lunch? I don't like making this many decisions in one day," she grunted.

He took a sip of tea, "I know..., so there's no pressure. I've given this a lot of thought and what I want to do is open your schedule up to six days a week, same hours, nine to two."

Lisa slumped; a threshold gaze in her eyes, "Nathan I can't. I'm already working two jobs with only one day off every two weeks."

"I know. That's why I'm offering you an open schedule. You can work as many days as you want, up to six days a week. The only thing I'll need is a few days advance notice so I can plan around you."

Lisa laughed, "Around me? Don't be ridiculous."

She stared for a moment and her lips tightened, "This doesn't have anything to do with what Henry Stewart said, does it?"

"It doesn't have a thing to do with him or anything he said, it has to do with what you said."

She began to shake her head slowly in refusal as she remembered her own confessions.

"Look Lisa, I understand that you don't like change, at least big changes. More hours here might let you ease away from your tenant situation with Troy and let you make decisions instead of reacting to which debt is due next. And if later on you'd like to find some place you could call your own, I'd be glad to help."

Her hand slid across the table, resting on top of Nathan's.

"Nathan, you're doing it again. It's too much too fast. I know your heart is in the right place, but I'd be trading a pot for a kettle."

"How is it the same?" he grunted. "Get extra money, get your Real Estate License, get your own place, and ultimately your independence."

She stared thoughtfully, daring herself to decide.

"Going once..., going twice...," he whispered, looking into her solemn eyes.

"Okay," she sighed. "I'll try it your way. One step at a time?"

"Think of me as your safety net, minus the payday loans and advances of course," he grinned.

It was a hard won battle. If he'd done what he wanted, to hire her outright as a fulltime employee, she would have turned him down completely. Lisa almost made him feel guilty..., as if he were coaxing and corralling a wild mare into a stall. There were no guarantees that she wouldn't pack her bags one day, hop in her pistachio green car and drive away. At least he would know that he had tried.

Nathan stretched his hand across the table and shook her hand, "We have an agreement then."

"I guess we do," she smiled.

♥

A one of a kind chocolate brown Audi Spyder was parked a few spots down from Heart Realty. As they stepped closer, Nathan took out his phone to make sure he hadn't missed his sister's calls, but there were none.

Caroline opened the car door and hurried up the steps of the sidewalk, throwing on her patented smile in the process.

"Nathan," she said with a grunt as she hugged her brother.

"I had no idea you were coming," said Nathan, hurrying with the office door.

"Neither did I until I parked out front of your office."

She grinned mischievously at Lisa, "It's good to see you Lisa. Has my brother been a good boy?"

Lisa chanced a glance at Nathan as he disappeared through the door, "More than usual?"

Caroline's eyes brightened enthusiastically, "Thank God. He's finally grown a pair of eyes."

She hugged Lisa briefly before hurrying inside to the ramshackle view of strewn maps, photos, and stacks of legal sized documents everywhere.

"I see you're busy. I don't intend to stay, but I need to talk to you for a few minutes if you can spare it," said Caroline, hurrying to take a seat in front of Nathan's desk.

There was no quick mention of Allie or any of the family and it was a little disconcerting.

Nathan looked at his watch, "As long as we're out of here in one hour. What can I do for you?"

She looked around the end of the partition to where Lisa was collating stacks of forms and binding them with heavy clips, then leaned forward closer to Nathan.

"It's about the photo. Is there somewhere we can talk?" she asked.

"We can talk freely here. Lisa has seen the photograph. She recognized Marion right away, the same as you did."

"Are you sure that's wise? If the wrong people managed to get their hands on that photo..., it would be awful," she whispered.

Nathan reached in his desk and handed her the envelope she'd sent him in the mail, "They're all in there. Feel free to keep them safe if you like."

Caroline flipped it open and rifled through the photos, stopping on the one of Marion Heart peering through the tall glass panes.

"Have you learned anything new?" she hissed, leaning closer.

Nathan nodded, "The ghost you saw is real."

"It is mother?" she gasped, her voice a little louder than she intended.

Lisa was suddenly standing behind her chair, peering over Caroline's shoulder at the photo.

"It is, but you can't ask me how I know," he said, glancing up at Lisa. "At least until I feel comfortable with explaining how I know."

The cat wasn't quite out of the bag, but Nathan could see its big green eyes peering out from the opened cinch.

"It has to be her," said Lisa, causing Caroline to jump at the sudden recognition of her presence.

"Have you seen her…, there…, in the house?" she asked cautiously.

Nathan smiled at her and shook his head, "No…."

It wasn't quite the whole truth, but it wasn't quite a lie. His answer was just truthful enough that his conscience wouldn't bother him later.

"But…?" she prodded with her sisterly radar. "You have to tell me something. It's been driving me insane."

Nathan pondered far too long with his internal demons before answering, "It appears I have some unfinished business…, and it seems to be centered around the one piece of inheritance I ended up with."

"The grandfather clock?" she asked.

"Lucky me," shrugged Nathan. "The one piece of furniture I can actually call my own and our mother isn't ready to let go of it just yet."

"I think that's precious," said Lisa.

Both Nathan and Caroline gawked up at her as she continued to hover.

"Well?" she grimaced. "Don't you see? It's the only thing you managed to inherit and it's like she's sticking around to make sure you know she wants you to have it."

Both Nathan and Caroline continued to stare up at Lisa with some strange disbelief.

"Okay, I know it's strange, but I still think its sweet," said Lisa, a little perturbed. She turned and walked back around the partition and continued noisily with her work.

Without warning, Nathan felt the first stages of vertigo come and go in an instant. He didn't feel the familiar dropping sensation, but there was some sort of confirmation in Lisa's statement.

"I think Lisa's right," he muttered. "I think she's absolutely right."

There was an immediate hush that fell over the office until Lisa peered back around to look at Nathan. Her face was gleaming with pride just before she spun back into hiding, working on her duties.

"I guess I'm supposed to feel some sort of relief," said Caroline as she stood up hovering over Nathan's desk. "You'll tell me if you figure out what this means? You promise not to treat me like a mushroom?"

Nathan laughed until he felt his lunch protest, "I promise."

Their chitchat turned mundane and friendly until it was nearly time for them to close the office for the day. Caroline seemed determined, even antsy, trying to watch what Lisa was doing.

"Lisa, you have a new fan," said Caroline, stepping back against the wall to get a better look around the partition.

"Me?"

Nathan could hear the smile in Lisa's voice.

"I've never had a fan club before."

"Allie and Katie, but especially my Allie. Whenever I mention her Uncle Nathan, you're the one she asks about."

"How did that happen?" chuckled Lisa.

"You must have said something. Allie raved on about...."

Caroline stopped suddenly, as soon as her eyes met Nathan's her mouth disengaged.

"Tell her to come see me soon, next time you're in town," said Lisa. "Maybe she can help me decorate this place for the holidays."

"I think she has other ideas on how she wants to help you," chuckled Caroline, glancing back at Nathan.

Lisa laughed, "I think Allie has me confused with someone else then. I'm afraid that train has already left the station."

Caroline's eyes turned sharp toward Nathan once again, "Really.... Is there something you haven't told me dear brother?"

"No. There's not," blurted Nathan, far quicker than he intended. It even sounded harsh to his ears.

He couldn't see Lisa, but he could tell from Caroline that some sort of silent communication was going on between the two women.

Caroline's face softened, "I'll make sure Allie gets to visit as soon as we're back from next week's vacation."

"Christmas won't be far off by then. I'd love to take her shopping with me," said Lisa.

Nathan closed his eyes and sat back in his chair, waiting for Caroline to quit spinning her web around him.

"Allie will love that," cheered Caroline. "That is if your boss doesn't object."

Nathan heard his cue and blandly cut in, "Her boss doesn't object. I'd like to see Allie too, even if I have been replaced."

CHAPTER FIFTY-FIVE

PRECISELY two p.m., Nathan locked the office door and turned the sign around to 'closed'.

The scrolls of maps and plats were all back inside clearly marked tubes and there were three stacks of forms ready for the following day's legalities.

"You've finished," he said with amazement.

"It's not rocket science; it's elbow grease," she said, shifting the strap of her shoulder bag up higher. She looked anxiously at the time as she inched closer to the door.

"Don't sell yourself short Lisa. Accept the compliment."

"Compliment accepted…, now can we leave so I have time to change before I get to my other job?" she begged.

Nathan handed Lisa his car keys, "I have to check the back locks. I'll be there in a second."

♥

"Did your sister really drive all the way here to find out about that picture?" she asked.

Nathan cranked the car, "Among other things."

He caught a slight grin on Lisa's face as he leaned to back out of the angle parking.

"You can't really blame her," said Nathan. "How would you feel if you found a photo with the ghost of your mother in it?"

Lisa shook her head and laughed, "I'd be happy to know anything about my parents. But that only proves that we are from completely different worlds Nathan Heart."

Nathan snapped a glance her direction, "Not so different."

She was about to put up that wall again and force him back two steps.

"You don't know everything that Caroline and I've been through together," he said cautiously. "You'd probably be surprised."

Lisa sat up straighter than before, her hands pushing nervously against her thighs, "Well..., why don't you tell me..., over dinner, later this evening? At my place."

Nathan heard a car horn blare behind them and quickly put his foot back on the accelerator.

"I'd like that..., very much -- Oh, blast it all," he grunted, in remembrance. "I already have obligations for this evening."

Lisa turned to look out her window, "Lindsey Stewart?"

"Lindsey? No. Heaven's no," he spat. "Why would you think that?"

Of course she would think Lindsey was more than just a friend, it would have looked that way from the very beginning. If he'd had any prior misgivings, Lindsey had already set him straight more than once.

"Don't get me wrong. I actually kind of like her. She treated me better than most friends I've known, almost like a sister. It's just..., well..., when the two of you are together..., you seem..., like a couple. It's none of my business," she sighed.

"Yes it is your business," he grunted back. "You asked me to dinner and I said yes.... Lindsey and I are very good friends and we have somewhat of an unusual relationship. It's complicated..., but we are not a couple."

Nathan groaned inside. This continual denial would only make matters worse, but he couldn't tell Lisa what he was going to be doing this evening. If the idea of Lindsey's overt friendship gave her a reason to turn away, what would Lisa think if she knew he'd be spending the evening being tutored by Sibyl Bates?

Not everyone would be open-minded enough to understand that he was learning how to control some sort of sixth sense barging its way to the surface. Preserving his future sanity was the most important item on his agenda and that was one secret he doubted he could ever share with anyone outside the Stewarts.

Still..., "Maybe I can get out of my obligations this evening. I'd really love to have dinner with you..., or maybe we could try another night? Soon?" he asked.

It must have taken every ounce of grit she had to invite him in and he was destroying it.

She shook her head, "It was too spur of the moment. I might have to work a closing shift tonight anyway."

There was no mention of a rain check; the wall between them had risen again.

'No. No. No. Not again', he groaned inside, 'Think Nathan, think'.

"Just out of curiosity, what were you going to cook for us?"

She looked at him in disbelief, "I hadn't thought that far ahead. Why?"

"I'd have to know what kind of wine to bring…, and what kind of flowers."

Lisa almost smiled, "I doubt you'd want to bring wine to what I'd be cooking."

"I guess that rules out flowers too," Nathan said with a nod.

"But…, why? I like flowers," she blurted.

Nathan shrugged slightly, "I suppose I could still bring you flowers."

Lisa turned away, staring out the side window once again; her emotions on a rollercoaster.

"Oh alright. What about Thursday?"

Nathan held his breath, "Thursday. Even if the earth cracks in half, I'll find a way to be there."

This time she did smile, but he could only see it in the reflection of the fogged over passenger side window.

"Can you pick me up tomorrow morning?" she asked.

"I have a full schedule tomorrow, remember? I won't be able to leave at two to take you home."

"I wish my car was out of the shop," she muttered.

"You'll get it back Wednesday, quit worrying."

Nathan put on his brakes and took an early exit a few miles short of Crab Cove.

"Nathan, where are you going? I hate listening to Troy gripe when I'm late for my shift."

He hurried underneath an overpass and turned down a connecting road headed toward his house.

"You won't be late," he mumbled to himself, standing on the gas.

In minutes, the Cadillac was idling by the stone gates of Heart Manor and he quickly slid out of the driver's seat.

"Are you going to tell me what you're doing?" she whined.

Nathan slipped his carryall over his shoulder and unsnapped the key to the Cadillac, still in the ignition.

"You're going to drive this to work tomorrow. I didn't waste my breath to explain, because I didn't want to hear you argue."

"Nathan, no…," she whined.

"I need the Yukon tomorrow anyway. Hurry…, get over here so you won't be late."

"But this is your favorite…, I wouldn't know what to do if I put a scratch on it."

Lisa's eyes were large…, terrified.

Nathan shrugged as he began to walk the rest of the way up the long drive, "Then don't scratch it."

♥

The cold air felt good deep in his lungs and he took his time walking up the gently meandering drive towards the house. His feet felt as if they were floating on air as he helplessly fought against a sudden teenage glib.

He had resisted Troy, rebelled against Caroline and yet somehow, despite his best efforts at self-sabotage, he had a date with Lisa. Why, he wondered. Not why was he interested in Lisa; that was self-evident. Her beauty mixed with such intense pure character was like a neon sign not yet ignited.

But why was his interest in her such a battle?

Lindsey on the other hand, whom he hadn't truly pursued, seemed effortlessly awaiting an indication of his undivided interest. Then there were the other irregularities; Lindsey frequently reminded him that she wasn't interested in a relationship with him, yet she clung to him like a past lover-in-waiting. Even the last words she spoke to him seemed like bait on a hook; announcing that she was beginning to find him interesting.

He had to admit, it was flattering and enticing to be around someone as alluring as Lindsey. Not to mention the immense wealth she was expected to command alongside her brother Henry.

Then he remembered one more item that stumped him; something strange and inexplicable happened whenever Lindsey was around. It was as if his usual senses were befuddled into complete helplessness.

"Seven," he muttered idly, as he walked across the porch toward the front door. His mind dropped the trancelike succession of puzzling thoughts. There were more important matters at stake this evening; more important than future wealth or companionship, even his livelihood.

"I didn't hear you drive up," said Madeline.

Once again, it was only her and Sibyl busying themselves in one corner of the living room as he urged toward them, unconsciously straightening his blazer.

"Hello Madeline, Sibyl. Are we going to continue where we left off yesterday?" asked Nathan, ignoring her unspoken question.

A few of the other Stewart family members, seated with backs turned near the library entrance, glanced his direction.

"As soon as you have a few minutes to relax."

At times, each of the other Stewarts seemed as nondescript as a seldom-opened family album, yet they milled about quietly in peaceful conversation. The raw contentment was disquieting. It was as if they were..., observing him.

Madeline closed the worn leather folder she was holding, placing it on a small similar stack beside her, "You seem a little anxious."

"I am. This is all new to me. Surely you understand that," he said, forcing a smile. "I'll hurry back down as soon as I change."

He did hurry away, all the while making a mental list of questions he needed answers to. It would be bitter medicine needing copious amounts of sugar, missing an opportunity with Lisa, spending the rest of his evening in didactic monologue. Answers to his dark questions would be his only recompense.

He dug out a pair of jeans and his favorite charcoal gray pullover sweater, quickly tossing his dress clothes over a chair.

Everything else in his room was immaculate; bed crisp, room dusted. As he wandered into the bathroom, it too was clinically clean with fresh towels in the open cubby beside the shower.

Nathan thumped some water on the spotless mirror with a grin after raking a comb through his hair. The housekeepers were making his transition away from this homestead much easier without even knowing it. It no longer felt like the home he grew up in. Well, at least there wasn't a mint on his pillow.

Nathan dug in his satchel and grabbed a familiar leather notepad and a pen. Reading between lines had been his specialty since grade school and this time he wanted a record of the new world about to open its' doors.

CHAPTER FIFTY-SIX

THE Stewart sisters were still busy with some items in a curio cabinet when he arrived downstairs. Madeline was carefully turning a small ceramic statue back and forth in her hands, then placed it close beside her and jotted a short note before she spoke.

"I trust your day was pleasant," she smiled. Her hand waved toward the expanse of the living room and one of the staff hurried over.

"We'll take supper out here this evening. Are sandwiches okay with you Nathan?" she asked.

She was planning on staying the course with their cataloging this evening..., or Nathan was in for an evening of nonstop training session.

Madeline didn't wait for a response from Nathan and shooed the lady away with a flick of the wrist.

Nathan sat in a nearby chair and slid his notepad in beside him.

"I suppose you may want to take notes for future reference, but I doubt it will be necessary. We going to repeat everything we do together until its second nature; perfect practice makes perfect. Sibyl?"

Her elder sister looked up from rearranging the shelf in front of her, "Start with Little Boy Blue. I'm almost through lining up the more promising ones over here."

Madeline nodded and reached beside her, then tossed the little ceramic effigy to Nathan. He caught it almost in a panic, seeing it shatter on the floor in his minds eye.

She laughed, "It's essentially worthless..., in itself. If it broke, the rubble would serve the same purpose for our needs. Do you remember how to begin?" she asked.

Nathan glanced at her before studying his first *Object* closer. It was almost three inches tall, a depiction of a little boy child, with a blue cap and trousers, carrying an armload of wood. It looked as if it came from a ten-cent garage sale in Middle America.

He sat back and closed his eyes, waiting for the sudden shift and spin that was already becoming second nature.

Suddenly, it was dark and very cold. He took in a deep breath to steady himself as he looked around in the bleakness and could see nothing, then everything around began to empty itself in a surge. Dim light began to fill what turned out to be a room, some sort of cabin and the surge he'd been feeling was water.

A body floated past him, dressed in a white suit with gleaming brass buttons, right out the open door and he felt himself getting dizzy.

"Nathan…, breathe," said a distant voice.

He opened his eyes to find Sibyl close to his face, a childish grin on her thin lips. He quickly turned his head and exhaled the breath he'd been holding, a natural response.

"Before you begin, always remember you're only an observer or odd things can happen to you," she said, backing away. "Start again…, and remember to breathe."

He nodded with a sheepish grin feeling a familiar calm. There was almost no spinning vertigo with his second attempt. Thrust immediately back into the draining room in the sunken ship, the lights were now bright on the wall. Nathan managed to recognize that he was in some sort of stateroom on a ship just as he heard a loud groan and everything on the floor righted itself onto shelves and tables. The reel playing in his mind was like so many other instances, in jerking fast reverse order.

The little statue he was attached to was now on a shelf overlooking a very neat and orderly room. With some effort, he separated himself from the *Object,* then wavered back and forth until he saw a round window. He willed himself out a porthole in the side of some sort of ocean liner and ended up on a deck outside where there were several people milling about. On the side of the ship was one word…, Titanic.

Nathan opened his eyes and exhaled slowly.

"Amazing," he hissed, his eyes fluttering open.

He looked back at the little object, much closer this time.

"It was on the Titanic?" he asked.

"Part of one of the first salvage attempts," said Madeline.

"I thought you said it was worthless," he scoffed.

"Relatively speaking. Somehow it ended up at an auction in Atlanta…, one of my favorites. However, it became separated from its letter of authenticity. And with no markings whatsoever on Little Boy Blue, he might as well be a dime-store reproduction from the 1920's."

"What a loss," said Nathan sadly.

"Yes…, indeed. Unless we find some other method of authentication, only our small group know of it's actual worth."

Sibyl was waiting anxiously to speak, "Uh…, why don't you take another look at it Nathan? Maybe go back a little farther with the *Object* this time instead of jumping ship."

She grinned at her intended pun and took a seat, now finished with her rearrangement of the curio shelf.

Nathan glanced at the time. The eight minutes he'd been seated with the two women seemed closer to an hour.

"Before I do, explain how time seems to stand still while I'm *Reading* an *Object*."

Sibyl lit up, "It's a curiosity and as you do more readings you'll find that even less actual time passes during your visit to an *Object's* past. Something that you'll come to appreciate when you get to be my age, Mr. Heart."

It wasn't a complete answer, but at least it was confirmation that he wasn't imagining the oddity.

Madeline flicked her fingers, "Please continue. Despite the incongruities of time, we do have several more *Objects* to investigate before supper."

Nathan grinned, "Slave driver."

He closed his eyes and watched time collapse once again, in reverse, faster and faster until he was seated on a shelf in a store, he knew not when or where. A little girl was perusing the wares and trinkets displayed on wooden shelving, alongside her mother. Her hair ringlets of gold, startling blue eyes and a beautiful frilly dress; she was as lovely as a china doll. She seemed to look him straight in the eyes curiously, frighteningly, then shifting her head to the side her smile grew warm and kind.

"This one mother."

The child's voice was polite and just as angelic, with a distinct New England accent. She reached to the shelf and grabbed the Boy Blue and thrust it towards her mother.

"You like this one?" her mother answered.

"Yes…, yes…, mother. His name is Nathan Alexander."

Nathan's eyes flew open and he gasped for air, still holding the ceramic doll for dear life.

Madeline was seated quietly, her fingers laced together in thought, but Sibyl was affixed with a gentle smile partially hidden behind her wrinkled hand. She'd been waiting for his reaction, obviously hiding her anticipation.

"How?" he whispered.

"A rare few of us can see forward in time just as easily as you and I see into the past," she answered.

The implications were overwhelming..., he had somehow been predestined to meet this child along a fixed timeline; one looking forward, one looking back.

Stunned, Nathan handed the little character back, but Madeline waved him away.

"It's yours, please keep him."

The odds that this simple little ceramic doll would travel from that little child's hand and voyage through the years to find its way into his hand was unfathomable. She had looked right into his eyes..., into his soul in that fleeting moment in time. Some switch flipped inside and he melted with wonderment as if this might be some calling placed on his life.

"The little girl..., was she the one attached..., did she die on the Titanic?"

He had no desire to go back and search out what he might find; those dazzling blue eyes in a dead stare, lost in the icy water underneath the ocean.

Sibyl answered somewhat sympathetically, "No, she wasn't on the maiden voyage, but her father was the Ship's Steward."

He looked at the Little Boy Blue and for once in his life, Nathan didn't refuse his gift, but slipped the treasured figurine into the seat beside him.

♥

"Again...," said Sibyl, shaking her head slowly. "You need to learn when to stay with the *Object* and when to take a detour into your surroundings. With enough practice you'll be able to sense when to stop and take a look around."

Nathan stood and stretched, looked down at six other oddities they'd already investigated in the past hour, "I need a short break."

"As do I," said Sibyl tiredly. "Madeline, I think I've run my course for the day. I need to get some rest."

Madeline rose quickly and helped her sister stand, "Of course. Would you tell Lindsey that I need her assistance before you lie down?"

She nodded, "Mr. Heart, it has been a true pleasure working with you. You are leaps and bounds beyond where I thought we would be at this stage. I look forward to seeing you again tomorrow."

Madeline followed Nathan as he walked out onto the front porch letting the fresh cold air rejuvenate his system.

"Sibyl is very fond of you," she began. "She wouldn't let me charge you for your time with her."

Nathan felt his eyebrows rise in shock, "Charge me?"

Madeline nodded, a shrewd smile on her face, "You couldn't afford her, even by the hour."

Nathan turned away slowly, a grin on his face, "I suppose this means that I'm indebted to you?"

It was just as Lindsey had warned him.

"Not to me…, exactly," she chuckled. "But in the future, if my niece and nephew should happen to find themselves in a situation where they needed some help, I would appreciate it if you could find the time to help them? After all, none of us are promised tomorrow."

It wasn't the sort of debt he had expected at all.

"I'd be glad to, Ms. Stewart. I'm sure you already know that Sibyl has settled several of my fears already. That alone was priceless."

"There's an old saying Nathan…, the best thing you can to for others is not share your riches, but reveal to them their own. I think the saying was plagiarism myself, but it's still better than the original version about teaching someone to fish; you get the gist."

Her attempted turn of word was so out of character for Madeline that Nathan turned to face her. Her nose was still crinkled at her own joke. He remembered Madeline detested anything related to fish as much as Lindsey.

She shivered and rubbed her arms briskly, her cue to hurry them both back inside.

CHAPTER FIFTY-SEVEN

THE house was a quiet as a tomb. Lindsey was seated where Sibyl had been earlier, an onus somber expression on her face.

"Thank you Lindsey. Your Aunt Sibyl was incredibly tired," said Madeline. "Did Sibyl get a bite to eat before she went to her room?"

Lindsey nodded quietly, looking over at Nathan as he sat down.

"Good then, we have about an hour before supper. Let's continue."

This was strange. Lindsey was obviously not happy with this duty and it was causing him some unrest just watching her expressions flux.

"Excuse me," said Nathan. "Lindsey is going to take Sibyl's place?"

"Of course. Lindsey's been working with Sibyl since she was fifteen. Her basic talents are nearly as sharp as Sibyl's already, in some ways better. Along with that, I'm sure she has some insights into the world of your generation that Sibyl and I aren't able to convey."

Madeline looked sharply at her niece, urging her on.

"What stage is Aunt Sibyl at?" asked Lindsey. "*Following Object*s to *Origin, Detachment, Clairaudience, Clairvoyance, Clairsentience*...."

"No, no..., no," Madeline interrupted Lindsey's stream of clatter. "Nathan's past all those. What I'd like for you to focus on at present is how he interacts with his awakened nature and his daily activities. He needs more practice getting in and out of a *Reading* so that if, say..., he were driving. We don't want him in an accident."

Lindsey's eyes flicked an instant of a frown at Nathan and back at Madeline, "He's already beyond the first five?"

"Don't be jealous dear," she cooed. "Aunt Sibyl tried to tell you that your resistance held your training at a standstill."

Lindsey pursed her lips into a moue, letting little bursts of air from her lungs in restraint.

"We can postpone this until tomorrow," said Nathan. "There's no need to rush. I can practice on my own if you'd rather not, Lindsey."

He could tell that Madeline and Lindsey were about to have one of their not-so-private heated conversations.

Instead, Lindsey turned a hard face to her aunt, "Has Sibyl worked with *Following* or *Interaction* yet?"

"Lindsey...."

The very inflection of her spoken name was some sort of heated warning between them.

"We're trying to help Nathan adjust. Not send him to the sanitarium."

Lindsey grinned maliciously, "Well if Nathan is this far advanced already, I don't see what harm it could do."

"That will be up to Sibyl. Please try and contain yourself to some basic repetitions and some sound explanations. We need to strengthen Nathan's confidence."

Lindsey stood and paced in front of the open curio cabinet, angrily snatching three or four new *Objects*. Nathan could feel the anger reeking from her very presence. Whereas she usually exuded peace and serenity when they were together; now it was just the opposite. This wasn't going to be pleasant.

"Am I going to need a wastebasket?" Nathan asked angrily.

Madeline frowned at the reference, the morning she tricked him into a *Reading* and he'd dove into the back yard to expel his breakfast.

"You might," said Lindsey, a lilting snap in her voice.

It sounded like a challenge.

"Have you met Mr. Oogah Booga?" she grinned.

"Lindsey...."

It was that same tone of stern warning.

Lindsey hurried across to the far side of the living room and grabbed the little ebony wooded statue perched on the mantle.

"I have," said Nathan. "Not a very friendly fellow."

"He was my very first experience with the art of *Reading*. Right, Aunt Madeline? Remember when I had nightmares for a week? I was only a child...." She choked the little warrior in her fist before she placed him back on the mantlepiece.

Nathan couldn't imagine meeting that scar-faced demon prodding at him with a spear at fifteen years old.

"Lindsey, calm yourself. That was an accident," scolded Madeline. "Nathan, I'm sorry. I suppose we'll have to wait until Sibyl is rested before we continue."

Lindsey stomped back over in front of her aunt.

"Absolutely not. I'll sit here until the sun comes up with Nathan if that's what you want. I just want him to know that all isn't peaches and cream where we're headed together," said Lindsey.

For once Madeline was silent. Maybe afraid to speak…, maybe too taken aback by Lindsey's sudden proclivity for the dramatic.

"I… think I'll go check to see where Sara is on our supper," Madeline said quietly before she stood. Her face had aged immeasurably in those last few seconds of conflict.

Lindsey brushed past her aunt and sat down in a chair next to Nathan, carelessly dropping her handful of *Objects* on a little table between them.

When Madeline was out of range, Nathan whispered, "Was that necessary?"

"Very. For both of you."

Nathan watched her as she closed her eyes and calmed her breathing.

"Now you have me worried," he mumbled.

"Good," she grunted back.

This was all wrong. Bright warning lights were flashing inside his head, sirens blaring in the void of his mind. Where was the amiable, meek, carefree Lindsey he'd come to know?

"Don't worry, I won't break you," she sighed. "I wouldn't dare do anything to damage Aunt Sibyl's new prodigy."

Nathan scooted his chair so that he could face Lindsey. Even when upset she was appealing to him, a mass of blond hair shrouding her kind face. She seemed worried.

"Lindsey…, the only reason I'm doing this is so I don't end up like my mother. In a few weeks you'll be gone back to your world, doing whatever it is you have planned and I'll just be a memory. I really do need Sibyl's help…, and your help."

Her eyes darted frantically around his face in thought, "Pick one."

She pointed to the little table and she tried to smile.

♥

"No Nathan, do it again," grumbled Lindsey.

Madeline walked back to where she'd left them for almost an hour. She seemed more composed, silent and observant.

"I don't speak French and I can't get past the silly man with the white wig and rouge on his cheeks," he argued.

Lindsey's head snapped to Madeline, "I don't see any other way except to let him *Follow* me."

Madeline closed her eyes and nodded silently.

"How…?"

Nathan's question was terminated when Lindsey touched his arm and he felt himself yanked from consciousness into what he interpreted as her version of a *Reading*. It was like turning himself inside out at the speed she was traveling. Images whirled past that he'd seen previously, stopping only for an instant at the pastie faced French nobleman that had thwarted his attempts to pass.

Back in reality, he heard Lindsey's noxious tone, "Will you at least try and keep up?"

Instantly, images became a blur halting at unknown indices set by Lindsey's progress. Seconds later, they halted and he observed her watching a grizzly looking character standing in a snow covered village.

"Nathan…," said a voice beside him.

He blinked his eyes madly for a second before Lindsey turned to Madeline, "Twelfth century Budapest, but it was handmade somewhere in the Carpathian foothills."

"Somewhere?" asked Madeline, as she jotted down the information in her ledger.

"You told me no *Interaction*," she answered, with a shrug and tilt of the head. "Do you want me to go back?"

Nathan felt as if he were the dead weight of an anchor Lindsey was dragging behind her. She handed the thin flute of hand carved bone to Madeline for her inspection and she quickly applied a stringed tag for identification.

"Any anomalies?" she asked Lindsey.

Lindsey gazed tiredly over at Nathan before she answered, "I was a little preoccupied."

Madeline sighed heavily and handed it back to Lindsey and nodded, "Take him with you. Be careful."

Lindsey's hand grasped Nathan's arm as they flashed backward in time to stand before the same bear of a man wearing heavily furred clothing that stank to high heaven. Heavy clouds were spitting snow on his already damp, stringy black hair.

To Nathan's amazement, Lindsey appeared beside him, her body translucent, almost glowing from within like a lantern concealing a flickering flame. She had to snap her fingers in the Neanderthal's face to get his attention. It was as if Nathan and Lindsey appeared as a phantasm to the ogres' wild untrained eyes. Fear blossomed, then rage, and a thickly muscled arm swatted in Lindsey's general direction.

When his hand passed through Lindsey's incorporeal body, a stream of Slavic grunts that even Nathan recognized as terror flew from his mouth. Lindsey placed a hand toward his ancient head, then almost angrily thrust it inside, as if listening for a moment. Then the big oaf dropped to his knees and pointed to a path leading outside the village.

In an instant, the two of them flashed as if pulled by the strings of a parachute to another village. High snow covered peaks glared down like the broken teeth of an ominous monster, angry mountains overshadowing several thatched dwellings.

One such hut had a mountain of enormous elk antlers beside it.

"Košice," said Lindsey, pulling Nathan back to the present.

The name sounded alien, the language foreign, as it rolled off Lindsey's tongue.

Madeline jotted down her information and tossed the delicate hand carved artifact aside.

"I'll send it to the university when we get home and have it dated. It might make someone a nice collector's piece."

"Excuse me…," stuttered Nathan. "What just happened?"

Lindsey looked over at Madeline, her eyes a question mark along with an 'I told you so' tilt of her head.

"We went to the *Origin* of the *Object*," said Lindsey, her answer an oblique disguise.

Madeline nodded and excused herself for a few moments, calling to one of the helpers zipping down the hall.

Lindsey frowned, pursing her plush lips into a thin line, "Can't you simply accept what you see without asking so many questions?"

Nathan shook his head, was about to protest for further information.

"But I saw you…, you had a body…, you did something with your hand. I don't know exactly; pushed it inside his head?"

Nathan's voice ended barely above a whisper. She obviously didn't want Madeline to hear her objections to his curiosity.

"We call it *Interaction*. He…, wasn't cooperating," she answered. "I merely treated his mind as an *Object* within an *Object*."

Nathan waited quietly for a more detailed explanation and received none. Evidently, this person from the past could actually see them, more exactly, they were visible to each other. Was he appearing like an apparition to these long lost people of the past? Was time just a huge lazy river that a few special people could navigate? His scattered thoughts centered back on the ceramic statue, Little Boy Blue. That little girl from the past had seen him, looked forward through time, even knew his name. These new questions were bringing on a migraine and he canceled them all.

Madeline returned; one of the staff walked up slowly with a serving platter as another quickly unfolded a table to set it on.

"Please bring us tea," asked Madeline as they walked away.

Lindsey looked over at Nathan's tired face, "At least you didn't puke."

Nathan reached for a plate and Madeline stopped him, "One more item of interest."

She handed him another *Object*, a wooden box, "What do you see?"

Nathan turned it side to side, "A puzzle box. Do I have to open it before I get a sandwich?"

It had no lid or obvious mode of entry, yet some unknown slid about heavily inside its hidden cavity.

Madeline grinned, "Nothing that dire. Take a walk with it, around the room; tell me what you see inside it."

Nathan gladly stood and stretched, walking toward the front door, yearning to leave. His evening already felt as if it should be well beyond midnight yet it was not quite six in the evening.

With each step, he tried his best to force that familiar little sinking sensation as he scrutinized the outer walls of the box. He turned and came back to where Madeline and Lindsey were already filling cups of tea.

"Well?" she asked.

"Nothing. Does this mean I don't get to eat?"

Madeline laughed quietly while handing Nathan a plate.

"Motor functions turn off the onset to a *Reading*, even walking. Something for future reference."

"I knew there was a reason I needed to get back to my evening runs," grinned Nathan.

CHAPTER FIFTY-EIGHT

NATHAN tapped a discolored spot on the corner of the wooden puzzle and it receded slightly. He grinned and handed it to Lindsey who immediately frowned as Nathan took a drink of tea.

Without a word, she sighed and closed her eyes, letting her palms slide around the edges. Much later, far too long for her ardent abilities, she reopened her eyes and tossed the box back to Nathan.

"You cheated somehow," she hissed.

"No, I took my time," he grinned.

Nathan had spent three tries Reading the box to learn how to unlock its mystery to no avail, then decided to give it a normal everyday once-over. He wasn't about to tell Lindsey that he hadn't seen the box opened along the timeline of its existence. It would ruin the last of the evening's entertainment.

He twisted the box a few times and tapped at two more spots, one of which receded until it clicked. Very pleased with their game, Nathan quietly handed the box toward Lindsey.

"Keep it," she huffed. "It doesn't prove anything."

"Don't be a sore loser, dear," said Madeline. "You know what they say about beginners luck."

Madeline took the wooden puzzle and looked at it curiously, "This can wait until tomorrow evening."

Lindsey stood, "Well then, if you don't need me any longer, I'd like to get a bath and relax. It's been a very long..., evening."

Nathan agreed with a nod. It was nearly eleven and yet it seemed they'd sat there for an entire day, maybe longer. It was enough to tax anyone's patience.

Madeline closed the ledger she'd been perusing through, "Yes, you go right ahead. Thank you, Lindsey. You've been so much help."

Lindsey had been acidic all evening. At first Nathan assumed she was somehow angry with him, then wondered if she was being forced to do something beyond her conscience.

Lindsey turned and walked away, then stopped short, "Where are my manners. Good night Mr. Heart."

She continued on in a huff before Nathan could reply, just as the front door opened.

"Hey Lens…," said Henry cheerfully. "What's up?"

His crooked grin dissipated slowly when she waved him off and clopped tiredly up the stairs.

Henry yanked off his coat and saw his aunt and Nathan seated underneath one of several lamps still glowing around the room.

"What happened to her? Ya'll aren't fighting again are you?" he asked.

He stopped several paces away. Nathan assumed to keep his aunt from trapping him into an all night conversation, but then he caught the scent of Henry's travels.

"No, it's a simple case of envy," said Madeline, then suddenly covered her nose with a handkerchief. "Oh my…. You reek. Please go away before you make me ill."

Nathan was right; the rife scent of beer on Henry couldn't hide the distinct strong current of lobster and garlic butter inching toward them. For someone like Madeline who didn't like fishy foods, it would have been pungent. It only served to remind Nathan of his usual evening in Crab Cove and the sacrifice he'd made to postpone his date with Lisa.

Henry's eyes flashed at Nathan and back to Madeline, "Good night then. Talk to you later Nathan."

Henry was almost to the staircase when Madeline removed the kerchief, "Henry, did you do what I asked?"

He never slowed, trotting up the stairs, "Working on it."

Throughout the evening, Nathan had sat quietly and obediently as one question after another was answered without his having to ask. Now a new flush of questions had him wondering.

"You did well today Nathan," said Madeline quickly. "If Sibyl is correct in her assessment, you should not only be able to handle most any unknown situation, but soon you'll be able to use your refined talents to see beyond the walls and shadows of your fears. I predict that your vocation is about to take a distinct turn for the better."

"I hope you're right," he answered thoughtfully.

Her long fingers intertwined as she gazed at him, "Very few empaths ever go beyond feeling sorry for others. Some choose vocations as doctors, or nurses, maybe even volunteers at a homeless shelter. The rest wander around feeling as if their ship has already sailed without them, finally letting that awful feeling of despair implode on them."

Her odd twist of topics worked magic on his mind and suddenly he'd completely forgotten the mounting questions about Henry.

"An empath," muttered Nathan, scooting to the end of his seat.

He tried his best not to make it a question as the term piqued his interest.

"One singularity all true *Sensitives* have in common is unparalleled empathy for others. They'd give their last dime to a perfect stranger seated on a sidewalk."

Nathan nodded thoughtfully. Either she was having him followed or she was dead on with his personality type.

"The thing is Nathan, most empaths are above average in intelligence, but without the right guidance early in life it's usually wasted. You obviously had strong positive influences in your childhood."

"Marion was involved with every facet of our lives," said Nathan. "Everything...."

"But you were her youngest, her last chance to accomplish something special. She knew you'd take care of all the others. What she didn't know was that you'd take that responsibility right down to your own destruction."

Nathan sat back in his chair, tiredly wiping his face with his hands, "You don't have much faith in my sense of self-preservation."

Madeline laughed, "Empaths have no sense of self-preservation. It's not in their genome, Mr. Heart. As I said once before, it's both a blessing and a curse."

Nathan sighed, "Curse or not, at least I know what's happening to me. After these few hours I've spent with Sibyl, I barely take notice of the vertigo..., and when I do, I don't fall into a panic. The unknown was more of a curse to me than simply accepting what was happening to me."

Madeline turned a curious gaze toward Nathan, "You haven't had any more episodes around your employee? What was her name?"

Guilt thumped heavily in Nathan's chest, "Lisa Evans. Once..., but it was of no consequence."

His voice caught as he reminded himself to keep his council close until he completely trusted Madeline Stewart and her motives. While he was learning a deeper respect for Madeline, he was also learning that she almost couldn't help herself when it came to controlling and manipulating her known world.

"I'd like very much to meet your secretary, Miss Evans," said Madeline.

For an instant, he almost told Madeline that Lisa would be with him at their Thanksgiving gathering. Then, he remembered that Lisa had told Lindsey she would see her on Thanksgiving. Lindsey hadn't told her aunt that Lisa was his dinner guest? Madeline obviously didn't know.

"I'll try and arrange that soon," he muttered.

Warmed by the thought of Lisa, he suddenly felt protective of her. For some unknown reason he wasn't ready for Madeline to inspect Lisa like one of her acquisitions. Maybe Lindsey felt compelled to protect Lisa as well.

♥

Nathan took off his house slippers and yawned so hard his jaw ached. The only light in his room was seeping in from the nightlight in his steaming bathroom and the flickering votive candle across the room he'd become so accustomed to. Next to the candle stood Little Boy Blue; something about the ceramic doll warmed his heart as he remembered the hauntingly innocent eyes of the little girl calling his name.

When he laid his head on his pillow, something crunched underneath his hair. As he felt, he drew out a small piece of paper and rolled over to turn on the bedside lamp.

It was a crumpled note that read:

Nathan, I'm so very sorry.
Please remember that I warned you.
Lens

If tomorrow didn't hold such a daunting schedule of events, he would have thrown on a robe and marched across the hall to wake Lindsey from her sleep.

Totally confused, he switched off the light and curled back under his covers. He was too tired to consider anything other than sleep tonight.

Mingled with the quiet murmur of the house, twelve gongs of the old clock in the vestibule were the last faint sounds he heard as he drifted off to sleep.

♥

The sound of tires screeching to a halt jostled Nathan from a strange dream. As he opened his tired eyes to the gray light of predawn, his mind grasped that he was seated upright against a wall, with an annoying steady clucking sound beside his head.

His eyes were bleary, his butt numb and ice cold, then came a succession of footsteps clopping his direction.

"Mr. Heart? Are you all right? What happened?"

Another timid voice chimed in, "I didn't mean to scream, I was about to open the front drapery and I saw him sitting there."

Nathan yawned and looked at his surroundings. He was seated in his pajamas, back against the wall, huddled against the old clock in the vestibule.

310

"What the blazes am I doing here?" he croaked. "Is this some sort of a joke?"

He leaned forward and every bone in his body was stiff from the hardwood floor and the unforgiving paneling behind him.

"How long have I been here?" he grunted, as several sets of hands began to help him stand.

"Looks like a bit of the devil's work to me," said Sara.

The devil? Nathan focused on Sara's face as he thanked the other innocuous house staff for their help.

"What do you know about this?" he grunted.

Why was Sara's tone so harsh?

"P'shaw, how should I know? We found you like this, seated in your bedclothes, no less. It's shameful," said Sara turning her head to look away.

"I'm as dressed as you are," he spat back angrily. "What does the devil have to do with me waking up on the floor? The last thing I remember, I was in my own bed with the covers up to my chin, listening to…."

The midnight chimes of the clock were the last thing he could remember.

"And ya expect me to believe you just up and took a stroll down the stairs and snuggled next to that old relic all by your lonesome?" she scoffed.

The other helpers began to slink away, disappearing into the gray light of morning creeping into the house.

"I've never sleepwalked in my life," he shot back.

Sara turned her back and began to walk away, "Maybe the devil was holding yer hand."

The devil again? What was her sudden obsession with the devil?

"I don't believe in your superstitious baloney," he hissed, as he started stiffly toward the staircase.

Sara spun back around, eyes in a tight angry squint, "You're telling me you don't believe in God, Mr. Heart?"

"What? Of course I do," he grunted, trying to get past her obnoxious blockade.

"If you believe in one, you have to believe in the other," she said smugly. She spun again and hurried toward the warm glow of the kitchen just in the distance.

Angry at her logic, stiff and cold from last night's sleeping quarters, he remembered some old quote, and blurted it out in retaliation.

"God sends meat…, but the devil sends cooks!"

Sara gasped, her finger suddenly shaking his direction, "Then I trust you'll not be poking your head in my kitchen looking for any breakfast this morning, Mis…ter Heart."

CHAPTER FIFTY-NINE

FEWER than fifteen minutes had passed when Nathan stormed out the front door, hurrying toward his Yukon, with several items thrown over his shoulder.

He barely cast a glance toward the house as he flew out the circle driveway, past the two suspended guardian lions.

This was not good. The step he had made toward settling his fears of insanity were thwarted by two steps backward last night. There were questions leaking from his mind like a sieve.

He jerked his head around toward the back seat. Had he remembered his all important day planner? Yes. Thank God, it was peeking out of the front pocket of his shoulder bag.

His cell phone. He patted the front pocket of his wrinkled t-shirt and felt the hard square of his smart phone. Suddenly, he remembered to turn on the heater as chills wracked his body.

Falling to pieces was not one of the items on his agenda for this Tuesday morning.

He had already stuck his key into the front door of Heart Realty when he acknowledged that the door was unlocked and the lights were already on. Black spots of cold rain dotted the gray t-shirt sticking to his body as he hurried inside.

Lisa was already on her feet, headed his direction, "My God Nathan…, what happened?"

Her hands flew up and straightened his scrambled hair as she stared into the dark circles under his eyes.

"You don't want to know…, trust me," he muttered.

Lightning flashed outside, followed quickly by a low rumble as he caught his breath.

"Your clothes…, you have clients this afternoon," she said quietly, following close on his heels.

"They're in my back seat. I'll change in a minute."

His stomach growled loudly and he looked at the time, a few minutes before seven, "You're early."

Lisa's eyes seemed concerned as she hovered in front of his desk, then Nathan perceived that he'd been staring at her for several moments without speaking.

"I'm starving," he muttered. "I hope it doesn't rain all day."

Food was the last thing he wanted at the moment, but he couldn't think of any quick explanations for Lisa and he didn't want his stomach grumbling while talking to clients.

"I'll get your clothes," she said, then hurried away despite Nathan's immediate string of protests.

What was he going to tell Lisa? As little as possible. Somnambulance was for pre-pubescent children, not thirty-year-old men. Maybe it was time for a doctor's visit after all.

He squeezed the bridge of his nose, trying to force his memory into action. How did he get down the winding staircase in his sleep?

"Nathan…," he heard the voice in his mind, soft, quiet, beginning to remember.

"Nathan?"

He looked up at Lisa standing in front of his desk once again. His clothes, on covered hangers, were carefully draped over a chair.

"You forgot your dress shoes. I looked everywhere," she said apologetically.

Nathan wiggled his toes and grunted with closed eyes. He was wearing his house slippers.

"The stores open in about an hour. I'll go get you another pair," she offered. "Nathan? Are you going to tell me what's going on?"

Lisa looked at his disheveled hair and the t-shirt once again. She'd never seen him this far out of sorts, not once.

He forced a smile and wiped his raspy unshaven face, "I'll go clean up. Be back in few minutes."

Morning duties were such a habit at his age, it should have only taken about six or eight minutes, but to his dismay, he had to deal with the morning traffic from the shared restroom of the adjacent coffee shop.

When he returned, still in his rough clothes, Lisa was seated in one of his chairs, carefully biting on a cuticle, deep in thought.

"I'm going to have to change clothes back here," he grunted, stepping behind the last half partition in the far recesses of the office. He noticed a tall stack of new cardboard boxes with several folded blankets and a pillow on top, all pushed neatly against the wall.

Lisa turned, directing her question into the dark, "Does any of this have something to do with your obligations last night?"

She was going to try to pick the information from him piece by piece. Lisa was his sister Caroline made over. Her voice wasn't accusatory with some hidden agenda, but it was obvious she wasn't going to let this drop.

"Yes..., no..., maybe..., I don't know," he spat, finally settling on an answer.

"Can I just say I had a bad night and leave it at that?" he asked.

"No. You expect me to trust you; I expect you to trust me," she answered.

All Lisa could hear was the jingle of Nathan's belt as it threaded around his waist.

"Did your obligations last night have anything to do with the Stewart's?" she asked. It was point blank.

Nathan emerged from behind his faux privacy screen, dressed for the day, bleeding from a razor cut on his left jawline.

Lisa snatched a napkin and began to daub at his face like a mother hen, waiting for him to answer.

"Yes," he said finally, wondering how much he was going to allow her to pry from him before putting up a defense.

"Was Lindsey there?" she asked, again without accusation.

He sighed, "Her entire family are there Lisa. Yes, Lindsey was there too."

Even though it was the truth, his chest ached with the deceptive intent of his answer.

Lisa nodded and pressed on a dot of tissue paper, "Leave that there for a few minutes."

He took a deep breath, "My meeting was with Madeline Stewart and her elder sister. It was..., something of a personal nature."

Lisa turned away quietly, "Personal. And you just happened to show up at the office this morning doing the walk of shame?"

He was both flattered and upset when he realized that Lisa was dancing around what sounded like jealousy.

"The walk of...? Lisa," he growled.

Nathan's anger faded like frost under a hot sun and he began to grin, "I walked in my sleep last night. The Stewart's cook found me downstairs asleep on the floor huddled next to my beloved grandfather clock at six this morning."

Lisa's jaw dropped and Nathan's mood elevated instantly. He looked out the front window at new light filtering inside.

"I'll tell you all about it over breakfast," he chuckled.

After a nearly two hours at a nearby restaurant, Lisa and Nathan were still huddled in a corner talking while teasing cups of coffee.

Lisa finally reached across the small table and yanked off the tissue tourniquet from Nathan's jaw. He winced with embarrassment; he'd been sitting there showing the world his postoperative surgical skills.

"We'd better get you back to the office before someone sees you in your slippers," she grinned. "What size shoes should I get you?"

"Fourteen, but I'd better do that myself."

"Fourteen? You wear a size fourteen? Those things qualify as boat paddles."

He grinned, satisfied that he had successfully diverted her questions away from the true depth of his newest concerns. In turn, his conversation with Lisa had made that morning's fears seem trivial.

"Lisa…, I noticed some boxes in the back of the office…, and I was wondering," he began.

"I'm storing a few things…. There was so much empty room back there, I didn't think you'd care," she said, very quietly.

"Of course I don't care," he said cautiously.

Something was offish in her response; he didn't dare push.

"I was thinking of putting in a few pieces of furniture and make some sort of waiting area back there for clients. You know…, a sofa and chairs, lamps, a coffee table, magazines, a mini-fridge, that sort of thing. What do you think?"

Lisa nodded slowly, "I think that would give the place a warmer atmosphere. You really are expecting more business. Is this what our Thanksgiving meeting is about?"

He wondered why he was so hesitant to answer.

"You know as much about that as I do," he muttered. "But you really should know…, Madeline Stewart is probably unlike anyone you've ever met before."

He hesitated for a second, "Nothing like Henry or Lindsey. She knows how to get under your skin."

Lisa nodded, "I can handle nosey people. Remember who I work for?"

She quickly covered her mouth, but Nathan segregated she was referring to Troy.

Nathan laughed, "Nosey…? More like a surgeon's scalpel."

"You don't like her?" asked Lisa. "I don't get it."

"It's complicated," he answered quickly, wishing an end of the subject.

"Complicated for you, confusing for me," she frowned.

He had to change the subject quickly, "I'm probably making more out of it than necessary. Uh…, you're welcome to use whatever space is left over in the back. I can help you with anything heavy."

His mention of the boxes worked perfectly, too perfectly. Her face fell back to ash.

"No…, that's about it," she said quietly.

"Good. Put the furniture on your to-do list. You're in charge. Have the delivery people butt the whole arrangement up against my cube wall. Use as much room as you like."

Lisa was trying to push past her internal distractions.

"By the way, what have you found out about your classes?"

She looked slightly distressed again, "Mid-January…, Portland."

He prodded further, "That's great. Have them send the enrollment forms to our office so I can cut them a check."

She still looked questionable, "I'm not putting too much on your plate am I? If you want to put off the classes until later, I'll understand."

"No. It's almost nine, we better hurry," she mumbled, standing up from their table.

Nathan waited patiently for Lisa's usual chatter to reconvene until they were walking down the sidewalk outside. As a last resort, he decided to use her own words to reopen their conversation.

"Lisa…, earlier you said that you expect the truth from me…, and I appreciate that," he muttered. "I can't help but notice that you seem a little troubled. Is there anything you'd like to share with me?"

Lisa looked up as she slowed their pace, "Maybe…. As soon as you tell me the whole truth."

With a hint of a satisfied smile, she walked inside a department store, "Go get your shoes. I'll see you back at the office."

♥

Nathan was out with his first clients of the day, the Clements, showing them their one property of interest, while still preoccupied with concerns about Lisa. She had never quite explained why she was at the office so early that morning. He could feel some distant pain she was hiding, but he had learned his lesson. Lisa was easily spooked. She would be long gone back to her other world as a waitress by the time he was through with his first appointment. Then there was his next appointment at three p.m. with the Harrison's; a large family, looking to relocate to the area.

Their breakfast confessions seemed to ease all the previous tensions. For the first time since they began the haggard dance of getting to know each other, he actually felt as if he were courting her. One last item was worrying him. There had been no mention of their Thursday night plans all morning.

Nathan was amazed that his first clients were ready to commit to a purchase despite his preoccupied daze. His second appointment only had to linger in the office a few minutes while he completed all the preliminary forms.

The Harrison's brought along two of their oldest four children, and Mrs. Harrison was quiet noticeably four months along with their fifth child. Three property photographs were in their grasp and one on Elk Drive, which they were most anxious about.

It was an older estate, on contract for over eighteen months, not nearly the age of Heart Manor where Nathan grew up. The owners had cut the price for the third time, quite dramatically; anxious to be done with the process.

The price relative to square feet made it the obvious choice for anyone willing to move a thousand miles across the country to a posh neighborhood six miles outside Salem's city limits. He unlocked the door and let the Harrison's peruse freely while he checked his cell phone for messages.

As he leaned against the outside doorframe, despite his mind drifting back to Lisa in perpetuity, he placed a hand on the abutment of the open jamb. A quick jolt, then a soft spin of vertigo caught his attention as he jerked his hand away.

There was something alive beyond the norm reaching out from the memories of the older home resting against his back. He suddenly had a decision to make, then placed his hand back in the same position on the freshly painted wood.

Fewer than fifteen seconds later, he removed his hand and took a deep breath. It could have just as easily been three seconds because he already knew more than he wanted.

Nathan walked back to his Yukon and punched in the telephone number of the current owner from his day planner.

After several minutes of denials, the owner finally conceded that there had been a gruesome double homicide committed within the confines of the house. Even if there weren't any Real Estate laws in Oregon requiring full disclosure of violent acts within a property, he had to dissuade the Harrison's somehow.

Sometime later, the family reemerged from their explorations of the property and Nathan was relieved that they wanted to see the other two properties before making a decision. Maybe he would get to keep a clear conscience after all.

CHAPTER SIXTY

THE day was trying, but ended on a much better note than the way it began. Nathan walked through the door of Heart Manor at seven p.m., after trying to call Lisa for the third time.

He wanted to check on her, but also had news of her vehicle, which would be delivered to his place late Wednesday afternoon.

Sibyl Bates met him as he was entering the house, "Mr. Heart, I'm glad you joined us."

"It's been a long day," said Nathan. "But I'm looking forward to more lessons in sanity."

"Nathan."

Madeline Stewart interrupted them from across the room, "May I have a quick word with you before you disappear?"

He shrugged out of his blazer and shoulder bag and begrudgingly met her where she was seated.

"Sara?"

Madeline's voice was borderline harsh as she called for her cook.

Sara emerged from one of the other rooms as if she'd been waiting for her name to be called by a clerk at the department of motor vehicles.

Nathan waited in silence until she made her way to where they were.

"Sara, you will apologize to Mr. Heart."

Nathan's gut clenched, "I don't see any need...."

Madeline put up her hand, "Also..., as long as you are in my employ, you will treat Mr. Heart with the same respect that you treat me or any other member of my family. Is that understood?"

Sara's face was blank of expression, "Mr. Heart, I apologize for my rude behavior this mornin'. I assure you it won't happen again." Her Irish colored dialect was in full display.

Nathan stared into Sara's eyes, wanting to wish the entire moment away. He felt it completely uncalled for.

"Apology accepted and please accept mine as well," he added quickly.

Sara nodded.

"Thank you Sara, that will be all," said Madeline.

Nathan sat down in the closest chair to Madeline and leaned closer, "Was that necessary?"

"Yes, it was. I heard some of Sara's unfounded accusations this morning. They were likely things she wanted to say to Sibyl or myself. Apparently, she has a very low opinion of our methods of conducting business."

He nodded, "I understand, but I'd rather not be used as your brandishing iron."

Sibyl inched closer and quietly chose a seat beside Madeline.

"Duly noted. Will you be joining us this evening?"

"Of course. I just need a few minutes to collect myself and I'll be right with you."

♥

"Of all the pompous, pigheaded things to do," hissed Nathan, as soon as his bedroom door locked.

Sara was out of place with her comments, but the predawn situation had been just as strange. Madeline's words echoed in his head during each step up the stairs. Sara had a problem with Madeline and Sibyl, maybe even Lindsey…, and now him?

"Perfect," he grunted, snatching off his red tie.

Sara seemed to be one of the few people he could count on for inside information, his only spy. Now he was about the devil's business in Sara's eyes and alienated in one fell swoop by Madeline's reprimand.

"Only a few more days," he reminded himself.

He changed clothes quickly and hurried down to continue his indoctrination into the world he was predestined for. One he certainly didn't choose. A life that was unwittingly thrust upon him just as certainly as it was his mother, Marion Heart.

Nathan's heart rate slowed as he descended the staircase. Sibyl's generosity had spared him a future of miserable uncertainty. Even Madeline with all her connivings and misleading conventionalities could have simply let him go on his merry way. It was hard to criticize the hand that was saving his life.

As with the previous evening, the aged Sibyl was anxious and spry, waiting to begin. Similar to last night's training, about an hour beyond the evening meal, Lindsey relieved Sibyl of her duties.

That same distant attitude was hovering between him and Lindsey, though she didn't seem as anxious to dethrone him as Sibyl's newest Wunderkind.

"…and that's the last of this curio cabinet," said Madeline. "I'd like to have you experience some of the older, more eclectic items in this room…, but another night. I'm not as young as I once was, Nathan, neither is Sibyl. It does me good to see you and Lindsey working so well together. I believe it was most fortuitous that our family found you when we did."

"You sound as if you're standing with one foot in the grave," scolded Lindsey.

Her hand eased over on top of her Aunts, patting it carefully. It was the first honest show of concern for her aunt that Nathan had witnessed since their initial meeting.

"Maybe you should slow down some?" suggested Nathan.

Lindsey was the one to give a quick chuckle, "Aunt Madey has slowed down. She limits herself to 80 hours a month in our private jet and stays away from small countries with sudden outbreaks of illnesses."

Headlights flashed past the front windows, quickly coming to a halt out front. Lindsey rolled her eyes dismally and stood.

"Speaking of sudden illnesses, it looks as if Henry's back," grunted Lindsey. "If you'll excuse me."

Nathan was about to excuse himself as well, with the unction to spend a few minutes catching up with Henry. Their friendship seemed at a sudden halt, surely because Nathan had become the sole property of two of his aunts. He and Henry seemed to have a great deal in common when it came to leisurely pursuits and sports.

"Aunt Madeline," grunted Henry, the door shutting far behind him.

He was already at a trot, heading to his room.

"Henry. What is your hurry?" asked his aunt.

"I've had a long evening, Aunt Madey. I don't feel up to visiting," he sighed, his feet still moving. "Besides, you'd only run me off after the platter of steamed shrimp I had for supper."

Madeline shook her head grimly, "Did you manage to shore up the business I asked you about?"

Henry finally stopped walking, watching Nathan's expression over their short conversation, "No. And it's not likely I'll be able to."

It was cryptic, like everything that had to do with Madeline Stewart, now with Henry participating. The underlying tension building between Lindsey and her brother seemed to be spreading between Henry and Madeline.

"Pity…," she sighed. "Good evening then. We'll discuss it tomorrow."

Nathan shrugged his observations away in his mind. The last time he stepped into their family business, he was accused of courting Lindsey.

"Henry?" said Nathan. "The replay of today's Washington - Giant's game should be on in about an hour if you're up for it."

Henry darted a look at his aunt, "Thanks, but I've already seen it. Wanna know the final score?"

Nathan raised both hands and grinned, "No spoilers. I haven't even turned on the radio today. I guess I'll catch you later."

"Yeah…, sure. Sorry Nathan," grunted Henry.

Then Henry was gone out of sight, with only his footsteps announcing his retreat.

♥

Lindsey's bedroom door opened about the same time Nathan reached midway of the upstairs hall. When she saw Nathan, she turned to hurry back inside her room.

"Lindsey? Wait," huffed Nathan as he hurried to her door.

"What?" she asked, pressing the door to a close.

"Where were you headed?" he asked.

Here eyes closed, possibly looking for some excuse to get away.

"Sara made something decadent. I was going to steal a bite before Henry destroyed it tomorrow," she mumbled.

"I could use a snack," said Nathan, a blatant hint.

Lindsey stared up at the hallway ceiling for a second, "I'm not really in a chatty mood tonight Nathan."

"I'll make us some tea," offered Nathan.

Lindsey started to close the door, then her shoulders slumped and she stepped out into the hallway.

"Come on then. I'll make sure Sara doesn't stab you with a toothpick."

Lindsey tried to smile as she led the way back downstairs. The mass of lower lighting was already dim, only twinkling nightlights dotting around several spots on the walls.

She didn't speak again until they were in the kitchen. One of the refrigerator doors blinked more light in the room, until Lindsey slid out a large covered platter.

"It's Italian Cream Cake," she whispered. "Sara spikes it with rum. There won't be any left by tomorrow evening."

She cut them both generous slices, while Nathan put on some water for tea.

The late nite meeting reminded him of their first collusion.

"What is it you want Nathan?" she said with a huff, plopping into a chair.

A bright red glow hissed underneath the teakettle on the stovetop.

"First of all I'd like to know what you meant by this," he said holding up the crumpled note in her handwriting.

321

"I thought it was pretty simple. For someone as bright as you seem to be, I thought you would have figured it out by now," she scoffed.

She shook her head and took a small bite of cake.

"For the sake of argument, let's just say that I have too many things on my agenda to understand anything simple."

She turned to Nathan, keeping her voice very low.

Lindsey licked her lips, "You know you'll never get away from Madeline now. You'll always be at her disposal. Is that plain enough for you? Everything and everyone are pawns to be used and directed for the family's better good. That's her cardinal rule."

It seemed that she was talking more about herself than Nathan.

He let her words soak in while he poured both of them some hot tea.

"What choice did I have Lindsey? Of all people, you should understand why I needed to get some answers. I didn't want to spend the next thirty or forty years in some mental ward."

She sipped her tea thoughtfully, "No, that much I do understand. But after you figured it out, why didn't you leave well enough alone?"

"Because I still have questions," he blurted angrily.

"Questions…," she huffed. "You've become her perfect game, her pet project. It's a pity you didn't listen to me."

He wondered if Lindsey truly was jealous, instead of trying to help him.

"If that's true then why are you telling me this?" he asked.

Lindsey took another bite of cake, finished her cup of tea and stood up.

"I've been asking myself the same question," she whispered.

Nathan thought he caught the glimmer of unshed tears welling in her eyes. Lindsey put the cake away and disappeared out of the kitchen without a single sound.

CHAPTER SIXTY-ONE

WEDNESDAY began much easier. It was the sound of Nathan's alarm clock, not the screeching voice of a stranger that jostled him awake.

When he arrived in Salem, the first thing he noticed was his red Cadillac parked out front. Anxious thoughts of seeing Lisa nudged him. A few of the office lights were on in the back as he carefully unlocked the door and eased inside.

"Lisa?" he called out from the open door. There was no reason to sneak in a scare her. There was only silence after the jingling of the bell above the door.

Lisa's laptop was already on..., a photo array of homes on the display. He looked at the clock on the wall..., eight a.m. Everything inside the office was squared away, neat, stacked, to a fault.

After dropping his belongings on his desk, he took a quick look toward the dark back storage area. There were unmistakable happy morning noises coming from the coffee shop only a brick wall away.

Lisa had already rearranged some of their filing boxes, moving them farther back, almost clearing a space for the new lounge area. A single new lamp-stand illuminated most of the empty slot.

Suddenly the breezeway door, shared with the coffee shop opened and Lisa hurried inside, clutching a soft bag in each of her hands.

"Good morning."

Lisa spun, wide eyed and startled at Nathan's unexpected voice.

"You're early..., again," he said quietly, his back propped against the red brick wall.

"So are you," she said, forcing a smile.

"Actually, I'm a little late," he continued quietly. "Before I moved my office to my home, I was at my desk at seven a.m. every day."

Lisa walked away without responding, hurrying toward the front of the office. He heard noisy shuffling at her desk, then..., nothing.

Her laptop was closed by the time Nathan sat down in the one chair in front of her desk. Avoiding direct eye contact, she sorted through a dozen manila folders, picked one, then began paper-clipping photos to the edge and making notes.

"Do you need something?" she asked quietly.

"Coffee and a danish would be nice."

She lay down the open folder and nervously pushed her chair away. Something was definitely wrong.

"Would you rather have a latte and cinnamon roll? They're on special."

She stood, expressionless; her clutch purse already in her hand.

"I didn't really expect you.... Why don't you sit back down for a minute? I'd like to talk to you first?"

Her posture was even more unsettling as she carefully sat back down.

"About?" she asked carefully.

"Didn't you get my voice mail yesterday?" he asked.

Lisa snatched open her clutch and tapped her phone display.

"Shhtt," she hissed through clenched teeth, then her eyes flew wide at Nathan.

He'd never heard her upset enough to come close to saying anything off color.

"You want to tell me what it says or should I listen to it?" she asked carefully.

If he'd learned anything at all about Lisa Evans, he knew she was easily jolted into rash decisions. Nathan sat uncomfortably for several seconds, staring at Lisa, searching a way to calm her sudden erratic behavior. Apparently, he waited too long to answer.

"Nooo..., not you too? You talked to Troy, didn't you? Did he call you?"

Lisa slumped in her chair and covered her face with both hands, only for a moment.

"When is my last day?" she asked quietly, sucking in a deep breath.

Nathan was flabbergasted, "Last day?"

"Oh, please...," her voice quivered. "Just give it to me straight so I don't have to spend all day guessing."

"I..., Lisa I don't have a clue what you're talking about," he stammered. "Do I need to talk to Troy?"

She shook her head nervously, her eyes stopping to peer deep into Nathan's, "You didn't talk to..., oh God, why am I such an idiot."

He was leaning back in his chair, fingers laced, truly worried for Lisa. She carefully withdrew her cell phone from her clutch and patiently listened to Nathan's message.

"You wanted to tell me…, about my car…," she sighed.

Lisa's face reddened and her mascara began to crawl down her cheeks. Nathan hadn't seen a woman cry since his mother's funeral, much less someone that he felt attached to.

He frantically snatched several tissues from a dispenser on Lisa's desk and handed them to her. At least he had the good sense to keep his mouth shut.

"Troy fired me. I…, I thought.…

Nathan closed his eyes in wonder. It had to be something massive for Troy to fire his favorite head wait staff. Then the stack of boxes in the back of the office flashed across his mind. Silence had benefited him more than questions, so he remained silent once again.

"Aren't you going to ask me why?" she snubbed, her tears slowing to a halt.

"Isn't that between you and Troy?" he asked.

Lisa looked stunned and it was her turn to get quiet. Despite his good intentions for Lisa's future career, he wanted what was best for her.

"Would you like me to call him and help you get your job back?" asked Nathan.

Lisa's lips tightened, "I'd rather sell pencils on a sidewalk than go back to work for Troy O'Bannon."

This was more than a simple rift.

Nathan shrugged, "Then I don't see a problem. Your schedule is open for forty hours a week here. More if we really get busy."

Lisa swallowed her sudden anger, her face flushing red once again, "I hope you feel the same after you talk to Troy."

How could their disagreement possibly have anything to do with Lisa's employment with Heart Realty?

"I didn't hire you because of Troy and I'm certainly not going to fire you because of him either."

Lisa wiped her eyes one last time and picked up a paisley colored handbag from earlier, "Then I guess I'd better go put my face back on."

♥

"The Blind Pirate doesn't open 'til ten. You can damn well call back then."

The phone call went dead with a loud snap and Nathan looked at the time. A quarter before nine and Troy sounded winded, hung over, and angry.

Nathan looked up at the threatening sky before he hit redial and waited as the phone rang six times.

"If you value your life, this had bloody well be an emergency," growled a harsh voice.

It was clear English or at least as clear a facsimile as anyone could expect from an old hungover deckhand.

"This is Nathan Heart. Do you have a minute?"

A car honked a horn in the distant street as Nathan sat down on the first step of the cold concrete curb outside Heart Realty.

"If this is about Lisa Evans, she'll not be settin' a foot back inside The Pirate."

"Troy, don't do this. You've been friends with Lisa for years."

"She can stay out the week, then she has to move. I won't be having her squatting in one of my rentals for free."

"You're kicking her out of her apartment?" asked Nathan.

He was stunned.

"Tell me what happened Troy."

"She didn't tell ya herself? Ha! O'course she didn't. Well let me fill yer ear full, Mr. Nathan Heart."

Nathan held the phone away from his ear as Troy went on a ten-minute long rant, explaining why he fired his best employee.

"...like a dog in heat, I tell ya," hissed Troy, ending his angry spew. "And it's just as much your fault. Didn't I warn ya?"

Nathan finally remembered to breathe. There had to be another side to this story. He couldn't believe that Troy would make up such a load of filth on the spur of the moment, but Troy was known for turning something simple into a steaming load of manure. There were two sides to his incredible story and Nathan had only heard one.

"I'll talk to Lisa..., but Troy? No matter what happens, Lisa's your friend. You need to cool off and reconsider how you feel, okay?" asked Nathan.

"That's mighty big talk..., considering the circumstances," said Troy, his voice suddenly quiet.

"I know you see Lisa like a daughter, but she's a grown woman. She has to make her own decisions, even if you or I don't like them."

Troy was breathing heavily, still listening, "I just don't want to see her make a foul mess o' things. She's come so far."

There was sniffling. Perfect..., two disasters in one day.

"Think about what I said Troy, will you? Lisa deserves friends that won't judge her even when she does something they don't like."

The empty silence was verification Troy was listening. That alone was major progress in such a short time with Troy O'Bannon.

At least Nathan wasn't the author, but he was definitely in the mix. He ended the call when he saw Lisa standing in front of his desk through the plate glass window of Heart Realty.

♥

"I guess that was Troy."

Nathan nodded, his spirit suddenly quenched and broken.

"I tried to tell Troy, but he wouldn't listen," she continued.

Nathan looked her in the eyes, "I'm listening."

He locked the front door and arranged two of the bigger comfortable chairs to face each other in his open cube. Something he'd learned from Madeline Stewart. He already didn't like the guilty look clouding Lisa's face. Several things were beginning to make sense, congealing in his memory. Things he didn't want to believe.

Nathan crossed his legs giving Lisa a little more space and waited until she gathered her thoughts.

"It all started late Monday afternoon. Henry Stewart walked in and began to shoot the bull with Troy at the bar like..., like he was suddenly his best friend. By the time the main crowd began to filter in, he was good and drunk. So was Troy.

"Henry waltzed over to my section and ordered a bunch of food.

"Well, apparently that wasn't good enough. He kept calling me back over to his booth..., just to talk. I tried to tell him I was busy. That was when he walked back up to the bar and slapped down ten one hundred dollar bills and bought out my entire section for an hour."

Nathan nodded. Nothing could get Troy's attention faster than a stack of money; something Henry had plenty of.

"When my section cleared out, I was stuck. I knew his family is important to you..., and I kept expecting to see you come in any second. Monday's..., you know..., your usual? Anyway..., he kept buying out my section until closing time.

"I guess that was about the time Troy started to sober up and figured out what Henry was doing."

Nathan was quiet. So far, her story was pretty close to Troy's.

"Nathan? Did you tell Henry that I was coming with you to their Thanksgiving Dinner?"

Nathan shook his head, deep in thought, "No. Why?"

Apparently, Lindsey had kept her mouth shut to everyone including her own brother.

"Because..., he must have asked me half dozen times that night," she mumbled. "He wouldn't let it drop. Said he wanted me to meet his family. Troy finally came over and escorted him out, but he was waiting outside in his car like some love struck teenager.

"When I left, he started to follow me in his car. I couldn't go home. I didn't want him to see where I lived. So..., I came here instead."

Lisa's head was lowered, staring at her hands as she went on.

"Henry followed me all the way here, but I went in the coffee shop and used my key to get in through our breezeway entrance. He sat out there watching the little shop next door until it closed."

Nathan stared up at the ceiling. Adding in travel time, that was about when Henry came back smelling of seafood and beer. His gut tightened in anger at Henry, then at himself. He'd made no claims on Lisa and rightly so..., she belonged to no one. Could he blame Henry for his interest in her?

"Did Henry have the lobster that night?" asked Nathan.

Just saying Henry's name caused that tightening anger again.

Lisa frowned, "Enough for three people. He was there for over four hours."

Before she could ask Nathan how he knew, he urged her to continue her story, "And that's why Troy fired you?"

Lisa's lips tightened to a slim line in frustration as her eyes darted up to Nathan.

"Yesterday afternoon, Troy was already on a tear from the minute I started my shift. Then Henry came in again. Instead of starting at the bar, talking to Troy, he walked right over and sat down at one of my tables. I sat down across from Henry to try and warn him about Troy, but he was already trying to get a date with me. Troy walked over and ordered me to get back to work, more than once.

"Henry finally ordered food and somehow made it last for hours, stopping me every time I passed his booth. It's like every time I sat down, Troy was watching us. Henry did everything but promise me the moon to try to get me to leave with him. Neither of us saw Troy walk up, but that was when Henry tried to kiss me.

"Troy was really pissed. He grabbed my arm and lifted me out of the booth, and of course Henry stood up and started an argument with Troy. If I hadn't stepped in between them, there would have been blood. I couldn't tell Troy that your Realty business had something to do with Henry's family. Even if Henry was being an ass, Troy thought I was taking sides. Then Henry had to start grinning like a fool.

"That was when Troy called me a... floozy. That was when he fired me. I left while they were still arguing and headed to my place, but it seemed so dead and quiet. So I took a shower, grabbed the last of my things and left."

There must have been other harsh words between her and Troy before that; otherwise, she wouldn't have needed to store her belongings in the back of the office.

"You spent the night here last night..., alone?" asked Nathan.

Lisa leaned forward, her face tightened in something that resembled anger or hurt, "Yes..., alone. I didn't have anywhere else to go."

Nathan felt his face smile with relief.

He was glad that Troy's assumptions were the byproduct of an overactive imagination. Troy had gone by Lisa's to apologize, but he'd found her place empty and assumed that Henry had swept her away in some lurid escapade.

Nathan leaned quickly across the seat where Lisa was, cupping her face between his large hands. Before Lisa actually fathomed his intent, her arms were at his sides and she was returning his kiss in kind.

Nathan backed away slowly, memorizing the feel of her lips, following her eyes carefully. Lisa seemed nervous, but at least she wasn't running for the door.

Unwilling to free herself from Nathan's grasp, she whispered, "Does this mean you're buying me breakfast?"

CHAPTER SIXTY-TWO

"...**A**ND remove the property on Elk Drive, west of Salem from our listing and from the website. We're no longer representing their property. I've already told the client we've cancelled his contract."

Despite their late start, it seemed as if he and Lisa had accomplished more that morning than the last two days.

"Don't forget you have an early appointment at ten tomorrow."

He looked at the clock..., it was just past noon.

"Why don't you plan on going with me? I want you to get some experience with the sale. I think it'll help you get into the mindset of what a buyer wants to hear on our ads."

"I think I'm already past that," said Lisa.

He had avoided the subject of homelessness for her sake, "Have you thought about where you're going to live yet?"

Lisa shook her head, "My friends at work all offered to let me stay with them until I can find a place, but I can't do that. If Troy found out he'd pitch a fit. So..., I spent all last night looking for apartments in the paper and a couple of local listings on the web. I can't stay here another night."

She was in panic mode just as he expected.

"What? It's not like I can afford anything you have listed for sale," she scoffed.

"Troy mentioned that you could stay out the rest of the week at your apartment."

"The rest of the week," she mumbled, shaking her head.

Lisa was getting flushed with embarrassment and Nathan was tired of the dance.

"Oh for heaven's sake, Lisa. Are you going to let me help you or not?"

Despite his good intentions, he couldn't think of any scenario that wouldn't be seen as inappropriate.

Lisa sat at her desk quietly looking out the front window.

Any local hotel would eat her resources and her pride wouldn't let him help. He was living in a mostly occupied house, the caretakers' quarters were inhabited, even the attic was outfitted for the house staff to cohabitate. But even if Heart Manor was empty, it would look far too bawdy to invite her to live there.

"At this point, I could use a few suggestions," she sighed.

"We'll take one thing at a time. Do you have furnishings you need to move?"

She grimaced, "Nothing I want to keep; I have a few more clothes to box, some trinkets I guess. Everything else is going in the dumpster."

This end-of-the-world depression had to go.

"Come by Heart Manor this evening after six and pick up your vehicle. I asked the repair shop to deliver it there for convenience sake. We'll take one step at a time."

A light came on in Lisa's eyes, "I get my baby back tonight?"

"Absolutely."

"Nathan..., what if Henry's there?"

Lisa saw the torment on Nathan's face.

"Promise me you won't do something you'll regret. Henry's just..., really dumb."

He'd tried to push down the emotions all day, hiding his angry feelings over Henry even from himself.

"You expect me to let him get away with what he caused?"

"No, but I do expect you to be the person I've come to respect. After everything you've told me, Henry might have been following orders."

As if someone dashed him in the face with cold water, he glared into space. He stuffed his hand in his jacket pocket and extracted a wrinkled note, then reread it.

Lindsey's apology..., Henry's peculiar behavior..., Madeline's cryptic conversations.

"Madeline...," whispered Nathan.

At once he felt like Troy, his imagination running full tilt. Then there was Lindsey's remark.

"Everyone and everything are just pawns...," he mumbled.

Nathan crumpled the little handwritten note back into his pocket.

"Nathan? What's wrong?" asked Lisa.

There had to be a way out of all the secrecy. He needed to share with someone.

"There's something I need to tell you. Do you consider yourself..., open minded?"

Nathan looked quietly at Lisa, then turned to stare out the front windowpane.

"Lisa…, you said you wanted the truth from me," he said quietly.

He turned around to see her face fallen to ash. What if he told her the truth and she thought him a lunatic? What if he lost her forever?

Lisa's expression turned to one of near fright.

"Please don't tell me I spent the best part of my day kissing some sort of Dexter. You haven't done something bad have you?"

Nathan grinned, "No. Of course not. It's something far more complicated than that and it's going to take a while to explain."

♥

The black Yukon eased its way to a stop at the top of an overlook. A quarter mile in the distance, a long white veil of water and mist cascaded down the mossy green hillside.

Lisa stuffed another french fry into Nathan's mouth and dug into a brown sack to sort through their lunch.

It always seemed easier for Nathan to open up while he was driving. Lisa was being a good captive audience and at times he forgot that she was even in the vehicle as he recanted his life from the few weeks before he met the Stewart family, to the present. So far she hadn't asked him if he was seeing a shrink and he'd already confessed to hearing voices.

"So…, you think Madeline Stewart orchestrated all this grief with Henry, just to try to meet me?" she grunted. "I don't see it. What could she possibly want with someone like me? Why didn't she come to the restaurant?"

"You think I'm overreacting?" asked Nathan.

That was the last thing on his list of worries. She seemed to be taking everything else he'd confessed in stride. There was no reason to explain Madeline's violent reaction to the scent of seafood.

"No. I want to believe you…, as crazy as that sounds."

Lisa's eyes froze at some point in the distance and she became still and quiet. She stuffed her hoagy sandwich back in the brown paper sack and reached for her clutch purse. After only a few moments, she yanked out something small, something hidden in the palm of her hand. Her breath became ragged and she turned to Nathan.

"Prove it," she said, holding out her closed hand. "It'll go a long way to making me believe you."

"What?"

"You're either a very good liar, you're insane, or you're telling me the truth. So prove to me which it is."

Nathan wiped the breadcrumbs off his hands and looked away from Lisa, holding out his hand. He didn't need to see whatever it was she was going to hand him.

Lisa dropped a small round object in his palm, already warm from her tight grip.

Immediately, he saw a weathered face, tired from years of a hard life. An older lady with carefully pinned salt and pepper hair was lightly dotting her cheeks with rouge from a little brass compact, delicate with designs.

Someone walked up behind her and Nathan felt himself take in a breath. A young lady, almost identical to Lisa slid an arm around the older lady's neck and kissed her cheek. Memories fluttered around like butterflies, the last of which were not pleasant.

Nathan opened his eyes and breathed, "Evelyn Crain."

As if wounded, Lisa leapt from the Yukon and hurried to the shelf of the lookout, a cold hard wind whipping her hair. Her arms were tight across her chest as she halted, her eyes affixed into the distant canyon.

Nathan followed quietly, walking cautiously up behind Lisa.

What might have once seemed out of place suddenly seemed natural as he slid his arms around her and drew her close.

"My grandmother's name was Evelyn Crain," she whispered, leaning back against him.

"You look just like your mother," said Nathan.

Lisa gasped and turned in his arms, "You saw my mother?"

She buried her face against Nathan's chest, "I wish I could see through your eyes. I don't even have a picture of her and I was so little all my memories of her are a blur."

Her head leaned back as she looked up at Nathan, "How?"

Nathan shrugged, "Did I pass your test?"

Lisa lifted his hands where she could see them, hands much larger than her own.

"What else can you see with these?" she asked.

Nathan warmed each side of her chilled face with his palms, "I can already see everything I need to without them."

♥

Light as a feather carried by summer winds; the heavy weight of secrecy was lifted, shared with someone he was learning to trust.

With their afternoon at Heart Realty cut short, Nathan was anxious to get back to Heart Manor. He'd considered dragging Henry Stewart out onto the sprawling front lawn to twist some truth from him, except for two things. The first was Lisa, asking him not to resort to physical violence; the second was more complicated. What percentage of blame should he throw on Henry? He'd come to the conclusion that it was Madeline putting him up to his nefarious exploits while she and Sibyl kept Nathan occupied with other events. Then there was Lindsey...; who surely knew something was going on, but clearly wasn't choosing sides.

Even if he was overreaching, there were too many coincidences.

He felt the crumpled piece of paper in his pocket once again. Lindsey was even more complex...; he had no concrete indication of what she had been apologizing for. His one attempt to find out was met with cryptic conversation over a midnight snack.

As Nathan stopped his Yukon in front of the garage, he saw the sheriff's cruiser parked near the front steps.

"Now what?" he grunted.

Sheriff Kern was slowly walking down the steps, a legal sized sheet of paper in his hand, trying to read and watch his step at the same time.

"Ben..., what brings you out this way?" said Nathan with a nod.

The sheriff waved the piece of paper, "I decided to take Ms. Stewart up on her offer. It's her list of movers."

Evidently, the sheriff's investigations had run aground.

Nathan closed the gap and shook the sheriff's hand, "I doubt those guys had anything to do with your dead guy. I talked to everyone of them, even helped them move most of the stuff inside. They were all just honest Joe's."

Ben folded the paper, "People can fool you. Every time I think I have folks figured out, they surprise me."

Nathan grinned in agreement, despite himself.

"I did what you suggested," he continued. "I found where my perp was staying. A run down four-unit lodge about five miles away from here. That was a pretty good call Mr. Heart."

This perked Nathan's interest, "Find anything?"

Ben shook his head dismally, "Paid by the week... in cash."

Nathan was itching to ask the sheriff if he'd checked to see who he might have called, but remembered the warning from Madeline Stewart. He caught his breath and shook his head to hide his verbal intent.

"You have any other bright ideas I might have overlooked?" asked the sheriff.

Nathan shrugged his usual shrug, "I can't imagine what the guy's motives were unless he was a thief or a creeper."

The sheriff's brows raised, "See? Now that's exactly why I haven't let this drop. Something's been bugging me about the whole thing. This guy was caught red handed, hauled off to jail. He never once talked or even lawyered up and as soon as he posted bail..., poof! He disappeared.

"Now here's what bugs me...; most small time rodents like him turn on whoever hired them after the first hour behind bars. It was as if he had some personal interest in whatever he was up to..., or maybe he was afraid."

Nathan waved toward the house, "Well..., the house is full of museum quality valuables."

He hated himself for this diversion. Nathan wanted to find a way to tie
Stäkkr to the sheriff's inquiries, to find a way to get him prying into the one
he'd seen screaming into the telephone at the dead man.

"You know…, you're right," perked the sheriff. "If he was about to
steal something like that, he needed to unload it fast. I think you might
have helped me after all, Nathan."

Sheriff Kern drove away, with Nathan standing in the circle drive, hands
in his pockets.

There must be a way to involve Eben M. Stäkkr without drawing
attention to his family's wrongdoing.

Nathan ducked his head at the amoral judgment; wouldn't his mother
be proud of him for pointing guilt at a Stäkkr, while trying to protect the
criminal activity of his own family. Were the situation reversed, the *Big
Three* would likely throw him under the bus without hesitation.

Still, they were family, his only family, and he owed it to his mother.

CHAPTER SIXTY-THREE

MADELINE Stewart was standing just inside the living room...,
waiting almost impatiently when Nathan entered.

"I see you had a chat with Sheriff Kern," she prodded.

Nathan grinned, "Don't worry, I sent him off in a circle."

She sighed in what appeared to be some sort of relief, "I suppose that's
for the best, considering the eventuality may have led back to one of your
siblings."

Nathan's breath caught. Her train of thought was coinciding with his.
The associate his sister Josie had been involved with could easily have paid
Stäkkr to investigate him. At this point, it was the most likely answer. He
thought of consulting the little notepad of secrets once again, now that he
knew more about how to navigate through the ether of the past. But the
notepad was probably long gone by now.

Nathan shuddered, undeterred in his mission, "Is Henry here?"

Madeline's eyebrows rose, "No. Henry's not one to let the grass grow
under his feet for very long."

Nathan racked his jacket by the door, "I need to speak with him as soon
as he gets in."

"I thought you might," said Madeline.

Nathan spun to face her, his anger building, already showing in his
darkening eyes.

"You mustn't blame him for his actions...," she began.

There was already a small table with cold cuts and iced tea waiting where
she began to walk. Nathan followed closely, his anger building with every
step.

"You put Henry up to stalking Lisa Evans, didn't you?"

Madeline sat down and frowned, "Henry...," she shook her head, "Henry has all the grace of a bull in a china closet when it comes to the female persuasion. He thinks if he charges in and makes a display of wealth, the world will bow at his feet."

"Did Henry tell you he was responsible for Lisa Evans getting fired from her job?"

"Please sit..., have some food," she motioned. "I'm sorry to hear that. But..., I suppose it could free up time to benefit her position at your Realty office."

She was already sidestepping the issue, about to leap away in diversion and he was going to have none of it.

"What exactly is your interest in Ms. Evans?"

Madeline finished her sip of tea before she answered.

"Lindsey approves of her. The fact that you've taken her as an employee..., let her drive your vehicle..., tells me she's trustworthy. I'd like to meet her," she answered coyly.

Nathan was still standing in front of the proffered chair, angry adrenaline beginning to die away at her summation.

Madeline looked up at him, "Oh, my.... I had no idea that you were interested in Ms. Evans personally. Lindsey assured me that your interaction with her was..., strictly professional."

Nathan made a point of not acknowledging her accusation either way.

"Had I known...," she sighed.

It was all beginning to make sense. Henry was acting on Madeline's wishes, to kill two birds with one stone so to speak. With Henry interested in Lisa, he could bring her around for Madeline to scrutinize. Luckily, Madeline didn't know how obstinate Lisa Evans could be.

Nathan finally sat down and took one of the glasses of tea. Madeline wasn't off the hook just yet.

"All you had to do was ask me," said Nathan. "Wouldn't it have been much simpler? You could have dropped by my office with Lindsey."

Madeline chuckled, "I'm sorry you don't approve of my methods. You see, I've found that the direct approach is rarely as productive as a slant. Most people immediately raise their protective shields; form all sorts of preconceived ideas. I prefer to make a less spectacular entrance. It's much easier to learn what a person is made of if they don't know you're watching."

She still hadn't explained what her interest was in Lisa Evans. It was unlikely she would, even with another hour's worth of twaddle.

"Not if someone like Henry manages to run her off completely."

It was the first time Nathan had seen Madeline shift from her stanch reasoning, as her eyes darted up at him in a quick glance.

"And leave her employment with you? Where would she go?"

Nathan grimaced and shook his head from side to side to hide the smile that was hiding inside him.

"I haven't a clue. Someone like Miss Evans, with no other resources could easily disappear without a trace."

Madeline set down her drink, still clearly rattled, "Not without a trace. Anyone can be found eventually, especially if the trail is warm. When did she say she was leaving?"

Nathan stood, "I never said she was leaving, only that she shouldn't be cornered."

She pursed her lips as soon as she recognized Nathan's deception, but he'd made his point. There was no reason to start a war.

"Lisa is dropping by around six this evening to switch vehicles," said Nathan.

It wasn't the best of circumstances. At least Lisa wouldn't be blindsided by Madeline or Sibyl, especially after his lengthy disclosure of confidence earlier that day.

"Well then..., how delightful," perked Madeline. "I'll tell the staff to prepare another setting at supper."

Nathan chuckled, "After her experience with Henry, I'm not sure that's a good idea."

Madeline waved a hand, as if shooing away his negativity, "Introduce us and I'm quite sure I'll be able to persuade her to join us. Now..., we have at least three hours to continue our other pursuits. If you're still interested."

♥

Sibyl Bale held out the little wooden puzzle box to Nathan. It still had two small spires jutting out that he'd managed to unlock. Her tired eyes smiled with grandmotherly patience.

"Until now, I've only exposed you to *Objects* which were...," she struggled for some correct word, "...benign in nature. But I would be remiss as your tutor or your friend if we didn't press on. It's time to begin the next stage of your training with some of the darker elements you will likely incur."

Nathan looked over his shoulder at the ebony statue, "You mean things like the fellow with the spear?"

Sibyl chuckled, "Oh Lord no.... He's all hot air and show. The worst thing he might do is give you a fright."

Lindsey confessed that "Mr. Oooga Booga" had given her nightmares for a week. Nathan was more inclined to agree with Lindsey.

"As usual, I'm not sure I understand," grunted Nathan.

"You will," she sighed. "I believe it's time to enroll you into elementary school. You've passed kindergarten with flying colors."

This certainly didn't bode well.

"You have to be kidding? Kindergarten?"

"One step at a time Nathan," she said encouragingly. "The puzzle box you've been toying with is going to be your first task. I was going to force my way inside and make sure that it's safe, but instead it may prove to be good primer for you. Now as a reminder…, I'll be right here with you the entire time. You'll only need to remember to breathe as usual."

Nathan looked at the pristine little box with dismay as well as some renewed interest.

"This thing?"

"Why don't I make you an offer as an incentive?" she continued. "Whatever tidbit you find inside the box you can keep…, if you get past the *Object's Guardian.*"

What could be so intimidating about this little wooden box?

"Great," mumbled Nathan. "Where do I start?"

"The same as always," she began again. "Use what I've taught you and resurface if you need any help."

Resurface…. What an appropriate term she'd used. Sometimes it felt as if he was drowning in a vacuum.

Nathan sat back and closed his eyes.

He was immediately confronted with…, nothing.

His eyes blinked open, then had an idea and snapped them back shut.

The box shuffled around in his hands, with some hidden article thunking noisily around inside its inner sanctum. One index finger settled on the first pin he'd discovered, then did the same to the other. He pushed harder with his fingers and the second pin moved a bit further.

Nathan was about to open his eyes, to gloat and find the next key the same way he'd found the first two.

A gruff voice shouted at him, "Dumm Scheißkerl!"

The language he recognized as deep guttural German as well as the "dumb" reference. Nathan heard his own voice as if it was far away. "Same to you buddy."

Suddenly a bleak skeletal shaped face appeared to Nathan. His teeth looked shaved or ground evenly across in an evil smile. Midnight blue eyes, filled with hate and loathing couldn't disguise this lost soul's most striking feature. There was a swastika the size of a silver dollar on the center of his forehead. At first Nathan believed it a tattoo or a self-inflicted scar…, but it was neither. It was a brand…, burned deep, burned proudly onto the front of his bald head, announcing his loyalties and true nature to the world.

"Eindringling!" he yelled into Nathan's mind.

Intimidating as he was, he was no match for the darkened antics of his first experience with an unfriendly Guard. Nathan considered himself lucky he couldn't understand his nemesis.

Nathan ordered him much the same way he had the aborigine from the ebony carving to 'Go sit in the corner'.

The daemonic face smiled, "Scheißkerl. Beschissen Dieb," then railed on in what must have been a string of profanities."

Stymied by his defiance, Nathan remembered what Lindsey had done to the ogre in a bleak Carpathian past and reached out his hand toward the marred and disfigured head.

The grinning face turned to one of pure hatred, gnashing at his hand with blunt teeth.

Nathan retracted his hand and his eyes flashed open.

He could hear a calm voice urging him back to the present.

"Nathan?" said Sibyl for the third time.

Nathan took a deep breath, surprised by his own calmness at the situation, "Some Nazi just called me a shithead..., I think."

He was unconsciously rubbing his hand and Sibyl reached out to him.

"What happened?" she asked, urging him on.

"I did what I saw Lindsey do. I tried to..., touch..., the *Guardian* so I could understand him," said Nathan.

Something inside him warned of divulging Lindsey's secret. He'd tried to push into the *Guardian's* head and take whatever he pleased.

"Let me see," she grimaced.

Nathan raised his hand, to reveal a slight curved bruise on the rim of his meaty palm.

"He bit you," she hissed.

She took the box from Nathan, "When did you see Lindsey do that?"

"Yesterday? The day before?" he answered, unsure of how all the days were running together. "That thing bit me?"

"You *Followed* Lindsey?" whispered Sibyl, ignoring his question. "She *Interacted* with a *Subject* while you were *Following* her?"

Sibyl turned angrily toward a silent Madeline, "You knew this?"

Still Madeline was quiet, which was unusual.

"Well..., it appears we're much farther down the road than I was aware of," she muttered. "Yes..., an animus spirit can inflict damage on you if you don't know how to protect yourself."

Sibyl turned once again to Madeline, "Where did we get this box?"

"Hidden inside the spinet," said Madeline.

Sibyl closed her eyes, her face flashing both regret and disgust.

"We should have burned it," gritted Sibyl.

"It's safe in the Zürich Museum," argued Madeline.

Nathan looked at his hand again; the bite mark was already fading into a strange memory. He reached over to the box and shook it, thunking the entity inside it noisily.

"Tell me what to do," he said to Sibyl.

She took a deep breath, her eyes compassionate and full of thought.

"Are you a Christian, Mr. Heart?"

What an odd question. What could his views on religion have to do with any of this?

"I haven't been to any services in years," he said, shaking his head.

"That's not what I asked."

"Then…, yes. I've had my disagreements with God after my mother's passing, but I think I've settled those issues."

She seemed overtly pleased, "Good, then we don't have to worry about possession."

Nathan resisted the urge to stand, "Possession?"

Maybe he'd been too quick to judge Sara and her accusations of devils after all.

Sibyl's voice was calming, "Good overcomes evil, Mr. Heart."

CHAPTER SIXTY-FOUR

"**G**o back and tell him his Fuehrer is dead. No…, on second thought, tell him he is dead. That bit of information sometimes shocks them into remission. Can you remind me how to say dead in old Germanic, Madeline?" asked Sibyl.

"Would you like me to ask for Lindsey?" grunted Madeline. "She wouldn't be trying to have a conversation with an evil spirit."

"Lindsey and I disagree on her methods of running roughshod into the past," said Sibyl tiredly. "I fear terribly for my sweet little niece."

Nathan let the two sister's drone on in argument as he angrily picked up the box again. He was tired of the whole of the matter, ready to smash the wooden box to pieces and be done with it.

A snarling scarred face was already waiting for him as he closed his eyes. Sibyl might not approve of Lindsey's methods, but Madeline was right, her method worked.

Nathan remembered what Lindsey had looked like. A transparent angel with a flickering lantern glowing inside her. He visualized his anger, seeing himself reaching out to this monster that had been a madman and renowned serial killer in life. If it worked for Lindsey, it should work for him.

The animated hatred on the face of the branded Nazi suddenly turned to awe as he stared at Nathan.

"Geist…, poltergeist," it hissed, eyes glazed in fear.

This thing didn't know it was dead.

Nathan used the moment of bewilderment to ram his hand inside the spirits face, then in that same moment wished he'd never heard of anyone named Stewart.

All the evil perpetrated by whoever this evil man had been, began to leech into his memories, the atrocities he'd ordered for his Vaterland, the murder and torture…. Worst of all, the pleasure this creature had derived from it all was sickening.

The shaking skull disappeared, dissolved, leaving Nathan gasping for breath as he opened his eyes once again.

"Tote…, geist," he whispered, answering Sibyl's question.

His hands flew at the box, pushing angrily at the sides as another hidden pin jutted out, then another and another.

Six spikes were standing out as Nathan slid the end gate open, revealing a three inch by three-inch compartment inside the puzzle box. The once felt-lined interior was beaten bare by the years of constant abrasion due to the contents of a small leather pouch.

Nathan already knew what was inside it; he abhorred it already because it had cost an old jeweler his life.

He lifted the pouch, "Ein toter Hund beißt nicht."

The once foreign language, now ingrained in him, seemed to flow naturally out of his mouth, full of inflection. Chills raised all the hairs on Nathan's arms and the nape of his neck.

He toppled the open box to the floor in disgust and took several slow breaths.

Unwilling to show Madeline the contents, he stuffed the leather pouch inside his pocket as he rose.

"Ich mussen…," he stopped himself. "*I need*… to clean up before my company gets here."

He heard the conciliatory voice of Sibyl behind him, begging him to stay, to explain what transpired, and the shocked silence of Madeline as he hurried away…, up the stairs.

♥

His bedroom door latched and Nathan felt his large hands trembling. He dropped the pouch, his treasure, onto the bed carefully.

He'd watched Lindsey do the same thing to a man easily three times her size while in that altered state. He was beginning to peer into what Lindsey tried to spare him from and what she must have endured at Madeline's prompting. In that fleeting moment, his heart was broken for her…, for what she must have endured.

Clothes angrily flew off his body as he hurried to step into a blazing hot shower. Somehow, he needed to feel clean again. The filth he'd experienced still hovered over him like a stench.

The blast of hot water seemed to soothe him as he forced his thoughts toward Lisa Evan's impending visit. It was far too late to help Lindsey, but somehow he needed to protect Lisa from any usefulness that Madeline might deem good for her family.

Nathan's thoughts drifted away as a tune replaced his musing.

Ade, mein liebes Schätzelein,
Ade, ade, ade,
Es muß, es muß geschieden sein
Ade, ade, ade,

It wasn't until he twisted the knob, turning off the shower, that he heard himself. He'd been quietly singing a song he'd never heard, in a language that he'd never spoken before in his life. His thoughts were drifting back and forth between his native tongue and some version of early Germanic, as if he was native born to both regions. Nordlicht, somehow fell proudly into his mind..., northern Germany, High German not low.

This new unknown was terrifying. His pulse was still uptempo, as he toweled off, remembering how Lindsey had repeated the name of some Scandinavian village, with the same inflection as the villager they'd encountered.

A side effect of *Interaction*? What else would he collect? And for how long?

Nathan was stuffing his shirt into the waistband of his trousers when someone bumped a fist on his door.

"Jesus," he whispered, feeling his pulse rise in fright.

He'd never been skittish in his life, it was an unwelcome emotion.

"Just a minute," he barked.

"You have a visitor, Mr. Heart," said a friendly voice he didn't recognize.

"I'll be right down," he answered loudly, angrily finishing the last two buttons on his shirt. He was compelled to hurry downstairs as some unknown protective mode overtook him.

On the bed was the little worn leather pouch, his treasure. He snatched it up and placed it beside the ceramic Little Boy Blue on his chifforobe.

♥

No one was at the front door, which worried Nathan immediately. He heard no conversations humming about in any of the adjoining rooms.

He hurried to look out one of the window panels beside the door and saw Lisa, blue jeans, tennis shoes, and long overcoat removing several items from the trunk of his red Cadillac convertible..., aided by Bolton.

Nathan was down the front steps at a quick clip, listening to the mysterious man's glib chatter, watching every inflection of Lisa's face as he hurried closer.

"Lisa!"

She spun and her face lightened, "I was afraid you weren't here."

Nathan slipped both his arms around her waist, giving her a quick kiss.

"You're early," he said, backing away slowly.

He watched her eyes carefully, shocked by his own forward behavior.

A crooked little grin forced a dimple on one of Lisa's cheeks, "I can leave and come back again."

She reached up and straightened Nathan's rumpled shirt collar, her hand taking its time down his chest.

Nathan caught the nervous fidgeting of Bolton out of the corner of his eye.

"Bolton."

Nathan turned and shot out a hand, "I hardly see you anymore."

Bolton brushed away what looked to be white dust from sheetrock onto his coveralls and shook Nathan's hand, his face expressionless and tired. His hair had flecks and strands of yellow insulation braided in it, undulating in the breeze.

A cold wind whipped angrily against the garage doors causing the three to turn and stare as the nearest ones creaked in protest.

"I was just telling Miss Evans that I had her car put in the last stall of the garage," said Bolton, pointing. "You wouldn't consider selling it would you?"

Lisa sidled next to Nathan, "Are you kidding me? That's my baby. I might as well sell an arm or a leg."

"Can't fault me for trying," he muttered, his eyes darting to Nathan. "I left the keys in the ignition. I..., guess I'd better head back to work."

"Hey Bolton, when you come up for air, if I'm here, say hello."

His dust caked face creased in a smile, "I'll do that."

After quick goodbyes, Nathan was left alone with Lisa, followed by several moments of silence.

"When did you get so territorial?" she asked quietly, looking past Nathan around at the deserted garage.

"I..., don't know what came over me," he shrugged apologetically.

"That wasn't a complaint."

Lisa hugged against his side, "Where's your jacket?" Then just as quickly, "Are you going to let me see my car or keep me in suspense for the rest of the evening?"

"Promise you're not going to jump in it and drive away?"

Lisa slumped, "That was the plan."

Nathan felt his face shift in thought, "How would you feel about staying for..., dinner?"

He could hear Madeline's southern dialect say supper in his head and just as quickly its German alternative.

"Uh..., I don't know. Right now? This evening?" she stammered.

Nathan nodded with a slight tilt, "Your name happened to come up and...."

Lisa gasped, "Nathan, you didn't get into it with Henry did you?"

Something about her concern made him grin. His anger at Henry had been misplaced, "No..., I think that might be settled..., even though Henry doesn't know it just yet."

"So my name came up all on its own? With who?"

"Well, not exactly on its own. Madeline and I had a heart-to-heart. It appears she was trying to play matchmaker between you and Henry."

"Me? With Henry? She doesn't even know me."

"Apparently Lindsey's opinion carries a lot of weight with Madeline," he explained.

"Lindsey...," she whispered. "Wow..., that's...."

Nathan could see that this conversation placed Lisa in an uncomfortable position. She needed time to think.

"Come on. Let's get your car out of the garage."

♥

Four boxes of belongings and a sleeping bag fit easily in the enormous trunk of the Buick Special; the last of Lisa's personal belongings. The Buick was repaired to its original condition except for one missing hood ornament, lost somewhere in the pacific ocean at Black Shoals Beach.

Lisa stalled on the front steps just long enough to give one of the stone lions an endearing pat on the head, followed by her traditional, Nice Kitty.

Reluctantly, she'd agreed to walk inside, say hello and test the water before deciding on whether or not to stay and visit.

Once inside and out of the cold, Lisa slid a hand along the side of the huge clock, watching the bright pendulum rock to and fro through the glass front.

"It really is kind of pretty."

She grinned mischievously at Nathan and turned to the window beside the door, "Hello Marion, it's so nice to see you."

The clock immediately gonged once..., as if answering her announcement. With the half-hour announcement hanging in the air, Lisa gasped, clutching her chest.

Nathan caught her, kept her from tripping over her own feet as she reeled backwards.

Nathan began to chuckle and Lisa spun, slapping at his arm, "That, was, so, not, funny."

"But it was good timing," he shrugged.

He turned and gave the old clock a quick wink before they walked out of the vestibule.

Sara was pacing just inside the living room. She seemed anxious, more so than usual, hurrying over to stand patiently while Nathan helped Lisa out of her coat.

"Sara, this is Lisa Evans," said Nathan.

"Excuse me…, hello Miss…," she nodded toward Lisa. "Mr. Heart, could ya tell me if the lady will be joining us for supper? It's not a problem, but Bolton's had the gas shut off downstairs for half the afternoon and now one   the   ovens   is   givin'   me   fits."

Sara snapped around looking to make sure she wasn't being overheard.

Lisa looked to Nathan, "Maybe this isn't the best time for me to drop in like this. I should probably go."

Sara looked very alarmed, "Ooh…, noo. It's not a problem Miss. I'm making roast duck and I can lay it off on Bolton if I'm delayed, but I really need a head count…."

There were voices in a discussion coming down the hallway and Sara backed up quickly.

"Never you mind…, it's a good thing they've been marinating all day. Maybe I can throttle Henry and there'll be seconds for everyone. Sorry I troubled you," she nodded, hurrying off back to the kitchen wringing her hands.

"Poor thing. Is she always like that?" whispered Lisa.

"Never," said Nathan. "Sara and I go at each other like family most of the time. I don't know what's bothering her."

Lisa looked around the huge room, "I thought there was a bunch of people here. Where is everybody?"

It was a good question. The house seemed deserted.

Nathan shrugged, "Back in the den, watching TV?"

CHAPTER SIXTY-FIVE

NATHAN was holding Lisa's hand, ambling toward his old office to show Lisa the antique roll-top and writing desk, when Madeline and Sibyl emptied out of the downstairs hallway.

Madeline's perfectly practiced smile hurried toward them and Nathan gave Lisa's hand a soft knowing squeeze before he let it drop.

"You must be Miss Evans," she cheered, before Nathan could offer any sort of introductions.

Lisa extended her hand to the older lady, at least an inch shorter than herself. Madeline looked as deceptively formidable as a teddy bear to Lisa.

"This is Madeline Stewart," said Nathan, as they shook hands. "And this is Mrs. Bates…, her sister."

"So good to meet you. Call me Sibyl."

Sibyl stepped around quickly as her hand reached out and clasped Lisa's.

After a few moments, Sibyl's eyebrows lifted questioningly toward Madeline.

"Please, make yourself at home," said Madeline. "Would you like something to drink, maybe a little wine?"

"Do you have tea?" asked Lisa.

"Certainly. I'll have Sara make some fresh and bring it right out," said Madeline.

"Oh…, no…, don't…," Lisa looked up at Nathan. "Don't go to any trouble. I guess wine would be nice."

Nathan knew she was worried for Sara's already frazzled state.

"Why don't I make us some tea?" said Nathan. "Any preference?"

He'd be leaving Lisa alone, but surely Madeline would behave with Sibyl on her heels.

Lisa grinned at Nathan, "Anything hot and sweet sounds great."

"Ladies?" asked Nathan.

"My usual," said Madeline.

She'd come a fraction short of her usual condescending tone.

"Why don't I help you?" said Sibyl. "I'm not sure what I want."

This was an about face Nathan hadn't expected as he hurried away with Sibyl slowly following behind him. It was rude of him to scurry off ahead, but so was the two sister's ruse to get Lisa alone with Madeline.

"Won't you have a seat?" was the last thing Nathan heard Madeline say as he stepped beyond the staircase toward the kitchen.

"Sara, may I use one of your empty burners?" said Nathan, already filling a teapot with water.

She saw Sibyl follow him through the door and nodded politely.

"Nathan, I didn't get a chance to apologize for our short session earlier," said Sibyl.

Sibyl sounded cryptic. Was it for the sake of their audience hovering near, topping baked yams with seasoning? Nathan ignored her probe for as long as he dared, wishing the water to hurry a boil.

"Why would you feel the need to apologize? I took it upon myself to hurry us along."

Nathan readied a salver with cups, sugar, and cream. Sibyl was brooding over her thoughts, watching him for quite some time, expecting him to spill some unknown to her. It was the first time he'd seen Sibyl this antsy.

Sibyl set out several tins of various teas, "Would you like to share the details with me?"

Nathan shook his head, "Eigentlich nicht, (not really)."

"Excuse me?" said a shocked Sibyl.

Nathan raised the boiling kettle from the stove and looked at Sibyl oddly, "I said not really." Then he cringed; he must have slipped into his newly acquired language.

"Your German is very…, natural," she continued. "Did you spend time abroad?"

Nathan grinned, plucking two Orange Blossom teabags from a tin and dropping them carefully in some cups.

"No. Ich tat nicht, (I didn't)," he finally answered, not bothering to translate.

He quickly poured hot water over his and Lisa's tea as Sibyl continued to stare at him.

"Would you like to choose your tea?" he asked.

♥

Lisa was seated across from Madeline, her legs crossed and fingers laced at her knee. She seemed absorbed in some tale issuing from Madeline's lips, which ended as soon as Nathan sat down the tray.

Lisa took the cup Nathan handed her and sniffed, "Oh..., a man after my own heart. Thank you."

She casually placed a hand on Nathan's knee and sat up straight, "Was that when your family decided to come to this country?"

Madeline lifted her teacup, almost poetically, "That very year..., the fall of 1748. We still have the first family ledger preserved at the Stewart Family Historium in Charlotte. But..., I didn't mean to prattle on about our boring family chronicle. Tell me a little about yourself."

Lisa grinned and glanced over at Nathan, "Sorry, I don't have a pedigree. There's not much to tell. I haven't been able to trace my roots past my Grandma."

"What about your parents?" she prodded.

Lisa shook her head as a sudden darkness fell, "I left my foster home as soon as I was of legal age, then lived with friends until I finished High School. I moved here. The rest is even less interesting."

"What a pity..., and such obvious potential," muttered Madeline.

Nathan hid his thoughts with a drink of tea; such subtle flattery mingled with disdain.

"I'm glad you think so," said Lisa. "At least I have a promising job, thanks to Nathan."

Lisa didn't exhibit one ounce of sarcasm in her obvious sting.

Madeline didn't bite, but casually turned to Sibyl, "Did Sara mention when supper would be served?"

"Seven'ish," answered Sibyl, somewhat coldly.

Madeline looked at her diamond-encrusted wristwatch, "I admire tenacity Miss Evans. I only wish that my niece was as resolved to her talents."

"You mean Lindsey?" asked Lisa, twisting a frown across her face. "She's a darling. She's one of the nicest persons I've met in years."

Madeline looked over her shoulder and waved at some hidden wraith. One of the younger house staff appeared from out of the hallway and hurried over.

"We'll take our supper in the den. We'll need..., six settings. The rest of the family will be in the dining room this evening."

The young lady nodded silently and hurried away back down the dark hallway.

Lisa looked nervously at Nathan, her eyes speaking volumes. She wanted to jump in her Buick Special and drive away; Nathan wanted to go with her.

A loud bustle banged against the front door, which happened to be on the far side of the living room from where they were seated.

"The prodigals have returned," muttered Madeline.

Lindsey rushed through the door with an ebullient shrill; several bags dangling on both arms, with Henry's booming voice close behind. Both seemed happily exhausted.

"Children."

Both Lindsey and Henry stopped like deer in headlights, looking for the source of command.

"Aunt Madey," said Lindsey, rearranging her prizes as quickly as she did the surprise on her face.

Henry's face flushed the moment he saw the back of Lisa's head seated next to Nathan.

"Supper is in fifteen minutes. Please join us in the den," she ordered. "You too Henry."

Nathan felt Lisa's fingers twitch against his leg..., a nudge..., maybe a plea.

Nathan casually grinned as he resolved to view the entire process as some grand theatrical performance put together for their entertainment.

Madeline's ideal facund returned to her face, her chin tilted up slightly, "One of my staff mentioned that you are in the process of moving."

The faint party on Nathan's face slowly dwindled. Bolton-the-spy was still on duty.

"In a few days," said Lisa, cautiously.

"Well then..., congratulations are in order," said Madeline.

Nathan tried to get Lisa's attention, to stop her, but it was too late. Lisa took the bait.

"I wouldn't go that far just yet," said Lisa, her voice becoming steel. "I'm still deciding on my next address."

Nathan was impressed. Even with all the opportunities, Lisa still hadn't mentioned Henry's complicity in her predicament. However, her emotions were starting to ink through. It would only be a matter of time before Madeline found Lisa's niche and blood would spill.

"And you only have a few days to decide on something as important as your next residence? How awful," Madeline sighed.

Then her face positively began to glow, "I have the perfect solution. We have one room upstairs that's vacant, next to Lindsey as a matter of fact. Would you consider staying with us until the end of the month? It might give you the extra time you need to make a quality decision."

"I'm sure we'll find Lisa a nice place in Salem in a day or two," blurted Nathan.

This charade had gone far enough. He wasn't going to sit there like some silent lackey, while Madeline continued to manipulate yet another life to her unknown benefit.

"Why..., I think that's very kind of you," said Lisa, a bright smile appearing on her face. "Don't you think so Nathan?"

Nathan felt his muscles constrict so tightly he couldn't swallow the lump of air lodged in his throat.

"Are you sure I wouldn't be intruding on your family?"

Madeline wove the fingers of both her hands together, "Lindsey speaks very highly of you. I think it's the perfect solution."

Lisa's smile stupefied Nathan to the point of total silence.

"I'd love to get to spend some time with Lindsey..., and it would give me more time to look for my next home."

Madeline smiled back at Lisa, "Well then..., it's settled. I'll have one of the staff prepare your room and you can move in as soon as you're ready."

"That is so sweet of you," cheered Lisa. "What about..., this evening? I've already stored all my things from my apartment."

"Don't you want some time to think it over?" asked Nathan, quietly.

A bell dinged from the hallway and Madeline looked at her watch, "Where are those children?"

Nathan felt his insides turn sour as he stood, "Why don't I show Lisa where her room is and give her a chance to wash up?"

"Excellent idea," said Madeline, "...but do hurry. Supper is about to be served."

CHAPTER SIXTY-SIX

"**H**AVE you lost your mind?" gritted Nathan.

He was having a hard time keeping pace with Lisa trotting up the stairs. He was having a harder time understanding what was going on in her mind.

She ignored him until he could take no more, pulling Lisa into his room and closing the door.

"What do you think you're doing?" he sighed, his voice turning into a plea.

"Shut up and play along Nathan. That old battle axe is out of her mind and I need time to figure out what's going on," said Lisa.

"And you think staying here is the answer?"

Nathan slumped into his plush chair, "I want you to change your mind and get out of here."

"After..., I figure out what's going in that head of hers," spat Lisa.

She paced the room for a few seconds, staring into oblivion, obviously not listening to Nathan.

"Look..., I'll give you some cash and you can leave tonight. Drive into Salem, rent a hotel for the week. I'll help you...."

Lisa shook her head, interrupting him, "I could go back to the apartment for a day or two if I thought that would help."

"Then let me find you a place in Salem. I can sell it back to you at cost."

Lisa sat next to him on the soft chair arm, "Don't you get it Nathan? She snaps her fingers and people appear and disappear. How long do you think it would take her to have someone find me?"

What had Madeline said to throw Lisa into such a defensive spin? Of course he wanted to keep Madeline from manipulating Lisa. But surely she didn't think Madeline was capable of something so clandestine?

"Madeline Stewart is a control freak, but I can't picture her doing anything that far fetched," muttered Nathan.

Why did he suddenly feel he had to defend Madeline? Bringing Lisa here was a horrible mistake.

Now she was overreacting to Madeline's odd supercilious air of superiority. Nathan was raised around arrogant families with money to burn; this culture clash wasn't something that could be taught.

Lisa shook her head, "You ran off and left me there with her. You didn't hear everything that was said. She's the cat and everyone else are mice. I need some time to figure out what it is she's after."

"Lisa…, I warned you about Ms. Stewart and her family. That was part of the reason I shared my secrets with you today. I know this is going to sound crazy to you and they actually have helped me, but I don't want you caught in their web."

She took a deep breath and leaned against Nathan's shoulder; at least she was calming down…, listening.

"Lisa…, Madeline Stewart may be everything you say she is. I might be blind to what's going on, but my gut is telling me its something else completely. I'm only trying to protect you from being interrogated."

Lisa carefully turned his face around with her palm, "You still want me to leave? All my things are already packed."

"No. Of course I don't want you to leave. I want to leave with you."

He didn't like the compromise. If only she hadn't jumped at Madeline's offer.

Lisa slid from the chair arm into his lap, "I guess if I'm wrong…, I still get a free room near you…, and we can ride share."

She grinned and kissed Nathan before he could say something to ruin the moment.

"We'll compare notes later. Right now I want to see my new room and I'm in dire need of a potty break."

♥

Henry ignored Lisa. Lisa ignored Henry. Thus began their supper in the isolated den, mere feet away from the rest of the Stewart family.

Worker bees buzzed around almost invisibly, delivering one course after another.

Henry was still oblivious to Nathan's change of heart and with no one else to listen to his baritone chatter, he buried himself in conversation with his Aunt Madeline.

With Madeline seated directly across from Henry, Sibyl facing Lindsey, it left Lisa seated across from Nathan, while rubbing elbows with Sibyl.

Sibyl held several polite conversations with Lisa, always touching Lisa's arm or shoulder to convey her private comment.

By the time desert arrived, Nathan, Lisa and Lindsey were involved in a somewhat congenial conversation.

Lindsey leaned across the small table once again, while placing a hand on Nathan's arm beside her.

"Please come with me, Lisa. I'll finally have someone willing to ride the trolley to the top of the Eiffel tower."

"It really sounds amazing," confessed Lisa. "But I have a meeting with my unofficial fan club the first week of December."

Lindsey giggled, "You have a fan club?"

"Nathan's favorite niece is coming to visit me. A promise is a promise," said Lisa.

"How old is your niece?" Lindsey asked Nathan.

It was the first time he'd seen Lindsey this much aglow with interest about anything. It was almost a physical relief to see her tortured beauty put to rest for these few minutes with friends.

"Allie turns seven the thirty first of December."

"She's such a sweetheart," said Lisa. "You'll have to meet her. She's this little...."

"Oh no...," sighed Nathan.

His life had become such turmoil, he'd forgotten to write his niece Kate.

Both women were staring at him now, he had to explain.

"My niece Kathryn..., Katie," he mumbled. "I always write her about the middle of each month. I'm her and Chuck's only source of mad money. With everything that's happened lately with her mother, she's going to think the worst."

"She will not. She's family. We'll do it first thing tomorrow," said Lisa.

"She sounds sweet..., so lucky...," muttered Lindsey.

Lindsey took in a slow breath, visibly disturbed, as an array of emotions flashed across her face. The beautiful smile turned crestfallen, then lost, finally to bitter with a dash of psychotic, as if life had suddenly forgotten her, or vice versa. She turned to look across at Madeline, interrupting Henry's incessant drone.

"Aunt Madey, will I ever be allowed to have a family? Or will I end up an old crone like you?"

All conversation halted at once, then the chatter and movement in the adjoining dining room fell to hushed whispers.

Madeline's burning eyes were still framing an equally cutting reply when Lindsey stood, throwing her napkin onto the table.

"That's what I thought."

Lindsey stormed out of the room as quickly as her feet could carry her.

"Lens!" yelled Henry, running after his sister.

Nathan felt that same horrible aching empathy, forcing his gaze toward Lisa. Her eyes held the same sadness he was feeling for Lindsey.

At the same moment, both Nathan and Lisa rose from the table, "Would you please excuse us?"

Madeline nodded, her expression dead as a codfish.

♥

Lisa was gripping Nathan's hand tighter than she had realized, but refused to let go, "Which way do you think she went?"

"Let's try her room first," he offered.

"This is what you meant when you said your relationship with Lindsey was complicated," said Lisa. "I think I understand it better now."

Nathan held his commentary as they hurried down the upstairs hallway.

"I'd rather die than live the rest of my life like this."

Nathan and Lisa stopped just outside Lisa's closed door, catching Lindsey's private declaration.

Henry's low mumbling response was just beyond recognition.

"No Henry, it's never going to change. Just get out. I need some time to think."

"Don't do anything stupid, Lens," boomed Henry.

"Don't be ridiculous..., I know first hand what happens to suicides. It's even worse than this. Just go! Get out, please."

The bedroom door opened and Henry didn't seem surprised to see Nathan and Lisa standing there, round eyed, cautious. He hurried away back down the stairs, soon followed by the slamming of the front door.

"And I thought being orphaned was bad," whispered Lisa.

Nathan slid an arm around her waist, "What do you think we should do?"

"We can't stand here all night," she answered, letting out a gush of pent up breath and emotions.

Lisa opened Lindsey's door and pushed Nathan away, "We need some girl time. Go on. Don't forget, I'll be right across the hall."

She tiptoed up and kissed Nathan, "Go on. I'll take care of this."

The door closed as Nathan sucked in a deep ragged breath.

♥

He might not be able to console Lindsey, but he was well versed, even quite comfortable at head-on family conflict. Anger built like steam as Nathan replayed the conflict. He could no longer stand by idly and watch Lindsey buffeted by some hidden stranglehold, with no advocate....

His feet were moving even before he consciously made the decision to confront Madeline..., to settle this. The worst thing that could happen would be getting kicked out of the house and his contract with Madeline destroyed, which in itself would be a blessing.

Nathan took off down the stairs, passed several of the Stewart family in huddled conversations spread across the living room.

His footsteps must have been ignored as he neared the den. Stopping in the doorway, he noticed that the table had already been cleared and the two women were huddled with their backs to the door.

Sibyl's concerned voice spoke low, "I did Madeline..., several times. I found nothing remarkable whatsoever. She seems to be just what you see; a very likable young lady. But we need to discuss Nathan..., very soon."

"Very well..., I need to address Lindsey's latest display for attention," muttered Madeline.

Nathan cleared his throat, causing both the elder women to flinch, "I'd like to speak to Madeline..., alone please?"

CHAPTER SIXTY-SEVEN

NATHAN closed the doors to the den without invitation, "You understand that your niece has contemplated suicide? Lindsey isn't an apparatus placed on this earth for you or your family's disposal. She's a human being."

"Bah. She's smarter than that. It's nothing more than another one of her rude tantrums...," huffed Madeline.

"It's not a tantrum; it's a plea for help," said Nathan leaning forward. "What I can't understand is why all the other Stewarts aren't in here having this discussion with you instead of me. I'm only a stranger in the middle of this, but even I can see you're pushing Lindsey right over the edge...."

Nathan posed himself right in Madeline's face, "You're going to lose her."

"You don't understand Nathan," she hissed back. "Our entire family will one day be dependant on her and her decisions."

Nathan stood in anger, "When will it be enough? Haven't you amassed enough fortunes to let one generation have a normal life?"

"That's not up to me," she answered quietly.

The headache Nathan was feeling was turning quickly into a migraine, more noticeable as he shook his head in disgust.

"I need to check on Lindsey."

Madeline's voice seemed tired.

"Lisa is with Lindsey. She'll be fine," said Nathan. He lowered his voice, forcing himself to calm down.

"Have you considered letting Lindsey have a normal life and if..., God forbid..., one of her children show themselves to be as extraordinary as Sibyl or Lindsey...."

Madeline shook her head slowly, "You don't understand Nathan and I'm not privileged to explain. Far weightier things hinge on our family and its talents. Sibyl is getting old Nathan. I'm getting old. Do you honestly think that I would purposely wish my life or Sibyl's to fall upon Lindsey or Henry? Yet it has. I can't tell you any more than that. At least not yet."

Did he see tears forming in Madeline's eyes?

♥

Nathan sat alone in the den for several minutes collecting himself. So many other things he had wished to say inched into his mind as his emotions cooled. His time wasn't wasted though. He'd seen it in Madeline's eyes before she hurried out. He had reached her, some part of her.

"Would you like a hot cup of tea?"

Nathan looked over at the open door to where Sara stood fidgeting nervously.

"If you'll join me."

She nodded somewhat reluctantly and disappeared.

His eyes closed, so many imminent conclusions on the horizon. How could his world have gone from zero to full throttle in these last few weeks?

Sara inched into the room balancing a small tray carrying two large steaming cups.

"I hope ya don't mind. I made use of the microwave to hurry things along."

"Thanks…, Sara, I've been meaning…."

"Don't be telling me your regrets Mr. Heart. I'm the one that owes you a real apology. I couldn't help but overhear you taking Miss Lindsey's part and it appears I may have misjudged things a mite."

Nathan finished his sip of tea, "Somebody had to do it."

"That may be so, but it was you that had the spine t'do it."

She nervously took a sip of her tea, turning her head to listen toward the hallway.

Her voice was low and measured, "Ya asked me awhile back to let ya know if I heard of anything peculiar about the place."

Her eyes rounded and she nodded toward Nathan, "Young Annie was up straitenin' the room for Miss Evans earlier today."

Nathan sat bolt upright, "What do you mean…, earlier today?"

"I cannot say to that, Mr. Heart," she whispered. "But just before supper, Annie was carryin' fresh linen and towels up to the room and…."

"Sara?"

A distant voice called to her from the kitchen and Sara stood abruptly, "Thank you for the company, Mr. Heart."

She disappeared before another word could be spoken.

"Sibyl…," grunted Nathan.

♥

"What an evening…," sighed Lisa. "Never a dull moment around you is there Nathan Heart?"

Lisa flopped backwards across the end of her bed.

"Once upon a time," he groaned, stretching his arms high over his head. "I'm sorry you were dragged into my personal nightmare."

"Are you really?"

Nathan looked around her room, choosing a loveseat, then fell into its cushion clasping his hands.

"I'm not. But I have to say, you really know how to pick 'em. I keep expecting Herman to walk out from under the staircase."

"Herman?"

"The Munsters? Reruns? Never mind," she said with a yawn. "It took me forever to calm Lindsey down. It felt so strange for me. I'm only a year older than her, but I had the feeling I was the mom talking her teenager down off the roof."

"She didn't have much of a childhood. I thought she might explain," said Nathan.

"No…, she went on about how all she ever wanted was a normal life. She just needed to vent…, about some things…. But some of what she said didn't make any sense. Like not having a choice…, and being cursed. Do you know what she was talking about?"

Nathan nodded, "I do, but it's not my right to tell. I'm sure she'll explain it to you when she's ready."

Lisa sat up sharply with a loud gasp of breath, "She's like you, isn't she? She can do that touch thing you do?"

Another trait was emerging in Lisa, she was tenacious as a bear. Nathan lowered his head. There was no reason to deny it, "Since she was fifteen."

"Oh…, my…, God…. Now it makes perfect sense. No wonder she was drawn to you. What if you thought you were a freak and suddenly you found the only other person on the planet that was just like you? Not that you're a freak…."

Nathan's eyes rose to stare at Lisa.

Her eyes drew to slits, staring back into a sudden depth in his brown eyes, "You're not the only ones…?"

One of the few things Nathan didn't share with Lisa was who and how he was being helped by Madeline and Sibyl.

"No…, we're not."

"Am I going to have to drag it out of you?" she asked.

"Sibyl."

"The sister…, so that's what she was doing," muttered Lisa.

"What do you mean?"

"At dinner..., she kept..., touching me. My arm, my shoulder, or my hand. Every time she said something to me. I thought she was just being sweet, like some older folks do. Was she trying to do that same thing with me?" she asked.

"Only inanimate objects...," his voice trailed off.

That wasn't the truth. When they first met, Sibyl had held his hand, read him like one of their artifacts. Was that what Sibyl meant about him only being at the kindergarten stage of learning?

"She can..., can't she?" said Lisa. "It's all over your face."

"Maybe..., I..., I don't know for sure," he stammered. "And I wish you wouldn't do that. My sister Caroline does that to me all the time."

Lisa smiled as if paid the highest of compliments, "Really.... Maybe I'll get a chance to talk to Caroline when she brings Allie to see me. I'll make sure we get a chance to compare notes."

The room suddenly felt chill to Nathan, barely noticing Lisa's taunting smile. At least he'd diverted her interrogation without her noticing.

"I'm sure she'd like that," he said listlessly.

Suddenly uncomfortable, he looked around the room, taking note of the different furniture, the thick curtains which were arranged and tied decoratively to either side of the windows.

"Caroline's always asking about you," his voice trailed off.

Shrugging off the odd sensations flooding his senses, he stood, "Its getting late. I should let you get some rest. What about your things? Would you like me to run out to your car and get something?"

Lisa seemed bewildered by his sudden shift and shook her head, "Look in the dresser..., and the closet. Lindsey loaded me up with some of her things. Most of them still have the sales tags on them."

That would be just like Lindsey. She'd spent most of her life buying friendships from those she liked.

"Well..., goodnight then," he said shuffling to the door.

"Nathan? I meant what I said earlier."

She followed him to the doorway, "I'm not sorry you let me in."

♥

Lisa's kiss was still lingering on his lips when he flipped on his bedroom light. The first thing he noticed was the fresh scent of vanilla and a new candle flickering on his chifforobe, next to his accumulated treasures.

Nathan stepped over and picked up the small brown leather pouch, feeling the heft in his hand. Carefully, he untied the cinch and let the prize tumble into his palm.

The blood red ruby was just smaller than a half dollar, delicately shaped into a teardrop, with more symmetrical facets than he'd seen on any diamond. It was truly a treasure in itself, not withstanding its historical value.

Against his better judgment, he closed his fist on the gem, letting it speak to him.

He opened his hand with a shudder, "Sie ist edler denn Perlen."

He recognized the quote, instantly saddened. The old jeweler had spent months crafting the gem as an anniversary gift to his wife. That was before the horror of war, before his execution.

"She is far above rubies," he said as he slid the gem back in its protective sheath.

♥

Sleep had fallen like a stone in a pond, with the ebb and flow of spiraling dreams. Nathan was lost in the grip of yet another when a hand began to shake his shoulder.

"Nathan," whispered a soft voice.

"Nathan!" it hissed louder, now two hands trying to rouse him.

"What," he grunted as his bleary eyes opened.

One of the small hands that had been bullying his arm clasped over his mouth, "Sshh."

"Someone was in my room."

Nathan opened his eyes wider, finally recognizing Lisa's features from the dim light of the candle on the far side of the room.

"Who was it?" he asked, managing to keep his voice lower.

"How should I know?" she hissed. "Somebody lifted my window a few inches and it's freezing in there. I..., I..., thought I heard voices."

Nathan slumped back into his pillow, recognizing old oddities being resurrected.

"Don't you dare go back to sleep. I'm scared," she whined.

Nathan took in a deep breath and let it out, "Alright. Sleep here then."

"What?! No."

Lisa whined at him angrily, "I'm not that kind of girl."

"I know you're not, Lisa," he grunted, pushing back the covers.

"I'll take your room. Come on...," he muttered. "Try to get some sleep."

Lisa slid in where he had been, pulling the heavy covers up to her chin. Her eyes were still wide with uncertainty as she scrunched into the unbelievable warmth where he had been.

"You're going to leave me here alone?"

Despite her intensity, Nathan yawned and nodded his head, "Unless you want to sit up the rest of the night. I need some sleep."

"But...?"

"You'll be fine. I'll lock my door on the way out."

Lisa slid deeper under the covers up to her nose, slowly inhaling the comfort of his scent.

"The alarm's set for seven. Come wake me in the morning."

Lisa watched him in disbelief as he casually shuffled out of the room and shut the door behind him.

Lisa's bedroom door was still partially open when Nathan stepped inside. True to her word, it was a good fifteen degrees cooler, probably more. He casually walked over and closed the window by the bed, turning the two latches, knowing it would do little good to keep it shut.

With a quick glance around the obviously undisturbed room, he slid in where Lisa had been, the bed still warm under her covers.

It was as if Lisa's presence was still there as he caught the soft clean scent of her hair on the pillow. How quickly his feelings had changed toward her and lately it seemed hers were changing as well.

Something had finally ignited between them, some unseen spark was evident in her kiss, the way she kissed, the way she let herself cling against his body.

He snatched the covers tighter and rolled over on his side.

Those kinds of thoughts would keep him awake until morning if he allowed them persist.

"Goodnight Marion," he whispered.

CHAPTER SIXTY-EIGHT

HE didn't hear the knocks at the door before it opened, "It's seven. I hate your alarm clock. It was…, hissing at me. Why don't you use the buzzer like normal people?"

Awakened from yet another peaceful dream, Nathan turned over to face Lisa.

"It woke you up didn't it?" he grunted.

"It's evil. I unplugged it," she spat back.

Any war with Lisa would be a losing battle.

"Did you sleep better in my room?"

"Oh yeah," she grinned. "It was…."

Lisa blushed from cheeks down to her neckline, quickly turning around. She began to dig through the top dresser drawers, "You need to get out so I can get dressed."

There was one solitary knock at the door before it opened and a head with a blond ponytail swished inside, "Lisa, come down and have some breakfast with me."

Lindsey's smile turned to utter shock when she saw Nathan, his face flushed, fighting with the quilt on Lisa's bed.

Lisa gasped, "Lindsey…, it's not what it looks like."

Lindsey stepped inside the room and closed the door at her back, "Alright then…, what exactly is it?"

Lisa turned toward Nathan, waiting for him to speak up, "Lisa was scared…."

"So you naturally just trotted down the hall and ended up in her bed?" scoffed Lindsey.

"No! No…, I stayed in his room last night," said Lisa.

Lindsey's lips were pursed tight and bloodless as she turned back to Nathan. Some sort of jealousy shrouding her every expression.

Nathan sighed, "It was Marion, Lindsey."

Lisa spun, "Marion? As in your mother? That Marion? But I thought...."

"That ghosts were only wisps of imagination?" said Lindsey.

Lisa nodded, "Yeah, something like that."

Rumpled from yet another jagged night's sleep, Nathan threw himself out of bed, not bothering to add any more to the conversation.

"I'll meet you downstairs for breakfast."

♥

Nathan was seated alone in the kitchen, idly scraping at some scrambled eggs on a shallow plate when he heard the clatter of Lindsey and Lisa coming down the stairs.

Lindsey was still in the throes of describing some travel adventure in Great Britain when the two joined him.

Both women sat on either side of him, nabbing several homemade items under covered warmers.

"How long has the house been haunted?" asked Lisa.

It took Nathan a few seconds to compose himself. Weren't there better ways to open a morning conversation?

"Probably since my mother passed away."

He felt her hand, warm and soft slide across his lower back.

"When did you figure it out?" she asked.

"The photograph. The one you saw. That was when I knew for sure it was Marion reaching out."

"And before that?"

Nathan turned to catch Lisa's gaze, "I thought I was losing my mind."

Her hand slid away as she began to eat, "Where did it happen?"

"Where did what happen?" he said, stiffening.

He knew very well the painful question Lisa was asking.

"You don't have to talk about it...," she answered quietly.

Nathan pushed away from the table, not looking at either of the women. Why not? Today was as good as any other day.

"In her bedroom. When I found her, she'd fallen, hit her head on the windowsill. It happened sometime before morning, while I was asleep. I should have checked on her. I usually checked on her, but..., I slept through my alarm."

There it was, his guilt, never before confessed to anyone outside his family.

"It wouldn't have changed anything, it wasn't your fault," said Lindsey.

"Then whose?" he asked quietly.

"It was an accident," said Lisa.

♥

The telephone didn't stop ringing the entire morning at Heart Realty. Lisa was content to stay and keep vigil while Nathan whisked off with his ten a.m. consignment. Immersion into his work was the only thing that had managed to hold all his fragile pieces together.

Before noon, her appointment book was filled through mid-December with both anxious consignees as well as interested buyers. She tried to explain that there were only so many hours in a day to a few irate inquiries and that the office would be closed during the upcoming holidays.

Nathan bustled back in, minutes before noon with an excited couple on his heels. Lisa laid the appointment book back down, which she had been waving at Nathan, as her telephone rang once again.

She thought of asking for a raise, then grinned at the huge vase of bright flowers on her desk and changed her mind, "Heart Realty."

Her own voice sounded like a recording ringing in her ears.

"Caroline..., thank God," chuckled Lisa.

"Busy day?"

"I had no idea it could be like this," whined Lisa.

"I don't suppose I can talk to Nathan?"

"He's...," she stood with a grunt and peered over their partition, "...in the middle of signing some contracts at the moment."

There was a heavy sigh over the phone, "We're leaving for Seattle first thing in the morning on our vacation. I was hoping I'd get to talk to him for a few minutes. Can you have him call?"

"I can try..., but it's been crazy here this morning."

"Okay..., well..., just tell him we love him. Tell him we'll get together and have our own Thanksgiving with him as soon as we get back. Do you think you can get Nathan to invite you to come with him?"

Lisa's face tightened into a smile as she pulled one of her gifted flowers close to scent it's fragrance, "I think I can manage that."

"Oh. Oh, that's..., wonderful," said Caroline.

Caroline seemed more relaxed as they continued on a few more minutes. Lisa scribbled the message into the mix of the days notes, destined for Nathan to review. Caroline's message ended with, "Ask Lisa to come with you" and a smiley face beside it.

She sighed a long breath, then looked at a stack of a dozen manilla folders she'd left in her desk tray. They were the consignments she'd argued with Nathan over in her exuberant attempt to attract more business. She was insanely thankful he won that argument.

Nathan and company walked past her desk, hurrying out the door, when he spun, "Lisa..., would you please call and check to see the new requirements for getting your Notary License and add it to your to-do list?"

Before she could complain or ask what a Notary was, the door closed.

♥

A late lunch was followed by the sun squinting past the early morning clouds. Lisa set up her camera, took pictures of their storefront, with both of them standing near the front door.

One more item off her constantly growing to-do list. Ever so thankful she had decided to wear some of the clothing offered her by Lindsey. She'd almost dragged Lisa back to her room after breakfast, dressing her in a knee length skirt, blouse, jacket and matching heels. The more Lisa protested, the more Lindsey seemed to enjoy adding to her ensemble.

The next two afternoon hours were spent with return calls, then Nathan sat down with Lisa for a few minutes office training. Patiently he explained their standard realty contract to Lisa, eighteen pages, section by section until it was time to lock the door.

Happily exhausted, both had honored their mutual agreement not to make the entire day's conversation around the Stewart family drama.

As soon as the doors to the Yukon shut, "I suppose you intend to cancel our date tonight."

Lisa bit her bottom lip to keep quiet. She'd hoped Nathan had forgotten about her offer. That was when she had two jobs, an apartment, a little bit of organization. The bouquet of flowers that morning was a dead giveaway he remembered.

"My car doesn't have an oven or a dining table."

Nathan grinned, "I thought you might use that as an excuse."

Lisa looked a little uncomfortable, "I know we sort of agreed not to discuss it, but I'm living in a houseful of strangers at the moment. Can I give you a rain check?"

Nathan chuckled, "Only if you put it in writing."

"Fine...," she sighed.

Nathan caught a slight smile on her face as she turned to look away.

"We actually agreed not to spend the day jumping to conclusions about yesterday, but there's something I need to ask you."

Lisa arched her brows in an 'I told you so' accusation, "I knew something was bugging you all day. Does this mean I can ask questions too?"

"Maybe...," he grunted. "Did you happen to mention to anyone besides me that you were looking for a new apartment?"

She frowned, "Bolton?"

"No..., before you came to get your car yesterday."

"Nobody. Not a soul."

Nathan stared at the road in thoughtful silence.

"Are you going to tell me why you wanted to know?" she blurted.

"Not yet."

Lisa shook her head, "Then I'm not answering any more of your questions."

"It has nothing to do with you and me, Lisa."

She turned and coughed out a laugh, "It as everything to do with you and me. I'm already trying to figure out Ms. High and Mighty Stewart. I sure don't want to walk around with a blindfold over my eyes just because you don't think I can handle one more secret. I'll have you know, I've been taking care of Lisa Jess Evans since I was five years old. You think I can't deal with some rich old broad with a power complex?"

Lisa's chest was heaving and Nathan saw her heading off the rails again. After all the progress they'd made together, the wild mare was pacing her fence again, ready to jump and run.

Nathan nodded quickly, "You're right. I guess it was too much to ask for you to trust me."

He let his stinging words settle as Lisa's breathing became more controlled.

"I do trust you," she grunted. "Sort of..., well..., more than anybody else I know."

"Then I'm going to trust you not to repeat what we talk about just because you get upset, alright? If you do, innocent people could be hurt."

She slumped in her seat and turned to gaze at the scenery flying past on the interstate.

"You have options Nathan. I don't. I'm kind of backed into a corner here. Can't you see that?"

"Of course I do, you're my main concern at the moment." He quickly dove into what was on his mind, "Sara confided in me last night that they had prepared your room early yesterday morning. Before you came to pick up your car. Well before Madeline made you the offer to stay in the empty room next to Lindsey."

Lisa's frown looked painful, "That's it? That was your big secret? That's not so big a leap. Henry got me fired. He knew I'd lose my apartment. He also knew that Nathan Heart would fly in to save the day. So we're right back where we started, Sherlock, trying to figure out what she wants with me."

Nathan chuckled. Her response was so anti-climactic and logical, he felt a little silly.

"What's so funny?" she grumbled.

"You're just full of surprises, Lisa Jess Evans. I don't remember seeing a middle name on your employment record."

She slumped even lower in her seat, "It was my Grampa's name, okay? Jess Crain. Can we skip the family history?"

Nathan let the breath he hadn't known he was holding, then let his hand slide over and lace fingers with hers, patiently waiting for her to relax.

"I won't tattle on Sara."

Lisa calmed a little more, wiggling her fingers in his hand.

"Since we're sharing secrets...," said Lisa. "There's something you should know."

Nathan could tell that whatever it was must be weighing heavily on Lisa.

"It's about Lindsey," she muttered. "I found out what had her upset. I wasn't sure if I should tell you. I guess I'm still not."

Nathan wondered if he was going to have to extract her secret surgically, as if it were a thorn in her hand.

"Her boyfriend..., well I suppose ex-boyfriend would be more precise.... Some guy named Jon called her yesterday and told her he was getting married. Even invited her to his wedding."

Nathan slumped, "Getting married?"

"You knew him?"

"Knew of him. He was nothing more than a player, but I think Lindsey actually had feelings for him. No wonder Lindsey fell apart at the seams."

"They were close?"

Nathan nodded as he remembered his futile attempt at helping her.

"I guess Madeline was doing the right thing all along."

He didn't want to explain the sordid tale to Lisa and a dozen questions were settling into her eyes. No doubt Lindsey would tell her when she was ready.

"By the way, have you called Troy?"

Lisa glared at him, shocked away from her forming list of questions, "Of course not. Why should I?"

"Because Troy has too much pride to call you, and he needs to apologize."

CHAPTER SIXTY-NINE

THE Yukon rumbled to a stop inside the garage and the humming radio went silent. Before they got out, Lisa scribbled a note in her planner and ripped the page out.

As they were walking toward the house, she folded it in half and handed it to Nathan after a lengthy contemplation.

Barely legible, it read, "I.O.U. One Dinner Date. Lisa J. Evans."

Nathan grinned and stuffed it inside his wallet for safekeeping.

A large white panel van was parked out front, bearing a familiar black shield that read, Industry Standard Security inside the logo. The security service technician was back.

Nathan had received no text messages from the security system…, and rightly so; it had been disabled since the eighth of November.

The Stewart family seemed to be contentedly milling about the house, giving a somewhat friendly nod or two as Nathan and Lisa passed by. All were conveniently ignoring a heated conversation emanating from the general vicinity of the kitchen.

Lisa tried to pull Nathan toward the stairs with her, to ignore the two male voices, with little results.

"…and I told you. I've already ran the conduit, pulled the new wiring, and relocated the security panel in the basement."

The same young technician Nathan had met once before was shaking his head, red faced, "But my company can't guarantee your work, no matter how fine you think it is."

Bolton leaned into the tech's face, "Then replace it all or would you rather I tell the owners you sold them an outdated and reconditioned security system with at least six dead sensors?"

"I think you just did," said Nathan.

Both men turned in an instant to the new voice coming from the kitchen doorway.

The tech stood silent, while Bolton gave him a sly grin, "I was just explaining to our security expert that we need an upgrade."

The young fellow snapped open his cell phone and walked toward the backdoor, "I'll call my manager and setup a date."

"Next Monday," barked Bolton.

Nathan grinned at Bolton as the disgruntled tech disappeared, "Is there anything you don't do?"

Bolton grinned past his tired, dust-caked face, "I still haven't learned how to pick my battles."

"Join the club," Nathan chuckled. "By the way. Are you through building your dungeon down there?"

"I'm almost done. You're welcome to see."

Nathan followed Bolton down the staircase into a very different scene than the mass of framing he'd seen before. The outer cellar door was replaced with a set of steel, spring-loaded monstrosities worthy of a fallout shelter. Gone were the stacks of plywood, sheetrock, cement panels, and the other building materials. There were six new small rooms, each with large metal doors, standing three by three facing each other across a wide expanse. The area for firewood was still intact, still full for the final winter months.

These new rooms weren't for wine, there was already a set of sturdy racks near the staircase, fully populated with vintage wine.

"Is this some sort of storage?"

"Containment cells," said Bolton.

The word containment conjured visions of monsters, madmen, and biochemical atrocities.

"Ms. Stewart said that she'd explain what they're for next week," he added, postponing Nathan's next question.

Bolton opened each steel door to the pristine twelve by twelve cubicles, with red grit for a floor like the rest of the basement. One cell was lined with wooden shelving, each layered with thin black rubber matting over the sections of white pine.

"I've never heard so much as a sound from down here," mumbled Nathan. "I'm amazed."

"I've had plenty of complaints during the day," grinned Bolton. "I had to make a little noise so they'd appreciate all my hard work."

As Nathan trudged back up the stairs he had a feeling that Bolton, with no last name, was probably very appreciated.

♥

"We're going out. We have some shopping to do and errands to run," said Lindsey, tugging at the hesitant elbow of her new companion.

Lisa's expression was screaming for help and Nathan couldn't contain his grin as they passed each other on the staircase.

"I really should stay...," whined Lisa. "I'm still looking for...."

"You can parade yourself in front of Nathan tomorrow. We have more important things to attend to this evening," she whipped. "Have fun with Aunt Sibyl, Nathan."

Lindsey was running interference for Nathan's time with Madeline and Sibyl. It made perfect sense. There would be no way on earth to contain Lisa from trying to observe something that would be inexplicable to her..., without war.

"Do you want my car?" he asked, jangling his keys on a finger.

"Henry's driving us.... Don't worry..., I'll make sure to keep them separated," said Lindsey. "Don't wait up."

His grin became a chuckle when he heard Lisa's outrage at her new friends' accusations. It was the closest thing to normal he'd heard inside the Heart home in a decade. He all but expected to hear Marion call out to tell them to be sweet to each other, remember that they're family.

It was a different kind of family, but there was an immediate bond of sorts that was forming; different kinds..., different levels. Nathan shook his head at his own wistful thinking.

He'd changed clothes, plugged his dark alarm clock back in and found an empty hissing spot on the tuning dial, all before he received an expected knock at his door requesting his presence downstairs.

Both women were waiting in the den together when he finally found them.

"Since we don't know how much time we have this evening, I'd like to get straight to work," said Sibyl.

There was a small stack of weathered books on the table beside her, wrapped in delicate cloth. He assumed they were the *Objects* of their studies together that evening. It might be a simple repetitive boring session, but he was tired and ready for something easy and simple.

"If I may, Sibyl," said Madeline. "How is Ms. Evans adjusting to her new surroundings?"

"Disturbed...," he answered, with a shrug. "She feels that she has been manipulated into her current position..., and as much as I want to argue the point, I think she may be right."

"Ms. Evans is highly intuitive. Another trait I admire. And..., she is quite right," said Madeline.

Nathan could hear the rollercoaster of drama clicking to the top of its first hill inside his chest, "Then it's true? You admit it? Henry wasn't just playing the fool when he managed to get her fired and evicted?"

Madeline nodded and sat back, elbows perched, fingers laced, as if ready for the primed onslaught of angry questions and accusations.

"It's all for a very good reason, I assure you. And if you can assuage Ms. Evan's impertinent nature for a few days, let her acclimate herself to her new surroundings, I'll explain everything."

Nathan sat forward, "Lisa isn't…, like us? Is she?"

Sibyl shook her head, "Not in the slightest. She's a very bright, extremely lovely young lady, with a very troubled past, but as far as I can tell, she isn't remotely *Sensitive*."

He didn't know whether to be relieved or saddened at his first assumption, "Then…, I don't understand…."

"If you can contain yourself as well, for a few days, Mr. Heart?"

Nathan felt as if the blindfold had been slipped over his eyes as he nodded, "I don't like it, but I'm going to trust you. But let me warn you…."

"No need for ultimatums, Nathan. For the next few days, please make sure that Ms. Evans is accompanied by yourself or someone you trust as much as possible. Do your best to limit her time alone, preferably without her knowledge."

"Is she in some sort of danger?"

Nathan felt his pulse continue to rise.

"Have you mentioned or made any sort of display of your recently awakened talents to anyone else?"

It had something to do with him, "No…, of course not."

"Except Ms. Evans?"

Nathan nodded reluctantly. Lisa must have confided in Lindsey and the links of the chain whipped back to Sibyl and Madeline.

"Good. I thought I made it clear when we began this journey together that what we do…, has far reaching implications. Apparently, you need a reminder. You must not expose what you do, or what you are capable of to anyone, friend or family…, without serious forethought."

Nathan felt a pulse of adrenaline, "Then I'd better have a talk with Lisa as soon as possible."

Madeline closed her eyes and nodded, "That would be very wise of you. Please let me know when you've done so, then send her to me. I have some forms for her to sign."

"Forms? What kind of forms?" he frowned.

"Nathan, what you choose to do, who you choose to tell is your business; but anything connected to the Stewart family is not. I'll explain the rest at our formal meeting next week."

Sibyl grunted her displeasure, "Now can we please begin?"

♥

The hardest thing to remember was to breathe. The night's hellish training was almost at an end. Facing one formidable spirit after another in a duel of wills, mental screaming matches, wasn't something he had expected.

More than once he had secretly used what he'd seen Lindsey do, what he'd done to a nasty war criminal, to bully past his given *Object's* opposition.

Each time he bullied past these particular evils, Sibyl would frown, asking for specific details. It was that stubborn will he'd seen in Lindsey that made him skirt the truth. If Lindsey had been working with Sibyl since she was fifteen and had kept her secrets from Sibyl, then it must be for a very good reason.

When the last *Object*, a worn, almost ragged first edition of Dante Alighieri was complete, he felt his resolve give way; he was spent.

The book's *Guardian* had finally relented. Some long dead spirit posing as a demon from hell, insane in life and deluded into believing what was written in the author's fictional version of hell. Nathan's relief was palpable when he ordered the red-skinned imp to the lowest level of Dante's version of hell, shrieking in terror.

After that..., it was simple to see that the inscription and signature inside the hard cover of La Divinia Commedia was authentic. The handwritten copy, in faded Italian, was offered as a memorial to Dante's beloved wife Beatrice and had taken him nearly twelve years to complete. Seeing the actual placid face of the author, once a Prior of Florence, was worth the effort.

Nathan sat back in a slump, yielding to the cushion in the chair. With this outlay of internal energy, he knew exactly why Sibyl was always looking for daytime naps, late breakfasts, and quiet moments away from others.

"1316," he began. "The entire poem was written in memory of his deceased young wife."

Madeline scribbled the information, listening for more precise details.

"He died soon after it was completed; this was one of the first copies, in his own handwriting."

Madeline nodded, "The inscription was to Pope Benedict, did it ever reach his hands?"

Unbelievable..., she wanted more. Nathan took the book back from Sibyl's gloved hands and closed his eyes as the new search played out before his minds eye.

Moments later, he carefully handed the book back to Sibyl.

"What a clot of self-righteous tyrants!"

"I take that as a yes," said Madeline calmly, scribbling in her journal.

"It was meant as a work of art, a literary allegory. They hid this copy as if it were some heresy, in a dark place..., a catacomb for over a century."

Madeline scooted forward in her chair, "You didn't happen to see the whereabouts of that particular catacomb did you?"

"Maybe if I went back and slowed down the whole process...," he sighed, shaking his head. "I'm exhausted."

"You did as well as anything I could have done," said Sibyl. "Now that the *Guardian* is gone, I can dig around in the books past."

Now that the *Guardian* was gone. That had to be the specialty Lindsey was capable of that Sibyl was unable to perform or too timid to try..., or maybe Sibyl had limitations she wasn't willing to admit.

CHAPTER SEVENTY

"**H**OW did you manage to sneak past the *Guardian*?"

Sibyl's lingering question rang in Nathan's mind as the hot water of the shower pelted his face. Her question was the confirmation to his. She didn't know, or according to Madeline's implications, Sibyl wasn't willing to face some of the dark evils standing in opposition.

All he knew was that he could now do it, Lindsey could do it, and she was mind-numbingly, sickeningly fast. Whereas he could manage to plod through the more difficult *Objects* in fewer than sixty seconds, Lindsey would already be at the source, gazing around like a lazy tourist at the required information. She was the newer ninja version of Sibyl.

Nathan turned off the hot water and stepped out of the shower.

He swiped away a patch of steam from the mirror over the sink and stared at his reflection.

What was Lisa going to think when he told her she was right all along? Madeline had plotted and nudged her toward staying in the same house as the Stewarts. It wouldn't be good. Especially after he made her take a vow of silence about his secret.

Then there was Madeline; he could just imagine the subtlety she would employ with Lisa.

The knock at the door was welcome, awakening him from dreary suppositions. He tightened his robe and cracked it open.

"Sara said you looked like you could use this?" said Lisa.

She held up a plate, a slice of one of Sara's creations and a glass of milk. It was probably another peace offering from Sara.

He opened the door and let Lisa inside.

"Have you been back long?" he asked, taking the napkin from the plate.

"About ten minutes. You miss me?"

He nodded, "You have no idea."

She hadn't talked to Madeline yet…, good.

"Did you enjoy your trip?"

Nathan's eyes couldn't seem to stop their inspection of Lisa's transformation: Tight jeans, luxurious burgundy sweater, wrapped in a soft lipstick red leather jacket that reminded him of his first view of Lindsey.

"I guess. Lindsey took me shopping. You like?"

Nathan broke his gaze and nodded, "Most definitely."

"Of course now I feel like some sort of charity case," she smirked. "Not because of Lindsey…; it was…, it doesn't matter."

Henry must have been his usual charming self. She seemed as tired as he felt and rightly so, it was getting late. Lisa slipped off her heels and sighed as her toes wiggled on the cool hardwood floor.

Nathan felt a pang of guilt, "I should have given you my card to take with you. That was my fault."

Lisa rolled her eyes, almost a mimic of Lindsey's reactions, "And I thought I couldn't feel any lower."

"Consider yourself fortunate and enjoy it while it lasts."

"How do I ask her to stop? She's already bought me an entire wardrobe…, and we're going again tomorrow," she squeaked.

Nathan listened patiently, quickly finishing his snack.

"We're both tired…," he sighed. "And there's something I need to talk to you about."

Lisa flopped backwards across his bed with a grunt, "I suppose I'm not going to like this am I?"

Nathan set down the plate on the floor beside him, "No. You're not going to like it at all."

His quick explanation about Madeline's maneuvers was no surprise, but he reminded her that under no circumstances could she tell anyone about the secrets he'd shared. He used the excuse of not wanting to become a circus act or hounded by the media, which was true and something Lisa would believe.

It was when she heard that Madeline wanted to speak to her, and what about, that she came unglued.

"Tonight?" asked Lisa.

"I'm sure it can wait until morning. Do you want me to go with you talk to her?" he asked.

His reason was to protect Lisa from flying off her hinges, but of course Lisa took his offer askance.

"Don't you think I can handle one old woman? I can't wait to see what she has up her sleeve next."

Nathan sighed tiredly, "I think you could handle a hurricane single handedly. At least take Lindsey with you. She seems to calm Ms. Stewart, even when they're toe to toe."

"Wait. You're afraid I'll act like Henry?" she stared angrily. "You're afraid I'll do something crazy?"

Nathan shook his head, "Madeline and her sister are getting old. Older people think that their experiences qualify them as experts in everything, particularly other people's lives. I'm only trying to keep the peace."

Lisa seemed to relax as she contemplated his wisdom, then stood up, glancing at his robe.

"Well…, put on some clothes then. No use waiting until morning. I won't sleep a wink if I don't get this over with now. Especially if the ghost of your mother makes us switch rooms again."

♥

Madeline was indeed waiting, in Nathan's old office at the foot of the stairs.

"Please, have a seat," said Madeline, as she quickly shuffled a folder to the lip of the heavily marred desk.

Madeline looked up at Nathan, "I see you brought moral support."

Lisa rolled her eyes, "I tried to tell him I'd be fine. All you want is for me to keep my mouth shut, right? Where do I sign?"

A wry grin wiped years from Madeline's tired face, "Let's chat a few minutes first…, alone if you please?"

Nathan raised both hands in submission, "Let me know if you need me."

His first thought was to meander across the living room and pretend to rifle through one of the daily copies of the Wall Street Journal. At least there, he would be able to extinguish any burst of flames erupting from the odd meeting in his old office.

Instead, his feet led him toward the vestibule, to the regular tock of the huge antique clock. As if on automatic, he reached for the key looped through the gold chain around his neck. The lock to the large glass door clacked quietly, giving him access to the mechanics.

The crank, securely wedged into its cubby below the pendulum gave him pause. He hadn't felt the usual vertigo as the large glass door swung open, in fact he'd completely forgotten the past effects of the clocks touch.

He quickly undocked the crank and shoved it in each slot, carefully cranking the three heavy shining brass weights to three quarters of their free travel from the top. He'd watched his mother perform this ritual every few weeks for as long as he could remember.

After stuffing the crank back in its niche, he hurriedly shut the door, then paused.

As if drawn, he placed both hands on each side of the clock, not daring to close his eyes. The last time he'd threatened to see into the clocks' secrets, he was catapulted dizzily backwards in shock.

"Hello mother," he whispered..., then further compelled, closed his eyes.

Every hair on both arms lifted as if brushed with a gentle breeze, freezing him in the moment.

"Nathan...," whispered softly into his ear.

He dared to peer deeper, then was met with a sharply outlined silhouette of a lady, and a gentle brush of cool fingers across his cheek. Fingers he quickly recognized as those of Marion Heart.

As soon as it began, it stopped.

He lifted his hands and relocked the clock's outer door.

Sara had mentioned to him that Sibyl didn't like the clock. Sibyl's wariness of an *Object's Guardian* was likely the reason. But had Lindsey been coerced into accessing whatever secret lay behind the antique clock's past? Surely she would have told him..., or was that yet another part of her multifaceted apology note?

He'd seen her..., *Followed* her, watched her bulldoze through obstacles with hardly a pause while in a conjoined *Reading*. If anyone was capable of forced entry, it was Lindsey, yet something unspoken reassured him that this was one lock left unbreached.

Nathan quietly walked past the closed office door, wishing to be a fly on the wall, to hear the muffled conversation. The mere fact that their chat was muffled and controlled offered some sort of belayed comfort.

He paused at the foot of the stairs, still unwilling to abandon Lisa to some unknown joust, then forced himself up to his room.

Lindsey was standing inside next to his chifforobe carefully lighting a fresh vanilla scented votive when he entered.

He halted in the doorway watching her pace slowly in the opposite direction, her gaze observing nothing in particular. Her hips swayed curiously inside the clingy silk evening gown. Very few women he'd known were oblivious to their innate allure, yet he was now dealing with two such startling anomalies at the same time.

Past Lindsey's obvious beauty, she exuded both innocence and fragility, which had been the hook in Nathan's jaw from the very beginning.

"I think what you're doing with Lisa is very kind, but don't you think you're overdoing it just a little?" he asked.

Lindsey spun, heavy concern in her expression.

"On the contrary, I'm returning her kindness in the only way I know how," she answered. "I'm sorry if our friendship makes you uncomfortable."

Nathan eased into his bedroom, ignoring her baited reply, "I see it's you I have to thank for the candles."

Lindsey grinned, "Actually...," she halted before she started, placing the small cache of matches back on top of the cabinet. "You're welcome."

It seemed that every mysterious reply was filled with open-ended innuendos begging for attention. He noticed that she didn't ask the whereabouts of Lisa, nor was she squeamish about invading the privacy of his bedroom not knowing when he'd return, unless....

"I suppose I should warn you that Lisa has an aversion to gifts..., or maybe it's just the ones with strings attached," he prodded, skipping back to where he began.

Lindsey shrugged and seemed a little hurt, "There are no strings..., and I don't want to discuss my friendship with Lisa. There are more important issues you and I need to discuss."

Nathan glared at her, "Such as why you told Madeline that Lisa was aware of my secret?"

"Nathan, what were you thinking?" whined Lindsey. "Of course I had to tell Aunt Madeline. Do you see what we do as some sort of parlor trick? As much as I despise what I am..., I cannot change it. For your own good, please look past your own nose and see the dangers."

He shook his head, "You still don't get it. Look, I have no desire to be the object of some three-ring circus any more than you do. But don't you think your private conversations with Lisa should have been confidential?"

"Yes..., of course I do, but...," Lindsey whined.

"It's okay Nathan...," said Lisa, as she entered the room.

CHAPTER SEVENTY-ONE

NATHAN and Lindsey both spun their attention toward Lisa. She closed the door and tiredly flopped on the side of Nathan's bed.

She'd been listening to Nathan once again running to her defense. Instead of the instant disapproval it might have prompted in the past, it somehow felt..., endearing; her eyes opening to how he felt about her.

"We have no secrets between us," she continued. "Your Aunt Madeline just made sure of that."

Lindsey rushed past Nathan and hurried to Lisa, crawling across the bed, "What did she do?"

Lisa fell on her back, staring at the tall ceiling, "Not much. Gave me a quick review of my entire life since birth..., asked me to sign some forms."

"And?" prodded Lindsey, looking down at Lisa. "Aunt Madey must have dangled something in front of you."

"And..., she promised to help me find out if I have any living relatives," said Lisa.

Nathan, tired of being the silent observer, collected a few of his things and headed for the door. He'd probably end up in the room at the end of the hallway before the night was over anyway, and it was getting late.

"Nathan, wait...," said Lisa. She propped up on her elbows, her face drawn and tired. "Thank you Nathan. For everything."

Completely taken aback by Lisa's uncharacteristically quiet remark, Nathan stopped in his tracks.

Lindsey slid off the bed, "We still have things to discuss before you run off...," looking cautiously back at Lisa. "Now that we don't have any secrets between us."

Nathan dropped his cache of bedclothes to the bare wood floor in exasperation, "What could we possibly have to discuss?"

He eased over and sank into his favorite paisley chair waiting for Lindsey to explain herself.

"For one thing, Aunt Madeline is getting more than just a little curious at the progress of your training sessions. I told her I didn't have a clue what she was talking about, at least until I had a chance to talk with you."

"Training sessions?" muttered Lisa.

"What is it that has her so worried?" asked Nathan, barely hiding the curve of a grin at the corner of his mouth.

"Sibyl told her that you were somehow getting past *Guardians* that terrified her," said Lindsey.

Nathan sat in silence waiting for her to be the first to give up more information.

"What are you two talking about?" asked Lisa, a little more perturbed.

"She said that you were hiding something," said Lindsey.

Nathan sat forward, "Only the same thing you've been hiding from her. Isn't that right?"

It was only a guess, but it had to be the reason.

Lindsey cautiously remembered their sessions where he'd been dragged along behind her in a *Following*, during several of their *Readings* together.

"You watched me. Is that how you figured it out?" she asked.

With a tilt of the head, Nathan raised both palms in the air as if to say, 'You tell me.'

Lindsey shook her head and knelt near the chair where Nathan was seated, "Madeline can guess all she wants, but you must never tell her..., or anyone that you know how to do what you saw me do. Do you understand?"

Her voice was quivering. Nathan looked up at Lisa now perched on the side of his bed in silence.

"Nathan, I'm begging you. There are people that will misuse what you and I can do. No one must ever know."

"Madeline knows," he smirked.

"Aunt Madeline suspects," said Lindsey. "Unless you told her."

Once again, Nathan was caught off guard, this time by Lindsey's sincerity. He only nodded as a deep frown creased his forehead.

"No..., I didn't tell her," he answered finally.

All Lindsey's breath seemed to exhale at once, then she looked back up at him in pallid shock, "You haven't *Interacted* with a *live Subject* have you?"

Nathan's eyes became large painful circles at the implication and only one word came hissing out his mouth.

"What?"

Adrenaline began to pump its poison through his system as he stared nervously at Lindsey.

Lindsey struggled to get up, trapped by her long gown, "I've said too much."

Nathan grabbed her arms before she tripped and fell, "No. Lindsey you have to explain what you mean."

"I can't...," she hissed, her eyes gathering tears as she struggled.

Nathan didn't let go of her, but turned and helped her sit in the chair where he had been seated.

"I'm tired of all the cat and mouse games Lindsey. If you really do value our friendship, then you'll explain yourself."

She brushed away a few clinging tears from her cheek and jawline, then nodded slowly. She pointed to the door, getting Lisa's attention, and whispered, "Make sure we're alone."

When Lisa nodded, her back against the door, Lindsey continued. "What you and I do in an *Object's* past can also be done in an *Object's* present. If they are unguarded."

Nathan frowned, baffled and began shaking his head.

Lindsey became angry at something she believed to be utterly simplistic to understand, "Do you remember the night you walked in your sleep?"

"Of course, but what does that have to do with...?"

"It was a..., suggestion I gave you..., Madeline asked me..., to see if I could use you to get past the *Guardian* in your antique clock."

Nathan felt his fingers sliding through his thick hair, his feet on automatic, pacing towards the veranda door.

"You were the reason I walked in my sleep? That's ridiculous. "What's so important about that blasted clock?"

"Sshh," waved Lindsey, trying to calm his sudden booming voice.

She glanced warily toward the bedroom door once again, "Maybe nothing at all, but once my Aunt Madeline's curiosity locks onto something, she can't let it go."

Still in shock, he almost skipped right over the more important implication, "You..., suggested.... You controlled me? Like some sort of zombie?"

Lindsey nodded, "I'm so sorry Nathan, but now do you understand why I was so worried?"

"What if I'd fallen and broken my neck down the stairs?"

"Not likely," she scoffed. "I was there to..., I mean...."

Nathan urged her on with his eyes blazing.

"It's not that pleasant of an experience, I can assure you," grunted Lindsey. "It makes vertigo seem almost enjoyable."

The plethora of questions inside Nathan's mind began to spin. He placed both hands on the cold glass panes of the veranda doors and peered out across the lighting on the dark front lawn. Mere weeks ago, the serenity of that second story view could have easily settled his nerves.

"What else haven't you told me?" he asked calmly.

A knock on Lindsey's door across the hallway disintegrated their moment of shared honesty. Lindsey was reluctant to utter more than a few whispered goodnight's before sneaking across to her room.

Lisa sat, wobbling and silent; completely indifferent to Nathan and Lindsey's concourse. She had her own revelations to ponder. Indeed most of their cryptic conversation about *Objects and Readings* drifted away like a mist. The very idea that she might have a living relative out there somewhere, something suggested by Madeline Stewart, gave her reason to hope. Yet it was the possibility of another hope that had her transfixed in thought.

She had entered the office ready to pounce on Ms. Stewart, retaliate for this odd woman's interference in her livelihood. All Madeline had done was hand her the little two by three inch photo of her mother and all Lisa's breath, all her angst, all her anger dissipated.

Madeline had used the photo as if it were a playing card, an ace she had up her sleeve. Lisa knew it, yet she couldn't care less. She would have signed away five years of her life for a glimpse of her mother's face. Somehow Madeline had discovered that empty spot lingering inside Lisa and knew how to disarm her without a single word.

Lisa carefully withdrew the photo from her jacket pocket once again, studying the worn image. The face looking back at her was so much like her own reflection, yet there she was.

Somehow afraid to look away, afraid that the photo would disappear and it would all be dream, she memorized every detail.

It was Nathan's distant voice that coaxed her from her sleepy meditation.

"May I see?" he asked.

Lisa glanced up at his face, unphased by his sudden closeness beside her. She handed him the photo and watched for his reaction.

"Where did you get this? Madeline?"

She nodded slowly and felt the comfort of his large hand slide around her waist.

Nathan was going to ask how, but knew the answer already. With Sibyl's direction and Madeline's vast resources, she could have found this discarded photo of Lisa's mother no matter how obscure its location. Why hadn't he thought of doing the same thing?

He let himself drift into the photo, watched the image come to life just as someone told a charming elder version of Lisa to smile. Detaching himself from the photo's past, he hurriedly looked about the room, somewhere in Illinois by the stack of unopened mail on a table by the front door. In an instant, the room was vacant except for cobwebs strung across the corners of the room.

Of course, Sibyl must have already done this…, and much more. Madeline's scouts were no doubt ages ahead of him, scouring for more information.

Lisa's fingers jarred him back to the present, taking the photo from his hand, laying it aside.

When she tilted her chin to meet Nathan's kiss, it was as if years of carefully laid walls of protection fell into rubble inside her.

Much later, as their lips parted and time resumed its calculations, she let him hold her in his arms for several moments, until her breathing returned to normal. With the side of her face resting against his chest, she wondered why it had taken the scornful remark of a stranger to make her see what was right in front of her eyes.

Madeline Stewart's many faceted talk, after the disarming gift of her mother's photograph, left her weak and defenseless. Yet she felt stronger now than all the other twenty-six years of her solitary existence put together. Something as simple as a photograph had given her life substance, meaning, and an anchor to reassure her that she had value.

CHAPTER SEVENTY-TWO

THE house had been as quiet as a mouse Friday morning. Nathan and Lisa lazied through breakfast, after the tiring late nite escapades. The door to Heart Realty clicked open a quarter after nine that morning, with the happy sound of the tiny bell over the door heralding their entry.

Both of them headed directly to their stations, listened to messages, made the appropriate notes, while keeping their conversation strictly on the day's business.

Shortly before eleven, Nathan decided to walk the few blocks to the county clerk's office to do some filing, hoping a brisk walk would clear the last few cobwebs from his mind. Normally, he would have sent Lisa, but remembered Madeline's strange advice to keep a careful watch over his secretary.

With one foot on the sidewalk, he spun back inside and flipped their dangling sign to 'closed' and locked the door.

He glanced at Lisa, refilling her flower vase, "We're closed until this afternoon. Don't let anyone inside no matter how much they gripe. We're booked solid for the next three weeks."

Lisa didn't ask or protest as she began shuffling another thick stack of completed forms on her desk, ready to be scanned. She punched the button on the answering machine to let it screen all incoming calls and sighed contentedly when it rang seconds later.

She unstapled the first stack of legal sized forms and queued them into the scanner's tray, ready to be translated into their software database. This first set would take about ten minutes to process before she could edit any mistakes on her laptop.

Her coffee cup was empty when she shook it and she stared at the first long page of the document as it slowly disappeared into the scanner bay.

Someone with an odd accent was leaving a message on the machine and she gingerly tapped the mute button, looking outside at the gloomy skied morning.

Lisa grabbed her purse and keys, then hurried to the restroom breezeway in the back. With any luck she'd be back from the adjoining coffee shop before the last page was through the software vacuum.

When the short line of customers shifted, she almost ordered two cups of coffee, but Nathan probably wouldn't be back until it was mid-lunchtime.

The barista in the coffee shop was always pleasant and fast. Her coffee was ready as soon as she finished paying. As she was hurrying back toward her exit, she noticed a tall blond gentleman bustle through the front door, hurrying toward the counter. His dark gray business suit was crisp and professional; at least it looked expensive to Lisa. There was rigid determination etched into his hard face; a man on a mission or maybe something last minute.

Over the din of conversations, she heard him ask about the realty office next door. That was her cue to scurry back through the breezeway and make sure the door was locked behind her.

Not being the type to skulk away from confrontations, she hurried back to her desk, in full view of the front window. The scanner was beeping crazily and she fell into her chair to untangle the jammed paper feeder, whirring away at the last crooked sheet of her stack.

As it ground forward, a face peered through the glass window, hands cupped around the eyes.

"I need to speak to Nathan Heart," the odd muffled voice blared. There was that same accent she'd muted on the answering machine.

Lisa pointed to the sign, "We're closed."

He stood back stiffly, looking sternly at the sign as Lisa re-stapled the finished document and began to check it against the data on her screen.

The fellows' knuckles rattled the little panes on the front door once again.

Lisa sighed, then put on her practiced waitress smile. The one she used for irate customers when she was about to refer them to the unlikely glare of her ex-employer, Troy O'Bannon.

Seconds later, she was looking directly into a set of startling midnight blue eyes, through the front door panes.

"You can come back around two. Mr. Heart should be back in by then," said Lisa.

"This is important. I need to speak to him as soon as possible," he grunted. "Can you give me the number to his cell phone?"

Lisa pointed to the number painted on their window sign.

The man stepped back once again, thoroughly agitated, "I already called that number."

Lisa shrugged, then almost conceded to let him wait in Nathan's cubicle, then remembered what Nathan had ordered. Another strange dark memory passed through her mind and she tested the dead bolt to make sure it was secure.

The gentleman reached to his inside lapel pocket and slid out a business card, forcing a smile, "Would you give this to Mr. Heart? Tell him it is of the utmost importance that I speak to him today."

He held it up to the door..., as if waiting. Lisa instinctively reached to unlock the door, then stalled at Nathan's warning voice inside her head. Nobody was supposed to get inside, but surely Nathan wouldn't care if he sat inside and waited.

Instead, she pointed to the mail slot in the door. Why was he so insistent on getting inside and waiting for Nathan there? Maybe it was just her imagination..., or maybe it was something she would never have to think about again.

With the smile erased, he stuffed the business card through the slot and walked away uttering some unintelligible gibberish.

Lisa peered out the door once more before cautiously digging the card out of the mail trap..., "Eben M. Stäkkr."

♥

Lisa was proofing her third set of documents when there was a loud rapping on the front door, making her heart skip a beat.

Expecting to see manicured blond hair and close set blue eyes; she scooted her chair to the side, then hurried to the door.

Nathan had his satchel strung over his shoulder, a large sack in one hand, while balancing two drink cups in the other.

She took the drinks and sniffed the sack, "Mmmm, Barbeque?"

Nathan grinned, "...and fries. I caught Bartlet's just as they opened. Any calls?"

Lisa set down their drinks and snatched a card off her desk,

"One. Not a happy camper either. Said it was important."

"Stäkkr?"

Nathan's anger flared, obvious in the way he spat out the name.

"Strange guy. Nice enough to look at, but he gave me the creeps," said Lisa. "Said he'd be back."

When Nathan continued to stare at the card, Lisa took their lunch and hurried to Nathan's cubicle, "Do you know this guy?"

Nathan shuffled behind her, snapped from his trancelike stare, "Our main competitor in the Northwest."

And he was involved with the snoop he and Bolton turned over to the sheriff, now dead, possibly buried in the closest potter's field.

"That's where I've seen that name before," muttered Lisa.

"On every rundown property in a five hundred mile radius," grunted Nathan.

Lisa stared for a second, "That's a little harsh don't you think?"

"We have a bit of history," said Nathan. "You didn't let him inside did you?"

She shook her head and mumbled with her first bite of sandwich.

"Good. I don't want him inside our office unless I'm here."

The little bell jingled over the front door.

"We're closed," grunted Lisa.

"Yes..., I see that."

The voice was unmistakable.

Lisa groaned, "Speak of the devil."

Nathan stood quickly and motioned for Lisa to take her food around to her desk.

"Herr Stäkkr. What brings you to Heart Realty?"

The strangest sensation nudged at the back of Nathan's mind. The automatic switch inside his head was flip-flopping to and fro in his newly acquired language.

Lisa blundered past as quickly as possible, leaving the two men alone in an odd staring contest.

Nathan relented and motioned Eben to a chair, without offering his usual friendly handshake.

"I need to speak to you about something that concerns both of us..., most urgent..., a very private matter," said Stäkkr.

Nathan's visitor nodded toward the front of the office, toward where Lisa had disappeared.

"Gewiß (certainly)," said Nathan, lowering his voice.

Stäkkr flinched almost imperceptibly, "Du spreche...?"

Nathan motioned toward Lisa, "Einzig mir (Only me)."

Stäkkr nodded at the implication and began to explain his irrational behavior in his native German, "I realize we haven't been on the best of terms, but what I'm going to tell you must stay between us. Do you agree?"

Nathan nodded.

"Very well. Several weeks ago, I received a telephone call from a man, asking me for information about a house that was for sale..., your Manor. I explained to him that I had no dealings with the sale of that estate, that he should contact you, Mr. Heart. He seemed pleased that I wasn't involved, then asked me several very personal questions about your estate, which I assure you I declined to answer."

Nathan felt the frown across his forehead tighten. Stäkkr was coming to him about the spy? During his session with the confiscated notepad, he'd seen Stäkkr yelling violently into the telephone at the decedent criminal.

"I can tell by your expression you are aware of the person I'm referring to."

Nathan nodded, "I caught him trespassing on the property, taking photographs of the contents of the house and the people. I held him until the sheriff arrived and arrested him."

There was no need to mention Bolton as a corroborator.

Stäkkr nodded thoughtfully, "A few weeks after his initial call, he telephoned me once again. He asked me if I would be interested in purchasing some valuable antiques..., collectibles, at a very reasonable price. For the sake of argument, I told him I might be interested. Then he explained to me that he would require payment in cash and that I should store whatever I purchased for a few months if I decided not to keep my purchases. I told him straight away that I was not interested in purchasing stolen goods and that if he called again, I would report him to the local authorities."

Stäkkr didn't kill the man? Nathan felt the agony of guilt pricking his conscience. As crude a businessman as Stäkkr was, he was no murderer.

"You do realize he's dead," said Nathan.

Stäkkr nodded, "That is why I'm here. I was paid a visit by the sheriff from Lumberton just yesterday. He seemed very interested in some telephone calls I received from a certain lodge near Lumberton. He also showed me a picture of an unshaven vagabond with black stringy hair and a rough face. I explained that I'd never seen him before, but he didn't act as though he believed me."

Nathan nodded, "That sounds like him, but what exactly does this have to do with me?"

Eben M. Stäkkr took a deep breath, "During my last conversation with the dead man, he let two names slip other than Heart; one was Stewart, the other was Bogart; people he was very angry with. I neglected to mention these names to the sheriff, until I had a chance to speak with you."

The Stewart name was expected; they'd purchased the place, but Bogart would eventually lead right back to Charles and Josie Heart.

"I don't understand why you didn't simply tell the sheriff what you remembered," Nathan prodded further.

"Because..., both of us have something to lose should an investigation arise. Regardless of our..., past differences, neither of our reputations would survive a scandal involving a murder investigation. And should the sheriff happen to ask questions..., say about Stäkkr Realty, I wouldn't want you to be skewed by those past differences. I wanted to be open with you so that neither of us would be cast into less than favorable light."

Stäkkr was afraid that Nathan would point every finger of suspicion his direction. Regardless of his feigned attempt at openness, he was trying to cover his own posterior and nip the entire thing in the bud. Withholding the names he had heard was his only bargaining chip.

Stäkkr continued, "I was able to account for most of my time..., you see my wife has been bedridden for several weeks and I have to pay someone to watch after her when I'm not available to be at her side."

Nathan was lost in thought for several moments; unmistakably conflicted about which direction this conversation could turn. Stäkkr was also very disturbed, maybe even scared for his livelihood.

"The Stewarts are the new owners of Heart Manor," began Nathan. "I can't see why our dead man would be upset with them. As for Bogart..., I...."

Stäkkr interrupted, "The sheriff said you and the Stewarts were the ones that pressed charges on him after he was arrested. That might make a swindler like him want revenge."

Nathan felt his entire body relax, "So this guy called you the second time, after he posted bail and was out of jail?"

Stäkkr nodded, "He seemed desperate for money. I also did some checking on the name Bogart, but there was nothing to speak of except an investment group with that name that recently went under."

Also.... Had he also figured out who the Stewarts were? That much money and its underlying power would be enough to scare someone like Stäkkr into oblivion.

Nathan sighed, hiding his relief, "I think you did the right thing Eben. The dead man probably had more enemies than you or I combined."

Eben grinned and nodded, "Then we'll let sleeping dogs lie. I see no reason to blacken our reputations over the misfortunes of a thief."

♥

"Guten Abend," said Nathan as he closed and relocked the front door.

The moment Nathan had shaken E. M. Stäkkr's hand goodbye, he felt one singular emotion pass between them..., relief.

"Are you going to tell me what that was all about?" asked Lisa.

Nathan shook his head, "No."

"I didn't know you spoke German. You're not going to add a class in German to my to-do list are you?" she whined.

"Nope," he grinned.

"Oh, thank God," she whispered. "I can barely speak English."

Nathan sat on the corner of her busy desk, "Your English is good enough for me. Now where did you put my sandwich?"

CHAPTER SEVENTY-THREE

NATHAN had no idea where the little notepad from the thief had disappeared to. The last he'd seen of it was when he kicked it across the Library's hardwood floor to be rid of it. Now..., with more experience under his belt, he wanted to search its history more carefully.

It was Lisa's voice that broke the silence as they passed Salem Oregon's city limits.

"Nathan, what exactly is a consortium?"

He shrugged at her quizzically, "A group of businesses..., investors..., that sort of thing. Why?"

"Ever hear of something called the Trifecta Consortium?"

"Not that I remember, where did you hear about it?"

Lisa furrowed her brow, "I took a few minutes to search the business directory and I even looked on the internet but I didn't find anything there either."

She remained quiet and thoughtful until Nathan reached over and wiggled her shoulder with his hand.

Lisa relaxed and smiled, shuffling closer to him, "It was at the top of my vow of silence I signed last night. It had a symbol kind of like the one at the courthouse..., a circle with a triangle inside, with a lady holding the scales of justice inside the triangle."

Nathan cringed, "Sounds like a DOJ symbol?. Did you happen to read the document before you signed it?"

"Didn't have to. Madeline read the whole thing to me like it was her favorite bedtime story. She said she wanted to make sure that there were no misunderstandings."

"Would you mind telling me what you remember about it?"

"I can do better than that. Madeline gave me a copy. She said it was a standard confidentiality, non-disclosure contract. There wasn't much legalese mumbo-jumbo in it. I'll show it to you later."

Lisa slid closer to Nathan, watching the shifting emotions playing on his face.

"You need to quit worrying," she muttered. "I think I'm pretty close to figuring out Madeline Stewart."

Nathan barked out a laugh, "Tell that to Lindsey."

"She's too close to the forest to see the trees, has been all her life."

His hasty chuckle tapered off into silence.

"Maybe you are too," she shrugged. "It's not your fault..., I think she blindsided you. You see..., Madeline puts on this act of being strong, pushing and shoving, but I think she's something more like a puppet. What I haven't figured out yet is who's holding her strings."

Nathan tilted thoughtfully at Lisa's insight, "...for the good of the family."

"Huh?"

Nathan shook his head, "Something Lindsey mentioned once."

♥

When they drove through the stone gates, displaying a brass plate heralding Heart Manor, a food delivery van halted to let them pass.

"Looks like Sara's going to have her hands full this week."

This was the fateful week of Thanksgiving. Eight more days and the house would be empty once again. It surprised Nathan at the sudden realization that he wasn't looking forward to the caving silence of an empty house.

Nathan felt Lisa's warm hand on the back of his, "You're quiet. Is everything alright?"

His foot was still on the brake as the vehicle idled to a stop, still a fair distance from the front of the house.

"That last year..., with Marion..., I'd planned to take her to visit Caroline, at Thanksgiving. She'd been especially distant..., lost in herself for weeks. I was worried how she would take the sudden jolt of being surrounded by Caroline and her family.

"The night before, I woke up and heard a clamor coming from downstairs. Marion was down in the kitchen..., cooking. She had a ham in one oven, a turkey splayed open on the counter. She was elbow deep in preparing a huge bowl of stuffing, chicken dressing..., pies..., yams, just as if the house was going to be filled with family the next day."

Lisa was watching him intently, "What did you do?"

He shrugged and looked over at her, "What could I do? I got dressed and helped her. It was as if she was Rip Van Winkle suddenly awake and unaware that the house was empty except for the two of us."

Lisa sighed and slipped back to her seat, "If everything you told me is true…, about you…, then I think you did the right thing. Getting help, I mean."

The Yukon began to slowly move again, "I hope you're right."

♥

"But it's Friday night, Lisa," whined Lindsey. "Wouldn't you rather spend the evening out on the town instead of moping about here in this old house?"

She was trying to convince Lisa to abort her empty plans and go with her and Henry to parts unknown for the evening.

"Nathan's going to be busy with my Aunt Sibyl all evening. I guarantee you my offer will be much more interesting. Please?"

Nathan opened his bedroom door and propped against the opening, "Lindsey's right. You deserve a night on the town."

"Eavesdropper," hissed Lisa.

"Thank you Nathan," sighed Lindsey. "I've been trying to pry Lisa out of her moldy shell, but she's just not listening."

Lisa walked over and casually handed Nathan an envelope, while still trying to build a defense against Lindsey's persistence.

Lindsey was tapping her foot like a petulant child waiting for an answer, until Lisa conceded, "Fine…, help me pick out something to wear."

With their controversy ended, Nathan put away the envelope and continued on downstairs to where two anxious elderly women were waiting in the cluttered library.

Madeline seemed different, more relaxed. Nathan presumed it could be because the potential leak of their family secret was sealed or she had gained an unprecedented advantage with her games.

Lisa's slight knowledge of the Stewart family antics was successfully captured by some unknown quid-quo-pro agreement. He couldn't help but feel guilty for dragging Lisa in, instead of shielding her as he had intended.

Lisa's observations concerning Madeline must have been lingering in Nathan's mind. He couldn't seem to shake the fact that Madeline seemed worried about some unknown danger for Lisa…, thus the warning about her safety. Maybe there was even some guilt involved, if someone truly was holding Madeline's strings…, someone dangerous.

Wishing that he had a few more moments to contemplate these new enlightenments, he greeted and sat down near his tutors.

Instead of the usual beginning to their session, "How was your day today Nathan?"

"Interesting."

"Really. How so?"

"I was paid a visit by someone I would have never expected to grace my office. Eben Stäkkr."

Sibyl glanced at her sister, "He's the realtor...."

"Yes, I remember. He wasn't left alone with Miss Evans by any chance?"

Shaking his head, "Of course not, I take all your advice seriously."

Nathan gave a shortened version of his meeting with Stäkkr and began to notice a few almost imperceptible nervous reactions from Sibyl.

When he was through, Madeline asked, "Did you happen to consider that he could be lying?"

"Actually, I did. And I hate to admit my lack of scruples, but I despise the man. However..., he seemed more genuine than I can ever remember. We haven't so much as spoken to each other in several years. What would he gain by concocting such a story and then visiting me at my office?"

Madeline leaned back tiredly in her chair, "To gain your trust? Which apparently he did."

"If everything he said was a lie..., he's a well oiled snake. What makes you think he was lying?"

Madeline looked to Sibyl, who nodded some hidden ascent to her sister.

"Mr. Stäkkr has very recently been making inquiries into the Stewart businesses and holdings. I doubt he mentioned that little bit of trivia in his visit."

Nathan leaned forward, responding quickly, "Only in passing. As a matter of fact he made it a point of mentioning the name Bogart and that they recently went belly up."

Madeline nodded and closed her eyes, "Sibyl?"

Sibyl reached in the pocket of her cardigan wrap and handed Nathan the notepad he'd been pondering since E. M. Stäkkr's visit.

"How did you know...?"

"It was only a matter of time...," she said, patting his hand in a grandmotherly fashion. "Now can we begin?"

Nathan slipped the notepad in his shirt pocket. The information he wanted from its past would take some time and careful interpretation.

Sibyl reached to the floor and retrieved a long narrow box. Inside was an enormous black feather, carefully arranged on black velvet. With a closer inspection, he noticed that the quill end was oddly stained as well as crushed and splintered.

"A word of advice Mr. Heart. I wouldn't follow this *Object* to its *Origin*, unless you're less afraid of heights than I am."

A rooftop maybe, or the top of a building, but the heights that an eagle might soar could cause quite a bit of undue stress.

"I see your point."

♥

Nathan was naming the fifty-six individual hands, which had used the feather as an instrument of freedom, from John Adams, to George Wythe, when Lindsey and Lisa stepped closer. They looked on as silent observers as he described the signing of the Declaration of Independence.

When Nathan was through, "It was John Hancock that stomped the end of the quill. He said it signified the end of British tyranny."

Nathan still unaware of the ladies behind him, pinched the bridge of his nose and took a breath, "I still don't see how you'll be able to verify anything I've seen. It's just a…, feather."

"You'd be surprised what our specialists at the university can do with a sample of the ink, now that they know where and when to look," said Sibyl.

Henry rushed in and quickly stepped forward, "We'll likely be out late. Call if you need anything."

It was the first time Nathan had seen Henry in a suit and tie. His dark gray trappings looked a little out of place to anyone familiar with his boyish face; nevertheless, he looked as if his athletic form were poured into it.

Nathan's breath caught and his eyes were instantly on stems.

"Ladies…, you look…, very nice. Where exactly are you going?" he stammered.

Lisa's eyes seemed to shimmer at him; when she smiled, his head swam refusing to let him stand.

Henry grinned knowingly, raking fingers through his perfectly trimmed hair, "Dinner, shopping, and the theater if Lens doesn't try to buy everything she sees."

A jealous knife stabbed Nathan to the hilt at Henry's proud proclamation. Lindsey was her usual glorious self, but it was the radical transformation of Lisa that overwhelmed him.

Henry took a quick glance at his wristwatch, "We should get going."

He heard giggles from the two women as they disappeared into the long hallway.

Forcing an about face, Nathan turned to see the two sisters carefully examining his expressions.

"Do you think you'll be able to compose yourself enough to continue?" asked Madeline.

"I…, yes of course I'll be fine," he snapped unexpectedly.

CHAPTER SEVENTY-FOUR

IT was late. Nathan had been distracted all evening, worsening as the time dragged on. He found his mind frequently sliding backwards to the surprising glint in Lisa's eyes, her shy smile, as well as every other clothing enhanced feature of her body.

Sibyl was getting restless as well, especially after they'd been served their evening meal right where they sat.

Using her foot, Madeline slid a worn wooden box across the Persian carpet toward Nathan, "I think we should make this the last item for the evening."

Sibyl seemed to perk up, "I'm not sure Nathan is ready for one of the Containment Projects."

Sibyl sounded nervous. Where had he heard that term used recently? At this point in time, he couldn't care less. Madeline had spoken the magic words that this would be the last.

"Take this one very slowly," said Sibyl. "No need to rush."

He lifted the twelve-inch cube to a knee and turned the latch, lifting away the hinged lid.

It contained a piece of metal barely the size and shape of his thumb, either untarnished copper or brass and its end was broken from some larger article. It was pitted with time or the crude manner in which it was crafted.

Nathan carefully lifted the dull nub of metal, feeling its weight..., fairly heavy for its size.

One deep breath and he saw the rest of the *Object* this was broken from. Too difficult to describe, he asked for a pad and pencil to sketch the irregular shape.

"It looks like the lid to something," said Madeline. "Despite the decorative design on top."

Nathan cupped it in his hands, becoming more impatient, finally seeing the other piece of the puzzle.

"It's the lid to some sort of metal pot," he grunted, tired of the whole exercise.

Madeline handed him a pad and pencil, and after some coercion, had him sketching the rest of its entirety.

"It looks like…," hissed Madeline.

She raised herself tiredly from her chair and perused one of the bookshelves. After a few minutes of sleep inducing silence, she sat back down, swishing hurriedly through the large pages of some ancient tome.

"It is…," she exclaimed. "It's an urn. Possibly from the Urnfield Period, 8th or 9th century B.C. If we knew where it was buried, there could be several more. Remember the King's Grave at Seddin Germany?"

Sibyl nodded thoughtfully.

Before either of them prompted, he grasped the nub of metal, ready to end the night's adventures. There was no *Guardian*, no nightmarish obstacle to try to scare him off. It was just an ugly piece of metal.

He was suddenly standing in a meadow beside a lush green hillside, still attached to the *Object*, watching as four workers, two in thick leather robes, the other two with wooden paddles being used as spades.

Quickly, the urn was placed in the hole that was prepared, while the ones in ceremonial clothing grunted some sort of guttural singsong chant.

Then it was dark.

Seeping cold, dark, and very, very quiet.

Nathan took a breath and opened his eyes.

It was still pitch dark, absolute and cold.

All he had to do was release himself from the *Object* and look for the all important landmarks or indicators of where this burial ground was located.

He took a slow practiced breath and blinked hard at his eyelids, but the unrelenting ink of the vision was still upon him.

On the precipice of panic, he remembered that Sibyl was still seated close by, ready to jostle him back to the world of the living.

Then he heard something shuffle in the distance…, in the dark.

Now…, one other thing was certain.

Wherever this was, he was not alone.

♥

Once again, for the hundredth or was it the thousandth time…, Nathan had scurried through a vast uneven terrain of blank darkness, shifting away from his unseen companion. Had it been hours…, days…, weeks? Not one to easily panic, he listened to the whispered incoherent ramblings of some sort of incorporeal being somehow trapped in this hellish tomb.

"Hello," he hissed, instantly frightened by the warbled distortion of his own voice.

Nathan heard an unmistakable hissing laughter and once again he began to hurry away to the periphery of its origin. Whoever…, whatever…, was entombed with him, had somehow realized that Nathan was sharing the domain.

How long could this continue? Why weren't they shaking him awake? What if they couldn't wake him from this dark place?

Cold, damp fingers snaked around his wrist and Nathan recoiled in horror, screaming, running blindly until his legs would no longer sustain him, his heart pounding in his chest. Stars formed in front of his eyes, the kind one sees as they drift from consciousness.

More hissing laughter only feet away brought an ugly reality to bear. This could very well be the end of Nathan Heart.

♥

Blinding light caused Nathan to groan in pain as something warm and wet quickly covered his eyes.

"Don't try to open your eyes."

Nathan tried to move, pushing past a foray of aching muscles all over his body. His left hand was throbbing, wrapped in some sort of binding that prevented his fingers from twitching. He imagined an IV plunged in a vein, taped to his wrist while trapped in the months of darkness.

Of course, it was itching madly.

"Where am I?"

"In your bed. Don't try to move or get up. You need to rest."

Nathan finally recognized the voice as the one of Bolton.

His listless body was wrapped in a constriction of sweat-drenched blankets from neck to toe and a violent shiver brought him another inch toward reality.

"What day is it?"

"Sunday, now stay there and don't do anything stupid. I need to tell the others you're awake."

Sunday meant absolutely nothing. Nathan scourged himself for not asking what month and year it was.

"Nathan?"

This voice he recognized immediately.

"Lisa? What happened?"

Soft lips pressed against his, then his cheeks and the tip of his pointy nose.

"You had me so scared. I thought you weren't ever coming back."

He felt warm drops of water touch his cheeks. She was crying.

"How long Lisa?"

"Two days, it's Sunday morning."

Nathan felt his body quiver as he exhaled. That wasn't possible. He'd been gone months, possibly a year..., no longer.

"Bolton managed to get you up here with the help of Henry and some of the other men. We started to take you to the hospital, but Lindsey worked some sort of miracle after Bolton pried the piece of metal from your hand."

Nathan tried to move but the blankets cocooning him were so tight..., so heavy, and that nasty dampness made them cling to his skin.

"Hey, I'm sorry about your hand Boss," said Bolton from somewhere in the room. "You have a grip like a vise. I had to use two screwdrivers to force your fingers apart. Bent both of them silly before I pried that thing out of your hand."

Nathan felt his body slump, "Two days.... It felt like years."

Lisa's warm body draped over his as she held him tight, "I'm really glad you're back."

There was some rattling noise and commotion Nathan wasn't able to distinguish, "Well, look who's returned to the land of the living."

Lindsey leaned heavily on the bed and gave him a peck of a kiss on his cheek.

"I brought you some food. It's only soup, but don't you dare complain. Sara made it especially for you. You need to eat as much as you can, but slowly, alright?"

"You're the one that pulled me out of that hell hole?" he asked.

"None other. We'll talk about that later."

"Wait..., my eyes. What's wrong with my eyes?"

Lindsey patted him on his thick chest as Lisa shifted away, "They think you've been in pitch darkness for a very long time. The light sensitivity should wear off in a day or so. Lisa's going to feed you now. Now quit complaining and eat something, then we'll get you out of those blankets and clean you up. I'll be back to check on you later."

♥

Before the room could fill up with questions, Lisa spooned another scoop of broth into Nathan's mouth.

He shivered. Why was his room so cold?

"I did a few things around the office Saturday. They wouldn't let me help you..., you know..., I had to do something. I bought stuff for the waiting area, a couple of couches..., a table, the stuff we talked about. I figured I'd clear a few things from my list."

She sighed, resting the back of her hand on his forehead before another spoonful went to his lips.

"Are you going to tell me what really happened?" Lisa whispered.

He nodded and swallowed painfully. There was no reason to keep anything from Lisa at this point.

Every movement of his body was an unpleasant task and his legs felt like rubber weights. Sitting up, his back against a stack of pillows, made his stomach feel like he'd done a marathon of sit-ups.

"Want me to close your door?"

Nathan shook his head gingerly, "What would it matter? There's no secrets around here."

She set down the empty bowl on the tray beside the bed.

"Remember how I held your grandmother's compact and saw a few things? Well, I've been practicing on antiques for Madeline, with Sibyl explaining the process; the training I mentioned."

Lisa carefully sat near him on the bed, placed a warm welcome palm on his bare chest, then decidedly stretching alongside him. She seemed to be giving him time to gather his thoughts.

Nathan draped his unwounded hand around her unexpected show of affection, wincing as his muscles contracted.

"I was holding the piece of metal you heard Bolton talking about and everything was going as usual. It was a piece of a bronze urn and I was trying to see where it was buried, but somehow I managed to get trapped inside it. At least I think that's what happened."

He heard Lisa's intake of air, "You were trapped for hours in an urn..., buried in the dark?"

Nathan took a deep breath, not willing to expose her to the rest of his torments.

A soft knock on the door brought their attention away from each other. Lisa sat up and straightened her sweater but didn't offer to remove Nathan's hand from her waist.

"I think I can explain some of it," said Sibyl.

The grandmotherly woman walked in and sat down in one of the many chairs edging the periphery of Nathan's bed.

"When someone such as Nathan or I step into the realm of an *Object*, time almost comes to a standstill. A few seconds feels like several minutes, a few minutes..., hours. You can use your own imagination what several hours or even a day might feel like. Anything you do while you're there seems to be amplified when you end the session and anything you manage to pluck from the tree of your experience tries to cling, whether good or bad."

That's why he was so sore. He'd spent most of his time running and crawling, trying to escape some unseen monster in the inkwell of darkness.

Sibyl looked past them, toward the door, "Lindsey dear, would you like to explain to Nathan where he erred?"

"Do you mean other than not joining us at the theater Friday night? Why I'd be glad to."

Lindsey's arms were crossed spitefully, chin raised in an air of superiority. Then she relaxed and took a seat with a sly grin.

"I realize that at first it's going to feel like all this was a very long time ago, but if you trust your mind to sort things out it'll begin to make sense. Picture your life traveling along on a straight timeline and all of a sudden, you stopped and took a detour, but now you're right back where you started. Go back to the moment when you put the relic in your hand, when you dropped into its reality. Do you remember seeing a burial ceremony?"

Nathan nodded painfully as he dredged up seemingly long past memories, "Four men."

"Good..., now do you remember the ones wearing those interesting leather robes with all the symbols burned into them? They were performing a ceremony to seal the spirit of the dead inside the urn. The *Object* you were attached to at that moment. You my friend..., happened to pause your *Reading* at the pinnacle of their duties and joined the dearly departed in his miniature tomb."

Nathan forced himself to sit forward, feeling his abs protest the sudden movement, "That was another person in there with me?"

She grinned at his blind eyes, "You were in no danger. The poor soul couldn't understand you but he was so glad he wasn't alone all he could do was laugh."

Nathan slumped back against his pillow, "That would have been nice to know."

He took another deep breath before his raspy voice asked one last question, "Lindsey, what would have happened if you hadn't pulled me out of there?"

Sibyl patted his leg gently, "That is precisely why we couldn't leave you here alone without someone else that understands your uniqueness. Someone that can call another for help without involving..., those that might not understand, or more importantly..., the ones that shouldn't."

She nodded toward Lisa, despite Nathan's closed eyes, "Madeline will explain the rest in a few days."

Lindsey sat back trying not to think of the horror; the many threats that they both shared with the few others of their kind. "His mental state is intact. I won't need to lead him through a restoration sequence. It looks as if Mr. Heart will be back to normal in a few hours."

CHAPTER SEVENTY-FIVE

EVEN with the sleep mask of Lindsey's and his eyelids closed, the light bleeding in was painful most of the day. Sunday happened to be one of the few days on the northwest coast where there was a clear blue sky. Bright sunshine glared through the upstairs windows and veranda doors most of the day, accompanied by a howling wind that promised some radical change to come.

With Bolton's help that morning, he'd managed to shower and change from his sweat soured pajamas. By the time he emerged, his bed linens had been stripped and replaced with fresh and he could tell the room had been aired by the crisp cold temperature. It was an humbling experience he didn't want to repeat any time soon.

By that evening's twilight, the eye mask was gone and he was accustomed to the dim candlelit glow of his bedroom.

Lisa tapped on his open bedroom door, "Do you need anything?"

Everyone had already been waiting on him, hand and foot, to the point of embarrassment.

"I need out of this bed," he grumbled. "I'm sick of feeling like an invalid."

"Want me to help? Lindsey and I are about to eat something Sara put together in the kitchen."

His stomach growled anxiously at the very thought of something substantial to eat. Nathan grimaced quietly as he threw his legs over the side of the bed, careful to keep the covers intact.

"No..., I should take care of a few things..., by myself first," he grinned. He raked his hand across his stubbly face, scratching at the itching growth.

403

"At least let me help you to the bathroom door."

He counted the twenty-five paces to the doorway, his strength returning with every step. Lisa leaned against the outside of the closed door with arms crossed.

"Want me to come back up and get you?"

"I'll be fine," came muffled through the doorway.

Afraid he'd fall and do some real damage, she lingered just to be on the safe side.

"I called Troy yesterday. You were right. He spent nearly fifteen minutes apologizing and begging me to come back to work for him."

A loud shuffling ensued as Nathan hurried to the opposite side of the door, "You're not going to are you?"

Nathan sounded distressed, his voice louder through the thick wood.

"No. I have other interests at the moment."

"Lisa?"

"Yes."

"Could you uh…, step away from the door?"

♥

His trip down the stairs was less than graceful, but at least it was unattended. Nathan had yet to speak with Madeline after his episode with the entombed and subsequent resurrection.

He flexed his bruised left hand, feeling the aftereffects of Bolton's handiwork. Bolton…, full of surprises. Nathan added yet another line to the bottom of the unusual man's résumé, wondering just how much of the Stewart's activities he was privy to.

Nathan had intended to ask if what had happened to him was some sort of fluke or an anomaly, but the more he thought of it the less it seemed plausible. The way Madeline had slid the box across the off-white Persian rug to him with her foot, as if it was tainted, that should have been his first clue. Then there was Sibyl's remark about a Containment Project.

Madeline knew something. She was pushing the last of their frayed relationship out on thin ice.

Nathan adjusted his stature before stepping into the kitchen, pasted something between a smile and a grimace on his face.

Forcing his shoulders back, he felt his chest and abs tighten like stone, while the backs of his thighs and calves contracted in rebellion. His reflection in the full-length mirror hadn't been lying after all. The constant marathon of running and crawling for months upon months in faux captivity, trying to evade an unknown assailant, had honed his body to his college year's physique.

Upon entering the kitchen, both women hurried forward to help him, but he waved them off with the flick of a hand and what he hoped was a smile.

After extracting a plate from one of the cabinets, he steadied himself to the table, where there was already a table setting and silver waiting for him. Both Lindsey and Lisa were watching him as inconspicuously as possible, so his act wasn't quite as convincing as he had hoped.

When he sat, they both visibly relaxed and took his ubiquitous plate, loading it with Sara's mish-mash of scrumptious leftovers.

Nathan cleared his throat, "Is your Aunt Madeline where I can have a quick word with her?"

Lindsey flicked her caramel brown eyes at Lisa and back to him before answering, "She and Henry left..., they should be back by Wednesday evening or early Thursday morning."

He sat quietly looking at his plate without moving for a few moments, while Lisa dropped two rolls on his napkin.

"Is there something I can help you with? If it's an emergency I'm sure I can get her on Henry's cell phone."

"No," he muttered, finally picking up a fork and poking randomly at a piece of roast beef.

"Your eyes are still hurting?" asked Lisa.

He shook his head to the contrary and opened his eyes from his careful squint, precariously stuffing in a bite of food.

"Your motor skills should be back to normal in a few more hours. They're the last to come back on line," said Lindsey. "It's like riding a bike, you never forget."

His next question was avoided. Lindsey had answered it. She'd had the same thing happen to her once upon a time. But who had saved Lindsey from her psychic dungeon? Certainly not the timid Sibyl. And neither of them were willing to answer Lindsey's remark about his mental state.

Lisa scurried to the walk-in fridge and hurried back, setting a bottle of imported beer on the table.

"I found Henry's stash," she grinned. "Won't he be surprised?"

He slipped his good hand to her arm and gave it a gentle squeeze of appreciation.

"You miss waiting tables?" he asked.

Lisa laughed at his intended implication, "Not especially."

He swallowed his bite, then sipped, his movements slow and thoughtful, "You know..., if you really want to go back to work at the Pirate, I won't try to stop you."

Nathan had done more than play hide and seek in the pitch blackness for those insufferable imagined months.... There had been many hours spent soul-searching decisions that affected those around him.

Lisa chuckled, surprised at his sudden openness, "As if you could. No..., I'm right where I'm supposed to be at the moment."

He couldn't help feel that he'd altered Lisa's future for his own selfish pursuits, much the same as he had accused Madeline of doing. His self-deprecation almost caused him to miss the sudden shift in Lisa's attitude.

"Nathan you shouldn't be so hard on yourself. Life happens and we have to deal with what we're given," sighed Lindsey. "Which is why I finally made peace with Aunt Madey. I've decided to step into my role as the family *Sensitive*..., at least for now."

Nathan tried to hide his surprise. Was her usual defiant impudence broken due to Madeline's continual dripping? The defiant self-willed Lindsey had given up? Something unknown must be in the mix. Yet..., Lindsey seemed..., more relaxed and at harmony not only with the circumstances, but with herself.

"At least for now?" he repeated.

Lindsey smiled and nodded; no explanation.

♥

Sleep wouldn't come and the room seemed as bright as twilight due to Nathan's persistent mydriasis. Wispy shadows seemed to move and shift with some ethereal life, dancing to the rhythm of the silent candle flame.

"Nathan?" whispered softly from the hallway.

He sighed, then realized the voice was familiar to the living instead of the dead.

"Are you awake?" the voice persisted.

"Come in."

"I can't sleep," whined Lisa, very quietly pulling a chair close to his bedside.

"Neither can I," he grunted, shuffling on his side to face her. "Is something on your mind?"

"Yeah..., everything. All at once."

"Is your bedroom bothering you again?"

He watched her awed expression shift, "No..., not really. I'm sort of used to it now."

They sat in silence for a few moments, watching each other's expressions.

"You want to talk about what's bothering you?"

Lisa shook her head, "Not really, but...."

Her head dropped as she contemplated her words, "Nathan, I've been wondering..., a lot lately. What exactly it is that's going on..., between us I mean?"

Nathan chuckled, "I'm not sure. I spend most of my time trying to find a way past all your defenses. I have to admit, you're like a minefield."

Lisa huffed, "Not one to beat around the bush, are you?"

"Actually..., I am. However, being patient doesn't seem to be working very well for me. I haven't even had a chance to cash in my I.O.U. yet."

It was either the late hour or the product of his soul searching..., Nathan couldn't believe the words he'd just blurted out.

"Does that mean that you're really interested..., in me?"

Unbelievable.... Apparently it was going to take a billboard in lights.

"I thought you would have figured that out by now. Why is that so hard for you to believe?"

"A simple yes or no would have worked," she muttered.

Now she looked more worried than she had when she'd sneaked into his room. Nathan shut his eyes..., and was about to turn and stare back at the ceiling in frustration when he felt the bed shift.

"What if I told you that it was a bad idea?"

Lisa's chin was propped in her two cupped hands, inches from his face.

"This isn't easy for me," she grunted. "I've never really let anyone this close to me before."

"Oh, for heaven's sake. Kiss her and tell her that you love her so I can get some sleep!" barked Lindsey, just before the door across the hall bumped shut.

CHAPTER SEVENTY-SIX

HEART Realty remained closed Monday, while Nathan and Lisa shuffled schedules and meetings forward to the following week. Both Lindsey and Sibyl had warned him not to make any major business decisions until the lingering effects of his escapade with death were gone.

Nathan argued that his strength was back as if he'd recovered from a recent marathon, his light sensitive eyes were covered with shades, and most of the bruising on his left hand was gone.

Neither of the women seemed convinced as he and Lisa hurried out the door, with Nathan grumbling about being coddled.

Lisa drove them into Salem because he couldn't get the Yukon's key aligned with the door lock or the ignition slot. Thankfully, Lisa wasn't smug, not like Lindsey would have been if she'd found out.

Before they left the office at noon, his fingers were contacting the correct keys on his keyboard and complaining that the room had begun to get dark. That was when Lisa removed the sunshades covering two dark-brown smiling eyes.

After a private lunch, most of the afternoon was spent in light conversation. Nathan explained his complex relationship with his family and Lisa complaining about her lack of relatives, while trying to coerce him to get to a barber.

They crept back in to the old Heart homestead two minutes after the clock by the door announced the fourth hour of the afternoon.

"Well..., how was your little afternoon soirée?" asked Lindsey.

The smile was there, despite the slight tone of jealousy they were coming to know as Lindsey's root personality. She was seated by the front window in the waning sunlight with a stack of rumpled magazines at her side.

"Oh Lindsey..., I forgot that Henry was gone or we'd have come by to get you," said Lisa.

"Don't beat yourself up. I had my family and my magazines to keep me company."

This time the sarcasm was thick enough to cut with a knife.

"All you had to do was get in the car with us this morning. You were more than welcome," added Nathan.

She shoved the stack of slick-bound magazines to the end of the couch.

"Oh..., I'm not upset with you. I had to stick around and wait for Aunt Madeline to call with her instructions. Then there was the equipment for the new security system that arrived this morning."

"It's just as well. I knew the parameters of my duties before I accepted them.

So..., tell me. How many times did Nathan drive you into the ditch before you took over this morning?"

Lindsey was grinning from ear to ear, waiting for Lisa to tattle.

Nathan shook his head, "Lisa drove. I needed to make some calls."

Lisa snickered when Lindsey's expectations turned into a pout.

"I guess my day was a complete disaster after all," she whined.

"It's just as well. I..., get to be your tutor for the next three days."

Nathan perched on the end of her couch, "Tutor? I assumed that since Madeline was gone..., and after what happened Friday...."

"The great and mighty Nathan is skittish?" she scoffed.

"No..., it's just..., I didn't exactly enjoy my last class very much."

Lindsey nodded, "And yet here you are..., passed along into my capable hands."

Lisa chuckled and Nathan felt her warm hand on his shoulder, "I need to catch up on a few things. You two have fun."

"Oh... no...," drawled Lindsey. "Your presence is required during all said future training sessions, per her majesty, Aunt Madeline. If you have a problem, take it up with her."

Lisa laughed at her court gesture, "What could you possibly need with me?"

Lindsey tilted her head slightly before she spoke. She was obviously enjoying her new role a little more than she should.

"It appears that you have more of a vested interest in the student according to Madeline and your role has changed somewhat. Aunt Madey said that you would understand."

Lisa seemed stunned, as if some confidence had been broken, "Well..., I..., I guess I could sit and watch whatever it is you do," she answered sheepishly.

"Excellent! We'll meet back here at five. Sara is making us burgers and home fries at seven. Since I had a say-so in the menu, I picked something that I like for a change. As for the rest of them..., *Let them eat cake!*"

♥

"She's taking this new position a little too seriously, isn't she?" mumbled Lisa.

"I guess we'll have to wait and see," shrugged Nathan. "I can always say no thank you. It's not like I signed some contract forcing me to continue on with these sessions until the end of time."

Lisa had turned away, her cheeks were flushed, her eyes set in deep thought.

"Lisa...," he stopped her in the hallway. "What's the matter?"

"Nothing. I need to hurry and change. See you in a few minutes."

As soon as Nathan closed his door, he wondered if Madeline and Lisa's quid-quo-pro extended further than Lisa's voluntary silence. Call it a hunch or some sort of knowing; the idea tried to invade his thoughts as soon as he stopped Lisa in the hallway. Now he wanted to know exactly what Madeline had promised and what was expected of Lisa.

He threw off his jacket, "Blast it all."

Lisa knew how Madeline operated. Why would Lisa willingly step into one of her traps? Whatever Madeline had offered must be something so rare to Lisa that she would have forfeited anything.

"Family...," hissed Nathan. That's what she'd told Lindsey.

That's all Lisa talked about. Madeline had offered to find any of Lisa's living relatives. Come to think of it, Lindsey had a meditative preoccupation with the same subject.

"Madeline..., what have you done?"

♥

"Where are the *Objects* we're studying?" asked Nathan.

He looked about the floor for a stack of trinkets or some chest of carefully tagged items to pilfer through.

"Aren't you tired of doing the same old thing over and over?" asked Lindsey. "For the sake of time, we're going to tell Aunt Madeline that you are officially in the second grade."

Apparently, it was as condescending a judgment as she could muster at the moment.

Lisa yawned and settled down against the arm on her end of the long grand couch by the front window, thinking of a dozen things she'd rather be doing.

"Then what exactly are we going to do?" he asked.

"You and I are going to take a little trip, as my invited guest. If you'd kindly give me your hand, we'll begin."

Nathan's eyes became glazed as he took Lindsey's hand. A fresh scene appeared in his mind, blanking out everything his eyes should have been seeing in the natural.

A wispy thin little girl with shoulder length blond curls was seated on a wooden park bench. Her bright blue dress was whipping in the breeze as she reached into a paper bag and threw a peanut onto the sidewalk in front of her. As soon as it bounced, a large fat gray squirrel shot from a moss covered oak, tail brushed and whipping as it scurried for its prize. Just as it reached the offered food, a long-legged boy dressed in dark slacks, button down shirt and tie bolted out and lunged at the barking rodent.

"Henry!"

Nathan's focus was immediately back in the chair across from Lindsey, his hand sliding away from hers. The young girl's shrill voice was still echoing in his ear.

"Welcome to *Reading People 101*," said Lindsey.

Nathan knew he shouldn't have been surprised, but he was stunned, "That was you?" Something unexpected was conveyed, still lingering…, a caving vacuum of sad emotions.

"Who did you expect it to be?" she laughed. "That was two years after mom and dad died. We were at the cemetery paying a visit."

He didn't have a clue what to say. Nothing seemed appropriate at the moment, especially an, 'I'm so sorry.' Yet why had she chosen that precise memory to share with him?

"Now that was an invited memory, from a willing *Subject*," she continued. "It could just as easily been some fantasy of me walking on the moon and it would have appeared real to you."

"Then what's the point?" he asked, glad that the uncomfortable moment had passed.

"That was what I placed in the forefront of my mind. I led you there. If no one is aware that you are probing their conscious thoughts, that's the first stop. If you can get a quick peek there, it means that the barn door is wide open."

Lindsey waved her hands and sat back, "Don't get too excited. Think of that initial contact as checking the lock and those first thoughts as their visitors lounge or waiting room. Most of those little trips are fruitless…, just ignore them. They either want you to shut up so they can talk or hurry to the bathroom, they have groceries to buy, or they're sizing you up."

"I'm guessing that these aren't the thoughts we want to see?"

Lindsey grinned, "My but you are the bright one aren't you? You're on the right track, but don't get ahead of our lesson plan. There's a means to our madness and if we jump too far ahead, you won't have a solid foundation."

Lisa's shoes slid from her feet with a clop and she stretched out on the couch where Lindsey was seated; her eyes were droopy and glazed with boredom. To her..., absolutely nothing had transpired, only a quick brush of hands, then a bunch of odd expressions and conversation.

"This time I'm going to tell you what to look for," Lindsey continued.

The next half hour was simple and repetitive, but extremely enlightening. A simple quick touch, while looking for something pinpoint specific, was as easy as plucking merchandise off a department store shelf.

"I think that was an adequate introduction," sighed Lindsey. She turned and looked at Lisa and smiled.

Lisa's face was shifted to the side against the couch, lips slightly parted and dozing peacefully.

"Well..., we've bored this one into oblivion," she muttered quietly.

Nathan grinned, "She didn't get much sleep last night."

"Yes..., I remember," grunted Lindsey, with a patented roll of the eyes. "Did you settle all of her..., anxieties?"

"In time," he answered, pushing away Lindsey's frissive insinuation.

Lindsey carefully pinched one of Lisa's big toes and wiggled it, "This little piggy went to market..., this little piggy...."

"I can hear you talking about me," muttered Lisa.

CHAPTER SEVENTY-SEVEN

"I don't see why you need me here," grumbled Lisa.

Several trays of leftovers were looming nearby, waiting for some of the staff to whisk them away.

Lindsey leaned very close to Lisa for a semi-private comment, "Aunt Madey informed me that you had no qualms about your new arrangement. Have you changed your mind?"

Lisa's eyes rounded into a silenced plea, then she wiggled her head almost imperceptibly.

"Good. Nathan...? Now that you're comfortable with Part one of our lesson, it's time to begin part two..., entitled: an unwilling *Subject*."

Lisa gasped and shrank away from both Nathan and Lindsey, "This doesn't have anything to do with me, does it?"

Lindsey grinned, "Be patient, you'll get your turn soon enough. Besides..., if Nathan wanted to peek inside that pretty little head of yours, he's had ample opportunity lately."

Lisa's cheeks flushed crimson and her head snapped to look at Nathan. He'd never seen Lisa back away from any sort of confrontation..., until he became ingrained into her life.

Lindsey hurried next to her friend, laughing and patting her hand, "All in good fun..., I forget sometimes you didn't have any siblings or cousins nipping at your heels when you were little. I'm sure Nathan could tell you what that was like."

"She was only teasing, Lisa," said Nathan in what he hoped was his best calming voice.

"Now..., I want you to query my mind for an image of my 2009 Graduation Ceremony. What a *jubilant day* that was."

Lindsey's sneering sarcasm was back in full force, "Everyone was so amazed that I'd raised my grades out of the gutter and made it into the top ten of my graduating class."

Lindsey offered her hand to Nathan. This time he saw nothing but a gray wall, something like a mist that was useless to try to see through.

He shook his head, "Blank, it was empty."

"Locked…, not empty I assure you," she chided.

"What did I do wrong?" he asked.

"Refer to Part one of our lesson. Did you look for the lounge before you tried the penthouse suite? Or did you, like the typical alpha male, go straight for the goods?"

It was Nathan's turn to feel heat creeping around his collar, "I pinpointed the event the same way we did earlier."

"I wasn't blocking you earlier. Always, try, the lounge, first."

She extended her hand once again. Once again nothing appeared, as sheer frustration pelted his mind, he dropped her fingers and shook his head.

"I didn't see anything at all this time."

She grinned slightly, "But what did you feel?"

"Honestly? I was frustrated."

"And you assumed those were your feelings?"

"Instant anger, excitement, fear…, any raw emotion you didn't begin with can be your personal back door into your *Subject's* mind. Now start over. Treat that *emotion* as if it was one of the rudimentary *Objects* you were peeking into for my Aunt Sibyl."

Lisa's previous boredom had waned, not only by Lindsey's initial threat, but she was listening to a demonstration of how Sibyl had been traipsing around in her mind the first time they met.

Upon touching Lindsey's manicured fingers, the gray wall appeared, then a lounge also empty of memories, except for a definite hint of anxiety. He quickly converted the emotion into his *Object* and a vast ocean of sights and sounds opened before him. Colorful vivid images were playing on the panorama of Lindsey's mind at multiple points during her lifetime. This new scene was warm and welcoming, with a special invitation written just for him. The temptation to explore Lindsey's life and how she came to be in this role was almost overwhelming. Even more disconcerting…, he felt her lower all barriers of resistance in one overwhelming droop of energy. Refocusing…, it took every ounce of energy he had just to remember what he was supposed to be looking for.

"You and two others were wearing a white cap and gown up on the podium. The other graduates were wearing the tradition royal blue," he said as he forced himself to let go of her fingers. "I thought you said you were in the top ten."

Letting go of the wash of emotions was like shutting off Niagara Falls in one turn of some imaginary faucet.

"I was...," she shrugged. "Honorary Salutatorian is in the top ten, is it not? My grades were better than that other snit, but my attendance and..., anyway now you understand how to get past the most prevalent lock of the mind. Lisa?"

She whipped the conversation away from herself, instantly back on some unseen track.

Lisa jumped, already anxious with eyes fluttering, "What?"

"Are you ready to play too?" she asked.

Lisa swallowed and nodded, then scooted up next to Lindsey.

"This isn't going to hurt is it?" muttered Lisa.

Lindsey grinned slyly, "Think of it as getting a tetanus shot. All you'll feel is a little pinch."

"Lindsey," scolded Nathan, as Lisa slumped backward. "No Lisa..., you won't even realize anything happened."

Lisa slapped a chuckling Lindsey on her arm and moved forward once again.

When she'd regained her composure, Lindsey leaned nearer Lisa, "Tell Nathan the steps and what to look for. Remember our little talk?"

Nathan wondered if it was the content over the lesson or if it was the reference to Madeline that Lindsey was referring to.

Lisa looked a little perplexed at first, "Uh..., the visitor lounge first, then..., Oh. I need to pick some memory don't I? Oh, not that..., no...."

Lisa blushed and glanced up at Nathan, "I don't like this."

Lindsey was at the end of her patience, "Oh for heavens sake. Show him what you were thinking when he kissed you last night. That's a good place to start."

Lisa stood, "I'm not doing this."

Nathan scowled at Lindsey's instant cheshire grin.

"Lisa, please. Just pick some moment in time that's clear in your memory," said Nathan.

Lisa slowly reseated herself on the sofa, but not before thumping Lindsey on the shoulder in protest. She extended her hand toward Nathan and grimaced comically as if expecting an electrical shock.

Nathan took her rigid hand and gradually helped her relax, then heard the words, "No, no, no, no, no, no, no...," singing in endless repetition.

"Lisa, please," he grunted.

Nathan ignored Lindsey's sudden barking curiosity and Lisa relaxed at the feel of Nathan carefully caressing her hand.

Lisa's waiting room was gray..., blocked, with uncertain fear hovering like the scent of strong coffee in a room. After a moment he adjusted his port of entry and the gray dissolved. He saw a younger version of Lisa in her waitress uniform, at the Blind Pirate, seated in a booth across from..., Marion Heart.

His mother was holding Lisa's hand and patting it with the other, deep in conversation. Fraught with emotion, Nathan slowly released Lisa's hand as the scene completed.

It took Nathan even longer to regain his composure after witnessing this particular scenario, "Mother told me she lost her favorite Cameo pendant. She gave it to you?"

Lisa's eyelashes fluttered slowly and she nodded, "I thought you knew. She told me it would keep me safe until the right one came along. I still have it. In fact I wear it all the time."

The image was still vivid in Nathan's mind. It was an oval solid gold pendant surrounding the traditional sardonyx black with an elevated white silhouette. Decades old, the Cameo had been passed down to his mother, as during each previous maternal succession.

"I tried to refuse her," continued Lisa. "But she made me take it. I guess you can have it back if it means that much to you."

The moment was suddenly uncomfortable as all three of them sat in silence, staring at one another.

The antique clock in the vestibule began to chime....

While ten evenly spaced blows were hammering away, Nathan felt every pore of his body stand to attention, gooseflesh rippling up and down his spine. So accustomed to the clock's hourly chime, no one had given it the slightest thought..., until that moment.

"No..., uh..., I'm..., pretty sure mother wanted you to keep it," stammered Nathan.

Lindsey cleared her throat as her two students continued to stare at one another, "I believe we're done for the evening. If you'll both excuse me."

♥

"When are you going to tell me about the other agreements you made with Ms. Stewart?" whispered Nathan.

He was standing in Lisa's room with the door carefully pushed to a crack so that he could see anyone advancing down to the end of the hallway.

"Please Nathan, I'm so tired," she whimpered. "And part of my vow of eternal silence has to do with keeping everything Madeline and I talked about a secret."

"Does it have something to do with me?" he asked.

"Nathan, please. She'll know if I tell you."

Nathan stood steaming for several moments looking at Lisa's pleading expression.

"No she won't," he grinned slyly. "Because you don't have to tell me."

He peeked out into the hallway once more and shut the door quietly.

Lisa's eyes rounded as she backed away, "Now Nathan…, what is it you have in mind?"

"You won't feel a thing," he hinted.

Lisa gasped, "No. Don't you dare touch me. That's the same as telling you."

"Not if you don't know."

"Oh that is so not fair…, now you stay back Nathan Heart."

Giving up, he backed away. What a paradox of ideals; the one thing that could potentially bring them closer was pushing them apart.

"Does this mean that you're never going to let me hold you or kiss you ever again?"

"What? No. Of course not…, but…, maybe if you promise me that you'll stay out of my head."

Nathan felt all his resolve melt. Now there was a fresh minefield surrounding this new love he'd found. He had kissed her, he had shared every secret with her, everything but a blatant confession of his love, yet here they were once again. It was as if every circumstance was constantly finding ways to separate them.

Saddened, hurt, and bruised, Nathan took one last look at Lisa's wall of defense and left her room, pulling the door closed behind him.

CHAPTER SEVENTY-EIGHT

WORK Tuesday was torment. Nathan was out of the office most of the day showing properties in an all but constant drizzling rain and relentless tearing wind.

By the late afternoon, the temperature plunged and the wet precipitation was turning into white speckled miracles.

Spitting snow began clinging to the windshield as Nathan and Lisa drove toward Heart Manor in abject silence.

Lisa had carried out his every passing directive at work as if waiting for some sort of axe to fall on her head. Instead of telling her how lovely she looked, how much he wanted to make her a part of his family, he bit his tongue. Nathan made absolutely sure he didn't come within range to so much as brush against her, refusing to hold her hand, or touch her cheek more than a dozen times. He knew it was petty of him and this sort of relationship was doomed to end in flames, much like all his other attempts at finding someone that cared for him more than their own motives and desires.

Somehow letting go of Lisa was going to be harder than anyone else he'd come to care for; especially working so closely with her on a weekly basis. Not to mention the horror he would ultimately face from Caroline's family and Troy O'Bannon. They'd naturally blame him..., but that was nothing new. He had broad shoulders for a reason.

"Are you going to talk to me?"

Lisa's voice cut the silence, her voice raspy and hoarse.

"What would you like to talk about?"

"Thursday."

"The Dinner Meeting?"

MINUTES

"Do you still want me there?"

Nathan's eyes never twitched from the road, "Yes. You still work for me. I need you to be there."

He didn't intend his answer to sound so cold, but maybe it was for the best. He'd done everything but beg Lisa to trust him.

She didn't ask the question he knew was itching inside her, glad that she used her own restraint to stay away from bringing up his wants and desires. That was moot point.

"I need to have my dress pressed..., it was stored in the back of the office in the box you gave me."

"I'm sure Lindsey knows more about that than I ever will."

Nathan reached and turned the windshield wipers up another notch, whisking away the advancing snow.

The ultimate silence that followed was too much for his racing thoughts and he tapped the radio to banish his demons.

Nathan stopped next to the front steps of Heart Manor to let Lisa escape the heavily swirling mass of white, spitting from the sky. She seemed desperately relieved to be rid of her captivity as she ran up the slick steps without looking back..., or saying hello to one of the favored roaring lions wearing a white fluffy blanket.

Lisa didn't show up for supper, nor did she make an appearance during his Tuesday night session with Lindsey.

Lindsey proved herself to be a master locksmith of the mind. During this night's session, Nathan understood why she only let him playfully graduate to the second grade. There was an immense amount of tenure lurking in the background of someone as young and disarming as Lindsey.

She had yet to hint at how she'd broken into his dreams and used him as if he were a dime store remote control toy. That was probably third grade curriculum. This evening was filled with the mechanics of exploiting every weakness known to mankind to garner access to hidden knowledge and motives of the mind.

It was brute force hackery of the human soul finely tuned into an art and Lindsey promised even more pristine corruption for the following Wednesday evening.

♥

Lisa was late coming down the stairs Wednesday morning. Her cheeks were raw and eyes puffy, even with her cleverly applied mask of powders, creams, and hues.

Nathan was standing in the vestibule, glancing at the time on the old clock, thinking of his mother's pet timepiece in an attempt to thwart his anxiety.

Lisa clopped past him, avoiding his gaze. She looked like a jellyroll in her new neck to knee tan overcoat.

419

"Did you eat?"

"Not hungry," she answered, as the open front door unleashed a twenty-degree chill factor upon her grief.

Nathan tightened the lid on his coffee mug following closely behind Lisa just in case her perilous pace on the ice caused her to spill. She wouldn't accept his help, but it would be better than a broken arm or leg. Her years of slipping and sliding the six or so blocks to the Blind Pirate must have paid off as she skated the last three feet to the garage door.

The ride to Heart Realty was a repeat performance of Tuesday, with some annoying morning talk show idiocy blaring on the radio.

Lisa stood back at least three feet from Nathan as he unlocked the Heart Realty entrance, further enhancing his annoyance. After yesterday's performance and the current declining temperament between them, she could have stood a breath away and he wouldn't have moved to breach the distance. With the door pushed open for Lisa, he hurried on down the melting slush of the sidewalk to the coffee shop.

♥

"I have two early appointments this morning. Remember to keep the door locked while I'm not in the office."

Nathan sat down a cup of her favorite latte from next door along with a hot-buttered cinnamon roll. After locking the office door and turning the sign to closed, he marched stiffly on toward his desk.

He heard the paper sack rattle and tear as she spread it into a pseudo-plate for her breakfast.

"Is there some ulterior motive for keeping the door locked?"

Lisa's voice was muffled by the last of her chewing a bite.

He started to use his previous answer, they were booked, which was the undeniable truth, but why should he lie? At this point, it really didn't matter.

"Madeline told me to keep an eye on you. She said that I shouldn't leave you alone for any reason unless you were in a safe place."

Little things shuffled and fell in a clatter just before Lisa appeared in front of his desk.

"And you didn't think that was important enough to tell me?"

She was leaning over his desk at her waist, closer than she'd allowed herself to him in the last two days.

"I didn't want to alarm you…, or have this particular talk."

"Did she say why?"

Something close to fear was etched across her changing expressions.

Nathan shook his head and backed his chair up a few inches, creating a little more space between them.

"No, she didn't."

Lisa's eyes shifted from dark to thoughtful as she backed up, realizing she was breaking her own rule of space. Nathan's brain felt as if it was going to explode at any moment.

"Lisa…, are you in some sort of trouble?"

Her pupils dilated once again, agitated, terrified, or just old-fashioned fear. She nodded once, hard and fast watching for Nathan's reaction.

"Have a seat."

She shook her head, preferring to stand.

"What does Madeline have to do with all this?"

Lisa shook her head again, "I can't tell you."

This was going to take all day and he still had business to conduct, business he could not put off, in just under an hour.

"I want to help you."

"You can't."

"Is it because of me? Are you in trouble because of me?"

"Quit trying to guess Nathan…. No. It has nothing to do with you. Not really."

What was it Sibyl had mentioned? Lisa had a very troubled past.

"I'm sure Madeline Stewart is going to tell you all you need to know tomorrow."

Nathan looked at his wristwatch angrily, once again trying to make a decision over something he had no knowledge of.

"No," he said, his chair clambering against the wall behind him. "I'll find out right now."

He had nothing to lose and everything to gain, especially some perspective on what was going on. Lisa slunk toward the back of the office looking for an exit.

"You should have sat with me last night during our training session, Lisa. It was very enlightening."

Nathan wasn't pursuing her, but walking to her desk.

"You see…, I don't need to actually touch you to learn what I want to know."

He walked to her desk and scrambled through her strewn belongings, spilled across the desk. He could hear her clambering closer behind him, quickly closing the gap.

He picked up Lisa's hairbrush and held it in his hand, backing away from her. Strands of her soft brown hair came free into his hand and he closed his eyes…, only for a few breaths.

"No…," whispered Lisa, as darkness engulfed her. She slumped to the floor in a dead faint.

♥

Lisa awoke stretched out on one of the new couches in their faux home-style waiting room. Nathan was carefully dabbing a cool damp cloth over her face and neck watching her bleary eyes beginning to focus.

"Are you satisfied?" she asked, not bothering to raise her voice above a whisper.

"No, of course not."

Nathan kissed her cheek and began dabbing her face with the cool cloth he had robbed from one of Lisa's storage boxes.

"You didn't see?"

"Of course not. I would never do something like that."

"You mean you lied…, about…, touching my hair?"

"No. That part was true. That would have been simple enough, but I didn't. I respect your privacy. I thought you might tell me what's bothering you. I'm sorry about that."

Her body melted into the couch. He had never intended to rob her of her secrets and now she wanted to disappear from embarrassment.

"I might as well tell you. Ms. Stewart is going to tell you soon enough."

Nathan kissed her forehead, then her cheek, and carefully arose from his squat beside the couch, "Do you need to see a doctor?"

Her eyes batted furiously as she checked herself, "No…, I'm fine."

"Then you need to order us a carafe of fresh coffee from next door and get back to work. I have two meetings starting in about…, twenty minutes."

Nathan squeezed the last few drops of water out the cloth into an old scarred plastic bowl, swishing with soggy remnants of paper towel.

"I made a mess out of some of your storage boxes. Paper towels aren't much good as a compress."

"Help me up," she grunted, as the soft couch tried to hold her down.

Her arms were around him as soon as she stood; then somewhat hesitantly, she squeezed herself against him in a soothing hug before hurrying to her desk. With every step, every tear that fell, she wondered how she managed to find someone as faithful a friend as Nathan Heart. Not since Troy O'Bannon had she trusted anyone this much.

She cleaned her desk in a rapid succession of snatch and grab, then phoned the coffee shop. When she hung up the phone, she sat frozen, wondering. How could someone as crazy good looking as Nathan Heart be interested in someone as messed up as her?

CHAPTER SEVENTY-NINE

THE office door stayed locked each time Nathan was gone and for the first time since moving in, she lowered the white louvered blinds over the front window. She barely noticed that the sky looked as if it would start snowing again at any moment.

Was it possible that her past was catching up to her?

Unable to think or work, Lisa felt her head droop until resting against her desktop.

The photograph. She was the one that had taken the photo of herself and Nathan in front of Heart Realty; placed the AD in the Salem Chronicle herself. The newly purchased cell phone was listed under Heart Realty, but sub-listed in her name.

Those items alone might not be enough for someone to track her down. The title to her car, now in her name; that was in a national database. Maybe it was some combination of all these.

How could she have been so stupid? For nine years no one knew where she was, carefully hiding under Troy O'Bannon's umbrella. Now she regretted not changing her name the way Troy had warned her. He always paid her in cash, always under the limit to file taxes, utilities in his name, always so careful.

She looked at the paycheck Nathan had given her for the past two weeks..., it was more than she made in a month at the Blind Pirate.

She could already hear Troy's I-told-you-so, but no..., he wouldn't do that. In fact, it was Troy's idea for her to step out and try to make a life for herself.

Lisa sat up and let out a tired breath. She wasn't going to run again. She had friends here, real friends.

Then there was Nathan Heart. Nathan, the man that made her heart do flip-flops every time he looked at her. The man she pushed away every time he tried to get close to her.

It was possible that she was jumping to conclusions anyway. After all, it had been twenty years since she'd testified against the man that murdered her mother, right in front of her eyes. All over some gambling debt her father owed, before he was found floating face down in Anchor Bay, Michigan.

As a little six-year-old girl, the last thing she remembered was the growling promise in the courtroom to have her join her parents' graves.

Apparently a patient man, it was nine years after her testimony when Lisa had been tracked down to have that promise executed. After that..., more attempts assured that she was shuffled like a deck of cards throughout the CPS circuit. None of the foster families wanted the responsibility of a kid with an X on her forehead.

Detroit's finest couldn't keep her safe so at seventeen years old she chose the underground circuit to help her disappear from her assailant as well as the corrupt system giving away her location. With the help of perfect strangers much like herself, Lisa headed west until she ran into the Pacific Ocean.

Lisa snatched her cell phone; she had to be sure.

♥

Nathan had to jiggle the key twice to get the glass paned office door to open. His mind relaxed as soon as he saw the extra warm lighting of their waiting area beyond his cubicle wall. Something new had been added.

He locked the door and shuffled through the unopened mail in Lisa's inbox.

"I have one more sale for you to remove from Mr. Lucas's website. I've never seen anyone as indecisive as these people were. They ended up choosing the first house I showed them."

He sat down his satchel in one the chairs by his desk and peered over the partition to see what was new. The other couch, some lamps, and a coffee table had arrived, all arranged into an inviting den. He had been expecting to see Lisa stretched out admiring her handiwork or with her laptop on her knees.

"Lisa?"

It was past time to close up for the rest of the week. Tomorrow was Thanksgiving. She was probably next door grabbing a quick coffee for the drive home.

His eye caught a yellow sticky note on the back of his leather chair accompanied by an instant sick feeling in his gut.

Nathan,
I finished the filing. The rest of the stuff
came for the lounge. Hope you like it.
I had to leave early.
Troy came by and we needed to talk.
See you at the house around 5.

♥ Lisa

Nathan frowned and looked at his wristwatch. It was after four already; far past the time he'd intended on closing up shop for the day. He had wanted to talk to Lisa a few minutes before they left that evening.

"Blast it all," he muttered, throwing a few last minute items in his shoulder bag.

With a quick circle through the office, switching off lamps and checking the back door. He happened to glance over and noticed that something was different or missing.

The stack of boxes he'd dug into that morning were all gone. In fact, all of Lisa's storage boxes were gone. Instead, a wire rack shelf was in their place with several towels of various sizes along with some light kitchen supplies.

Nathan's chest heaved painfully in a moment of thought. Had Lisa given in to her urges and disappeared? Surely she would have said goodbye. He snatched the note back out of his pocket and reread it. This wasn't the note of someone about to skip town, he was being foolish, yet his heart caved at the very thought of it.

♥

Nathan ignored most of the town's traffic signs and broke most of the speed limits as he rushed toward Heart Manor.

Why hadn't Lisa just called him on his cell phone? He dialed her number in a fury and it rolled instantly over to voicemail.

"Blast," he grunted.

She'd probably forgotten to charge her phone again. He tossed his cell into the passenger seat with a loud thump, then snatched it back into his hand.

He searched his call history and dialed the Blind Pirate, but it rang until it went to Troy's annoying answering machine. Troy wouldn't answer, his restaurant would be humming from all the pre-holiday traffic.

All Nathan's anxious ideas only served to keep him occupied until he screeched through the front gates of Heart Manor. There were no signs of life except for a small ridge of unmelted snow following the rim of the drive. Bolton must have spent the morning clearing the runway for Madeline's triumphant return sometime that evening.

The moment he drove inside the garage, he saw Lisa's green Buick parked in its usual place. Part of him wanted to exhale a gross weight off his chest, but another wondered if she talked Troy into helping her. Then in some sort of mad dash to escape some unknown, she'd abandoned her vehicle. That wasn't likely either, she loved her baby Buick, as she liked to call it.

When he jumped out of the Yukon, the rest of him collapsed in another stage of relief. At the front of the Buick on the concrete slab was the neat stack of Lisa's belongings, still in their boxes.

♥

Nathan hurried through the vestibule, draping his leather coat on the rack just through the archway. He heard a loud chirp behind him..., a new keypad for the security system was blinking on the wall by the door. Nathan grunted at more of Bolton's efficiency and hurried on inside.

Next to the hearth of a crackling fire sat Lindsey and Lisa, playing a game of cards across one of the server's tables. With the confirmation of Lisa's physical presence, Nathan felt the last stages of tension finally relax.

Unwilling to display his post-apocalyptic surge of emotions in front of two very intuitive women, he headed to the stairs with a wave of the hand.

"Did you get my note?" asked Lisa.

"Got it. You should charge your cell phone."

"Sorry. Did you like the office?"

"Yes, it's nice."

"Nathan?"

Nathan stopped walking about midway up the stairs and turned to look at the obstinate mystery calling his name.

"Is everything alright?" she asked.

Nathan snorted and headed back up the stairs, "Peachy."

He didn't intend to slam his bedroom door, at least he told himself as much before he turned the lock to keep everyone out.

Somewhere in the back of his mind, he was getting a constant reminder that he should reign in his emotions. He stopped to glare out across the veranda, his palms steaming the cold glass panes.

For once in his life, he didn't want to smother the rage he was feeling, but he had no focus to vent upon.

There was a gentle crackle and sputter in his suddenly quiet room and he shot a glance to his left. The little votive candle flame was swimming widdershins in a macabre dance, the crackle manufacturing a steady tune.

With the intentions of extinguishing its display, he hurried over to his chifforobe. About to suffocate the flame from the disgruntled candle, he noticed that it was once more frozen and quiet. There on top of the chest, next to the candle, was his recent collection of absurdities huddled against each other in a neat display.

Little Boy Blue, a leather pouch, and a rumpled notepad sat evenly dispersed across the polished and dusted surface. He snatched the notepad, flipping through random pages, looking at the scrawled text. He'd all but forgotten it, especially after his recent evils, yet someone had placed it here, cataloged it somewhere appropriate for him to find.

Nathan parked himself in his straight-back dressing chair and gripped the notepad hard enough to press the ink from the pores of the paper.

CHAPTER EIGHTY

ONLY a slither of vertigo ushered Nathan Heart into his first true solo *Reading*. All three of his eloquent tutors had forewarned him never to consider even the simplest journey without a *Handler* nearby. Ignoring their warnings, his first vision appeared.

The spy named Smith was seated bedside in his hotel, yelling into the telephone, where Nathan had seen him last. Instead of taking the bait and following the natural course of curiosity, he stayed with Smith for a few more moments before pushing ever so slowly forward in time.

Smith in excruciating pain, humbled to his knees with a thumb carefully driven into the junction of his cervical nerve and subclavian artery. Smith's right arm was useless..., numb.

Back further on the timeline, ever so cautiously, the scene turned to almost complete darkness. Smith was holding the camera, focused on the thinly veiled windows of one of the cottages beside Heart Manor. He was nervously pressing the camera button repeatedly as Sara and Annie were in the last stages of getting dressed for bed. Mudsill thoughts had Smith mesmerized until he heard Bolton call out from somewhere close behind him.

Before he could turn, deep pain radiated the back of his right leg, a well-placed kick from Bolton, caused him to drop the camera. With his sciatic nerve in shock, Bolton swept Smith's left leg, causing him to crumple to the ground.

Unable to speak through his pain, Smith looked up at his attacker as Bolton pinned all the fingers of his right hand into a blade, raising it a careful angle.

In a blur, Bolton's left hand grasped Smith's hair, steadying him for a single strike as his voice warbled into the nearly unconscious Smith, "Who are you?"

The tone was both menacing and final. It was the hand of a trained killer, ready to strike a final careful blow.

"Who sent you?"

Unwilling to wait for an answer, Bolton's axe hand opened and swept forward grasping Smith's lower jaw with vice like fingertips, his thumb compressing the zygomatic nerve under the orbit of his eye.

"Who sent you? Was it Ethos?"

As Smith tried to answer through the blinding pain, only a whimper eructed.

Seconds later, with Smith deemed useless, Bolton was dragging him towards the front door of the house.

Farther back in time, Smith was outside the Manor, scribbling notes in a strange almost illegible code. Farther still..., seated in a dusky blue sedan, trying to stay awake, Smith was watching Nathan walking to the garage.

Nathan exhaled slowly, letting his eyes focus on his bedroom.

"Ethos...."

This was taking too long. He wanted at the root of this poison, yet terrified where it might take him. Lindsey had taught him to trust his instincts, to pinpoint what he wanted to know, then let the images swim past in a blur until the destination solidified into view. The problem was, he wasn't sure what he was looking for.

Nathan flipped the notepad to the very first page, brushed the ink with his thumb and shut his eyes.

It was suddenly blazing hot..., somewhere in a desert setting. Only weeds and nightmarish Joshua trees around a monstrous old house. Smith was viewing the dilapidation through binoculars, sweat stinging both his eyes as three people exited the building, hurrying into a black limousine.

Nathan recognized the three immediately.

His eyes opened, "Madeline..., what are you up to? Why was Smith watching you?"

Why hadn't he seen this the first time he tried to learn the truth? Was it his inexperience, or his preconceived ideas that led him to the vision of Stäkkr? Or could it have been Sibyl forcing him to detour away from the truth?

No..., he was the one that chose the page in the Spy's notepad that first time; he chose that last scribbled entry himself.

There were suddenly too many variables. He shook his head angrily trying to arrange his thoughts. If it were some dire secret pertaining to the Stewarts, Sibyl would have surely torn the pages out of the notepad.

He flipped to the next page and continued. He had to find the mysterious intersection between this man Smith and his family.

The next scene was one of a luxuriously sprawling estate, lush green manicured lawns, moss laden boughs of live oaks. It didn't take a genius to realize that this was one of the Stewart Family strongholds, somewhere in North Carolina. Again, the view was skewed with the help of a pair of expensive binoculars.

Suddenly Nathan understood that this man wasn't spying on him..., he'd been following the Stewarts, pacing their every move while on this continent.

He flipped forward to a random page, once again viewing the trio of Madeline, Henry and Lindsey, entering a remote house of unknown location. He watched Smith as his stubby pencil etched out some garbled notation..., which suddenly made sense.

It was a combination of the Greek and English alphabets, forming a phonetic dialect. Verbal charades turned into a cypher that only Smith could read; a personal version of shorthand. It was choppy, but very creative.

Nathan opened his eyes and began to read the scribbles of a well-trained spy.

♥

Page after page was dedicated to surveilling the Stewart family's travels, trying to ascertain some secret. Every entry ended with, "Unable to determine source."

Thirty or so pages into Nathan's study, he noticed an abrupt change.

Even the writing on the pages was hard, angry, jagged. It took a quick journey beyond the written information to learn that Smith had been fired. He had been terminated due to his lack of investigative prowess and lack of any confirmed information.

Nathan carefully rubbed the page, delving back into the dark mind of his only source of information, trying to see exactly who this mysterious employer was..., but was met with a strange dark cushy nothing that led nowhere.

With his source of funding cut off, Smith panicked and began looking for other sources of revenue; someone that might pay him for his due diligence. He had a gold mine of addresses and locations he had watched the ultra rich Stewarts ravage. If they were of such importance to his employer, surely they would be to someone else of like mind.

Smith the spy was also receiving tips from some anonymous source, pointing him to the Stewarts next acquisition. Every time Nathan tried to take the adjunct rabbit trail, he was met with that same velvety black void. It was noteworthy enough that he made a mental note to ask his mentors of the meaning.

In the next few pages, it took Smith little time to make a connection to Bogart Investments and he was back on the gravy train. However, every other page noted that Smith believed he was being followed to the point of paranoia; shadowed by someone interested in his continued pursuits of the Stewart family.

Nathan sat back in his chair, rubbing his bleary eyes. Barely any time had passed, but it seemed as if another day had escaped him. Sadly, the ties of his family to Bogart Investments was almost a given.

Then Nathan found the first entry mentioning Heart Manor. His name was registered…, then Lisa Evans. A sudden need to know surpassed his exhaustion as he sat forward in his chair.

He encountered pure frustration when the only tie to his name was Realtor, and to Lisa - waitress, then no more entries, coupled with that strange black wall. He and Lisa seemed to be nothing more than a passing embolism in Smith's interest. If that were the entirety of the matter, then why was Madeline concerned for Lisa Evans and her safety?

Angry, Nathan stood and stretched, strolling to the veranda doors to let his mind rest. Rest didn't come as he continued to ponder the sequence of events. Something didn't add up, something was missing, standing like a shadow in the valley of his mind.

Something Eben M. Stäkkr had said. The last time he allegedly spoke to Smith was in the hotel after Smith was arrested. If that were true, then the notepad's remnant memories wouldn't have recorded the angry conversation Nathan had seen. Nathan was in possession of the notepad when Stäkkr supposedly had that final verbal confrontation. So…, either Stäkkr was lying, or he'd somehow seen into the future, which wasn't likely.

Nathan shook his head; skipping forward in time wasn't one of the lessons Nathan had been led through, not yet, even if it was possible.

What did any of this have to do with Lisa Evans?

All he would have to do to solve that mystery is break his own moral code, break his promise to Lisa and invade her privacy. In a hopeless surge of intuition, he wished for a single strand of hair from the head of the spy John Smith.

Nathan gasped, remembering something that he'd seen, then ran back to take a seat. After flipping to one of the first pages in the notepad, he saw a brown dot staining the page. It was blood. Smith's blood.

♥

Nathan stood from his chair immediately, "Blast it all."

The thick notepad went hurling into the wall, adding a few more wrinkles to its weathered pages.

John Smith never saw his assailant.

The last thing Smith saw before eternal darkness fell on his existence was the luggage he was carrying while leaning inside his car.

In a frantic interlude at his hotel, Smith was throwing his belongings into the back seat of the ugly blue sedan, anxiously scrambling to escape the guillotine awaiting him in Lumberton.

Then nothing.

Nathan tried releasing himself from his human *Object*, to hover around and view the scenery and circumstances. Once the connection was terminated, Nathan was forcefully ejected from his *Reading*.

That same velvet black wall shrouded whatever mishap befell the infamous John Smith.

CHAPTER EIGHTY-ONE

THE clamor of familiar voices downstairs shocked Nathan from his funk. Evidently, Madeline and her troupe had returned in force.

Nathan halted at the top of the stairs, peering down at a couple of new faces in the mix as luggage and boxes hurried in the front door. All of the Stewart clan were mingling in light conversation, helping with the arriving party.

A blast of frigid air managed to whisk up to where Nathan stood before it was finally closed and locked shut.

With the cool mix of air came the comforting scents of both Sara's ovens hard at work on tomorrow's feast. The giant Manor smelled of home.

When Nathan came to himself, Lisa was standing at the foot of the stairs looking up at him. Everyone else seemed to disappear from view as he watched her frozen next to the bannister. Consternation on her face, she called to him with her eyes, begging him to come speak to her. He'd ignored her since his arrival, more than an hour of seclusion in his bedroom.

If Nathan was good at anything, it was forgiveness. With a deep sigh, he smiled sheepishly and started down to meet her.

As he neared the bottom of the staircase, Madeline turned from her animated conversation nearby and hailed him.

"Nathan, so good to see you. Would you and Miss Evans care to join us for a little informal supper?"

Nathan stopped beside Lisa, slipping an arm around her waist and pulling her close. He felt her sharp intake of breath before she melted comfortably against his side.

"I can only answer for myself, but I'd be happy to join you," said Nathan.

"Miss Evans?" prodded Madeline.

"Sure. I mean…, I'd like that," she answered, glancing up at Nathan.

Nathan felt the heat of Lisa's open palm press against his back and once again, all in the world was set upright.

"Very good. I understand that appetizers are already on their way to the dining room. Thankfully, there will be no caviar for those of you with that deplorable habit, but there are other aquatic delicacies I'm sure you'll enjoy, Mr. Heart."

Madeline handed off the last of her bags to waiting hands and hurried over to where Nathan was standing.

"Miss Evans, if I might have a word with you in private?"

She waved a hand over toward the open office door, "Sorry to steal your dinner date so abruptly Nathan. It's for a good cause."

Madeline spun once again, "Henry? Would you be so kind as to bring me my satchel? Lindsey, would you join us? This will only take a moment or two."

Nathan felt the warmth of Lisa's hand slide from his back as she disappeared into Nathan's old office with the other three Stewarts.

He shook his head, "Now what?"

Apparently, there would never be an end to the clots of secrecy when dealing with Madeline Stewart.

"Mr. Heart. Would you care to join me?"

Sibyl Bale took his hand and began to tug him toward the dining room.

"Running interference?" asked Nathan, looking over his shoulder at the closed office door.

"Running for the broiled shrimp before they all disappear," she whispered loudly. "Not all of us have an aversion to seafood."

Nathan chuckled at her honest gesture.

Once in the dining room, a few of the other family members actually made an attempt at light conversation, but Sibyl seemed to be hovering, keeping him occupied. She made no reference to or apologies for her absence over the course of the last several days.

"You seem a little preoccupied, Nathan."

"I have a lot of things on my mind," he nodded. "And I have a few questions for whoever will be in charge of this evening's session."

Nathan felt himself cringe inside when he realized that he had resorted to Madeline's method of asking an indirect question.

"I'm sure it can wait until after the holidays. Lindsey says that you're almost up to speed with both of us."

Nathan laughed openly, seconds before shoving an hors d'ouevre in his mouth, "According to her, I'm just starting the second grade."

Sibyl frowned, always careful before speaking her mind, "Lindsey likes to be first at all things, Nathan. She rarely likes to lose…, at anything. Even though she's somewhat enamored with you, she still sees you as her only worthy competition."

Sibyl froze into some sort of thoughtful repose, "You should be cautious that she doesn't playfully shove you into the mud, just to watch you flounder."

Nathan chewed thoughtfully, then sipped at his glass of wine.

One major question was answered immediately. Aunt Sibyl Bale had no concept of how advanced her niece Lindsey was or just how far she was willing to go to prove it. Lindsey's skills seemed only to be limited by her imagination, which was quite vivid.

Another question was raised. Was Lindsey truly enamored with him?

Madeline and her tight knit group bustled in the door with mixed expressions. Henry was his usual bright delightful self, greedily eyeing the bon vivant before him. In seconds, he had some of the elders around him chuckling in spite of their mastication.

Lindsey seemed to be closed off into some sort of swirl of thought, hiding. She glanced up at him for a moment and almost smiled, almost, before turning to answer a question from one of her less prolific aunts.

Madeline tapped Nathan on the shoulder and he twitched in surprise.

"Can I borrow you for a few moments? You can bring your food along if you like."

Nathan set down his plate of shrimp and calamari, knowing it would send her into a tailspin. With wine in hand, he followed closely behind Madeline.

After traversing the entire length of the living room, she opened the office door for a trailing Nathan. Inside, Lisa was quietly seated in a stiff little chair, her face unreadable.

Madeline shut the door behind them.

"The reason I brought you here Nathan, is that I've made an offer of employment to Miss Evans. However, she refused to give me an answer without speaking to you first and considering the parameters of this position, I agreed with her."

Of course…. That was why Lisa couldn't talk to him about her meeting with Madeline. The entire blasted mystery was about a job for the Stewart Clan, yet this was the woman Lisa had proclaimed crazy as a bat only days ago.

"I suppose I need a few weeks to find someone to replace you," said Nathan. "I'm not sure what to say, but congratulations."

Despite his best efforts, his rote sounded short and a bit angry.

Lisa was still mute, but looked strangely at Madeline as her mouth opened to speak, "Nathan…."

"Lisa's employment with me won't interfere with her employment with you," rushed Madeline. "It will however, require you to give her..., certain freedoms from time to time for travel."

Nathan carefully straightened his tone, "Lisa has always been free to do whatever she chooses. She's made quite sure of that."

Madeline's face flushed slightly, "I didn't expect this announcement to turn into a counseling session. Do you need to discuss this in private with Miss Evans or should I stay and mediate?"

Immediately angry with himself, Nathan let out a deep breath before continuing, "You'll have to excuse my outburst. Today as been one of the most trying days I've had in quite a while. Of course, Miss Evans can have all the leeway she needs to do whatever it is she'll be doing for you. I don't suppose I'll be privy to whatever that is, will I?"

"On the contrary, you'll know exactly what she's doing at any point in time," corrected Madeline. "Is that acceptable to you?"

Nathan looked at Lisa's questioned expression and nodded, "I wouldn't want to hold Lisa back from anything that might benefit her."

Madeline relaxed and pushed a stack of forms over the desk to Lisa, "Are you ready to go to work?"

Lisa seemed both pleased and hesitant, then began a sequence of initials and signatures across several pages of the employment document.

"Good," said Madeline, with a quick handshake. "Welcome aboard Miss Evans. Training begins this evening with Henry and I."

Nathan felt an immediate twinge of jealousy and just as quickly let it drop. Lisa had made no commitments to him, despite her occasional show of affection.

"I'll get you copies of your contract. Oh..., and don't forget this," said Madeline, handing a sealed manila envelope to Lisa.

Lisa's face lit like a bulb and she clasped yet another mystery to her chest with both hands.

Nathan stared in disbelief. The contents of the envelope must be the culmination of Lisa's change of heart toward Madeline Stewart.

♥

Madeline walked away from Nathan and Lisa, back toward her family gathering in the dining room. Lisa smiled energetically, turning in a pirouette with her frabjous prize high over her head.

"That your signing bonus?" asked Nathan.

"My freedom," she beamed. "I'll explain it all to you someday. If you'll be patient with me."

She stepped close to Nathan and looked up as if seeing him for the first time, "Can we skip the kippers and go for a walk?"

"What about your training?"

Lisa ignored the slight as if nothing in the world could ruin her secret celebration.

"Just to the road and back. We don't have to stay long. I want to see what it feels like to have a future."

Wasn't he offering her a future with his company? Whatever was in the envelope must be life altering, yet she wasn't ready to share it with him. Maybe this walk, asking him to be with her was her way of sharing her secret with him.

Disgruntled as he was, Lisa deserved whatever good was filtering her direction and he'd be hanged if he was going to spoil it. The last thing she needed was another Troy O'Bannon in her life.

"Better grab your heavy coat," grunted Nathan.

CHAPTER EIGHTY-TWO

LISA hurried down the seven front steps, swiping the fresh snow out of the stone lion's mouths. The air was damp with promises of a heavy flurry before morning and the temperature was already hovering just below the freezing mark.

Nathan swore he could feel the old clock in the vestibule sigh in approval as he walked past, as if it were a living entity.

Lisa waited for him and held out her hand, pulling Nathan close to her side, curling up against his arm. Her breath puffed out in steady fluff's of steam as they walked in silence.

Nathan rehearsed the entirety of the previous conversation in his head, still confused yet trying to share in Lisa's excitement. It was difficult for him to celebrate something he had no inkling of, but Lisa seemed happier than he'd ever seen her. Some unseen weight had been lifted and that was enough.

Half way down the drive, snow began to drift downward. The air was perfectly still, causing the flakes to hover as aimlessly as feathers around them.

"Nathan?"

"Hmm?"

"Thank you for believing in me."

Her grip on his arm tightened and Nathan took a deep breath. It was now or never.

"You shouldn't brag on me too quickly. I thought you left me today."

Lisa stopped dead in her tracks.

"The office was empty, your personal things were gone.... I nearly lost my mind until I saw you seated by the fireplace with Lindsey."

"I left you a note...."

He nodded, "That's the only thing that kept me sane after I tried to call you."

"That stupid cell phone.... You nearly lost your mind?"

Nathan ducked his head, feeling like an idiot for his childlike confession. "I don't know what I'd do if...."

Lisa's arms circled his neck, struggling on her tiptoes to reach his lips. Her head was swimming as she accepted that they actually might have something real together, now that the hovering threat of her past had been dealt with.

They kissed each other once again, after a brief contested stare into Nathan's troubled eyes.

His eyes did everything but put sound to the three magic words she'd never heard before. If he could be patient with her, she could be patient with him.

♥

Only the few sets of eyes seated near Madeline seemed to notice their late arrival to the informal meal. Several bottles of wine sat at the ready and conversation was light and cheerful.

Madeline raised her glass to Lisa with a nod when Nathan helped seat her chair closer to the table.

Their quick stop by the fireplace hadn't removed the rosy blush from their noses and cheeks, but had melted the snow into mist in their hair.

The long ebony table was nearly at capacity and Madeline had reserved two seats for them while she had taken a seat at the end.

Nathan was curious to notice that Sibyl had been casually demoted to the middle of the crowded table aside her husband and seemed all the more happy for it.

Henry and Lindsey were directly across from them, already in some light debate. Lindsey, closest to Madeline, "...and when did you plan on telling me that my old friend Clarissa was at the top of your dating list?"

Henry turned from his cheerful conversation, "I hadn't planned on telling you at all. You would have noticed on your own if you weren't so wrapped up in your own scheming. Clair tried to call you last week. She was one of Jon and Judith's bridesmaids in their wedding."

An instant plethora of expressions flashed across Lindsey and Madeline's faces.

"I hear they...," he grunted, "...had to get married."

"Henry, that's quite enough," muttered Madeline.

The food service arrived and Nathan took the opportunity to clasp Lisa's hand under the table. He could tell by the look in Lisa's eyes that he wasn't the only one saddened for Lindsey. She was hiding her devastation well, smiling carefully up at her server as her plate was set.

Other than simple sibling rivalry, Nathan couldn't fathom why Henry would be rubbing Lindsey's nose in her loss. They were after all a team, working together now, for the good of their family.

"I'll make sure and give Clarissa a call next week. I'm sure she'll be interested in your new responsibilities."

Lindsey smiled down at her plate and took a small bite. Her eyes glanced up at Lisa, then over at Henry as she chewed her tiny portion.

Henry snorted a laugh and turned back to his previous conversation, ignoring Lindsey altogether. It was grueling to watch brother and sister have at each other.

In that moment, Nathan knew exactly why he felt the need to help Lindsey, to console her woes. Aside from the obvious, that all *Sensitives* had a bond…, Nathan had always been Caroline's protector and consolation when they were attacked by the Big Three. Perhaps it was some combination of the two that made the urge to help Lindsey almost irresistible.

Their collective meal was over quickly and Madeline ushered the five of them into the library and closed the doors.

"Sibyl is on sabbatical for the next few weeks," she explained. "Lindsey, would you care to explain where you left off with Nathan's training?"

Everyone took a seat, Lisa close to Nathan, while Lindsey circled, looking somewhat restless.

"I'm afraid you'll need to take another seat, Lisa. Maybe over by Henry and Aunt Madeline? Being too close to a normal person can result in unpredictable results."

Lisa stood quietly, releasing Nathan's hand and moved to the couch between Henry and his aunt, while Henry shook his head in some sort of unexplained disgust.

"We just completed pinpointing a query into *Objects*," said Lindsey, finally answering her aunt. She failed to mention that the query was directed at live *Objects*. Lindsey took a seat on a tiny ottoman close to Madeline.

Nathan reached in his pocket and retrieved the crumpled notepad he'd been working with, "Before we get started, I have a quick question. I was going to ask Sibyl…."

He tossed the notepad to Madeline, bypassing Lindsey's suddenly outstretched hand.

"I spent some time practicing with that today. I'm sure you remember where it came from."

"Of course," nodded Madeline. "Were you alone at the time?"

It was very perceptive of her, however he ignored the obvious answer, "I noticed something that I've never come across before, not in all my sessions with Sibyl."

"Please explain."

"I seemed to run into dead ends that shouldn't have been there," said Nathan.

"There are limits to an *Objects'* attachments," spat Lindsey.

Nathan refuted her explanation, "It wasn't a limitation. I've seen those at least a hundred times in my exercises with Sibyl. I met with a sudden darkness where the information terminated. It had a..., velvet feel to it, like it had somehow been erased."

Madeline sat forward quickly, suddenly mortified, "Erased? Are you sure?"

"In several places. I can go around that piece of time, but I can't get to it from either direction."

"The notepad was probably damaged," huffed Lindsey.

Madeline looked strangely at her niece, "You know that wouldn't affect a *Reading* Lindsey. Can I keep this for a day or two Nathan?"

He nodded, reluctantly.

Madeline put it close beside her, "You've been warned not to try a *Reading* alone, Nathan. There's really nothing to be gained from searching out any information here. Your family is finally healing..., the sheriff has dropped his investigation."

Nathan didn't respond to how Madeline knew that, "So all's well that ends well? Stäkkr goes free? Just like that?"

Nathan happened to break his discourse with Madeline, long enough to see Lisa's eyes as round as fifty cent pieces.

"There would be repercussions," she added quietly.

"Stäkkr? That man that came by the office?" blurted Lisa. "What does he get away with? I don't understand?"

Lindsey chuckled, pulling her knees together with laced fingers, "Why Nathan. Have you been keeping secrets from your new *Handler*?"

Madeline's eyes went dull with anger as Nathan focused on Lindsey, "My *Handler*?"

"Why of course. I just assumed that Lisa told you about her new position in the Stewart Family Machine?"

Nathan snapped to Lisa seeing her sudden change.

"I was going to tell you tomorrow..., after I knew more," whined Lisa.

Madeline stood and addressed the situation, "Stop. Lindsey? Lisa was instructed not to discuss the details of her new position until I had a chance to talk to Nathan tomorrow at our meeting."

"Oops," said Lindsey, a sly grin appearing. "I guess some of us are just a little more open about ourselves than others."

Nathan's head swam with sudden forced memories. He remembered the vision of Lindsey's mind, the warm open expanse of who she was. Lisa had never offered anything but tiny glimpses of her private life.

"Henry, haven't you spent any time explaining Lisa's duties?" Lindsey continued.

"That's quite enough, Lindsey," barked Madeline.

"Why do I need a Handler?" spat Nathan.

Was this some ploy to keep her hooks in him for future use?

"Nathan, imagine being stuck in limbo for weeks until someone reports you missing or the unlikely event that your family might drop by to check on you," said Madeline. "It would make the twelve hours you spent in that urn seem like a picnic."

Nathan's eyes blinked in fear at that fresh memory.

Lindsey leaned into his field of vision, "There'd be no one to call me to rescue you."

Henry was leaning back on the couch, eyes closed and pretending sleep while fighting to hide a grin on his face.

"Henry. You too?" spat Madeline.

His eyes flew open, hands raised in faux innocence, "I haven't opened my mouth about any family business to anyone. I'm only enjoying the show."

Madeline looked old and tired when she sat down.

"I'm ashamed of both of you. God help us. To think our entire future family enterprise is hinging on the both of you."

Madeline snatched the notepad and waved it frantically in her niece and nephew's faces.

"Do you realize the implications of this? I had such high hopes, but both of you are acting like circus animals."

Henry stood, "I'm sorry Aunt Madey. Lisa and I can use the office. I'll give her a quick overview as a Handler."

"No," spat Madeline. "I need to speak to Nathan and Lisa alone now, thanks to the both of you. Please close the door on your way out."

Lindsey stood, winked at Nathan, then took her time leaving the library with Henry on her heels.

CHAPTER EIGHTY-THREE

"**I**F either of you wish to rethink your relationship with my family, I would completely understand."

Madeline Stewart was almost in tears..., she'd called for Sibyl who was seated close, holding her hand.

"Honestly? This is all too strange for me to make a decision," said Lisa. "If Nathan is still in..., then I guess I am too."

Madeline nodded, then looked to Nathan for his decision.

"I'm..., confused. I'm not exactly sure what's going on anymore and I've been sitting here day after day with both of you. I know you've offered me far more help than anyone else I've met, so I'm not ready to jump ship just yet."

Before Madeline could assume his answer was yes, "I have to ask though, are you sure that Henry and Lindsey are ready for the responsibilities you're asking of them?"

"In that respect, I'm afraid I'm the one that doesn't have a choice in the matter," said Madeline.

Now things were beginning to make some sense. It appeared that this concatenation between aunt, niece and nephew was unlovely on both ends of the arrangement. In effect, she was working with what she'd been given.

"I'm willing to stay on if you believe you can make some sort of peace with Henry and Lindsey."

Madeline wilted against her elder sister, "Good. Good."

Lisa leaned closer, tentatively forming her question, "Can you tell me what's going on with Lindsey? Maybe I can help."

Sibyl spoke quietly and slow, "You my dear..., you..., are what's going on."

Nathan closed his eyes in a silent groan. How could he have been so blind? Lindsey was jealous of Lisa.

"Me?" whispered Lisa. "I still don't understand?"

Sibyl looked at Nathan and grimaced an acknowledgment of their common understanding.

"It's late," muttered Madeline. "Tomorrow's Thanksgiving and we have a four p.m. meeting to prepare. You'll understand what you need to know afterward. I suggest we all adjourn and get some rest."

♥

"Lindsey is jealous of me!?"

"Ssshh," hissed Nathan. "This house has no secrets."

"But why? I mean…, she's so…, she's perfect, she's rich, she's smart and I'm just…. I'm just me."

Nathan chuckled, "Then you're just as blind as I was about Lindsey."

Lisa turned and propped her head in her palm, "Did I detect a compliment somewhere in there?"

"Yes…, absolutely."

Lisa frowned and flopped back down on her pillow, "I still don't understand. I mean…, she had you first. She's the reason I…, well I wasn't about to poach another woman's man."

"I explained that to you," grumbled Nathan. "More than once."

"Just like every other man playing both sides of the fence would have," she added.

"Maybe, but I was telling you the truth," he huffed.

Lisa lay quiet, staring at the ceiling.

"Speaking of the truth…," she sighed.

Lisa turned and pressed her bare feet against Nathan's hip, shoving his bulk off the edge of her bed.

"You need to get out. I need to sleep. This has been one mixed up day."

Nathan playfully bounced her bed with his palms as he hurried around to her open door. Lisa reached under her pillow and drew out the thick manilla envelope she'd received from Madeline.

"Here…," she said quietly. "Bedtime reading…, it's called, The Truth About Lisa."

Nathan stared at it blankly.

"Go on…, take it. I'm not going to read it to you."

He took it from her hand and leaned to kiss her goodnight but Lisa recoiled, holding him at bay with her fingertips.

"Oh no you don't…, not tonight. You do that and the whole house will be talking about us by morning. Now go before I change my mind."

MINUTES

♥

In his most comfortable chair, Nathan turned on his reading lamp and slipped open the envelope.

What looked like one thick bulk was in fact, several parts. On top was a certified copy of Lisa's birth certificate, her mother's photograph, a renewed copy of her Social Security Card, Drivers License, and an unused International Passport.

Next was a single page report of her minimal dealings with the IRS, then a multi-page report from the Michigan Department of Public Safety and Social Services.

Nathan sat back and inhaled at photographs of Lisa as a child, crime scene photos of her mother and father, detailed transcripts of courtroom testimonies, including the threats against her life.

The Child Protective Services report was colorful and painted a very sordid picture of an angry, decisive, and headstrong young girl. Words like, unruly, impudent, aggressive, destructive, withdrawn, secretive, were repetitive and common throughout the pages. Nathan saw no mention of drug use or immoral behavior, though a foray of intrusive tests were performed on Lisa J. Evans on a regular basis.

After rereading the court proceedings and subsequent attacks on her life as a teenager, he recognized that one descriptive adjective had been omitted. Lisa Evans was a survivor.

It took several minutes to reign in his self-loathing for every preconceived judgment he'd levied against her.

He picked up the last of a few other documents, an exhaustive diorama of Lisa's family tree, all the way back to the Iroquois Nation and Irish ancestry. It appeared that Lisa did have a few living third or fourth cousins scattered across the Midwest, with names and addresses.

Nathan yawned..., it was after midnight. About to stuff away the records of Lisa's history, a paper fell from the bottom of the stack. A scar faced black and white picture of a man with numbers across his uniformed chest peered up at him. Stamped on the document in red was, Not Eligible for Parole, then written in red ink - Mandatory Isolation for the remainder of sentence. No outside contact permitted.

It was signed by the Department of Justice, with a fresh notary crest crushed into the paper, dated that previous Monday.

This was the face of the murderer that had haunted Lisa Jess Evans her entire life. Forcing her to run, forcing her into isolation for most of her adult life. This was what Madeline Stewart had used to bargain with Lisa, for her silence as well as her gratitude.

He carefully placed all the information back in the envelope and set it on his nightstand. He had a string of careful apologies to consider for both Lisa..., and maybe for Madeline Stewart as well.

♥

"No Nathan. It's your turn to take him potty."

The familiar voice made him grin as he grasped the small hand of the towheaded toddler.

"Dad," spat up at him, apparently the first of his new vocabulary.

Nathan lifted the smiling boy just as he received a soft kiss on the cheek from his wife. Her blond hair swept against his chest, her arms wrapped around him with promises of what he could expect as soon as he completed his parental duty. Hands touching places only a lover or wife would recognize as appropriate.

Dizzying thoughts flooded his mind..., he wasn't married, there was no child..., his thoughts continued building their case.

"But there could be," whispered the soft voice. "And much more."

It was a dream..., a lurid dream, vivid in all aspects of reality, other than the truth.

"Lindsey?"

There was a soft sigh with more melting emotions and sliding hands. He'd never experienced a more lucid dream.

"Lindsey..., stop this."

"I know you want me...," the voice cooed.

"Lindsey..., this is wrong."

"I could make it right. We would be amazing together."

Swirls of mortal visions tempted him to the point of cloying lust.

"Stop it...," he said at last. "You know I have feelings for...."

"Lisa?" the voice answered in a whisper.

The face in his dream shifted into the perfect oval of Lisa's, complete with soft light brown hair, doves' eyes.

"I can look like her for you."

Nathan tried to free himself of the grasp of his nightmare, "No Lindsey. You are right. I do care for you. But not like this."

A harsh voice spat back, "I don't WANT you to see me as your SISTER."

"It's all I'm willing to offer you. I'd do anything for you..., but not this," argued Nathan. "I don't care for you that way."

"Not like you do Lisa," whispered the soft voice.

Nathan's heart broke for that voice, feeling the emotions being thrust upon him, the intensity of the loss was too much to conceive.

♥

The alarm clock beside his bed began to hiss loudly. Nathan scraped it off onto the floor, hearing it bounce and something break before going silent.

He bounded out of bed, threw on a robe and headed out of his room. His initial destination was across the hall, but was nearly bowled over by a wide-eyed Lisa hurrying his direction.

She suddenly seemed angry, her small hands drawn into little knotty fists.

"Is it true?" she spat.

Nathan reached out and took her by the shoulders, "Is what true?"

"Are you in love with Lindsey? Tell me!" she shook off his hands. "Tell me right now or I'll..., I'll...."

"No. Stop Lisa."

Instantly Nathan knew what had happened, "You had a bad dream, didn't you?"

He grasped her shoulders once again and Lisa calmed somewhat, her eyes batting furiously, still burning holes in him with waking eyes.

"It was only a dream, Lisa. You are the only person I'm in love with. No one else."

"But I couldn't have imagined it. It seemed so..., real. So...," she gasped. "You love me?"

His hands slid down her arms, "Without a doubt."

She slid closer, "Say it again."

"I love you."

"Again...," she whispered, melting against him.

♥

With Lisa at his side, Nathan knocked on Lindsey's bedroom door once again with no answer.

"Maybe she's not there."

Lisa jiggled the doorknob, but it was locked. She looked up at Nathan and shrugged.

Nathan blinked in thought, then touched the doorknob, relaxed his thoughts and took in a slow breath. Lindsey's hand was the last to grasp the brass knob, strong thoughts of her destination.

He looked over at Lisa, "Better get your robe..., and bring an extra. She's out on the front steps."

Outside, seated only in her thin nightgown, Lindsey's tears had pelted drops in the snow between her bare feet. The once docile wind was now shoving snowdrifts crisscross over the drive, swirling in unsettled directions.

Nathan brushed away the frozen white powder and sat beside her, after draping a thick houserobe across her shoulders. Lisa stood behind them, arms across her chest, shivering from the blustering cold.

"Will I ever be happy?"

Lindsey's heartbroken sobs were barely words.

"I'm sure you will Lindsey. Sibyl is like us..., she seems happy with her husband."

Her head turned to Nathan, "Was it so wrong of me..., to want something more?"

"No..., of course not. But you can't force something that wasn't meant to be."

Lindsey ducked her head, "You must despise me. After everything I've done..., what I tried to do. I'm so sorry about last night."

"You did that?" hissed Lisa. "You put that dream in my head? How did you do that?"

Lisa stepped back, "I knew it. That dream about Henry..., the first night I stayed here. You did that too didn't you?"

It was Nathan's turn to roll his eyes in disgust. Lindsey had been a busy girl since the first day she arrived.

Lindsey only nodded at first, "I'm sorry Lisa. I thought..., if you and Henry.... I like you..., so does Aunt Madey. I didn't want to run you off, but I hoped you'd see my brother in a different light."

"That wasn't likely. Henry might be my age, but he's still a..., a..., little spoiled brat," grunted Lisa.

Lisa stepped close to Lindsey, leaning in her ear, "Does Madeline know about this?"

Lindsey gasped and spun at the hip, "No..., no, she mustn't. Please."

"Alright then..., I can forgive you..., but you better promise right now to stay out of my head."

Lindsey nodded, then shivered violently, "Well..., I've had my pity party. I'd better go inside..., if my ass isn't frozen to this porch. I hate cold places...."

CHAPTER EIGHTY-FOUR

"**I**'M nervous," whispered Lisa.

"They're the same people you've been stumbling over every day," grunted Nathan.

"Well…, this is different, and you know it."

"Lindsey will you take Lisa to her room and make sure she's at least presentable?"

Lisa slapped Nathan's arm while Lindsey gave out an uproarious laugh, "I'll see what I can do…, considering what I have to work with."

"I hate you both!"

Both women exited Nathan's room, still grumbling at each other. Jealous enemies, now best friends…, it was an untenable situation.

Nathan slipped his black tie around his neck, deep in thought as his practiced fingers swept it into a bow. So many strange events in such a small amount of time…, how his life had been altered forever.

He slipped the jacket of his tuxedo around his shoulders, noting how it fit a little looser around the middle. Most of his clothes fit looser around the middle since his extended ordeal in a historic Slavic Urnfield barely a week ago.

Raking his fingers through his hair, he wished he'd listened to Lisa and had it trimmed last Monday. At the time, he was in no mood to let someone near him with a pair of clippers.

A tap on his door and a glance at his watch reminded him it was almost time to meet downstairs for polite mingling before dinner.

The rubbing of elbows he could handle, the dinner he could handle, it was the unknown of Madeline's meeting that had him preoccupied.

He took a deep breath, one last look of encouragement in the mirror, and left for downstairs.

All the elder family members were holding flutes of light colored liquid, wine or champagne, and milling about just as he'd imagined them. All in their finest pomp, each looked like a throwback to a different era when men and women dressed in their finest before stepping outside their door.

Madeline swept over to where he stood at the bottom of the stairs and gathered him at the arm. The diamonds swirling at her earlobes were dazzling flames, brighter than the polished crystal of the chandelier.

"Nathan…, I have a couple of gentlemen I'd like you to meet."

She tugged him gently toward the two new faces he'd seen at Madeline's arrival last evening. The two men were dressed in similar formal attire, serious faces, deep in conversation.

Both of their expressions relaxed as Madeline stepped closer.

"Nathan I'd like you to meet Senator Wortham of Delaware and Congressman Hanneman of Iowa; this is Nathan Heart."

They shook hands in turn, smiling with politically correct measures, and complimenting Madeline for their accommodations.

Nathan's radar went on instant alert. What were two high-ranking politicians doing here in the middle of nowhere, instead of with their families and friends on Thanksgiving Day?

When they walked away, Nathan looked around for some sort of armed attaché anchored at the wall or in a corner. The only person he saw that looked vaguely out of place was humble Bolton, standing near the front door, in an older looking tuxedo, with hands clasped. It would have been easy to imagine the lump underneath his breast pocket as a service model Beretta.

Madeline gave his arm a little jiggle, "Relax Nathan, they're here for our meeting this afternoon."

"That's supposed to make me relax?" he asked.

Bolton caught his eye and tipped his head with a quick grin.

"I suppose not, but you should get used to such personalities in the future."

She looked around at the faces in a careful sweep, "I don't see your date. Miss Evans didn't get cold feet at the last minute did she?"

Nathan was still pondering why he should get used to hobnobbing with elite politicians, "I think the two women are working on being fashionably late."

"Oh…, here they come," she muttered. "And none too soon."

Nathan glanced to the top of the stairs where Lisa and Lindsey were having some last second discussion, then began to descend together.

Elegant as two smoky-eyed debutant starlets, both women's hair was pulled up high in curls, carefully watching each step downward.

Lindsey was in a blood red sleeveless dress with a careless plunge, its muted train sweeping the steps behind her; bright blond hair clashing elegantly against her choice of colors.

Lisa was adorning her midnight blue dress, a perilous smile on her full crimson lips. Her hair cascaded in playful curls as she spun to offer some unheard comment to Lindsey, who was steadying her arm.

Once locked on, Nathan's eyes couldn't shake from watching every cautious step she took downward. Seconds later, his head swam with his own personal torment.

"Nathan? I see your vertigo has returned."

He swallowed and looked down at Madeline, seeing her mouth move, but waiting for the words to reach his ears. Finally, all of them hit him at once.

"Why don't you go escort your date to the dining room? The bell just sounded."

He felt her squeeze his arm and give him a gentle push toward the stairs.

Nathan hurried over, gathering both the women on an arm apiece, praying that the spins didn't interfere with his balance on the way to the dining room.

"Well?" hissed Lisa.

Nathan breathed slowly and looked at her cautious face, then nodded, "You're beautiful."

Anything more than that would have been tempting fate and apparently, those were the right words, because she smiled up into his face. That was when he noticed Marion's gold cameo pinned to the front of her dress.

Seeing the pendant displayed on Lisa's heavily gathered upper bodice carried a certain warmth he hadn't felt in many years. It was with much difficulty that he resisted the compelling urge to kiss his date..., brush a finger across her smooth face.

Composing himself, he quickly complimented both women and helped them to their prearranged seating.

Henry gave him a quick shake of the hand and a warm smile, when Lindsey took her seat beside him. As childish as Henry was, he'd had no part in Lindsey's plotting and scheming. Still, it would have been hard to hold a grudge against his childish impudence.

He and Lisa filled the next two seats along the table.

Two enormous golden brown turkeys were at either end of the setting, the rest of the expanse lined with an array of traditional vegetables and delicacies. Nathan's first thoughts were of his family, how he missed the closeness they once shared..., once upon a time.

Lisa patted his arm, then took his right hand about the same time Lindsey clasped his left. One of the Stewart elders stood and offered an eloquent prayer over the food and family, one that deepened Nathan's childhood memories.

Dinner itself was mostly unremarkable except for the constant attention of Lisa, her playful conversation, and the light atmosphere of all company present. Indeed, it was Lisa that kept him from falling into a melancholy stupor, centering his thoughts elsewhere…, on her. He'd only seen her this happy one other time…, when she held the manila folder in the air and spun, celebrating her freedom. Her eyes flashed at him with such intensity, it was hard for him to hear or see anyone else around them.

"For those of you that have room for desert, you may remain seated," said Madeline. "Some of us need an intermission. Please remember to reassemble in the den at four o'clock sharp."

She and a handful of others arose from their seats and disappeared into the cavern of the house, while the rest ogled over Sara's decadent creations.

♥

Several sectional tables had been brought into the den, the ends linked together to form a thin rectangular line around the room. To augment the sparse room for seating, even the hearth cover was in place over the front of the fireplace.

The conclave was alive with chatter, some attendees daring to cast a wary glance at the bound stack of paper in front of them.

"Nathan? Aren't you nervous?" asked Lisa.

It was five minutes before the hour and he looked at his watch once again, "A little."

He'd felt that same vertigo wash over him time and time again, usually when he concentrated his attention on Lisa Evans. Wasn't his vertigo supposed to be avoided when he was near someone he cared deeply for?

"A little…," she hissed. "My hands are shaking and I can't figure out why."

"They aren't going to execute us," he said with a grin. "We're guests remember?"

"So were the Thanksgiving turkeys. What if they ask me something?"

Nathan chuckled, "Your name is Lisa Evans. If you get confused you can read it from the card in front of you."

She spat his thigh softly with her palm, fighting away a grin, "I'm serious."

"Honesty is a virtue, but it's always appropriate to say, I don't know."

Albert Stewart stood and walked to the end of the room, speaking quietly to Madeline, after which Bolton walked in and closed the door behind him. One of the elder ladies took a seat in the corner where Bolton had come to rest. She switched on a stenotype, preparing to take the minutes of the meeting.

"Family, friends, associates, welcome to the Stewart Family's 270th annual board meeting.

We especially want to welcome our special guests, Nathan Heart, and our newest associate Lisa Evans."

A few smiles and comments were cast their direction before Albert continued. Nathan glanced over at Madeline..., wondering why she wasn't the spokesperson.

Albert's portly body danced anxiously as he had everyone turn to the first page of the report in front of them.

Section by section, references were made to certain holdings, businesses, and funds. Most were performing in the black, a select few were lagging and thus voted upon to liquidate or rehabilitate.

It was a traditional corporate meeting..., boring unless it happened to be your hundred million dollar business that was weighed in the balance. Votes were cast, tourniquet's applied, and after every considerable holding was discussed, the meeting was closed. Almost a trillion in assets covered in just under an hour.

"A transcription of the minutes will be couriered to your offices within the week," said Albert.

The stenographer tore off the end of her ticker tape and carefully wound it up for future replication, then inserted a new roll of paper.

"That's it?" whispered Lisa.

One of the family members was taking up the booklets from around the room, while replacing it with a smaller black folder.

"Surely not."

Albert Stewart took a seat and his brother George ambled forward with his cane to center stage.

When the last of the folders were exchanged, George addressed the group.

"Will the Trifecta Consortium please come to order."

George had the voice of a foghorn and the room quickly quieted. Evidently, this was where Henry inherited his genetic makeup.

"As we have quite a bit of new business to discuss, I'm reminded that our two guests are on a tight schedule, so without any more pomp, first please welcome Senator Wortham."

The Senator, which Nathan had briefly chatted with, stood and hurried forward.

"For the record, please present your request before the council."

Wortham nodded, and handed out a single page leaflet to the circle of dour faces.

"First of all, thank you for seeing me on such short notice. It has recently been brought to my attention that there is the possibility I have a mole within my advisory staff. I've taken the usual precautionary measures, but sensitive information has still managed to leak beyond the boundaries of my office.

"We've done the usual tests and sweeps for electronic devices, which leads us to the conclusion that it is a staff member.

"Normally, we handle this sort of problem internally, with such tactics as misinformation, but the true information in question seems to be filtering its way into the hands of rogue leaders in a few Middle Eastern and Central American countries.

"I've been authorized to ask for your assistance in pinpointing this mole…, as quickly as possible."

Albert shoved on his cane and stood to address the Senator.

"Did you bring the required *Objects* with you?"

"I did. They are in your Containment Facility."

"All in favor?"

The room raised their hands, then lowered them.

"Motion is passed. You'll be hearing from our contact within the week."

Wortham looked physically relieved and quickly gathered his things to leave.

Nathan felt his jaw fall slack and remembered to take a deep breath.

"Congressman Hanneman, welcome to our meeting. Please come forward and state your case for the record."

Congressman Hanneman looked as if the weight of the world suddenly fell on his shoulders as he explained that a member of the Secret Service, an operative in Asia, had gone missing. This person, no mention of gender, was supposed to have reported to their safe house in Hong Kong over a week ago, but hadn't been heard from since leaving Beijing.

When asked about the required *Objects*, he said that they would arrive by courier from China within a day, along with the pertinent information.

All hands approved the task and Congressman Hanneman, along with Senator Wortham exited the meeting, followed closely by Bolton.

Albert Stewart lifted his shaky cane toward Henry, "That's the last time I'm doing your job young man. I never have been much of a factotum."

"Sorry he wasn't prepared Albert, I've had Henry occupied," muttered Madeline.

After a protracted period of silence and listening to the incessant whir of the idling stenotype, Bolton reappeared and closed the door.

For the most part, Nathan and Lisa sat in total shock, barely nudging each other, as opposed to blurting something they'd regret having spoken…, and meticulously recorded.

With a nod of Bolton's head, Madeline stood and addressed the group.

CHAPTER EIGHTY-FIVE

As soon as the opening minutes were read, then the cryptic highlights of the last meeting, Madeline put everything aside and looked around the room at the group.

"Mr. Heart, before we begin our new business, I feel the need to apologize for the rushed manner in which you were introduced to so many radical extremes. Let me assure you it was for good reason you were placed under such regrettable duress; time was of the essence.

Please let me introduce you to the Trifecta Consortium's steering committee, which consists of three interconnected families.

Adelaide and Percy represent the Godwin family from Great Britain, Yvette and Carmen represent the Lamborghini family..., and wish to keep their origins private for the moment. Bolton Krae you already know..., is our multitalented chief security officer for the combined Consortium. The rest of us you are familiar with and it would be redundant to make introductions.

The reason you were allowed to witness the preliminaries was to assure you which side of the line the Trifecta Consortium stands on. We are not a subversive organization or cabal, working for the highest bidder, but you'll both get a booklet explaining our standards and operations at the end of this meeting.

Now..., I will attempt to answer your questions in what I hope to be a chronological order, with the help of the others seated here."

The box of questions in Nathan's mind remained closed, waiting for any of this to make sense.

"As you all know, I ran across an exclusive advertisement by a fellow that scouts for our group, Renaldo Lucas. He seems to have an ear for finding gems we may be interested in. When we saw the images of your advertisement, with your old clock in the background, Sibyl knew right away that we needed the property for our next stronghold."

Madeline raised her hand at Nathan's open mouth, "Please let me finish before you ask your myriad of questions."

Sibyl handed a printed photograph to her husband, which quickly made the circle into Nathan's hands. It was one of the pictures of Heart Manor from the website, with the clock in the vestibule. Nathan was about to set it   down,   when   Madeline   continued.

"Take a very good look at the photo Mr. Heart, specifically at the glass insert on the side of the clock."

Nathan held it up, shifting it underneath the beam of one of the recessed overhead lights. His chest thumped heavily as he glanced back up at Madeline.

"Marion…," he whispered.

It had gone completely unnoticed due to the many stressful circumstances; however, the transparent silhouette of her face was unmistakable in the clocks side panel.

Madeline nodded, "Yes…, and unfortunately Sibyl's trained eye wasn't the only one to see the image before we had Mr. Lucas remove it from his listing."

Nathan sat back and let her continue unabated.

"You can imagine our surprise when we arrived and discovered that not only was there a *Guardian* in this home, but a very reluctant *Sensitive* as well.

Sibyl duly noted your much-needed reasons for fleeing the premises as soon as it was sold. So once again, without being redundant, I won't explain how we organized a few circumstances to assure you would stay. For your own safety, we had to move things along at a brisk pace."

Nathan fidgeted, not willing to allow certain epiphanies to go unanswered, "My safety? The spy wasn't watching me. That much I figured out from the notepad. Who was he?"

"Patience, Mr. Heart. Your sister, Caroline Masters didn't arbitrarily win an all expenses paid cruise by accident either. We needed to nudge you in the right direction as quickly as possible. Unfortunately, the circumstances surrounding your elder siblings were none of our doing. We merely used their avarice to our benefit."

Once again, Nathan sat back, his head reeling.

Sibyl spoke up, seemingly out of turn, retracing Nathan's comment, "Out of curiosity, how did you get that information from that fellow's notepad?"

Nathan shrugged, "I read it. It was a simple cypher."

He was going to ask about the blank spots when Madeline prevented another interruption by her sister.

"As you surmised, the deceased was originally contracted to another organization...."

"Ethos...," barked Nathan, suddenly feeling tired, misled, and outright lied to. "Is that one of your competitors?"

He had finally struck a nerve; it was Madeline who was quiet for a few shocked moments.

"And where have you heard that name before?"

Nathan pointed, "From Bolton."

"You couldn't have heard it from me," argued Bolton.

"When you were interrogating that fellow Smith, behind the garage, the night you caught him. I saw it from the notepad's history. It was still on Smith at the time."

Madeline looked at the worn notepad on her table, then sternly at Lindsey. She had been a fly on the wall, sitting in silence during all the proceedings.

"Lindsey dear, is that true?"

When there was no response except for a rosy flush on Lindsey's face, "My bright young niece, our resident cleaner, was supposed to have removed that information from this notepad as well as the blank spots you discovered, Nathan."

Madeline sauntered over to where her niece was sitting in silence and dropped the notepad in front of Nathan.

Nathan grinned smugly as he stuffed it in his side pocket. Deception was circling him like flies. Evidently, Lindsey's speed was not always the right way to get things done. Thankfully for him, Lindsey had skipped through the information like a spinning stone on top of still waters.

"Ethos..., will have to be explained at a later date," said Madeline as she walked away. All seemed forgiven between her and Lindsey when she dropped the subject.

"Then they must have been the other group that saw the website listing for Heart Manor," said Nathan.

"You're jumping ahead again, but yes..., that's true."

Nathan shook his head, unwilling to wait for her circuitous explanations to answer his questions.

"What about Stäkkr? What did he have to do with any of this?"

Madeline's shoulders slumped at his lack of patience, "Jealousy..., greed..., but we believe that he's been contacted by a member of Ethos, after his unfortunate dealings with our dead Mr. Smith."

"Then he was the one that killed Smith?"

"Let's just say, Stäkkr knows who did..., and why. Fear for your life and loved ones can be a weighty advantage to blackmail. A person might be shoved into doing things they might never have considered. It would be wise of you to avoid any future interaction with Mr. Stäkkr, unless it could be molded to our advantage."

Nathan laughed, "So my life was turned upside down, all because of an advertisement I put on a website."

"Let's not forget that it was to your advantage, Mr. Heart. It would only have been a matter of time…, a very short time I might add, before you would have been suffering from deliriums you had no way of comprehending. At the rate your decline, you would have been institutionalized in under a year."

Nathan felt his gut clench before answering quietly, "I haven't forgotten."

Lisa raised her hand like a child in a classroom, "I'm almost scared to ask…, but what did I have to do with any of this?"

Madeline waved a hand to her sister Sibyl, "That is still as much a mystery to us as it is to you Miss Evans. You seem to have some inexorable tie to Nathan that I haven't been able to understand yet. When I discovered that someone was contracted to do you bodily harm, we had no choice but to intervene."

Lisa sat back quietly, realizing that her life had been hanging on a precipice, saved by some random chance that Nathan Heart cared for her. If Nathan had looked the other way….

Nathan was suddenly livid, aghast that Lisa had ignored the obvious question, "Someone is contracted to kill Lisa?"

"Was…," corrected Madeline. "As you noticed earlier, we have a large web of resources at our disposal. Miss Evans in no longer in any danger…, at least not from her past."

♥

Madeline handed Nathan and Lisa a slider bound packet apiece. Inside were photos and descriptions of properties from all across the United States, Canada, Mexico, as well as a few properties dotted in South America.

Most of Nathan's questions had been answered, to the best of Madeline's abilities. Even though Nathan still had a few nagging thoughts, they were mostly incidentals that could be answered in due time.

The interaction with high-ranking government officials was mostly self-explanatory, but worthy of some future investigation.

"One of our original strategies for purchasing this property was to incorporate your help with liquidating our spent Strongholds."

She had explained that their United States based operation used older inauspicious homes with auspicious value, mined them for their worth, then moved as soon as it was suspected they were being observed. If time permitted and there were no blatant attacks against their privacy by the mysterious Ethos, they would reinforce and renovate the property into what they referred to as a Stronghold.

Rarely did they get to stay in one location for more than one year before someone began asking questions that raised key concerns. They would move their current inventory to storage and look for the next potential base of operation.

"These properties have remained in the financial control of one of our shell corporations too long and our enemies may soon discover our previous holdings. We don't like to leave financial or paper trails, as you can imagine.

What we wish to do is turn these properties as soon as we leave them. Convert them into new ownership or into holdings with someone such as yourself who is free and clear of our family enterprise."

Nathan's eyes glanced over to Lisa, "Looks like your job security just went off the scale."

"Miss Evans has new responsibilities now…, more important ones that she still needs training for. As your Handler she is to insure your safety from becoming locked into an *Object,* which isn't as uncommon as you might think."

There were too many hidden assumptions lurking with that statement. One of which was his real need for a daily assistant and licensed partner.

"But Lisa is…," spat Nathan.

"Still under your employ…, helps you with your sales and buy's your morning coffee from that quaint little shop next to Heart Realty."

Nathan nodded and relaxed somewhat. He flipped through the folder making a mental estimate of the forty odd properties inside.

"It's going to take me some time to get the investment funding I'll need to take these properties out of your portfolio. I don't have the ready assets for all these."

"Mr. Heart, you sat in our board meeting…. We own several banking and lending institutions. A few in Portland and Seattle would be instantly available with one phone call from our attorney. And of course our private Tax Attorney will do your taxes from now on as well."

Nathan dropped the folder, "You have all this planned down to the cent. Why me? Why not someone else?"

"Anonymity, Mr. Heart. A rolling stone gather's no moss. Your realty business is established, respected. As our unofficial holding company, it shouldn't raise any eyebrows or set off any alarms among prying eyes. Think of Heart Realty as our…, property launderer. It's important that they disappear from our control as quickly as possible.

Please understand, should concrete evidence of what we do for our country reach the wrong ears, it would cause chaos among a few unsavory third world governments. It's in our government's best interests to help keep our group as something of the imagination.

Should your talents ever come to light..., it would be unsettling to say the least. One of Miss Evan's new duties will be to assure that something like that doesn't happen. I assure you she will be well trained and have the Stewart family's full resources at her disposal at all times."

Nathan raised his hands in submission, "Alright. When do we have to give you an answer?"

"You have until after this evening's meal to consider our offer and make your decision. We all hope you make the right choice."

CHAPTER EIGHTY-SIX

LISA'S hands were shaking, her voice quivering as she sat trying to hold a cup of tea.

Her view out the front picture window was spectacular as heavy clouds spread a flurry of white over everything in sight. She wished that the magic just beyond the glass panes wasn't tainted by the decision she was facing.

"Are you happy with what we're about to do?" asked Nathan.

"I don't know what I am. I'm scared shitless and your sitting there like this kind of stuff happens every day."

Nathan inched closer to Lisa, placing his arm around her back, "We both traded a nearly fatal past for the futures we've been offered.

Lisa..., I still need to know if you understand how much time we're going to be spending with each other."

"Why do you think I'm so scared?" she hissed.

She turned quickly, looking at Nathan's hurt expression.

"I didn't mean that the way it sounded."

Lisa set down her rattling cup and kissed his cheek, "I just imagined that we would take things a little slower..., between us."

"We still can..., as slow as you like."

"You mean that don't you?"

"Of course I do."

Lisa shook her head, puffing out the breath she was holding, "You're the most patient man I've ever met."

♥

Nathan left Lisa seated on the huge couch alone with her thoughts. He still needed a few more answers to his questions before he consigned his future and possibly Lisa's to a very unknown trek.

Once in his room, he decided to commit the unpardonable and try one last Reading alone. He slipped the notepad Madeline had returned out of his pocket and took his favorite chair.

Before he began, he sat quietly, rehearsing every detail that had been spoken during both meetings. If there was some gaping deception, it wasn't readily evident. It appeared that the Trifecta Consortium was exactly what it claimed.

A slow breath later, notepad in hand, his thumb on the last page, the vision opened. Working slowly backward, he watched himself and Bolton on the front porch. Then time jumped back to where Bolton was questioning Smith, skipping over a blackened snip of time. Bolton was about to ruin the peeping tom's sciatic nerve with a swift kick to the leg.

Curious…, Nathan released himself from the *Object*, pushing himself toward Bolton. He'd seen Lindsey do this…, and much more. The forced contact with the living memories had a stretchy-sticky texture as he invaded Bolton's past. The web sprang softly in his touch as memories came to life. Bolton was standing in an office with an emblem on the floor, peering down. As he raised his head, former President Clinton had just draped a Medal of Valor over his neck.

An act of unselfish duty was rewarded with Presidential congratulations while on the President's personal detail.

It was surreal to be viewing a place Nathan knew he would never stand, yet it was as real as his own bedroom.

Pushing backwards, he saw Bolton in scenes of military training, skirmishes of live armed conflict, then academic training for the Secret Service. Nathan experienced Bolton's tired body pushing past the pain of rigorous training in several styles of combat. Amazed, Nathan felt the fluid peace of performing rehearsed Kata for his Sensei and fellow classmates.

Nathan carefully freed himself from the vision of Bolton…, he was exactly who he claimed he was and much more.

Suddenly tired, Nathan had one last venture to pursue…, the darkness.

Lindsey was supposed to erase that piece of recorded time, but instead, she'd blackened over it…, smeared it…, covered it like words in a redacted document. If his guess was right, that meant the information was still there underneath it all.

When he reached that piece of time, he pushed, pulled, even kicked at it with his mind with no results. It was pitch black and velvety soft, yielding to his attacks, yet unwavering.

Something Sibyl had said once kept trying to reach out, almost annoying, like a constant tapping on the shoulder.

"…you're accustomed to looking at the world with your natural eyes. What we do, what you'll have to learn to do, is feel around in the dark and see things with the light that's inside you."

"Light...," whispered Nathan.

With an outstretched ethereal hand that looked nothing like his own, a glowing flicker danced through transparent skin. He slid into the blackness, pierced the darkness, and cautiously stepped through.

A wealth of time appeared as he watched and listened to things he didn't want to hear, wished he'd never heard..., then....

"Lindsey! What have you done?"

Nathan grasped the notepad with both hands in a death grip, pinpointing his queries to every point of darkness along the timeline and dove into each one, scouring the information.

With a violent leap, he stood from his chair and looked out the window onto the snow below gathering his thoughts, then threw the notepad to the floor. Lisa..., where was Lisa?

Three steps at a time, he lurched down the stairs, looking over the alarmed heads of the lingering family.

The couch where he left her was empty, the teacup still where she left it.

"Where's Lisa Evans?" he blurted.

"Nathan? What's wrong?" asked Madeline, following Nathan over to the grand couch.

"Has anyone seen Lisa? Is she...," he cut off his violent rant and placed a hand on the couch where Lisa had been seated barely a half-hour before.

Racing toward the front door, he said a quick prayer, then flung it open to the white expanse of the yard. Two small sets of fresh snow-filled tracks were headed toward the garage.

Nathan sprinted to the middle door and snatched it open. Lisa had been headed to her car, to sit in privacy..., her choice of solitude. A place where she could make an unclouded decision about her future.

The big green Buick's driver side door was standing open, the dome light glaring, but the car was empty.

"Lisa!"

Nathan's voice echoed through the long garage.

He strummed angrily through his hair, trying to force some calm into his thoughts. Where would she be?

In his visions he'd seen the unthinkable..., John Smith was angry..., but not at Nathan or Bolton that night. He was angry at his partner, standing in the distance watching him being subdued by Bolton.

Sheriff Ben Kern had been right from the beginning, there was an accomplice.

Halloween night, when the security system was going wild with movement, that same man was running through the second floor in a fury, due to the hurling pumpkin brigade out front.

That day the service technician was scratching his head at the belligerent security nodes, he was not alone in the house. The man was a skilled reconnaissance expert and assassin. He was also John Smith's anonymous source of information for some strange group.

In that last segment of darkness, this unnamed man had singled out Lisa as his target, his leverage for information.

"Ethos...," whispered Nathan.

"Lisa!"

Nathan was about to run back toward the house, then happened to notice Lisa's purse in the seat of the car. Rushing a hand along the seat, he saw the unthinkable. A bruising hand had slipped around her throat and was dragging her away....

The metal hinges to the back garage door flew apart as Nathan's shoulder hit it at a dead run. There were tracks in the snow..., two sets, one set walking, one set being dragged.

He hurried along as quickly as he could, not considering what would happen when he caught up to a trained killer.

Stopping only once to catch his breath, he heard Lisa arguing and the loud smack of a palm on skin, then a muffled shriek.

She wasn't far away. Brushing away snow laden spruce, he struggled through the tightening thicket, suddenly realizing they were headed to a bend in the nearby road.

If they reached the road.... If there was a waiting vehicle....

A sudden thrust of limbs and Nathan was barely ten feet away from a struggling Lisa and her attacker. Her long dress was shredded from her fearful resistance and her flailing high heels, as she fought her assailant every step of the way. A high bruise on her pale cheek, blood on her bottom lip, she was wrenching against the hand that held her wrist.

Nathan lunged forward, just as the man from his previous visions saw him coming.

A pistol arose from his side, directly in Nathan's face and he threw Lisa to the ground with a swift sling of his other hand.

"Let her go."

The man grinned. His face was surprisingly ordinary, plain. Average height, dark hair..., average in everyway, totally unremarkable. Except for the gun he was holding.

He could have been seated in the coffee shop every morning and Nathan would have never given him a second thought.

"I'm afraid she's coming with me."

Nathan saw Lisa's bruised face, quiet from shock, trying to crawl backwards on her elbows through the snow in her long formal dress. All common sense left his thought processes and a sudden peace poured inside.

"Take me..., I'm really what you're after," said Nathan.

Nathan relaxed and stood upright, no longer in the threatening linebacker's crouch from moments before.

The man glanced at Lisa, "I'll have more fun transporting her."

Nathan grinned, "She'll claw your eyes out."

His feet inched closer, barely a movement, barely noticeable.

"Maybe, but she'll talk more…, freely."

He raised the semi-auto higher and snapped back the hammer with his thumb.

Without realizing his own actions, Nathan's left foot twisted down through the snow as an anchor and his right snapped upward in a quick fluid motion kicking the gun just as it discharged into the air.

One moment later, the gun was sailing into an embankment of snow, and his opponent was coming at him.

As if in slow motion, the attackers right hand came out, fingers locked and pointed, aimed upward into Nathan's throat.

Some new automatic reaction was taking place…, some sort of flow taking over as Nathan shifted easily to the side. His right hand grasped the attacker's wrist, thrust him off balance to his right, while Nathan's left hand grappled this innocuous person by the nerve complex under his right arm. Nathan swept the attackers nearest leg, and pushed him face down into the snow with a loud huff of exhausted air.

Before Nathan comprehended what he was doing, the attacker's arm was pinned behind his back to the point of breaking.

Suddenly, someone was calling Nathan's name from behind him, repeatedly, softly, quietly, carefully bringing him down from some adrenaline rush. Nathan had already heard the gristle in his targets' elbow and shoulder crunch loudly as sounds began to trickle into his pounding ears. His left hand was clutched in a claw-like grip on the base of the man's neck, carefully crushing.

"Nathan…," warbled into his head, and he turned.

Bolton was standing over him, gun drawn, "You can let him go now…, he's down. It's over."

Nathan looked down at the unconscious man, felt his knee purposely digging into the man's spine, the pleasure of giving him pain.

All that was left was a little more pressure from the fingers on his left hand and he could stop.

"Nathan? Look, I'm putting away my gun. It's over."

Nathan heard the words penetrate his thought process and swallowed. His left hand released its grip moments before he crushed the ganglion, separated the spinal column and ended a life.

Reality clarified and he dropped the limp broken arm in his grip and stood, Bolton offering him his hand.

♥

Lisa was crying…, not from her ordeal, her swollen cheek or cracked lip, but from her shredded dress. She was poured against Nathan's overheated body as he held her tight.

"I'll get you to a doctor as soon as we get back to the house."

Lisa shook her head…, as her sobs ended, "I'm fine, just bruised. I hate emergency rooms. Besides, I've survived worse than this."

Nathan kissed the top of her head, "Don't ever do that to me again."

Bolton was turning the unconscious man over, looking for identification.

"You did a helluva job on him. I didn't know you were Special Ops, Heart. What outfit were you with?"

Nathan looked at him blankly and shook his head, "I've never served."

Bolton grinned, "Yeah, keep your story straight. In the mean time, we need to drag him back up to the house and call support. You just disabled your first Ethos agent."

Lisa gasped, making both men jump, scanning the area with their eyes.

"My pendant…, it's gone!"

She circled looking at the thousand tracks in the snow.

"No…," she whispered.

"I'll get you another," said Nathan. "Let's get you back inside, you're freezing."

"No…, it won't be the same…, it was your mother's."

"Alright then Handler, stand still and I'll see what I can do."

Nathan laid his hand over the ripped spot on the front of her dress, where her prized pendant had been attached. Lisa placed both her hands on top of his and leaned against him.

Reliving the scene of the attack was difficult, but watching the brutality of Lisa's ordeal was much worse. After what seemed a lengthy ordeal, he saw the little gold and black cameo fly to the ground. The last snow-burdened limb she'd been shoved through was the culprit.

He opened his eyes and smiled, walked straight to the dot in the snow merely feet away and lifted up the pendant.

In an instant, Nathan's world turned into a circling drain of vertigo and he plummeted to the ground.

CHAPTER EIGHTY-SEVEN

"**N**ATHAN...**, son?"

"Mother? What happened? Where am I?"

"You took a spill. You'll be fine."

Nathan didn't know if this encounter was real or imagined, but if there was the slimmest chance....

"I'm sorry I didn't wake up...."

"Now you hush..., clumsy me tripped over my house shoes in the dark. It was over as soon as I hit my fool head. Didn't feel a thing really."

"I miss you," he whispered. "Caroline and I miss you. I made a real mess of things."

"Mmm, that Josephine had something to do with it I'm sure."

"I don't know how to fix it."

"You leave that up to me and get on with your life."

"I'm trying."

"Tell Caroline I said it was good to see her. Tell her to quit worrying about being pregnant at her age. She'll be just fine."

"Does Chris know?"

He felt the smile on his mother's face as she winked, "Just us. Now you get back to taking care of things. You still have the family treasure after all."

Nathan felt himself smile at her reference to the old clock.

"She's a pretty thing isn't she?"

"I..., suppose so."

"Suppose? She's the best little girl I could find on the west coast."

"You mean Lisa?"

There was laughter, his mother's laughter he hadn't heard in over a year, "You didn't think I was still talking about that clock did you?"

She laughed once again…, "Now you take good care of her…, make me proud. Give me and Jonas some grandkids."

Nathan felt warm lips kissing his face.

"Marion?"

There was more laughter, "I'm not your mother, you fainting goat."

Lisa pushed his head off her lap as Nathan made sense of his surroundings. Bolton and Henry were lifting their groaning prisoner, readying to drag his uncooperative feet to the house.

Nathan jumped up, carefully grabbed Lisa by the arm, "Come on…, hurry, come with me now."

Lisa looked around in terror, expecting some other attacker to pounce from behind the thicket of bruised evergreens.

"Nathan…, slow down."

Nathan spun and lifted her in his arms, holding her close, legs still pumping at a blistering pace toward the house.

"What's got into you?"

"If there's a *Guardian* to the house, there must be something to guard."

"What? Did you hit your head on the ground?"

Nathan hurried up the steps and set Lisa down by the door, where a drove of faces were waiting for answers.

"Lisa dear…, are you okay?" whined an older voice.

He rushed past the onlookers, Lisa still in tow, and sat flat on his rear in front of the old antique clock. His mud stained tuxedo groaned as he urged Lisa closer to where he sat.

"Nathan, what are you doing?"

"I don't have a clue," he grinned.

He inspected the cameo pendant carefully; brushed away a few lingering specs of debris, then inserted it into the small carved recess in the front of the old clock's base. The silhouette on the pendant matched the face in the recess perfectly.

Nathan glanced once more at Lisa's curious face then gave the pendant a push and a twist.

With a loud clack, the front panel of the huge base groaned and pivoted forward, hinged at the bottom.

As soon as the ambient light hit the volume of bright yellow reflections, the entire group of assembled onlookers gasped.

Hundreds of thumb sized gold bars were reflecting the dim light like a beacon. The stabilizing weight in the bottom of the clock hadn't been cast iron or bars of lead…, it had been rows of carefully stacked gold.

"My great grandfather Jonah Heart hid his savings in the old clock when he built the house. That was why his money was never found and why this monster hasn't been moved since then."

Nathan handed the Cameo back to Lisa.

"Marion knew…, it was her gift to us."

Lindsey Stewart was guilt ridden and withdrawn as she said goodbyes to Nathan and Lisa. Nathan did his best to remind her how she had saved him from certain death, taught him what he needed to know to pierce the truth and save Lisa.

Nothing he said seemed to be enough to pry her from her remorse, until he held her close and let their strange common bond give her the peace she needed.

The Consortium members had already departed and only the Stewart family was left, still collecting their remaining things for the flight back to North Carolina.

"Mr. Heart…, it has been a pleasure," said Madeline.

"Likewise…," said Nathan, "…well mostly."

"Bolton has agreed to stay with you until our armored envoy arrives to transport your gold to our banking complex. I'm pleased that you don't want to convert it all into currency…, considering its rate of appreciation. Our tax analyst will find the appropriate shelters you'll need to keep it in your pockets."

"At least I won't have to worry about borrowing money to finance our venture together," said Nathan.

Nathan stared at the floor for a moment, remembering the sleek black helicopter that arrived from nowhere to transport the assassin, "What's going to happen to the man we caught now that he's in custody?"

Madeline shrugged, "There are some things I have no desire to know. But…, I imagine he'll be questioned and I doubt that he'll ever see the light of day again. That's none of our concern."

If Bolton hadn't talked him down from his ledge there wouldn't have been anything left for them to question, nothing but a lump for the authorities to cart off.

Nathan's face centered on Madeline's, "You knew about the gold, didn't you?"

Madeline smiled for a moment, "Let's just say…, Sibyl had her suspicions. But once we were certain about you…, well…, we have an unspoken rule among our creed. We don't poach from our own kind, regardless of how tempting it may be."

Lindsey had known for certain, bound by her allegiance to her family and her feelings for Nathan, she had been torn between the two. She had told him to make sure he didn't let the old clock out of his sight. She cared even back then.

"What about Lindsey? She needs…," he began.

"Lindsey will be just fine," she nodded. "I've already scouted several worthy young gentlemen, any one of which could make her quite happy."

"I was going to say…, Lindsey needs to mature if she's ever going to be Sibyl's replacement."

Madeline agreed with a nod, "I'm trusting that Miss Evans will be a defining influence on her when she arrives next week for her formal training. They seem to have bonded these last few days, don't you think?"

This caused Nathan to laugh outright, "Inseparable is more like it."

"By the way…, are you sure you don't mind Sara and Annie remaining behind? We will have to return soon, when our collection begins to accumulate once again. They seem to have acclimated themselves to this old house quite well."

"I think we'll get along fine together."

The thrust of what she implied forced another question, "The house is already full.…"

"Where will all the new inventory go?" she finished for him. "It will be auctioned off in stages to the highest bidder…, to a very elite group of investors."

"I guess I'll be seeing more of Bob after the first of the year?" he mumbled with a slump.

"I have one more question," he said quietly, after she left his rhetorical question unanswered.

"Only one? I quite doubt that Mr. Heart."

"Why didn't you have me sign your stack of forms? The ones Lisa signed were long winded and detailed. I haven't seen anything past our one-year agreement."

Madeline Stewart clasped her aging hands and nodded, "It's simple. Because I can't. After you study the booklet we provided, then we can discuss our arrangement in further detail."

"At the risk of sounding impatient, I'd rather you tell me now."

She ducked her head in thought for only a moment, "I'm only allowed to share a minimal of information until you've read the Trifecta Consortium Charter and signed the form on the last page."

"I'm not signing anything unless you tell me something."

Madeline nodded anxiously, as if she were waiting for him to force her to answer.

"As you are under the umbrella of my membership for the rest of this year, I can tell you this much.…

When our term of agreement as ended, then the Bidding Wars begin. The three families of the Consortium will each present you with an offer to join them.

Since we…, the Stewart Membership, discovered you, we will have first bid. It will be up to you to decide which branch of the Consortium you will join."

Nathan took a step back, then laughed, "I can answer that right now. I won't be joining any of them. No offense Ms. Stewart, I've grown to respect your family, even care about a few of you, but I have plans for my own future."

"That would be most unfortunate," she shook her head. "You see if you do not choose one of the three, then the umbrella of our protection would be removed. The governments we represent will not, indeed cannot allow a rogue *Sensitive* of your magnitude to exist at the risk of falling under the control of Ethos."

Nathan stood silent as the impact of her warning slowly seeped in. If he didn't choose a branch of the Trifecta Consortium, Nathan Alexander Heart would be eliminated.

"Does Lisa know about this?"

"She is your Handler, and as such she will be fully informed of all the ramifications of her duties over the course of this next year."

Madeline took one of his large, suddenly limp hands in hers and patted it gently, "Rest assured, I do not intend to loose the Bidding Wars. You see I already know what you value most."

♥

Nathan and Lisa were standing by the front door as the two stretch limousines eased away toward the main road.

Lisa leaned against him, "I'm going to miss them."

"You are kidding aren't you?"

Lisa's innocence was the most attractive part of her personality he'd discovered to date.

"Yeah," she grinned, turning to look up into his face.

His fingers carefully brushed the last hues of a bruise on her cheek, "Want to get out of here…, maybe get some seafood?"

"Definitely," she answered, with a quick peck of a kiss.

Nathan's cell phone chimed.

"Your girlfriend?" asked Lisa, a devilish grin on her face.

"My sister."

He hugged her close before tapping the screen on his phone, "Caroline…."

Caroline's rampant discourse left Nathan with little to say for over ten minutes as he listened to the details of their cruise.

Finally, when she had to stop for a breath, Nathan cut in.

"Caroline…, yes…, Caroline…, I have something I need to talk to you about. Can you keep a secret?"

Lisa watched carefully, pausing before she ran off to get a coat.

"Yes of course…, especially from the *Big Three*."

Lisa covered her mouth to keep from laughing.

Nathan described his discovery inside the clock, leaving out the majority of the details. After Caroline had recovered from her disbelief, there were a few other details he needed to share.

"It was Marion that led me to it."

There was sudden silence.

"Caroline? Still there? She said to tell you not to worry about being pregnant at your age…, you were going to be fine."

There was more silence, until Nathan finally hung up the phone.

"I think she fainted."

"What is it with your family and fainting?" grunted Lisa.

EPILOGUE

CHRISTMAS was drawing close and a year had passed in a whirlwind of events.

Allison Marie Masters was traipsing through the old Heart Manor, pushing her sleeping little brother in a carriage; following Lisa Jess Heart's every step around the brilliant lights of their Christmas tree.

Caroline and Chris were out shopping, thrilled to be spending the holidays with their new sister-in-law and enjoying the guilty pleasures of being coddled by family.

Nathan had done everything but beg Chris to move his business to Salem and help occupy the enormous estate.

Kathryn Clarion moved in with her Uncle Nate and Aunt Lisa immediately after graduation, now attending the University in Portland, much to the jealous rage of her younger brother Chuck. He was still over a year away from graduating High School in the elite Seattle suburb where his parents lived.

Lisa sat down heavily in the dark leather sofa encircling the blazing fireplace, leaving room for her niece beside her.

"Don't we have enough decorations?"

Allie sat down carefully, rocking the baby carriage slowly back and forth, "You can never have enough decorations. Now can I see your ring again?"

Lisa stretched her legs, closing her eyes, inhaling the scent of the freshly trimmed tree behind them. She draped her hand into the young girls lap allowing her to ogle the diamond cluster wedding band once more.

Allie's tiny cool fingertips were relaxing, almost to the point of sending Lisa into a nap. This was what home felt like…, this was family.

The back of the thick sofa collapsed behind Lisa and Nathan Heart's face drooped down to kiss her forehead, then her lips.

He whispered to Allie, "Sara just put some homemade strawberry ice-cream in the freezer."

His niece inhaled sharply and carefully pushed the sleeping infant's carriage closer to Lisa before she hurried off into the kitchen.

Lisa tilted her head back to look up at her husband, "The house is beautiful. Thank you for inviting the Masters to stay through the holidays."

"Did you notice the new group of presents under the tree?"

"Ughh..., there's more?" she groaned. "We look like a department store already."

"Let them have their fun. Allie and Kate will remember this for the rest of their lives. Speaking of..., what day is this?"

"Not you too? Are you going to keep this up?" she whined.

Nathan grinned and slid a small gift-wrapped box from the pocket of his leather jacket.

"The seventh day of Christmas," he sang, easing out of his chilled coat.

Lisa's eyes lit up. It was on the seventh day last year that Nathan had given her an engagement ring and proposed. The seventh day would always be one of expectancy from now on.

"You're spoiling me."

Nathan started to hand the small gift-wrapped box to her then hid it away, "This one comes with a short tale."

"Please tell me this one isn't sad."

"Well..., aren't most romantic tragedies a little sad?"

She twisted onto the sofa curling her feet into the deep cushion.

"There once was a fellow by the name of Heinrich Roth who was born in a little village north of Zürich somewhere around 1880. His father was an older man, both happy and surprised at the arrival of a son so late in his life. He was also a jeweler craftsman, with a fairly well known reputation among those circles. When this boy Heinrich came of age, his father struck a deal with another family and arranged for their daughter to become promised to his son.

Young Heinrich was a shy boy of twelve and was petrified when his father made the announcement to his mother and two sisters.

Everyone was happy except for Heinrich. The very idea that he had no say in the matter, that he had never even seen the girl angered him even more.

Instead of showing his anger, he formed a plan. He buried himself in learning his father's craft, all the while knowing that when he turned sixteen, he was going to run away from home.

Four years passed and Heinrich became his father's pride and joy, the best apprentice that his father ever had. Some of the old man's better clients were requesting Heinrich for specially crafted items of jewelry.

The day before his sixteenth birthday, his aged old father took Heinrich aside and presented him with a gift. It didn't look like much more than an opaque stone with jagged and sharp edges.

His father assured him that one day, if he was patient the stone would turn into something of great beauty.

Heinrich turned sixteen that next day, already packed, his hidden money secured away. He planned on using whatever gifts he was given to add to his treasury before he left his home.

Well..., that evening happened to be the day he was introduced to his fiancée, Mara Ellen Holt. From the moment Heinrich laid eyes on the young wisp of a girl, he was transfixed. It was as if someone had placed a spell on his eyes and his mind. His plans for desertion fell to pieces before the evening was done.

Soon after..., a World War erupted, claiming several lives including his father. Heinrich and Mara were married when they both turned eighteen, in a distressed war ravaged Europe.

That was the year that Heinrich remembered the stone and began to chip away at it. Patiently, he inspected each inclusion, chipping away at the dross until it began to take a shape in his hands. From then on, it became an obsession as the burgundy color revealed its true worth. Determined to create a worthy gift for his wife for all the years they had spent together, he was only days away from his perfect anniversary gift.

Then the Second World War erupted and his family was tormented once again, this time because of their heritage. Mara's family was still living in Stuttgart across the German border. In a desperate attempt to get them to safety, Heinrich set off on a two day journey to find them and secret them across the border into Switzerland.

He never made it back home."

Nathan handed her the gift box and Lisa's hands were shaking, tears welling as she pursed her lips tightly.

"True story?" she whispered.

"Open it."

When the lid slid away, Lisa lifted the delicate chain until an enormous perfectly crafted blood-red teardrop ruby emerged from the chiffon where it was hidden.

"Oh Nathan...."

"Merry Christmas...."

♥

"Why are you crying?" asked Allie.

Nathan was holding Lisa close to his chest as his niece shuffled back in with a half eaten bowl of strawberry ice cream.

Allie shook her head, "Never mind. My mom cried all the time when she was pregnant with Jonathan. I guess I should probably get used to it. Dad says you'll probably have a dozen right off the bat."

Lisa's sniffling gradually turned into deep chuckling laughter.

With soothing holiday music emanating into the living room, it wasn't long before Allie was fast asleep, stretched out along the cushions.

Lisa shifted her back against Nathan, letting his arms surround her.

"The Containment Facility is empty; the last shipment went out yesterday. Has anyone called you?"

Her voice was barely a whisper, as she monitored her niece.

Nathan slid his hands down her shoulders and arms, "It's been over a week since I've heard from anyone."

"Good, we're free until January," she sighed. "How is your head?"

"Better..., the headache only lasted an hour this morning."

Lisa turned her head to see him better, "Ms. Stewart thinks it's some sort of attack.... You do too, don't you?"

Nathan smiled, "You've been spending too much time with Caroline."

He reached inside his jacket stretched across the sofa and found the ornate envelope he'd been holding, handing it to Lisa.

"It came yesterday."

Nathan lifted her up, letting her rest in his lap as she inspected this new worry.

"I was going to wait until after Christmas, but since it concerns both of us I thought it best to show you."

Lisa didn't open the envelope right away. She glanced at the wax seal and gold foil edges as well as the ornate scripted handwriting before laying it beside her.

"Our year was up weeks ago..., why now? Why not wait until after the holidays?" she sighed.

"You know Madeline as well as I do. It's probably her version of a preemptive strike."

Lisa looked at the envelope once again, "I don't suppose its going to explode..., here..., you do it."

Nathan took the envelope and quickly crumbled the seal, flipping open the gilded flap.

Dear Mr. & Mrs. Heart,

You are cordially invited to attend the first installment of the
Trifecta Consortium's
bidding proceedings from January 15ᵗʰ thru the 31ˢᵗ.
We are pleased to announce that the Stewart Family will have the honor of
First Host at our beautiful Nassau Island Retreat. All
accommodations and travel arrangements will be forwarded separately.
Dress is formal for all meetings. Attendance is mandatory.

Welcome to the Bidding War.

Madeline Stewart

Lisa's body relaxed as soon as Nathan read the contents of the announcement.

"Well at least it didn't draw blood," grinned Nathan.

Lisa sat forward, easing the small carriage back and forth, as Allie's little brother stirred and stretched.

"Are you going to *Read* it or not?" she whispered almost imperceptibly.

"Patience is a virtue," said Nathan, letting his fingertips glide over the handwriting.

The vision opened with Madeline Stewart seated by a large natural stone hearth. Henry and Lindsey were standing at her flank; all in their finest, all smiling brightly.

"Hello Nathan. First of all, we wish you Merry Christmas. Also, it seems congratulations are in order. Please give Lisa our best wishes. I see you've wasted no time in the process of enlarging your family."

Henry grinned and gave a quick thumbs up where Madeline couldn't see. Lisa was not quite two months along, but Nathan had a good idea how Madeline found out, considering the mischievous grin on Lindsey's face.

That was when all their expressions fell somber.

"For all intents and purposes, the scheduled events will take place as ordered, but the day after I penned this invitation we received some unsettling news."

She looked over her shoulder and Henry stepped forward, "Hey Nathan. What we learned is that one of the members of the Lamborghini family..., that is..., they lost one of their members last week. It's no one that you've met..., she just didn't get up one morning. There was no obvious cause of death, but as you know so distinctly, that doesn't mean there wasn't foul play.

"What this mean's is..., what we're most concerned with..., is that Ethos may have recruited a *Sensitive* of their own. If that's true then that also means they know more than we originally believed. They know others like Sibyl, Lindsey..., you..., and a handful of others exist. It also means that they know how to damage an unguarded mind."

Lindsey stepped forward, "There's another thing you should know Nathan. The family member that the Lamborghini's lost was not a *Sensitive*..., it was her *Handler*.

I know that you've been getting the same headaches that Sibyl and I have. I don't think they intend to attack us directly..., I..., that is Sibyl and I believe they are trying to leech into our minds to identify our *Handlers*. Please be careful Nathan and keep a closed mind."

Madeline stood from her seat and looked straight-ahead, "Be on your guard Nathan. And when you arrive, be prepared for war."

ABOUT THE AUTHOR

David Pyle is the author of several supernatural tales and short stories, most of which are free for download at his website. Others are coming soon.
For more information please visit: www.pentwist.com

Coming soon:

Pitre

www.ingramcontent.com/pod-product-compliance
Lightning Source LLC
Chambersburg PA
CBHW051056030726
47504CB00006B/1653

* 9 7 8 0 6 1 5 8 6 0 5 1 0 *